A Moon Every Night

By Connie Kronlokken

The author believes that all quotations in this book have been used under the "commentary and criticism" fair use of copyrighted materials.

Published by

Lightly
Held
Books

19 Picadilly Court
San Rafael, CA 94903

ISBN-10: 0692094431
ISBN-13: 978-0692094433

DEDICATION

To you, dear Reader
For your patience

"The moonlight entered my door, and I got up, happy of heart. There was no one to share this happiness with me, so I walked over to the Cheng-tien Temple to look for Huaimin. He, too, had not yet gone to bed, and we paced about in the garden. It looked like a transparent pool with the shadows of water grass in it, but they were really the shadows of bamboos and pine trees cast by the moonlight. Isn't there a moon every night? And aren't there bamboos and pine trees everywhere? But there are few carefree people like the two of us." [Su Tungpo. Translated by Lin Yutang in *The Gay Genius: The Life and Times of Su Tungpo*, 1947]

A Moon Every Night

Paul held the wick of his candle to Mother's lighted one in church with his family on Christmas Eve. Mother's hand shook a little, but her brown eyes were soft and large as Paul took the flame from her. He then turned toward his wife Marie, whose smile lit her ruddy face in the dim light. Paul took Marie's available hand, feeling her thin, lithe body beneath her dark sweater. She knew exactly how he felt, both of them a bit subdued standing beside each other after midnight in the church pews.

The organist played "Silent Night" while the candles were being lit in the dark. The child Jesus, born in a manger, whom they had come to honor, brought symbolic light into the darkness. Paul took Mother's arm, but she was doing fine as they processed up the aisle. It was her church; its new head pastor, a woman.

The entry way was brightly lit, smelling of snuffed candles, the doors wide open to the cold night air. Mother clasped Pastor Susan's hand. "My Christmas gifts!" she said as she indicated the four of her six children who stood beside her, Ellie, Paul, Marty and Hanna. There were two spouses, Ellie's husband Bruce, and Paul's wife Marie, but only one grandchild, Ellie's tall, slim Rhonda with her new husband, Ethan.

Paul had thought Mother would be intimidated by the big St. Paul church, its congregation numbering in the thousands, which Ellie's family attended. Not at all. Mother seemed to relish these city people and the resources they so obviously had. She was sure of her place in it, the lineage of her Danish pastor father, her illustrious brothers and sister, and her own years of service as a pastor's wife all contributing to her quiet dignity.

Pastor Susan took each hand as it was offered. She looked warm and open, stifling a yawn. "I should have had another cup of coffee before the service," she laughed.

"It's way past our bedtime too," said Mother. "But we had to come."

Paul sniffed the cold crisp air. It had a bit of a bite to it. Mother limped a little on her bad knee, and Paul and Ellie on either side helped her down the snowy steps. It was a clear night and Paul was thrilled to be out so late. He looked up. The just past full moon had a hard crisp edge on it. The stars were tiny points of light, but Paul could make out Orion, lying against the horizon.

Bruce was waiting at the bottom of the steps in his new BMW. Mother and Ellie got in and they bowled off up the snowy street.

"Well, if that don't beat all," said Hanna theatrically, and she and Marty, Paul and Marie all laughed as their boots crunched down the icy street to Paul's beat-up Rabbit in which the heater barely worked. Ethan and Rhonda had already left.

"He told me it's going to last forever," said Paul. "But it's a little surprising he bought a foreign car."

"I don't even have a car," said Marty. "There's nowhere to put one in my neighborhood. They're a liability in San Francisco." She was wearing a warm white down coat, her thick dark hair set off by a red scarf.

"Me neither," said Hanna. She looked the most Norwegian of all of them, her long blonde hair spilling around her pale angular face. "We walk or take taxis in New York."

"I'm deeply glad for Bruce and Ellie," said Paul. "They make things much easier for Mother."

"Yes," said Marty. "Me too. I'm happy I don't have to worry about her."

"But Ellie shops at Costco!" said Marie, to her the ultimate in carelessness. Much of Marie's considerable artistry, of which Paul was the grateful recipient, went into gardening and cooking. She was an expert forager, and seemed to find fresh food even in the winter.

"That Christmas china!" said Hanna. "How could she buy that stuff?"

Paul laughed. He thought the china with its bright patterns of holly and berries, a sentimental scene in the middle, was garish too. Briefly the like-minded siblings discussed the spectrum of the family as Paul drove through the plowed streets toward Ellie's big house on Edgcumbe Road where they were all staying. It was only five minutes away.

"I find it interesting to see Mother being a pillar of her community," said Marty. "I think she always wanted that. It was really Dad who was the renegade."

2

"And we're the ones who got Dad's resistance to institutions, his nonconformity," said Hanna. "Ellie and Kristen are more on the conservative side."

Silently, Paul added his sister Line to the list of nonconformist Mikkelsons. Line had been the most outspoken, the leader, the arch-rebel. Hanna, the youngest, might not have been one at all if she hadn't been gay, thought Paul. Institutions didn't cotton to gays.

"It's wonderful to see Ellie happy, though," said Marty. "I wasn't sure she was ever going to get there."

"Yes," said Paul. "She's having a great time." After years spent in Italy and Chile, Ellie was now a high school English teacher, busy and officious, making the most of her life in Minnesota's twin city area, her children grown.

Line, the second Mikkelson daughter, who had been the leader of Paul and Marty's pack as a kid, was in Edinburgh that Christmas with her husband and two of her daughters. Line's son Christy had been with them in St. Paul earlier that evening, for dinner and the opening of presents, but he lived with friends near the university and had gone home. Kristen, older than Hanna by three years, completed the group of Lois Mikkelson's children. Kristen would come in from the farm she shared with her husband and kids for a Christmas celebration in a few of days.

Paul drove down the tree-lined street with its spacious lots and pulled into the wide driveway of the house, its windows edged with lacy Christmas lights. The branches of the great bare oaks were frosted with snow, lit by streetlights. The four of them got noisily out of the car and entered the house by way of Mother's downstairs apartment. Archie, Paul and Marie's border collie/shepherd, greeted them happily at the door, but Mother wasn't there.

"Just a minute," said Paul, giving Archie a good scratch behind the ears. "We're just going up to say goodnight." Archie wasn't allowed in Ellie's part of the house. Marie, Hanna and Marty were half way up the stairs already.

Bruce had put another log on the fire. Hanna and Marty would spread out sleeping bags in front of it that night. Bruce stood by the stereo, looking through his albums. Soft jazzy Christmas music played, and the lights on the tree glowed. Little piles of things stood about the room from the earlier festive opening of presents, but the paper and ribbons had been cleaned up. Mother sat on the sofa beside Ellie.

"Cocoa in the kitchen, if you want it," said Ellie. It did not look like anyone wanted to move from their comfortable spots.

"Such a nice service," said Marty. "It reminded me of going to Sarah and Abbie's ordination last winter. Did I tell you about it?" Sarah was about Paul's age; her father was Mother's brother David. The cousins had seen a lot of each other growing up. Abbie was Sarah's partner.

"Maybe at the time," said Mother. "Was it nice?"

"There were 20 pastors from all over the city, dressed in their ecumenical robes. They came to put their hands on Sarah and Abbie's heads. It was in one of the big downtown Presbyterian churches. Very impressive."

When Paul was growing up women could not be pastors, which is why the weight of being the only son in a family of girls had fallen heavily on him. He had resisted the suggestion that he follow in Dad's footsteps. Women were ordained by some Lutheran churches as early as 1970, though not by Paul's synod. The acceptance of women pastors was part of the recent merger of large Lutheran bodies into the Evangelical Lutheran Church in America.

"I wish I could have been there," said Mother. Abbie and Sarah's church, St. Francis in San Francisco, had been suspended by the ELCA for this ordination. Gays could only be ordained if they weren't practicing homosexuals. Sarah and Abbie were in an openly lesbian relationship.

"St. Francis is a beautiful church," said Marty. "Its white altarpiece stands out against a dark painted wall behind it. Nice stained glass. It was built by Nordic immigrants in a Nordic part of town. I used to go to the Finnish sauna there and you could buy Norwegian food! Now that area is known as a gay neighborhood."

"The next time I come to San Francisco, you'll take me, won't you?" asked Mother.

"Of course!" said Marty.

Paul wondered whether there would be a next time for Mother. She was not very mobile, and she had a tremor which affected her hands and her head. Uncle David had not lived to see the ordination of his daughter. He had not felt able to preside at Sarah and Abbie's earlier commitment ceremony. It was painful for their family; Uncle David was dean at the Lutheran seminary and had to uphold church doctrine. Mother must have sympathized, but now she found she too had a daughter whose sexuality leaned toward the love of women.

"Pastor Susan has been wonderful," chimed in Ellie. "She's been with the church for several years, and just became head pastor last year." Ellie had retained her membership in this church all during the time she and Bruce had been in foreign countries. She was on a stewardship committee.

Paul sighed. It was rather late in the evening for heavy discussion. Was his the only generation which had trouble with institutions? "Do you want something to drink?" Paul asked Marie, taking her hand.

"No, thank you," said Marie. "I'm too sleepy."

Paul and Marie went downstairs to the hide-a-bed in Mother's living room where they often stayed, Archie bedding down at their feet. Mother wasn't far behind.

Christmas Day dawned cold and clear. After church that morning, everyone helped Ellie cook a big turkey dinner. Paul talked to Bruce a while about jazz. He was always interested in other people's expertise and he loved some of the music Bruce chose. But it did seem that Bruce got his information from magazines and listening to records. He never went to clubs, of which Paul was sure there were a few in the Twin Cities. It was a sad thing, another instance of Bruce and Ellie's 'once-removed' life.

Was he being uncharitable to make such judgments? Paul wondered. Or was he just being human? Here he was, poor as a church mouse and unable to offer Mother the protection of a richly comfortable household as Bruce and Ellie had. But he and Marie had their own standards of authenticity, sustainability and care. Paul loved his sisters. Discrimination was simply part of one's humanity, Paul decided.

When the afternoon light began to go down, everyone gathered to watch Henry V, a British adaptation of a Shakespeare play which Bruce had rented because Ellie thought the family would enjoy it. Marty and Hanna seemed to be particularly wrapped up in it. Marty had seen one of the actors in Oxford, and Hanna knew of them also. Ellie worked on her needlepoint canvas during the show. Paul felt sorry for Archie, who was left alone downstairs in Mother's apartment.

The movie was long and Paul didn't know his history. As soon as the credits began to roll, he ducked out down the stairs to take Archie for a walk. "Good dog," he said. "You are a good, patient dog, and now you get your reward. Or rather, we both do!" Paul put on his parka and boots, a leash on Archie. Big cities were not a good place for dogs, even well-trained ones, as Archie now was.

The two of them walked down the tree-lined streets, the street lamps creating blue shadows on the snow. What had moved Paul about the movie was that all Henry had in his favor was his eloquent speech. He had invigorated his small band of troops when they went against a much larger French army at Agincourt, and also convinced the young French princess that he would love her. Language won the day, Paul reflected. But, of course, what did one expect from Shakespeare! Language was important. It was really all that made him different from Archie.

Not much was moving about on a freezing Christmas night. Many of the large, luxurious homes had elaborate Christmas light displays. One home had an entire nativity scene in its front yard, set close to the street. Archie sniffed the illuminated painted plywood sheep and the wooden manger, but what could he smell with the air below freezing? Especially on these manicured streets?

That evening, Paul was restless. "So, you guys in tomorrow?" asked Paul of Hanna and Marty as they all gathered for snacks. If the weather held, the four of them wanted to drive up to Lake Michigami, make a fire in the Ben Franklin stove and have a look at the lake. It was a long drive, three and a half hours on a good day, but Marty and Hanna didn't come often at Christmas and they seemed game.

"Oh yes!" said Marty. "I'm ready for an adventure!"

"I hope we get to see Grace," said Hanna. "I've got something for the kids."

"Okay," said Paul. "Early start, maybe 7 a.m.?"

"You should take my car," said Mother. "It's in better shape and you will need the heat!"

Early the next morning the smell of buttered toast and coffee rose in the air. Marie and Paul smiled to each other when Hanna and Marty followed their noses downstairs to Mother's kitchen.

"It's essence du Mikkelson," said Hanna. "The smell of wheat toast and butter always lead to a Mikkelson!" Black and tan Archie's nails danced on the tile floor. "Good morning, Archie," she said. "You know something's going to happen today, don't you."

Paul drank coffee and tuned to radio stations quietly, trying to find updates on the weather. Three days before they had gotten six and a half inches of snow, but since then the skies had cleared and it sounded like visibility would be pretty good. Mother's car had all-season radials on it. Paul was not worried. Marie cut bread and Hanna sliced turkey to make sandwiches to take with them.

Mother wasn't up yet, but Paul knocked on her door to say they were leaving. "Have a great time!" said Mother. "Give my love to Grace and her family." Paul knew Mother would have liked to come, but the snow and ice made everything arduous for her, if not plain dangerous.

Gerald and Grace, who lived close by in Bemidji, would go to the cabin and have a fire going by the time Paul's group arrived. The cabin wasn't well-insulated and the water had been drained so the pipes wouldn't freeze. They would have to go to the bathroom in the woods, but they would not stay more than a few hours. They planned to drive back late that night.

Taking all of the warm clothes they had brought and plenty of things to drink, the four of them followed Archie, whose tail wagged wildly, out to the car.

"Do you want to sit up front so you can see better?" asked Marie of Marty. Marty was the oldest of the siblings, two years older than Paul. "You don't get to see Minnesota country very often." She slid into the back seat beside Hanna.

"Thank you!" said Marty. "We could take turns. Hanna probably wants to see too."

Paul drove north, trying to get out of the city as quickly as possible. But there was little early morning traffic on the day after Christmas. The red sun popped over the lavender black horizon just as they got out of town. Snowy fields spread on every side, the long-angled sun throwing blue shadows beside bare-branched trees and telephone poles. Paul loved how bare and dry the trees were in winter, letting you see their bones. Mother's car felt like a big boat Paul was piloting, full of laughing sisters.

"So," said Hanna. "I don't want to tell Mother yet, because I'm not so sure how Faith feels about it, but I'm falling in love with a scientist. You'd like her, Paul. She's a biologist!"

"That can mean a lot of things," said Paul.

"Faith is getting a doctorate in immunology," said Hanna. "She's a research biologist. We're like opposites, but we love each other."

"Cool!" said Marie. "Does she go to the theater with you?"

Hanna was an intern at a theater in New York and worked at a bookstore to support herself. "Oh yes," said Hanna. "She loves it. I'm the story part of her life." Hanna patted Archie who was splayed in the seat between Marie and herself. "I think what really draws us together though is

7

that she grew up on a farm. Upstate. Her parents farm dairy cattle, goats and sheep."

"Have you been there?" asked Marty. "To the farm, I mean."

"Yes," said Hanna. "It's beautiful. We were up there last fall. It's in the Mohawk River valley; just your standard, beautiful dairy farm. Her dad's been farming for years. Faith ran off to the city to school. She lives in my building and she is always studying. We both have intense schedules. But we spend as much time together as we can. I'm getting pretty attached!"

"It sounds nice," said Marie warmly. "But it's kind of far from home, isn't it?"

"Yeah," said Hanna ruefully. "Yeah. I didn't really know this would happen. It won't make Mother happy." Hanna was the youngest in the family, the apple of Mother's eye.

"Mother likes to travel," said Marty. "She had a wonderful time in San Francisco when she came."

"That was a couple of years ago," said Paul. "I wouldn't count on that happening again soon. You guys wore her out!"

"Yeah," said Marty. "She said her legs felt like logs. We don't even think about it. We walk everywhere! But she did enjoy going out to Angel Island. It's a state park out in the middle of the Bay." She turned back to Marie. "You'd love it! You guys should come!"

"Someday," said Marie nonchalantly. Paul heard this with a tinge of pain. He and Marie were only just able to pay their mortgage. They had no money for traveling. Paul had once driven to San Francisco before his years in Alaska, but he had no idea how that could happen again.

Marie mischievously asked Marty, "And who are you seeing these days, Miss Marty?"

Marty groaned audibly. "Oh, God," she said. "I'm hanging out with a friend, thirteen years younger. We used to work together. We're just having fun. Neither of us takes it seriously and none of our friends know about it. He likes it that I'm so different than I was when I was working. He thought I was one of 'them'!" Marty's husband Erik had died in an avalanche several years before and they had no children.

"The establishment?" asked Marie.

"Yeah," said Marty. "I was a yuppie, making lots of money, holding myself in. But now I'm kind of a bum! Tai chi is great and I meet so many people. I get to dress like I want. I'm trying to find my very own self. But I am lonely. I've been trying to be really honest with everyone, but I still don't know anyone like me, exactly."

"Line should see you now!" said Paul. Marty was taking the year off, hadn't worked since the summer before when they had all met at the lake for Mother's birthday.

"I can't get away with anything," said Hanna. "I live in one of the biggest cities in the world, but because I'm in a communal residence, everyone knows everything! It's like a small town! The theater world is small too. And everyone can find me at the bookstore."

Marty continued, "I don't like being alone. I'm just not good at it. When no one else was enthusiastic about Will buying back his big old BMW motorcycle except me, he said, 'maybe we do belong together.'"

Paul tried to picture Marty riding around on the back of a big motorcycle. "That does sound kind of like bumming! Where do you go?"

"Usually out to the coast. Picnics and stuff. He's the safest driver, just a big gentle guy. Everyone I know right now is into making movies. Will's working for a production company. He wanted to get in to ILM. They made the Star Wars movies. But he got a job in a similar company. I'm taking some film classes too."

The straight, dry road began to be surrounded by stately pines, dusted with snow. Paul stopped for gas. "Bathroom break!" said Paul insistently. It would be a while before they got another one. He put the nozzle of the gas pump into Mother's tank, blowing on his bare, cold hands. He wished Mother didn't have such a gas guzzler. But it was warm, and safe. Paul enjoyed his sisters' exotic stories, but he was glad he was in Minnesota. He couldn't wait to get up to the lake. The ice would surely be strong by now, booming and cracking in the cold.

At last they turned onto the gravel road which wound around the southern shore of the lake. The woods lay bare and full of sun on both sides of the road. It had been plowed, which Paul was glad to see.

The snow in the driveway to their cabin was deeply scored by a single set of wheels. Gerald's Cherokee, thought Paul. It had four-wheel drive and a chassis set high on its wheels. Paul didn't dare drive down in Mother's car. He parked and Archie leapt out, running back and forth. Everyone loaded up the food they had brought and walked up the short drive to the cabin, trying to stay in the wheel tracks. Archie yipped and floundered in the snow, surprised it was so deep.

Sure enough, the Cherokee was parked in front of the frame building, its roof heavy with snow. Smoke drifted from the chimney. Marie took off trying to run, laughing as her boots sank into the deep snow.

Grace, Marie's daughter, came out on the porch with her kids. Little John and Dory looked like squat dwarfs, almost as wide in their coats as they were tall! Inside, Gerald, Grace's husband, stood by the black iron Ben Franklin stove, feeding logs into a blazing fire. Inches away, however, the air was still icy and everyone kept their outdoor coats on, the women chattering away.

"Thanks for making the fire," said Paul. Gerald was tall and dark, a steady, quiet presence. Half Ojibway, he had lived around Bemidji his whole life and now worked at the airport. "How's that pilot's license going?" Paul asked.

"Pretty good," said Gerald. "I'll probably get enough hours this year." He smiled engagingly. "Not much going on right now, except for shipping and people going home for the holidays. We'll have a few snowbirds in January, people flying south."

"That ought to keep you busy," said Paul. He went over to the window. Snow lay thick on paths and the empty piece of driftwood on the lawn, unmarked except by small tracings of bird and squirrel feet. "Think I'll go down to the lake," he said. "The light's not going to last."

Gerald stayed and fed the fire, but everyone else followed Paul's footsteps down the steep path to the lake. Marie carried Little John and Hanna put Dory on her back. They trooped out onto the ice where the snow wasn't so thick. The wind, sweeping across the big space, had thinned the snowpack on the lake.

Paul put up his hands to silence the group so they could listen. The lake was frozen solid. Paul jumped on the ice and Dory and Little John followed suit! Hardly any crackling resulted. It was about noon, just after the solstice, the sun quite low in the southern sky. The great northern silence had descended.

The aspens, birches and tall pines, bending and popping in the cold, were noisier than the ice. Paul walked along the shore, looking at the frozen icicles on the bushes at the edge, the patterns of tiny tracks. His boots crunched in the snow but he could not hear the water beneath the ice. Need an ice augur, he thought, to see how thick it was.

That afternoon the family had a noisy, festive meal by the fire in the cabin which warmed up just enough so they could enjoy their food. Gerald had brought hot dogs which they roasted over the fire, especially delicious in the cold. Marie set an old pan full of apple cider on the coals. The cabin was dark except for firelight, however. As soon as the sun went down, Gerald and Grace gathered up their children and left.

Paul dawdled, watching the fire go down. He did not want to go home. This was the Mikkelson place, the place on earth he knew best, the place he could never get enough of. He had certainly not seen enough of it in the winter. The moon was waning, would not be up until later. "Let's stay until the stars are out," Paul said. "Deep twilight. And then we'll go."

When the fire was almost out, they left Archie to enjoy the last of it and followed the snow-deep tracks they had made earlier in the day to the lake. The Milky Way was thrown out like a net in the center of the sky, thick and lustrous. Paul pointed out Rigel in Orion, Aldebaran in the nearby Bull, and Sirius, the dog star, the brightest in the sky.

Walking toward the middle of the lake, the sky was very wide. Paul headed for the places where the wind had swept the snow aside. "Wish we had skates," he said. Paul took Marie's arm on one side, Hanna's on the other. "Walk like a penguin," he said, leaning forward, lifting one leg and then the other. Marty grabbed Hanna's arm and they all walked across the ice like penguins, leaning a little and lifting their legs together.

"How about this one," said Hanna. "Duck walk! How low can you go?" She settled far down on her knees, and the others tried to join her.

"Dragon walk," said Marty. "We do this in tai chi, but we have to let go of each other. Just follow me!" She let go and stepped out, her open hands following as she opened her hips and her feet at the same time. "Take your weight on it, then shift. Stay low," she said. She walked out onto a fresh piece of ice covered thinly with snow.

Paul followed Marty, splaying out his hips and staying low, taking one step after another. All of a sudden he stopped, looking at the tracks they were making. What sort of strange animal was this?! He laughed, pointing the tracks out to the others. Even with no moon, the big expanse of snow was very bright.

"Remember, Paul?" Marie said. "Remember the Greek dances?"

"Of course!" said Paul. "I remember the sirtaki." He lifted his arms, putting one hand on Marie's shoulder and waiting for the others to fall in beside them.

"Ta daaaa," sang Marie. "Ta daaaa. Just copy us!" She lifted one leg, stepped and then crossed over with the other, slowly.

Paul could feel Marie's rhythm, hear the accompanying music in his head. Snow, stars, sirtaki, sisters. Paul felt the ecstasy running up and down his spine.

2

Line handed over a few paper Lire notes to the vendor at the outdoor market in Panzano and was given a roasted chicken in return. "Grazie," said Line, bringing out one of the few words of Italian she could muster. She put the wrapped chicken into a string bag and handed it to Christy, her only son, the light of her eyes, whom she hadn't seen for almost a year. "Here Christy," she said. "Will you carry the chicken?"

"Sure," said Christy. "Those deep-fried polenta look good," he mused over a sheet of honey-colored slabs.

"Yes," said Line. "Let's get some of that." She continued, buying arugula, bread, carrots and other vegetables, fruit for breakfast. It felt just like being in California! Fern and Ivy were bent over a jewelry stall. Fern tried on a necklace, which the gypsy-looking vendor was pleased to show her in an old mirror.

"I think I need a coffee," said Line, "before we go home." They had walked up the stony white road through the Vitigliano estate where they were staying near the small town of Panzano. Tuscany was being rediscovered, its derelict villas reclaimed, often by British and American owners. Suzannah, the owner of their rented villa, had told them about the Saturday market, only a half hour walk across the hills.

"Me too!" piped up Christy.

The four of them walked down the town's single street and stopped where they saw small tables set outdoors with red and white umbrellas saying 'Campari' on them. Line ordered a café latte and so did Christy. Fern and Ivy had gelato. Line fanned herself with a napkin. "I'm happy it is so hot," she said. "But it is unexpected! I had forgotten how it was!"

Ivy, who had twisted up her blonde hair into a bun on top of her head, handed Line a spoon so she could taste the mint gelato. "This will cool you off," she said.

Line let the cool cream slide down her throat. She felt euphoric. By this evening her entire family would be together for the first time in a year. Stephen had driven to Pisa to pick up Poppa, as his father was known in the family, and Heather at the airport. Line mentally crossed her fingers for their safety. She hated the Italian roads with native drivers going so fast they practically pushed you from behind in their tiny cars.

"So, which rock star's hair are you channeling?" Fern asked Christy, smirking.

Christy smiled widely. "Haven't got a lot of choice, have I?!" He brushed up his curls with one hand. "Kind of a Jewfro, after all," he said.

To Line he looked like his father, though Christy's hair was thicker. Christy was 23, exactly Stephen's age when Line met him. Her daughters, now 17 and 15, had long, untidy hair. They had benefited from being California girls in Edinburgh. So far, they seemed to prefer a natural look. Line hoped it would continue. So many of the kids she saw had odd hairstyles, strange piercings, dark clothes studded with metal.

"Don't worry about her," said Ivy. "She can't help it. She's a Steve Perry fan!" Ivy dissolved in laughter, but Fern glared at her.

"Journey?" asked Christy.

"Yeah," said Ivy. "Journey." She licked the last of her gelato.

Fern kicked Ivy under the table, but she was having trouble hiding a smile. Her brunette hair hung damp around her neck. "You wish!" she said.

"Any way you want it!" said Ivy, shaking her head from side to side, so her hair fell down. All three of them dissolved in helpless giggles.

Line smiled at them, barely knew what they were talking about, her attractive, almost grown kids. But their laughter was infectious. Line stretched arms and legs. Her muscles felt soft and sleek as butter in the warm sun. "Ready?" she asked.

Carrying their bundles they set off across the hills. Line put an arm around Christy's waist, walking in step with him, letting the girls go ahead. The green and gold hills rolled away from them in every direction, a patchwork quilt of vineyards and fields, greyer olive trees carefully tended. Tall, straight cypress trees formed the stitching at the edges of the fields.

"Are those poppies?" Line squinted at red flowers dotted among the hedgerows. Thick woods covered the distant hillsides. The sun beat down on them, but Line opened to it, her whole body drinking in the warmth.

"Looks like it," said Christy, whose eyes were probably better. "I see sunflowers!"

"Here we are, just like tourists," said Line, "out in the noonday sun!" They were hardly making any shadows.

"Mad dogs and Englishmen," said Christy.

"I'm so glad we are here!" said Line. "It was dark in Scotland for so long this winter. It was hard for me. But I suppose Minnesota is the same, isn't it?"

"Edinburgh is actually at least ten degrees further north, in latitude," said Christy. "I checked. And Minnesotans know how to have fun. You remember. I think it's warmer in Edinburgh, because of the coast, but definitely darker."

"Yes," said Line. "The wind is terrible sometimes. But the worst was I didn't have enough to do! I felt so homesick without a garden of my own, or anything to do but the shopping and cleaning." Line hung her head. After the initial euphoria of exploration, she had succumbed to days when she couldn't decide what to do with herself. But that was really more than Christy needed to know. She and Ivy had had the worst time adjusting. Stephen and Fern had settled happily into the intellectual environment. "It's better now," she confided. "I'm finally certified to volunteer at the National Health hospitals. It took weeks to get in! They're just very careful."

"So the National Health works?" Christy had a political bent. He was studying political science and sociology at the University of Minnesota, but spent all of his free time on political campaigns.

"It's pretty good," said Line. "I'm pleased to see it from the inside. There's a lot of bureaucracy, reviews and assessments; but people go in freely. It isn't like in the US where everyone is afraid to go to the doctor because of the costs." Line clutched at her tall, thin son as she stumbled on the treacherous rocks. Fern and Ivy were way ahead of them, disappearing over a little ridge.

"Paul Wellstone got into the senate this year," said Christy. "He's a big advocate of health and mental health care. But I can't see us getting universal health care any time soon." He laughed to himself. "Made me think of you and Dad during the election. His rival put out a letter to their fellow Jews saying Wellstone was a 'bad Jew' for marrying a shiksa and not bringing his kids up in the Jewish religion!"

"So?" asked Line. "He got elected anyway?"

"It was all over the media. Wellstone said, 'he has a problem with Christians, then?'" Christy laughed. "There are a few Christians in Minnesota! Nobody thought Wellstone could win, but he went around in this rickety green bus, visiting all the rural areas. And he stood up for things. We all love him!"

"Your Dad probably knows about him," said Line. It was what she lived for. Christy hardly ever wrote, might call with news, but mostly Line didn't know what was going on with him until she saw him. Certainly not the details of his wide-ranging life. Line longed to ask him about girlfriends, but there would be time. She could watch him. Perhaps he would betray some information if she was patient.

The villa they rented was set in a spacious green lawn. Line could not imagine the work that had gone into reclaiming it, from its red tile floors to its exposed timber roof. The fixtures and the aqua ceramic walls in the bathroom were gleaming. Each texture was beautiful in its historic context, earth-bound patinas showing age. Tasteful vases of grasses and flowers had been brought in. Line put the things they had bought at the market in their places in the kitchen, which had a stone fireplace at one end.

That evening, Poppa initiated Christy into his method of making the perfect Scotch, because, as Poppa said, if you only had one all day, it had to be perfect! All seven Cohens dragged chairs out onto the lawn and faced them toward the evening sun which would set beyond the wooded hills.

It was certainly the perfect setting. Line sipped a glass of lemonade beside Heather, whom she had also not seen for months. Heather was sun-kissed, her skin tawny and her hair glowing gold. Her legs looked brown and long in the evening light. "It's because I ride my bike every day," she told them. "I can't get around campus without it!"

Line could tell her younger sisters were a little in awe of Heather, now differentiated from them by being on her own for the past year in California. Line herself was remembering that each of these kids had once grown big in her very own tummy, that they had struggled to be the persons they were becoming.

Even the hairs on Heather's arms were bleached by the sun. Line pulled her chair so close she could touch them. "It's your time, my girl," said Line. "Enjoy it! But I hope you are using aloe vera on your skin. You don't want to dry up like a prune when you're older!"

Line had thought a lot about skin and coloring during the last year. She loved the tawny brown skin all of her kids were capable of, a legacy from Poppa and Stephen. Fern was the darkest, while Line herself was pale, all Scandinavian. In Scotland, pale was considered beautiful and many of the young people had dewy white complexions and flax-colored hair. Vikings all. But Line loved golden brown skin, wished she had it.

"What did you think of the Chianti?" asked Stephen, directing his question to Heather who was interested in winemaking. They had drunk the local red Chianti with dinner.

"A little astringent," said Heather. "But good with food. I'd like to try several versions."

"We're sitting in the heart of the Chianti Classico region it seems," said Stephen. "You'll have plenty of chances."

"It's mostly Sangiovese," said Heather. "With some sweet Malvasia Bianca grapes, which we grow in California, and also another red grape I don't know. I looked it up before I got here. I knew we'd be drinking it."

Heather, at 19, had been settled and clear about what she wanted for a long time. She wanted to work outdoors with growing things. She'd been influenced by a family friend who was part-owner of a small winery in the Santa Cruz mountains and had just finished her first year at UC Davis. UC Davis was traditionally the agricultural school of the University of California and had a degree in viticulture. Every vine that came into California from Europe had to pass through UC Davis' testing and quarantine program before it was accepted. Wine was big business in California and Heather looked to it for her career.

"I have to say," said Poppa, "it feels like California here. We could be sitting looking out over our own ridge!"

Line sighed. "Yes," she said. "It's the next best thing." She could hardly remember being so happy. Was it allowed? Or perhaps the contrast with the long Scottish winter made her feeling of well-being so strong. There was hardly any breeze, hardly any bugs in the grass or mosquitoes, though they had found a fat, spongy wolf spider over their bed when they first arrived. The warmth and the evening light felt totally benign.

"They're on about the same latitude," said Christy, the expert. "The sun is hitting us at about the same angle, I expect."

Ivy was having trouble sitting still, as usual. She bounced around, sitting on Poppa's lap, though she was a little tall for that, and then moving across the lawn to sit by Fern. A clothesline was strung at the edge of the field. Line could hardly wait to hang out clothes in the sun.

"And what have you been doing all winter, Poppa?" Line asked.

"Well," said Poppa decisively. "Got my film club going finally at the Nickelodeon. I've gotten Bill Raney's attention to my group and what we want to see. Bill's got his own ideas, but he listens! He was happy to set up a week night for us, Mondays. He gets pretty good box office. They've taught students from all around to love cinema. But he doesn't mind my input on the programming. And introducing them. I spend all my time studying! Sight and Sound especially."

"So how many people do you usually get?" asked Stephen.

"Well, it's kind of a geezer and blue-haired ladies night," said Poppa. "But these are people with amazing experiences! It's a rotating circle of people, depending on who's well. But maybe 30 to 50 most nights. We're having a ball!"

Fern had pricked up her ears. "Which movies?" Her hands were busy, braiding colored twine and beads into bracelets.

"Oh, we're eclectic," said Poppa. "All kinds of things. Sometimes it's a series about a director, or a country. We have our Jackie Chan fans, our Gerard Depardieu fans. Marty told me about some good Chinese films, and there are still some good French ones. And of course Bill's really tied in. He has lots of suggestions. Tarkovsky, from Russia. A Polish guy named Kieslowski. We've gone back and looked at Buster Keaton."

"Once a week?!" asked Stephen. "That's a lot of movies!"

"Well," said Poppa, "usually the movie's already chosen and I just study up on it and talk about it. But sometimes we put together a list and get Bill to see what he can do."

Ivy came and sat at Heather's feet, making her a bracelet of colored string. She tried it on Heather's ankle, and tied it off when it fit.

"What was your favorite movie this year?" asked Line.

"Oh! That would be hard," said Poppa. "Maybe Intimate Lighting. Sort of a comparison between living in the country and in Prague. Made by a Czechoslovakian in the 1960's. Ivan Passer. Just had such a light touch. Mostly non-actors. He's in America now, working in LA somewhere."

"I should be taking notes," said Stephen, taking a sip from his iced drink. "But I don't think I could take the time for it. Being in Edinburgh is such an opportunity, I can't waste time." He looked at Line ruefully. Line knew he felt a little regretful about how little family time he allowed himself.

The sun went down in the clear sky. Line realized it must almost be midsummer, the summer solstice, the longest days of the year. Slowly, as they talked, the sky pinked along the horizon behind the grey green hills and then turned lavender. The reunion of the Cohens had been planned all year. No one had traveled at the winter holidays, though Line and Stephen and the girls went down to London. Line expanded into the lovely summer air, wondering again if it was allowed to be this happy. She smiled at Heather and Ivy at her feet.

Ivy was not doing well in school. She was not as restrained as the northern kids had been taught to be, in their grey school jumpers and their little white blouses. Ivy slipped behind in her homework and her parents had found her a tutor. But even the tutor had a hard time getting Ivy to concentrate. There were tears. Even more so when Ivy couldn't penetrate the little cliques of girls who had grown up together and spoke in broad northern accents. Ivy had been happier at home with Line than in school.

But persistence, gentle rigor and patience had gotten them all through the school year. Fern was excited about history and had gone on an archaeological dig with her class. Her interest in academics impressed her classmates. Line was surprised at her daughters, fascinated by the changes in them. They would be in Edinburgh one more year. Line did not think a little adversity was a bad thing. Ivy would survive. This summer trip would revive her.

"Okay, Stephen," said Poppa. "Your turn. What are you turning your attention to?"

Stephen laughed. "I'm kind of playing the field," he said. "I'm like a kid in a candy store! This deep history I didn't know about. Like the northern kingdoms of Canute. He had an eleventh century North Sea empire, uniting England, Norway and Denmark. After the Norman conquest, he was pretty much forgotten. But he was a Dane, crowned king of England in St. Paul's cathedral when he was 22. And there is so much more!"

"We went there!" piped up Ivy. "At Christmas." She did not say that the significance of St. Paul's to her, and to Line and Fern, had been the song Julie Andrews sang about the little old bird-woman on its steps in the movie Mary Poppins. They had looked for her. The doves and pigeons had certainly been there, but there was no bird-woman. Tuppence probably didn't buy a bag of breadcrumbs any more, but every bit of England and Scotland was layered with so many kinds of history!

"St. Paul's burned in the Great Fire," said Stephen. "The one we visited was built in the 17th century. On the same spot. It's the hub around which London has turned for centuries."

"And now here we are!" said Christy. "On land that's been cultivated since before written history."

Line shook her head. It was impossible to imagine.

"Winemaking goes back that far," said Heather.

"Yes," said Stephen. "I've been concentrated on contemporary history for so long. I love looking back at this huge panorama of people who preceded us."

The wash of warmth and sunshine continued into the next few weeks. Line luxuriated in the long days. Some of them were spent at the villa, reading, talking, cooking, being lazy. And some of them were spent in the two nearest larger towns, Siena and Florence.

The road winding to Siena through the hill country was beautiful, oaks along the roadsides, vines on one side and olives on the other, the soil very red. In the town they got lost. Stephen drove up hills to a hospital and a church, then back down. The city was beautiful, factories smack up against old, textured buildings. Finally they found a place to park beneath the Medici fortress and walked up the narrow streets, looking down from the precipice to gardens below.

The Piazza del Campo was a huge space in the middle of town ringed by medieval buildings. They walked around the Duomo, looking at the amazing black and white facade and the marble flooring made by the Sienese. "Someone told me they didn't like Italy because it was all about churches," said Poppa.

"It was their home," said Stephen. "Their spiritual home. Everyone worked on the building as if it were their own." The Duomo was unfinished, however, the ambitions of the Sienese stopped by the plague. For hundreds of years the city states of Florence and Siena had fought for supremacy, but the Black Death put a stop to Siena's rise in 1348. Florence then conquered it.

Obviously people had been surrounded by saints and mystics. In Line's head Julie Andrews sang: "All around the cathedrals the saints and apostles look down as she sells her wares. Although you can't see it, it seems they are smiling each time someone shows that he cares."

St. Catherine presided over Siena. As a young mystic she had tried to make peace among the city states. Line stopped on the light, bright porch of her cloister looking down a steep, narrow street filled with Vespas, the ice-cream-colored Italian scooters everyone used. Washing, including fine embroidered linen, hung on lines strung across the street between upper floor windows. The place had been bypassed by the modern world.

When they went, on another day, to Florence, Line experienced that city as claustrophobic, the buildings ugly, so close to each other you couldn't get a view of them. The successful Medicis made Florence a thriving trade center, commissioning art and architecture to enhance it. Florence was direct and mercantile. Its appeal to tourists was tawdry. Line preferred Siena. Siena was about spirit, sitting light and airy on its hilltops, every sight thrilling.

"Siena won, in my mind," said Line to Stephen. "It's much more beautiful."

"I agree," said Stephen. But that didn't stop him from being avid about the sights, absorbing as much as he could and explaining things to his family.

The family also went to Greve the nearest town, with a spacious triangular main plaza, along the sides of which were shops and restaurants of all kinds. Line gravitated to the gardening and food shops, Heather to the enotecas, and Stephen looked for bibliotecas or libraries. Christy and Poppa tended to go with Heather, Fern with Stephen and Ivy with Line. Afterwards they all met for lunch at a restaurant with an outdoor garden, where they sat in the sweet shade of the trees, taking their time in the afternoon.

"I found a chessboard laid out in the park," said Christy as they sipped lemonade and soda waters. "They must use humans dressed up as the different pieces."

"Was anyone playing?" asked Poppa.

"Not at the moment," said Christy. "I've always wondered how you could see what you were doing if you weren't looking down at the pieces."

"Sometimes I think they do that," said Stephen. "They have a chess board in front of them, and then they call out the moves based on what they see on the board. Too distracting to look at people."

"But think how boring it must be to be a pawn!" said Poppa. "Or a rook or a bishop, waiting for your call!"

"Yeah," said Christy. "I bet they don't do it very often. I keep trying to beat Paul, but I've only done it once or twice so far."

"Paul?" asked Poppa.

"Line's brother," said Christy. "In Minnesota."

"Is he becoming a chess master?" asked Stephen.

"No," said Christy. "He says he only plays me! He's got too many other things going on. But he does like to play. He just concentrates really well."

"I'd like to be a pawn," said Ivy. "What do they wear?"

"You would make a terrible pawn!" said Poppa indulgently.

"White," said Fern. "Or black. I'd rather be the queen."

In a tree beside them, a speaker played Frank Sinatra singing "Strangers in the Night." Their host, Lucca, who spoke perfect English, told them Frank was his favorite. "There are no good singers or songwriters in Italy right now," he said matter-of-factly.

Poppa nodded appreciatively. "Ol' blue eyes," he said. "New Jersey boy. Hardly older than me."

Lucca, who looked to be not much older than Stephen, took a shine to the Cohens, bringing them first a delicate cauliflower soufflé with a creamy sauce and then tortellini wrapped around delicious roasted potatoes, also in a delicate sauce. Everyone shared, spooning small helpings from the platters. Poppa mopped the sauces from them with a piece of pane Toscano. A plate of tagliatelle with artichokes was followed by a salad.

"Amazing food," said Line. "So light and delicious."

"This is the best Chianti we've had!" said Heather. A drawing of a Tuscan building graced the bottle's label with the words 'Riseccoli Chianti Classico.' Heather looked closely at it.

"Let's see whether we can visit," said Stephen. "There are wine-making operations all around us." When Lucca came back, Stephen secured directions to the nearby family estate.

"Ah, yes, the Romanelli family. The winery is a little way east. They were artists!" said Lucca. "I'm not sure how much English they have up there. They do have an enoteca."

"Our daughter Heather is studying winemaking in California," said Stephen proudly.

"Ah! Meraviglioso! I think you like my food," Lucca said, retrieving the empty platters. "I have a Chinese cook making Italian recipes! He does very well."

Yes, indeed, thought Line to herself. He does very well indeed.

"And now," said Lucca. "Some coffee? Some Tiramisu? Ours is eccellente!"

Line nodded. She was pleased with her civilized family, sharing a meal together in Italy. Though they were spread to the four winds most of the time, they were united in her heart.

3

Marty tied the string at her waist which held up her wide blue cotton tai chi pants, and pushed the knotted cotton 'buttons' on her top through their loops. She stood in the women's dressing room next to several other women who were putting on the dark heavy clothing worn for aikido classes. How many days and nights had she stood quietly in this room, changing next to these women?

The aikido women knew each other, talked among themselves. The one Marty felt was most accomplished among them acted resigned to her fate as she tied the wide hakama trousers around her waist. It was repetitive to come twice a week and every Saturday to these same rooms, dress in the same clothes and practice over and over. But Marty found her tai chi class was never the same twice. She packed her street clothes in her backpack, buckled the flat Chinese cotton shoes and went out into the dark ballroom where her class met.

The building was ancient. Built in 1914 as a Young Men's Institute, it was a warren of rooms used by all kinds of people. A dance group met on an upper floor. Marty's group often watched Brazilian or Lindy dancers from the foyer as they waited for their turn to use the great ballroom with its hardwood floor. A few windows high up brought in light, and there were a few lights attached to the walls, but the room was never bright.

A person Marty didn't know in a new cotton jacket came up to her, asking who the instructor was. Marty directed her to Ernesto, a thin Hispanic gentleman with a little salt and pepper in his hair, and a grey Chinese jacket. She tried to be helpful to new people, but one never knew. Many people began class but didn't come back after the first few sessions.

Marty stood in the front of a grid with Anton, a thin, lithe Chinese man, on one corner and Stan, a large man wearing a tie-dyed t-shirt, his dark hair in a ponytail, on the far end. The people on the corners were the most accomplished, setting the pace for the slow set, a series of 108 circular movements made by the hands, the legs, the body. Marty stepped out, all attention, copying Anton, moving her weight slowly from one leg to the other. It was hard, not to say painful. Done properly, the Yang-style slow set took at least 40 minutes. Ernesto pulled out beginners to teach them in a corner of the room.

After slow set, the group took a break. Martin, a tall Dutch man, the oldest one in the group, wrapped a new air-splint around his ankle. People stood around talking. To the new person, Jean, who stood beside them, Martin said, "It feels really good, and," he whispered theatrically, "it's legal!"

Tim congratulated Anton, who was fluent in English, Mandarin and Japanese, on becoming the CFO of Gump's, the upscale San Francisco gift store full of Asian arts. Anton had brought Tim into tai chi because, as he pointed out, Tim had a "tai chi body."

Ernesto clapped his hands to get attention and bade the group push hands. Marty was paired with Betty, a large lesbian whose partner Charlene seemed to be the motivating force. But as Marty was deciding that Betty didn't care about what she was doing, Anton came over and pointed out that Marty wasn't blocking. She was just placing her hands in the two-person exercise. "Round your structure," said Anton, demonstrating with his own body. "Don't be afraid to block."

Three fast sets, in which the entire slow set was done in one tenth of the time, followed. Marty muffed many of the steps, but finished each one. Stan sat out the last, sweating, but there was nothing wrong with Marty's heart! The class finished with a salute and a clapping of hands. "Practice!" admonished Ernesto, as the group gathered up their things and left.

By this time, however, Marty was allowed to join the special class that followed. With Stan and small German Fredricka, Marty rushed across the street and bought a grapefruit juice to drink between classes.

Special class was just beginning the sword set. Marty had bought a collapsible one at an Asian bookstore. To open it, she swung it through the air, which delighted Ricka. "You could take it on the bus!" said Ricka. It was just made of coated tin, not as elegant as other people's steel swords with tassels on the end, but it would work for practice Marty hoped.

Ernesto demonstrated how to hold the sword, making the opposite hand into a 'sword' also, with two fingers held up. He taught the first three movements, which Marty must go home and practice. That was enough to get started.

For the rest of the class, Ricka worked with Marty on fast set. Ricka was small, golden-haired, and her tai chi was perfect. Ricka helped Marty slow the parry and punch movement down enough to understand it. But Marty was beginning to falter. Too many new things. She was spacing out. Tomorrow she would practice on her own, and the things she had heard today would come back to her.

Marty watched as the special class did two 'family' sets, made up by Master Liu's grandfather. They were beautiful, fast movements alternating with slow. The special class ended with a salute to the practice and to the lineage of the Liu family. Master Liu, who lived in Los Angeles, had taught the senior students Marty studied with.

Marty's legs, and especially the joints at her hips ached. She was also hungry! In the dressing room, she changed back into street clothes, jeans, a t-shirt and jacket. She went out into the foyer, and down the light marble steps into the bright October sun, where some of the special class members were talking about where to have lunch together. Several cars left for the Fountain Court restaurant on Clement Street, Marty in Ernesto's.

Parking on Clement Street, which was jammed with people shopping, especially Asians, was difficult. Ernesto eased them through the crowds with innate gentleness and courtesy, but also authority. He explained to Marty that tai chi taught him to get through a crowd easily! The air was cold and smells wafted through the street from many restaurants. Hot food, thought Marty. She was starving.

The Fountain Court was modern and cheerful, sun coming through the glass tiles at the entrance on the painted blue-green walls. Anton and Martin were already seated at a table. Anton ordered for them all: fried beancake, steamed pork dumplings with ginger, a soup of beef with thick noodles and five star anise spices, a whole fish cooked in a light sauce and wonderful spinach greens with garlic.

The food was light and delicious. "This is Shanghai food," said Anton. He spoke in Mandarin to the waiter, ordering an onion pancake to share. Marty dipped into the communal dishes with her chopsticks. She had eaten Chinese food ever since she came to San Francisco, especially with Meredith, whose family had been from Shanghai.

"I think I need some Mongolian beef," said Martin. But he had to eat most of it himself. No one else wanted it after the light, tasty food Anton had ordered. Martin had once told Marty of being forced by the Nazis as a teenager to work underground in the mines for 18 months, never seeing the sun. The story was still so emotional for him he could hardly bear to tell it.

That day the group talked of their travels. Ricka was going to Guatemala for a month to study Spanish with her husband. Ernesto was enjoying a leave of absence from his accounting job. Anton, whose wife was in Japan, had just gotten back from there. Gump's was now owned by a Japanese company. Marty realized that each of these people, except for herself and Stan, were foreign born. Ernesto had been born in southern Florida, in a cigar-making enclave more Cuban than American. Anton was from Taiwan, Ricka from Germany, and Martin was born in Indonesia. All of them had been in the US for years, but Marty felt surrounded by a terrific sense of internationalism. She herself had recently returned from Hong Kong.

The meal came to $14.00 each. "I won't tell my wife," said Martin. "She would have a fit!" Martin's wife was an English nurse he had met during the war. Marty did not mention that she herself was living that week on a VISA cash advance. She had taken almost a year off work, with some freelance work for old friends from Design Logic days. Marty wasn't worried, however. She would start working for another large architectural firm next week.

After lunch, everyone went separate ways. Marty walked down a block to the Green Apple Bookstore. She stood around disoriented, wondering where she was, what she was doing and what to do next. Special class was an experience! And then being with this remarkable group for lunch! The bookstore, a big warren of wooden shelves reaching to the ceiling over-filled with second-hand books, brought Marty back to her usual mental atmosphere.

Marty climbed the bare wooden stairs to the crowded shelves of books in a nook set aside for Eastern religions. Would there be anything there that she hadn't seen yet? That she needed to become aware of? Her eyes roved over the authors and titles. She should probably not spend money just yet, anyway. She must put some money in the bank!

What had she accomplished in the year she had just taken off, Marty wondered. Lots of tai chi. Lots of reading, classes in writing and even filmmaking, quite a lot of travel, and many deepening friendships. It was wonderful to have her own base in San Francisco and to have so much going on. Marty did not think she had changed much, just become more herself.

In fact she had just finished writing about the five books she had long ago chosen as an education in becoming a unique self. None of the authors were American. Rather, they were the world citizens Pasternak, Rilke, Virginia Woolf, Kawabata, Breton. They had been her teachers, helping her toward the life she wanted of mystery, coincidence, intimacy, individuality and domesticity.

Writing about the books showed Marty that particular vein was finished. New ones were opening up, mostly about Taoism. Taoism could only be experienced, but John Blofeld and Deng Ming Dao pointed the way. Tai chi helped.

The year off had been about freedom as well. About trying to find her way after Marty's long marriage to Erik, who had died in an avalanche a few years before. Ernesto was also taking a sabbatical. "It proves you're not a lifer," he told Marty with his typical dramatic flair. "They can see it in your eyes!" Ernesto was as an artist with many projects in mind.

Marty had begun to think about jobs as projects. Long term ones. They were essentially a contract between herself and an employer. In most of her jobs she had stayed a long time, since only after being there a while did one really figure out what was going on. Companies were like people. Small firms reflected the desires of their owners. Marty had seen several management struggles by this time. Her own path was different, but Marty still didn't know exactly what it was. She could not really call herself an artist, but she did like thinking of herself as the scholar warrior Deng Ming Dao described in a recently published book by that name.

For the scholar warrior, all of life was integrated. It began with the cultivation of the physical body, but all aspects of daily living could be understood as a spiritual path. The scholar warrior sought equilibrium in all aspects of life, with a strong focus on health and self-cultivation. This involved the study of many arts, including music and literature as well as the martial arts. "Discipline is freedom, and the companion to imagination," said Deng Ming Dao. The warrior part was not about fighting; it was about being prepared for what life put in front of one.

No one had taught Marty these things before. She had never known the meaning of her restless striving. In the eyes of the Taoists, one was responsible for one's own life and its direction must come from within. Having goals clarified one's personality, but in the end, the scholar warrior made accomplishments in order to then leave them behind. All of this made a great deal of sense of Marty. It left her with the rock solid knowledge that she was part of nature, that she would flower in some way, but that cultivating this unique flower was up to her.

Marty went down the steps of the bookstore. As she went past the cash register, she held up her hands to show the clerk that she had not picked up any books that day. She joined the swirling, shopping crowds and then took buses toward the city and her own apartment.

To the scholar side of her nature Marty turned that afternoon. Lonely, as usual, she took the ancient, noisy cable car over the hill, wearing jeans, a black woolen jacket, chocolate loafers and carrying the beautifully tooled chocolate-colored Italian bag she had bought in Hong Kong. The angled October light spilled in on people, old and young. The car was usually full of tourists, but a woman beside Marty was dressed in black cotton culottes, black stockings, antique black jacket. She wore a silver pin with turquoise beads hanging from it; her hair hung loose and she was reading The Painted Bird.

Here I am, Marty thought, among the terminally hip. Her loneliness carried her back into the kind of defiant, solitary sensuality which she had learned during her marriage. I will wrap myself into my personal mystery and come again to expect nothing, she thought, giving myself the fullest benefit of each day's sensual pleasure.

A scholar warrior might be lonely. Marty knew and admired many people who had learned to live alone. Though she had many friends, and was still occasionally sleeping with Will, the younger friend with the big BMW, Marty was not in a couple. She and Will were friends, comfortable, taking care of each other, but neither of them felt it was a 'real' relationship.

Marty got off the cable car at Post Street and walked to where it met Market. The October city was alive with shoppers, but Marty ignored them and went into the tasteful arch of the Mechanics Institute building. Built in 1910, the Institute was a conservative classic, with two floors of library space and a beloved chess room on the fourth floor. Marty climbed the circular marble staircase with its iron balustrade up to the library level, looking up at the smooth spiral which climbed nine floors.

Marty slipped the magnetic card which proved her a member in the door. Inside the library, it was very quiet. Matthew, a friend Marty shared intellectual interests with, sat behind the big front desk. Marty went up to him to say hello.

"Hey," said Matthew, talking quietly and brushing long, graying curls off his face. "Do you want to go over to the Vision Gallery tonight? I get off at 5."

"Sure," whispered Marty. "Sounds great!"

Tall white columns supported the ceiling in the large room, and light poured in from high windows. Wooden furniture and leather couches were arranged for comfort, and men in casual clothes sat about, reading the newspapers. Marty climbed the steps to her favorite desk behind a column on the mezzanine, in the stacks.

The library would forever be associated with Dawn, a beautiful, slim woman who had told Marty to read the biography of Su Tungpo by Lin Yutang there, many years ago. They had shared a growing fascination with the East. Marty borrowed the biography several times. It told the immortal story of an Eleventh century statesman, writer and painter, whose brilliance and insouciance endeared him to China.

In and out of exile his whole life because he would not keep silent about what he thought, the biography brought Su Tungpo to vivid life. One night, Su Tungpo, kept awake by the moonlight, went over to find his friend. Together they walked through the garden amongst the moon shadows of bamboo and pine trees. "Isn't there a moon every night?" Su Tungpo asked. "And aren't there bamboos and pine trees everywhere? But there are few carefree people like the two of us."

Today Marty did not pull the magical book off the shelves, or any book. She took a small wire-bound notebook from her backpack and began to write on its green-lined pages. From Natalie Goldberg's partly Zen-inspired Writing Down the Bones, Marty had learned that if she wrote without stopping or thinking, she might stumble on the contents of her own deep mind. Journal writing had become very fashionable.

Marty never needed to be told to journal. She had done it most of her life. She had only a few more days before she must go back to work, become an actor in the external world. Writing was precious. Marty bent her head to her pen and notebook.

Goals were fine, Marty thought. But there was one goal over which she had no control whatsoever. Matthew, sitting at the desk down below, was a reminder. It would have been so easy if Marty and Matthew could have become lovers. Matthew was a year older than Marty, a photographer who had managed to study in England at Sherborne, where J. G. Bennett had begun a school teaching Gurdjieff's Fourth Way. Though not well off, Michael had also gone to San Francisco's famous Art Institute.

Aside from the fact that Matthew loved Dawn, who had moved to Massachusetts, Matthew and Marty did not get along well. He was the oldest of seven kids, was wonderful at discourse when he and Marty got together with Phil and Shannon, as they often did. He was one of the few intellectuals Marty knew. But Matthew was prickly.

Much as she tried to tell herself that she liked living alone, the truth was that Marty did not. She longed for a friend of her own, who belonged only to her. She longed to have a life partner who met her at every point, body, mind and heart. But she had not met anyone who wanted to be her partner in full. Marty was making do with the friends she had, often on the verge of falling in love, but she was under no illusions that one of her friends would become her partner.

She was still friends with Nathan, but she did not go to Los Angeles to see him. She did not want to get involved with any of the many interesting guys she met in tai chi, because she wanted to be there forever. She couldn't afford to sleep with someone in that community and have it not work out, leaving trails of tears and pain. She thought of herself as a temple concubine, available to everyone and to no one as she tried to become her own impeccable, lonely self.

Marty had gone to Hong Kong and had taken a train trip deep into China because she thought she might study tai chi there. She had been very drawn to the East, and Meredith had allowed her to stay with her brother. But once there, Marty knew she did not have the mental energy to study Chinese, either Cantonese or Mandarin. She was better off studying tai chi in California. She thoroughly enjoyed her trip, and met many people who engaged her, but nothing about the trip changed Marty's life.

Back in California, Marty restlessly took classes, helped with a movie when Will and everyone she knew seemed to be interested in film, and had gone to Santa Cruz to see Heather and Poppa several times.

In August, Santa Cruz was laden with thick fog, but it was fun rattling around in Poppa's big house while the rest of the Cohens were in Europe. Heather had taken Marty up to the winery in Boulder Creek where her mentor Doug Henderson was part owner.

Marty could still see Doug in her mind's eye, tall, smiling, anxious to help. He had walked Heather and Marty through the rows of a fog-shrouded vineyard, collecting Pinot Noir grapes for testing. They took them back to the ramshackle shed that served as a lab, made a juice sample and read the brix, or sugar level. Doug patiently dripped juice on the lens and let Heather look through the refractometer.

"It's only 19 degrees," said Heather. Doug had told them Jeremy Barnes, the winemaker, wanted it up to at least 23 degrees for his Pinot Noir.

Doug had shaken his head. "Too cold this year. It's going to be a nervous year. The fruit won't get ripe very early, which makes us all jumpy. We'll have to wait out a long hang-time, hope the birds don't get them. We'll harvest late, before the rains come."

Heather nodded. It seemed old hat to her, but Marty was amazed at the technical expertise involved. There were many other ripeness factors too, Doug told them, talking about the colors of the seeds, the shape of the grapes, the way they came off the stem.

That year Marty paid more attention to the grape harvest, even becoming nervous herself! She had called Heather recently to find out how the grapes were doing, but according to Heather, a late warm spell had ripened them. Things were turning out well for the vintage.

Marty also met Doug's kids when Heather babysat for them. The oldest, Zoe, was 2, and the twins, Domenic and Natasha were just a year. They lived in an airy frame house up on the mountain. Their mother Mackenzie was young, and according to Heather, kind of wild. She did not like to stay home and sometimes went to rock concerts, leaving the kids with their grandmother for days. Marty did not see Doug with his kids, but Heather told her he was a great father.

From what Marty could see, Doug was a grownup, the exact sort of person she would like to have had for a partner. But men like him were married, already taken, mature and happy.

In a way, Marty's husband Erik was as alive for her as he had ever been. He was often in her dreams. But she had to admit their communication had gotten worse toward the end of his life. In Chengdu, in China, as she walked around a bonsai garden one afternoon, Marty listened as a man and a woman talked on and on in Chinese. She did not know what they were saying, but their measured, endless conversation had become a touchstone for what she wanted in a relationship. Someone with whom she could speak, about everything.

Marty hoped for a second chance for herself, but she had also resolved not to become involved with anyone who was not a match for her. This meant working on herself, as much as meeting people. Tai chi was helping.

Marty dragged herself back from daydreaming. Back to the city, her own life, where she would soon be at work in a big architectural firm, Designers International, which had both interiors and architectural projects, often for high-tech companies. Movies, wine, high-tech, these were California's products. Marty loved knowing about them and working around them.

At 5 p.m. Marty went out into the hall and sat on a marble step, waiting for Matthew. "Have you ever gone up to the top and looked down?" he asked her when he came out. The circular staircase, with its continuous wooden railing and crafted iron sides, was spectacular. "I've photographed it many times," said Matthew.

Marty looked up into the cupola. "It is amazing," she said. She was thinking about the circular escalator her last architectural firm had put into San Francisco Centre at Fifth and Market. "Circles are magic," she said. "Tai chi shows that as well."

They took the streetcar down Market Street and crossed over to Mission. Joe Folberg, wearing an old-fashioned tailored suit, strode about in his airy gallery with its wooden floors, brick walls and high ceiling. Smoke from his cigar wafted toward Marty. He had surely assessed Matthew, in his blue-jean jacket, and herself as connoisseurs, perhaps, but not buyers.

Matthew talked quietly as they looked at the huge framed photographs on the wall and then flipped through bins of photos. "They busted Jock Sturges," said Matthew as they looked at his photos. "The FBI raided his studio and confiscated his equipment. He was at the Art Institute when I was. Uses a big view camera, but he's been photographing on nude beaches. Especially teenagers. Some people don't go for that."

Marty looked at the long legs, the beautiful curves and the way the light accentuated people's skin. "They're beautiful," she said.

"I don't think he even poses them," said Matthew. "Even with that big camera. It must be hard to do on the beach. Pretty amazing."

They moved on. Marty recognized photos by Caponigro. There were also Brett Weston's strikingly graphic black and white photos and Ruth Bernhard's nudes and shells. "I thought that one was by Edward Weston," said Marty, pointing to a nude torso, the arms wrapped around the legs.

"She's been influenced," said Matthew. They walked around reverently, looking at the photos on the wall.

"I think I always liked Ruth Orkin," said Marty. "So much life in her photographs."

Matthew waved to Mr. Folberg as they walked out the door. "Yeah," he said. "I like street photography as well. I've been looking at my books again. Kertesz is so gentle in his photos of Paris, whereas Cartier-Bresson's are an attack!"

"Is Kertesz the one who did so many photographs of books and reading?" asked Marty.

"Yeah," said Matthew. "On Reading. A whole book full."

"I'm reading a lot less since I've been so involved in tai chi," said Marty as they walked down the street. "But I'm sure I'll always come back to books."

"So, do you want to get some coffee?" asked Matthew. "Or are you on your way home?"

Marty considered. Matthew lived in North Beach, not that far from Marty's apartment on Russian Hill. "I've got a bottle of wine at home," she said. "But it might not be up to your standards!"

Matthew snorted. He was a low-paid librarian and drove a cab at night as well, but Marty had drunk the best wine she ever had with Matthew over various dinners. "I can lower my standards, I imagine," he said. "What is it?"

Marty was chagrined to find she could not remember. "I guess we'll find out when we get to my place," she said. "Let's pick up some cheese on the way."

4

Paul stood at the back of Ellie and Bruce's big living room watching as Jack Morris, a Minnesota Twins pitcher, scowled at his manager who had come out to talk to him on the mound. It was the eighth inning of the seventh game of the World Series, and two men were on base.

"Oh! He's gonna pull him!" said Bruce, Paul's brother-in-law from the couch. "Morris doesn't want to quit!"

The tension was so high, Paul could feel it in the room. But Morris and Tom Kelly conferred and Morris seemed to agree. He let the next man walk, and with the bases loaded, the Twins made a double play on the next ground to first, sending the Braves off the field. Neither team had scored so far.

"It's a good thing they've got that dome," said Ellie, Paul's sister as she slipped into the kitchen. "Pretty cold out for a baseball game." It was almost the end of October. The Metrodome had a fiberglass fabric roof. Paul had never been in it, but he had certainly seen its white expanse from a distance.

Paul tore himself away from the room, smiling at Ellie, who came back with a tray of tortilla chips and salsa. She sat back down on the couch beside Bruce and picked up her needlepoint.

Archie's cold nose met Paul at the little wicket gate which prevented Archie from coming upstairs. Paul reassured Archie. There was plenty of life going on downstairs in Mother's apartment as well. Mother was entertaining Hanna and her friend Faith. Hanna and Faith had moved to upstate New York to Faith's family farm. They planned to start a cheese-making operation together, but Hanna wanted to introduce Faith to the Mikkelsons before their venture got going. Paul and Marie, and their dog Archie, had come down to St. Paul to see them.

Hanna strummed Paul's guitar in front of the fire. Marie was singing, but when Hanna saw Paul, she handed off the guitar she held in her hands. "You play it Paul!" she said. "You know Marie's songs much better."

Mother and Faith sat on the couch, hot drinks in their hands, listening. Faith, a small woman with olive-colored skin and wispy dark hair, looked more like Marie than blonde, Scandinavian Hanna.

Marie smiled at him and Paul took the guitar. It was a song Marie had just written about winter coming. Paul never felt very sure about the music, which he took back to deep folk roots, the best he could do. He was not much of a composer. But Marie's full-throated voice wafted out into the room, conquering space with its power:

> Oh, the wind will blow and the snow will fall,
> At night wool blankets warm us.
> We'll bank the fire and not be afraid.
> Our woodpile is enormous.
>
> I love to roast kabocha squash,
> Potatoes, greens and chicken.
> The kitchen smells rise in the air,
> They make my heart to quicken.
>
> Our skis are quick on sugar snow,
> Beneath the silver moonlight.
> We take the path round Miner's lake
> Our shadows share the cold night.
>
> My sister made my thrummed mittens,
> They're blue with white fleece threaded.
> They warm my hands with love and care.
> To family we're wedded.

Mother, Hanna and Faith clapped with delight. Marie laughed, self-deprecatingly and she and Paul dipped their heads in a grateful bow. "That is so great!" said Hanna. "I'm going to write down the words."

"What are thrummed mittens?" asked Mother. "I've never heard of them."

"You take bits of fleece," replied Marie, "and knit them into the mittens. Inside out, the mittens look like they are full of cotton balls or something. They're really warm!"

"Is that your sister in Sainte-Perpetue, in Quebec?" asked Mother. Mother was especially good at imagining other people's circumstances. She knew everything about Marie's family.

"It was Gilberte," said Marie. "They live nearby. She made them for me last Christmas. I've been thinking about them! But it isn't quite cold enough yet."

"So perfect, in a song," said Faith. She looked at Hanna. "I'm not much for knitting. But Hanna might be."

"Sounds intriguing," said Hanna. "But we have a lot of other things to do first! Where's Miner's lake?" she turned to Paul.

"It's about a block north of our house in Ely," said Paul. "It was made when the open pit mine was abandoned and filled with water. Some cave-ins too. Anyway, now there're trees and scrub beside it, with a path around it. It's kind of a sterile lake, but we take that path all year around. It's so close." Paul was feeling the pull of the World Series. Was it the last game? "There's a really good game going on upstairs," he said to Mother. "Almost over too. You might want to have a look!"

"You're right," said Mother. "I need to know what is going on with my home team!" She rose with difficulty from the couch on her stiff legs. Skirting Archie, who lay in the hallway, she pulled herself up the stairs, using the handrail. Paul followed her. When Marie followed him, Paul turned and stole a kiss in the crook of her neck, visible above her red sweater. Marie grinned back at him.

Upstairs they all knew enough not to speak as the television blared out the news. There had been no runs in the ninth either. The Braves pitcher had strained a muscle in his back, but the reliever managed to send the Twins down. The game was going into its tenth inning.

"I can't stand it," said Ellie. But she looked quite placid as she sipped a beer. She was wearing a sweatshirt blazoned with the word 'Twins' in red script across her chest.

"We're all gonna have to," said Bruce. He stood up and stretched, looking at the newcomers. He too wore a Twins ball cap with an old v-necked sweater. "Here Lois," he said to Mother. "Sit here," he said, giving her the best seat.

Mother sat down heavily. "Thank you, Bruce," she said. "So how's Kirby doing?" she asked. Kirby Puckett had hit the home run that won the Twins game six the day before. Puckett was popular in Minnesota for his friendliness and community service.

"Well, they walked him in the last inning," said Ellie.

The Twins pitcher, Jack Morris, was stubborn, rebuffing his manager's attempt to take him out. An announcer reported that Tom Kelly said, "Oh hell. It's only a game," causing laughs all around! But Morris retired the Braves' first three hitters, one after another.

Paul and Marie stood at the back of the room. Paul remembered how Dad used to do this when he was a kid. Dad thought watching television sitcoms was a waste, but he never forbid it, popping in now and then to see what was going on. Paul himself preferred radio. He listened to the news while he was driving, and sometimes a baseball game. He liked imagining the situation on the diamond. His favorite announcer, Halsey Hall, with his gravely voice, was long gone, but Paul had not forgotten him.

The first Twins hitter, Gladden, broke his bat on impact with the ball, and dashed to second while the ball hopped and bounced. "Wow!" shouted Bruce. Once again the pitcher walked Kirby Puckett. But Gene Larkin took his first pitch, driving in a deep hit, allowing Gladden, on third, to come in for the winning run. Even Mother gave a little cheer!

All of the Twins players erupted onto to the field, were joined by their families and then did a victory lap around the field in the Metrodome.

"That was quite a game!" said Bruce. "One of the best I've seen!"

"Sure kept up the suspense!" said Ellie.

Saying goodnight, Mother, Marie and Paul faded back downstairs. Hanna was playing a song Paul didn't know, singing softly, "Talk to me of Mendocino, closing my eyes I hear the sea. Must I wait, must I follow? Won't you say, come with me." She stopped playing. "It's a traveling song," she said. "Written by Kate McGarrigle." She looked toward Marie. "You must know it! She and her sister are from Quebec also!"

But Marie's face tightened and Paul knew what she was thinking. "I do know them," said Marie. "They sang in the same Montreal folk clubs I did, long ago. Kate is the same age as I am. But they were college girls. They knew what they were doing," she finished, looking sad.

Paul was solicitous, putting his arms around Marie's waist as she spoke. Talk of the McGarrigles evoked in Marie that painful time when she had come, friendless and alone, to the big city. And even worse, the craziness and violence she had experienced in trying to make a musical career in Los Angeles later.

Hanna tried to brush off Marie's sadness, blurting on, "We saw them at Café Lena in Saratoga Springs! A couple of home girls, we thought. So warm and real."

"Yes," said Marie. "They've had the success I hoped for. On their own terms too. They have a big Irish and French family behind them. I do love their songs," she finished.

"I'm sorry, Marie," said Hanna. "I had no idea. I was just trying to play this great song for Faith."

Marie sat down beside her, putting her arms around her. "It's okay, Hanna," she said bravely. "You didn't know, and I shouldn't let it bother me anyway. I'm happy now." She looked up at Paul, her eyes wet, but shining.

Paul knew Marie's long, tough story. She had gone to Montreal and Toronto as a very young girl to see what fortune her amazing singing voice might bring her. She became pregnant and had a daughter at her parents' farm, though living under the cloud of her eldest sister's, brothers' and the Monsignor's disapproval.

When she went back to the city to sing, she was coaxed into marriage and going to Los Angeles, leaving her daughter Grace to be raised by her mother in Quebec. She had a high-flying year singing with an up and coming band, but her husband, the lead guitar, got into drugs, alcohol and groupies. The drummer had fallen for Marie too. He was gentler, but the conflict had been paralyzing and Marie did all the cooking and cleaning in the house where the band lived together.

On top of it, Marie had trouble recovering from an infection from the IUD she was using to prevent pregnancy, and before she hardly knew it the doctors had taken out her uterus. When she was ready to leave the hospital, the band was on tour and Marie had no idea where her husband was.

Cheryl, one of the nurses, had taken Marie under her wing, bringing her home to live with her roommates. When Marie was still too sick to work after a month of recovery, and her husband didn't turn up, Cheryl sent Marie to live with her parents in Seattle. They had a grocery and delicatessen.

Slowly, Marie had begun working for them, recovering her health and her faith in herself. But the dream of making it in the music business was over. She got a divorce from her husband, the final defiance of her deeply Catholic upbringing, and started working in restaurants. Marie kept in touch with Cheryl and her family, who had been so good to her when she had felt she couldn't turn to her own. Not long after, she and Paul had met when she helped cook on the Adventuress, the two-masted schooner Paul crewed on for a couple of summers.

Marie still sometimes felt anxious and depressed, especially in the dark, cold winters. But becoming part of the Mikkelson family, reconciling with her own family and daughter, and having grandchildren had largely restored Marie's joy in life. Paul himself felt deeply lucky to have found this vibrant French Canadian girl who had taken him as her own.

Mother, who loved both Marie and Hanna, said, "You girls look so young and lovely! I love hearing you sing together!" But she did not sit down. "I think the next place I should be is in bed!" she announced. "If I sit down, I'll probably never get up! Good night, my darlings." All four of the rest of them, more mobile than she, got up to hug her good night.

"Tomorrow is another day," said Hanna, "as you so often told us!"

"Yes," said Mother. "Sleep well!" She went down the hall.

"You play," said Hanna again to Paul. "You're so much better!"

Paul took the guitar, strumming lightly the chords for Leonard Cohen's "Hallelujah." Most of Cohen's songs relied on the singer, not the music, but some of them were great. He wondered if he could play the percussive guitar required by the song he and Marie had been fascinated by. He looked at Marie questioningly. "First We Take Manhattan?"

"Oh yes!" said Hanna. "Now that we're into the Canadians." She put her arm around Faith on the sofa, pulling her close. "Faith's almost Canadian!" she said.

"Were you ever in Montreal?" asked Marie.

Faith nodded. "We were only a little closer to New York than Montreal. About half way between. And my mother studied French and got me to study French! So we went up there to speak it now and then. And just to be in a foreign country."

"And what made you want to make cheese?" asked Marie.

Faith smiled. "I found that it needs the same precise care as I use in the lab. In fact, you make cheese in a lab! With careful attention to chemical and microbiological processes in the milk. We're still investigating. I kind of mentioned it to my Dad and he was all over it. Especially when he started farming goats and sheep as well as cows. All of their milk makes interesting cheese. We're taking a cheese course when we get back."

"And how about you?" asked Paul of Hanna.

"I'm going to do the grunt work," said Hanna, laughing. "The farm is lovely. I'm not really a city girl, I don't think. And I've done more actual acting in Saratoga Springs than I ever did in New York. Shakespeare and summer stock. Saratoga is close to us. It all just makes a lot of sense for me," she said. "And my girl," she squeezed Faith around the waist, the dark and blonde heads pressed together.

"It sounds great," said Marie, wistfully. "I wish you all the luck in the world."

Paul began hitting the guitar strings rhythmically. "One more song," he said. "And then we better pack it in."

Marie began clapping and dancing rhythmically. "I chose this song," she said. "I just love the music." She whirled around, music in her head, the emotions touched off by the night visible in her mobile body. "And the words are interesting too!"

Marie came close to Paul, who sang as he played, deadpan as if he were Leonard Cohen. "They sentenced me to 20 years of boredom, for trying to change the system from within. I'm coming now, I'm coming to reward them. First we take Manhattan, then we take Berlin."

Marie, dancing around him and shaking her body, sang the chorus: "I'd really like to live beside you, baby. I love your body, your spirit and your clothes. But you see that line there moving through the station? I told you. I told you, told you. I was one of those."

There were more verses. Hanna stood up, clapping along. "You guys!" she said. "You have got this one down!"

Paul laughed. He did have a dramatic streak in him, somewhere. Where did it come from?

"What's it about?" asked Faith.

"It's about the fashion business," said Marie. "Leonard Cohen is pointing out that they've got some of their priorities wrong. His dad was a haberdasher, I think. That's why he always wears a suit."

Paul was beginning to feel that they were being too noisy. Mother might want to sleep! Archie too was drooping, his head on his paws. "Okay," he said, lifting the guitar strap over his head. "That's it."

In the morning, Paul and Marie left for home. A sweet, heavy sadness filled their little Rabbit as they drove north in the cold air, bundled up in warm sweaters and coats. Paul had wrapped Archie in a heavy woolen blanket in the back seat. Marie's mood of the night before hadn't lifted,

Paul could tell. "I'm glad we're going home," he said. He liked their quiet life.

"Do you think Hanna is settling for less than she could get?" asked Marie. "Could she be a starring actress, do you think?"

Paul looked at her. "Hanna is being realistic," he said. "She's a Mikkelson! I think Saratoga is a good choice for her. I have the impression it's a place where education goes on. Hanna likes the spotlight, but I don't think she needs to be a star."

"And how old is she?" asked Marie. "I guess she's 31 this year. She could certainly go further in theater, if she wanted to."

"Relationship is important too," said Paul. "This is an adventure for her. Maybe she'll make cheese commercials!"

"Well," said Marie, relaxing. "I do know how important good food is. And people are finally beginning to see it. The farm might be nice, too." She looked a little doubtful. It was interesting to Paul that Marie had invested in Hanna's success.

They pushed on, north from the city. Paul wished he knew something nice he could do for Marie, some comfort he could provide. A nice warm drink in their own house sounded best to him. Around them, the barren trees and the bare fields looked bleak against an opaque, white sky. The air in the car was not really warm enough.

Before long they were home. They warmed up the house and Paul took a moment to sit with his legs up, wrapped in a blanket. He had to admit they sometimes ached in the cold, especially his ankles where ligaments had been cut to repair his polio-damaged legs.

In the afternoon Paul went to the canoe outfitters. Not much was going on there. People stood around joshing each other, going over inventories and supplies as they shut down for the winter. Marie went to her little deli at the co-op to see whether her employees were having any trouble. The dark came early and at night Paul and Marie slept cozy together in flannel sheets under their heavy Hudson Bay blankets, Archie at their feet.

That week a cold front spread south and east and a low-pressure system moved up from the south. Early snow began to fall on Halloween. Paul carried the transistor radio around with him, listening to the news and the weather. He noticed that Marie had not brought her warmest jacket and her mittens to work. The car safe in its garage, Paul wrapped Marie's things in a bag and laced up his waterproof Chippewas. He and Archie walked across town in the evening to meet Marie with the warm clothes.

Snow was coming down heavily, beautiful under the street lamps, accumulating on roofs and in the trees. The sounds of cars going by were toned down and the air smelled fresh and damp. In the dusky light, small groups of kids, dressed as ghosts in white sheets, witches in black, superheroes and princesses passed them, going up and down the residential walks with their orange plastic pumpkins for treat collection, drifts of white collecting on their little shoulders and heads. Parents with flashlights accompanied some.

Paul saw a large carved pumpkin glowing within, snow crowning its cap. Archie wasn't spooked, but he was excited by a black Labrador, trick or treating with its family in a red blanket and a tiny red clown hat. Paul reassured Archie. "Don't worry, Arch," he said quietly. "I'd never do that to you."

At the co-op, Marie was clearing up. She had been working behind the big stove, making soup and baking breads and Halloween cookies. She looked elfin and mischievous; excited by the kids she had seen in costume. "My favorite was a little bat man," she said. "Not a bought costume, but a homemade one with a cape. Red hair sticking out of his black ski helmet and mask." She pulled on the warm jacket Paul had brought. "Thank you so much for coming!" she said. "I just didn't realize the snow was going to be this heavy!"

"I can't spoil you much," said Paul, handing over the blue mittens with white thrums knit like polka dots into them. "But I would like to."

Marie's eyes flashed with pleasure. "You are my prince!" she said.

On the way home, snow fell and the wind blew strongly from behind them. Marie, always present minded, lifted up her face, tasting the snowflakes like a child. The number of kids trick or treating seemed to have thinned out. Paul heard Marie's low voice singing:

> "Oh, the wind will blow and the snow will fall,
> At night wool blankets warm us.
> We'll bank the fire and not be afraid.
> Our woodpile is enormous."

They didn't have a fireplace at home, actually. Or a woodpile. Marie had been thinking of the Ben Franklin and the woodpiles at Mother's lake cabin.

It was early for snow, but it didn't seem to be stopping. Paul dug out his emergency supplies, flashlights, batteries, an emergency generator.

The heater and the stove were gas fueled. They would be fine, but it was nice to have light. Paul wanted to be part of the solution, if power lines went down, not part of the problem. He was glad for his tightly-built and insulated house, for the garage which protected the poor, old Rabbit.

In the morning the snow continued but the power stayed on. The Twin Cities was reporting more than eight inches of snowfall on Halloween and more to come.

"I wonder if Faith and Hanna are going to be able to fly out in this mess," said Marie, as she served up hot oatmeal. "Aren't they supposed to leave this weekend?"

"Tomorrow, I think," said Paul. He put the transistor radio, turned down low, on the dining table. "We'll call them tonight. See how they are faring."

Marie went to work, but Paul looked forward to a day of reading and thinking. Blizzards were great, he thought. There was no point in shoveling until the snow quit and nowhere he needed to go that day. It was no wonder that most technological innovations had come out of the north. For one thing, northerners needed them. For another, people in the north had more time to think!

After topping up the bird feeders with suet and seeds, Paul settled into a big chair by a window in his house clothes, a ragged woolen shirt over thermal underwear, wool socks. The heating worked well, but Paul kept the thermostat down, as a conservation measure and to save money. White light from the window fell on Paul's page as thick flakes fell and snow piled up around the house and in the nearby trees. A few birds turned up, but most would be hunkered down somewhere.

Paul was reading two books, as usual. For his serious book, he was reading Charles Darwin's The Power of Movement in Plants. In it, Darwin and his son showed that the ends of roots, the radical of the plant, was quite sensitive to moisture, touch or cuts, causing the plant above to react strongly to what was happening below. It helped show how Darwin's theories of natural selection worked.

But Paul was also reading Jim Kjelgaard's books about dogs, Big Red and his sons Irish Red and Outlaw Red. They were books for teenagers, but they were full of woods lore from Kjelgaard's time as a trapper in the Alleghenies early in the century. The beautiful red setters were important, but Paul also learned a lot from the human protagonist, Danny, walking silently through the forest, knowing the ways and manners of mysterious wolverines, lynx, martens, cougars, and fishers.

Paul was especially interested in the ways in which Kjelgaard described the Mustelidae family, the weasels, mink, otter, marten and fishers, with the fierce wolverine at the top. Helen Hoover and her husband had fed fishers and a small ermine in the winter on nearby Gunflint Lake in the 1950's, but Paul had never seen a fisher. The sinuous, long body of a marten chasing a squirrel was familiar, and Paul caught sight of the white fur of smaller weasels in the winter. But the weasel family was elusive, especially the ferocious wolverine. All weasels were vicious predators, as they had to eat almost a third of their weight each day, but the wolverine was legendary. There were few, if any, in Minnesota, but Paul longed to catch sight of one.

Marie arrived home early that night, saying that the co-op had been pretty empty all afternoon. Snowplows were out, but the thick snowfall didn't quit. The radio was reporting another ten inches at least had fallen in the Twin Cities. Paul called Mother's apartment. "How are you doing down there?" he asked.

"Snug as bugs in rugs," said Mother's warm voice. "But it doesn't look as if the girls are going anywhere!"

"I'll bet they're not too unhappy," said Paul. Marie stood next to him, her head bent over the phone to hear the voices coming over the line.

"No," said Mother. "Here's Hanna."

"Hey, Paul," said Hanna's voice. "And Marie? How is it up there?"

"Coming down pretty heavy still," said Paul. "So your flight is canceled?"

"Yup," said Hanna. "They can't plow fast enough to keep a runway clear. But it's fine. It can't last forever."

"No," said Paul. "You'll probably get out in the next couple of days." He handed the phone to Marie.

"We're thinking about you all," said Marie. "Hope you like snowstorms."

"Nothing this heavy happens in New York," said Hanna. "But Faith says they get plenty of snow on the farm. We made your lentil loaf today, Marie. It was delicious!"

"I'm glad," said Marie. "Did you convince Mother?"

"No," said Hanna. Paul could hear her teasing smile across the phone wires. "She doesn't like anything she didn't eat as a kid. You know, meat, ground meat, sausage, potatoes. We'll make a meatloaf for her tomorrow."

"So good to see you all!" said Paul, his mouth close to the phone. "Send us some cheese when you have a chance!" He wondered whether you could send cheese by mail. He put down the phone. "We should go visit that farm some time," he said to Marie, hope in his voice.

5

On a wind-blown, sunny day, Line wandered through a large glasshouse with her friend Kerry, a native Scotswoman with an adventurous streak. The place, run by old friends of Kerry, had large gardens and an orchard, plus a tearoom. Kerry's friends kept bees, which were beginning to be out and about in the blossoming trees. It was the sort of place at the edge of Edinburgh Line would never have found if she hadn't had a local friend.

Line tried not to touch anything as she walked around. It didn't seem courteous. Kerry, more proprietary, fingered the calendula, the marjoram and tasted the summer savory. She handed a bit of it to Line, who bit into the peppery leaf.

Everything was labeled by Rory, the owner and main gardener. How did he keep it all up? Line wondered. He had longish, grey hair and the wind-burned dark skin of someone who spent most of his time outdoors. Rory said little to them as he moved purposefully around, directing his helpers. Line had brought Stephen and her girls the previous fall during apple harvest, bringing home a bushel of the amazing Bloody Ploughman apples, so mild and sweet, which Line could find nowhere else.

Now, in April, people were carting the young sets out to the fields and planting them. It was a blustery day, as usual, but herbs had to be ready to handle it, to take in whatever patchy sun they were allowed over the summer. Line and Kerry walked through the orchard where the trees blossomed, sweet smells wafting on the breeze. Line was especially happy about the bees buzzing in the flowers loud enough to hear over the wind.

Line and Kerry ordered tea from Rory's wife Fiona and took the pots, mugs and scones out to a sheltered spot on the southern side of the glasshouse. Line was delighted to be outdoors after the long winter, sitting in the thin sunshine. "Oh my goodness," she said. "I am so happy out here!"

Kerry concurred. "It really is great!" she said. But she had just gotten back from a dogsled trek in the snow in Finland! She had loved it, but she told Line how much work it was to keep the dogs fed and happy. Kerry, a naturopath and acupuncturist; as thin as a stick and about the same age as Line, was interested in everything. She lived with her old Dad and his dog in a house at the edge of the city, leaving herself plenty of money to study and travel. Line had met her at the clinic where she volunteered.

Kerry lifted the strainer out of her teapot and set it on a saucer. "I always tell Fiona how much I like the loose tea they use here," she said. "Trying to buck her up a little. They don't get much business during the week."

"Yes," said Line. "Loose tea seems fresher." She smelled the bergamot aroma rising off the lovely cup of tawny colored Earl Grey tea in front of her. Today was special. Most people in Scotland were happy with limp teabags, which even appeared in tearooms. Line herself used the inexpensive Red Rose black teabags she found at Tesco's grocery every day. She looked around. "I hope they're doing well. It's such a wonderful place."

"Well enough," said Kerry. "The work is its own reward, but as Fiona says, they aren't as young as they used to be." She wrapped the woolen scarf she wore more tightly around her neck. She had the high, angular cheekbones and pale skin of an aristocrat, but Line knew her to be a gypsy at heart.

"They seem to have plenty of interested helpers," said Line. "It would be the perfect place for Ivy, if we were staying." Because they were not. The Cohens were about to pack up and go back to California. "Fern is staying though," said Line. "She wants to study archaeology, and there really isn't a better place than this."

"You're going to let her stay when you leave?" asked Kerry, putting jam on her scone.

"Well, she'll be 18 in a month," said Line. "She wants to go to the university here. And one of Stephen's colleagues, a professor's family, has agreed to look after her."

"Good!" said Kerry.

"It is hard on me," said Line. "My kids are so spread out. Heather's talking about an internship at a winery in some foreign country, my son is all over the place, and now Fern wants to stay here!"

"Well," said Kerry. "At least you'll have Ivy at home a little while longer. Cheeky girl," she said fondly.

Line looked at her darkly. "A little while," she said. Kerry loved Ivy. Most grownups did. But Ivy had not had a wonderful time in Scotland. She had been left with the outsider kids, which wasn't entirely a bad thing. They were often sweet to each other, but they were tough, had tattoos, wore leather and bleached their hair. School leaving age was 16 in Scotland. Most would go to work in shops instead of to university, already thinking of themselves as adults. Line and Stephen had had a tough time convincing Ivy not to prove herself by getting a tattoo.

Somehow the time in Edinburgh had been better for Fern. She had hustled and studied and hung out with kids with a brighter future. Line did not understand it. Ivy, who was so sensitive, was protected by these sweet, hopeless outsider kids, while Fern had toughened up and been willing to compete.

Line took a bite out of a buttery scone. "I think both of the girls are getting an education in drugs and alcohol. But the same thing would probably have happened in California," she said.

Kerry sighed. "Yeah. Seems like they have to do it. But they're so young!" She poured more milk in her cup and followed it with tea, stirring it with a slim, brown wrist. "We started it, after all, though," she said. "If we hadn't run around to so many different countries, figuring out how other people lived, including those hashish and opiate-ridden cultures, there might be less drugs around."

Line laughed. "You're right," she said. "I don't mind them knowing. 'Good sense, innocence, cripples mankind,' I remember we used to say. But I want them to get past it. To get to somewhere useful. I was glad when we got here that the kids were going to see different ways of thinking. We needed to shake them up a bit. But now, I think, it will be good for Ivy to get back."

"Fern can go to clubs when she's 18," said Kerry. "Seems like that's a danger point."

"Yes," said Line. "The whole club thing trickles down. They're all affected by it. I do think Fern has found a passion for herself, though. And she does see what happens to kids who don't have one."

"Why is the drinking age is so late in the U.S.?" asked Kerry.

"Because of cars, I think," said Line. "Kids have cars as soon as they can get a driver's license at 16. And keeping the drinking age high prevents accidents. I mean," Line backtracked, "They still get ahold of alcohol. And drive. But the consequences are steep. I think car accidents are still the highest cause of teen deaths there."

"It's the distance, then," said Kerry. "Here you can just walk home! Probably have to walk home. Or take the bus." She stood up. "Ready?" she asked. "You are brave to have all of those kids, Line."

Line smiled. "Yes," she said. "I suppose so."

"And what about you, Line?" asked Kerry. "Are you happy to leave?"

"I'll miss you," said Line, taking Kerry's arm in its heavy sweater. "And our talks. But yes, I want to get home to my own garden. I'm wondering about my persimmon tree. Poppa doesn't pay much attention to the things that are down below the terrace. It was rather new when I left. I'm hoping it survived."

Line did not say how much something in her longed to get back to California. It had become home, its pungent scents, its heat, the grey green cypress, iceplant and aloe, the golden hillsides and powerful blue sky. She had never realized how physical homesickness could be. How deep a place California had carved in her heart.

Stephen was terribly happy in Scotland. So much was happening in Europe and optimism about the new European Union was high. The Maastricht treaty had been signed, but would not go into effect for another year. Labour had lost once again to the Conservatives, but the Labour Party leader was resigning and a Scotsman, John Smith, a member of the opposition party shadow cabinet, bid fair to take his place. Everyone in Scotland was very proud of Smith. He was from Glasgow, but Stephen had seen him speak.

Stephen also loved being surrounded by ancient historical resources. He had opened books so old they had to be rested on a cushion, the pages turned with cotton-gloved hands. But someone in the family had to be flexible, Line thought. She was elected. And it had been a good move for the girls.

Line too had made the most of her time in Edinburgh, deepening her knowledge of herbal therapies and plants. She had found several small gardens which she loved, the Prince Street gardens on the other side of the castle; Dunbars Close, a small walled garden with rich plantings; and the wild, steep Dr. Neil's garden beside Duddington Loch. And if none of them were under her care, at least she learned from what was planted and how it thrived. Scotland cared much about its gardens.

They walked back to Kerry's tiny car and Kerry dropped Line at the Tesco's near her house. Line shopped nearly every day, as her storage space was limited. She and Stephen didn't have a car. They used bicycles to get around, buses, cabs and walking. Line took each day as it came. Who knew what would happen with her active family.

That night Stephen dined with his colleagues, but Fern brought a friend home, which meant four women making dinner together. Line cooked pasta and had Ivy help her with the sauce, while Fern and Annika made a salad. Something was eating Annika, Line thought. She seemed dispirited in some way.

The dining table was at one end of the spacious living room beside windows which looked out on the Meadows. Line blessed the evening light by which she could just see the explosive cherry trees, burgeoning pink on the avenues in the green expanse. She minded not being on the ground floor, not connected to the ground, but the views, the mists in the morning, the students strolling or playing games were a wonderful changing canvas outside her window. A month ago there had been acres of purple and white crocuses, and there were beautiful trees, beeches, chestnuts, cedars and ancient willows.

Ivy set the table in the spring light, placing napkins and silver with care for their guest. Line had met Annika before, a steady, sober girl whom Fern sometimes studied with. She wore dark-rimmed glasses, but had impudent freckles on her nose and a thick mop of auburn hair which was difficult to tame. Annika wasn't talking much, letting Fern and Ivy josh each other. But Fern too acted subdued. What was up, Line wondered. Was Fern in trouble? Was Annika?

When they all sat down, Ivy bubbled, taking up the space left over: "We're going to do the Millennium walk on the Isle of Man next week. It's 28 miles! But Dad promised Mum that we could do it in two days."

Line smiled, imagining herself walking so far. She was a good walker, but that was a long way. "It's a history project," she said. "As everything is around here. It commemorates one thousand years of the Tynwald, the parliament which was established in 1079 on the island."

Nothing seemed to interest Annika. "What is it with you guys?" asked Line. "You are generally so enthusiastic about everything."

Fern looked at Annika, who did not respond.

"You know there's nothing under the sun which won't be helped by talking about it," said Line quietly. "And we can talk about it right here." She looked warningly at Ivy, as if to say, be quiet. Give them a chance.

"I told you," said Fern to Annika. "I told you Mum would help." She turned back to Line. "Mom," she said balefully. "We have to ask you. Annika is pregnant. She hasn't had her period in two months."

Line was not exactly surprised. She leaned across the small table and touched Annika's arm. "Sweetheart!" she said. "Congratulations!" It was certainly a life-changing circumstance.

"I'm too young!" blurted Annika in her thick Scotch accent. "And I want to go to university!" She looked vulnerable, and a little indignant. Tears squeezed out of her eyes. She hadn't touched her pasta.

"Do your parents know?" asked Line. Her heart went out to the girl. But surely Annika was a smart one. "There's no reason you can't go to university and have a baby at the same time. How about your boyfriend? What does he think?"

"My parents don't know," said Annika. "But it makes Cull happy. He wants us to be a family. Even if we're young. He's kind of a grownup already."

"Good!" said Line. "That's half the battle!" She wondered what Annika wanted to ask her. "You should come over to the clinic, if you haven't been. Then you would be sure and a doctor could check to see that everything is all right." Line was volunteering at a clinic for mothers and children. She couldn't do much nursing, but she helped with reception and taking care of whatever was needed.

"But my mother or father would have to come with me, wouldn't they?" Annika asked.

"You have to tell them," said Line, simply.

Annika heaved a big sigh. "They'll kill me," she said. "They're quite religious. My dad is a deacon and he's always telling my brothers and me that we represent our family in the world. He would just die if he knew. And my mum believes everything he says."

Line looked toward Fern to see what she thought. "I doubt that either of them will die when they know," she said. "But you're going to need their help. Unless Culloden is independently wealthy! Or you want to run away. Which I doubt."

"My grandfather is Lutheran pastor," said Fern. "Mum told me that my brother Christy was sort of a surprise also. But then she and Dad got married before he was born."

"And everyone survived," said Line. "I was older. 23, I think. So it was easier to be clear about what to do. You have to know in your own heart what you want. It would help to know before you tell your folks about the baby."

"Or IF I'm going to tell them," said Annika, alluding to the fact that she could get a legal abortion, paid for by the NHS.

Line understood. This was the question the girls needed to talk about. The crux of human problems since time immemorial. At one time, when the earth was in need of people and disease was rampant, women needed to be pregnant all during their child-bearing years as so many children and mothers died in the process. But now, when the earth didn't need more people, and women and children were well cared for in first world countries such as Scotland, bringing children into the world wasn't quite so necessary. Line preferred contraception, however. Once a human life was conceived, taking it was a terrible thing for everyone.

"Annika's been thinking about the Marie Stopes clinic," said Fern.

Line looked over at Ivy, whose face was open and attentive. But she wasn't too young to listen to this conversation. "The one thing I would say," said Line, "is that you would always wonder. It is a very painful thing to know you've extinguished some little life. Especially one brought into being with someone you love." She felt grateful that the girls were willing to talk, that she had reached the place if life of being a wise woman whose advice they wanted.

"Yes," said Annika, looking down in shame. "I know. It was an accident! I just didn't think it would happen so fast!" She looked anguished.

"I think you have to make the decision with Culloden," said Line. "You share the responsibility. And you always will. What does he think?"

"He says I have to decide what to do about my own body," said Annika softly.

Line snorted audibly at this long-held 'women's rights' slogan. "Of course," she said. "But conception happens between two people. You need to make sure it has happened, and then decide how to handle it, with Culloden." Line's long-held beliefs came out clearly, in front of Annika and her own daughters. This kind of decision had to be made in the context of its circumstances. And should not be made alone. "And then your families, if need be."

Annika looked up at her balefully.

Line passed around the salad. "How long have you been worrying about this?" she asked.

"About a month," said Annika. Her face was blotchy and puffed up, her tears still visible. But she was eating her pasta.

"Good," said Line. "I don't think this is the kind of decision you make with your head. You sit with it, and you talk about it, and finally the thing that is right for you will become clear. There's no real rush. Medical care is very good here. That's the luxury of our rich country."

Fern and Ivy spooned salad onto their plates. The heavy air hanging over the dinner table had cleared a little. As it grew dark outside, the lamps inside became brighter. Line could tell that Fern had been living with Annika's decision as well. But none of them knew enough. None of them could help Annika decide; they could only bring it into the open by talking about it, trying to make it manageable.

"Human life is really precious," said Line. "Each of us is terribly lucky to be the product of such a long evolutionary history."

"We know, Mom," said Fern, reverting to her slightly superior status as a 17-year-old. "People keep telling us. Every day!"

"Lucky enough to have ice cream," said Ivy. "Do you want some, Annika?" She looked a little shy, honored to have been let into the company of women for an evening.

"Yes," sighed Annika. "It sounds good. Vanilla?"

"With strawberries," said Line. "I found some, though goodness knows where they came from." She turned toward Annika, "How have you been feeling?"

"Okay," said Annika. "A bit nauseous in the morning, but not too bad. I can't stand coffee any more. Makes me want to hurl." She looked sad and wan.

Ice cream lightened the meal further. Ivy put on some music and Annika even laughed. Fern and Ivy wanted to walk her home, which was fine with Line. She sat under a lamp in the empty house, having a late cup of chamomile tea. She was happy to be in a country where the issue of choices about birth were free and above board. But it would always be painful and an issue for families. Not so bad a thing, Line thought. It was the essence of being a person, really.

Line thought of Heather, so far away in California. But Heather had been well-educated about sex, Line hoped. And about Christy. By this time, many things might have happened to Christy that Line didn't know about. But he did seem to be responsible, from what Line could tell.

A few weeks later, the Cohen family stuffed themselves into a small rented car and drove down to Heysham Village in England, where they boarded a car ferry for the Isle of Man. Stephen thought the island a capsule of the early history of northern humans and wanted to walk the trail which celebrated the 1000-year anniversary of the beginning of the Manx parliament, the Tynwald. He thought it would be a great way to mark the end of their sojourn in Scotland.

Line was apprehensive, but Fern was excited and Ivy full of energy. They stayed in a venerable old hotel in Douglas and had a good old English fry up for breakfast the next day. Line was prepared to eat all of it, sausages, bacon and all, as they were planning to walk more than 15 miles that day. And some of it would be ascending. "Oh," she said. "Black pudding!"

"What is it?" asked Ivy.

Stephen tasted his, amused, saying nothing. "Have you never run into black pudding before?" he asked. "Try it!"

"It tastes sweet, just like the Norwegian blod klub my Grandmother Mikkelson used to make," said Line. "It was a treat for us at Christmas." Black pudding was animal blood, oatmeal, barley and fat stuffed into sausage casings. Slices were fried until slightly crispy. Mother wouldn't touch it, but Line loved it. No Mikkelson made blod klub now.

Ivy turned up her nose. She wouldn't eat haggis, the Scottish mixture of sheep parts with suet and oatmeal stuffed into a sheep's stomach, either. But Fern tasted the black pudding.

"You'll never make a hunter," said Stephen to Ivy. "Historians think that after a hunt, animal hearts, livers, and lungs were cooked up in the stomach for a quick meal. These parts were good food, but didn't last as long as the meat would."

"Historians rule," said Fern, somewhat ironically.

Ivy sighed and Line looked at her complicitly. It would be a long day!

The family took a bus to Ramsey, where the ancient Royal Way of the Manx kings began. Water was held back in thick cloud cover, but bursts of sunshine came through now and then. Tall grass on both sides of the path kept them from seeing far; but then the route opened up as they climbed a ridge onto open heather moorland. They could see as far as the sea, with Irish and Scottish mountains in the distance.

A little ways out, Stephen pointed out the wooded Scacafell, or Skyhill where a powerful Norse warrior named Godred Crovan, who dominated Ireland and the seas around Scotland, had hidden his men and defeated the Manx king in 1079. His rule was assumed to include a Norse-style parliament, or 'thing,' which was still the legislative power on the island. The history was all in the Chronicles of the Kings of Mann, a book written on vellum about 1262 at Rushen Abbey, which Stephen had seen in the British Museum.

The thin line of Cohens proceeded up the Way, Stephen and Fern followed by Ivy and Line. "You're carrying the ring," Line said to Ivy. "You're the most innocent." From behind, knapsacks on their back full of snacks and water, they looked like the travelers in The Lord of the Rings.

"Yes!" said Ivy. She reached out her arms to encompass the wide sky, the grasses and mountains. She had so much energy, she kept going back and forth between her father and sister up ahead, and her mother trailing behind.

Line tried not to think of the walk in terms of miles, but in terms of time. It wasn't hard, but they were climbing. She was often on her feet all day, she thought, especially when she worked at the clinic. She tried to think of herself as an ancient traveler, afoot on the paths of the world. Wearing tennis shoes made in China, she thought. The winds washed through her and hawks sailed overhead.

They did most of their climbing that day, with Stephen pointing out the sites. Fern was intrigued by mounds which were all that were left of Neolithic homes or burial sites. In the evening, they wandered in to the town of Crosby. Line was tired and her legs were throbbing, but she didn't say so. She didn't want the girls to think she was losing her stamina. The next day would be easier.

And it was! The second day the Way followed lowland paths and the banks of the Silverburn River. They crossed an ancient stone "monk's bridge," arched over the river to get to the ruins of Rushen Abbey, where the Chronicle had been kept by monks. Here they were in a medieval woodland, full of birds and spring flowers. Line relaxed. They were not far now from Castletown, their destination. She would surely make it!

Line followed Fern around the dilapidated grounds of the Abbey. "It's hard to imagine living here," she said. The buildings and tower were very small.

"It was built to the rule of the Benedictines in the Twelfth century," said Fern. "According to Dad." She touched the grey stone wall reverently.

"It seems sad to me that all the Isle has is its history," said Line. "Dad says there were people on the island 6500 years before Christ! But what do people do here now?" she wondered.

"History is important," said Fern. "Maybe they can convert it into income. Tourism is big business all over the British Isles."

"There were gardens here once," said Line. "Perhaps there could be again."

In Castletown, Stephen found the Old House of Keys, where the Tynwald met until it moved to Douglas. On Tynwald Day, about midsummer, the parliament met outdoors as most Nordic thing meetings had. Line's ancestors had been ferocious, but they brought a democratic process to the places they conquered, apparently.

That evening, Stephen and Line rested in their room for a moment before the family sat down to its last meal on the island. They lay beside each other on the old-fashioned bed, stretched out, resting their legs. Stephen said quietly into the crook of Line's neck, "Well, I'm proud of us for completing this adventure without incident! The girls did well hiking, and so did you, my love."

But Line did not think that her husband, whose head was often in some Mesolithic or Medieval time frame, should get away with saying this quietly to her. "Please tell us all that tonight at dinner," she said. "We've done well throughout the past two years. And it hasn't been easy for some of us." She was thinking of Ivy.

"Yes," said Stephen. "I know that some would like to be home in Santa Cruz. And soon we will be! But hasn't this been a fairly painless way to get to outside our complacent little lives?"

"Oh yes," said Line. "The world is a very large place. I'm glad we are able to show that to the kids."

6

A call from Doug Henderson surprised Marty on a July afternoon at work. "I'm up in Healdsburg, checking on some vineyards," he said. "I could be at your house by 6:30 tonight and take you to dinner. Didn't you say there were little restaurants near your place?" When Marty didn't say anything for a moment, he backtracked. "That is, if you're free."

"Okay," said Marty, floundering. "I'm usually home by six."

"That's on Hyde Street? Right?"

Marty realized he was looking at the business card she had given him with her phone number at Designers International on it. "Yes," she said. "2027 Hyde Street."

"Great!" said Doug's voice. "See you then."

Marty put down the phone. He had said he would call her. She kept running into him when she went down to Santa Cruz. Heather often babysat for his family, and he had set Heather on course for a career in viticulture. "You're easy to talk to," he told Marty. But Marty didn't really expect him to call. He was much younger than she was, and he had three kids.

The fog was rolling in when Marty took the bus home, feathering the edges of the sunny evening with wisps of cloud and chill. Marty went straight up the stairs. It was 6 p.m. What on earth should she wear? Where should she take Doug Henderson? There were several small, intimate places on Russian Hill. She settled on her black jeans, but tried to soften them with a rose cotton shirt and a grey cashmere sweater thrown around her shoulders. Her dark hair was about the right length, she thought, bobbing around her shoulders. She wore nothing but a little lipstick and some powder on her nose.

When Doug arrived, he looked relaxed in a short-sleeved sports shirt and jeans. He was a big guy, ruddy-faced and clean-shaven, his sun-browned hair long enough to look like it needed a cut. "Can I wash up?" he asked. "I've been out in the fields all day." He didn't look like it, except for his boots, sturdy black lace-up boots which showed a bit of soil on them. "Wow," he said, on looking into the living room of the apartment. "That is one spectacular carpet!"

They stood at the edge of it, looking down on the marvelous natural colors. "It's all I have left of my husband," Marty said. "He died in an avalanche several years ago." She tried to imagine what Doug saw in her quiet, city aerie on the third floor.

"I'm sorry," said Doug. He went over to the window and looked out through the thin blinds. He was a little too much life for the place.

Marty reeled off the restaurant choices, but Doug said, "I do like good food, but it all sounds good. I think you should choose." His voice, to Marty, had a ragged edge to it, emotional but upbeat and full of suppressed life.

"Maybe I Fratelli then," said Marty. Marty locked the door and they went down into the street. The sky was now uniformly grey. The cable for the cars which climbed Russian Hill clacked in its trough under the street.

Marty matched her steps to Doug's long, free legs which swung along the concrete.

The restaurant was a block away. Small lights were strung in the trees in front of it, and a few tables were placed on the sidewalk with candles glowing in red glass globes on them. Marty followed the host inside and they sat at a table with a blue checked cotton tablecloth. "The food is good, but not pretentious," she told Doug as she looked at a menu. "I really like the atmosphere. I can feel the family behind it."

"Hard to choose! I'll have one of everything!" said Doug. "I'm hungry!"

Marty tried to eat lightly at night, but she was grateful for a glass of wine. Most were from Italy, but they had a Spanish Albariño Doug thought she should try since she wanted a white.

"Refreshing," said Marty, tasting it. "Kind of grapefruity."

"Yes," said Doug. After a conversation with the waiter, he ordered a wine he said was from a Nebbiolo grape. He sniffed it, waiting for it to open up a little. "Jeremy, our winemaker, is always looking for new grapes. Not much of this one left in the world. Only in Italy, I think."

"So the winery is doing well?" asked Marty. She had very little idea of the wine world, which she was sure was intense in California.

"Oh yes," said Doug. "These are the salad days. There are three of us. Jeremy has the European winemaking education and taste. He loves the great traditions of terroir-based reds. But then we have Vince, who's something of a marketing genius, pushing us to produce enough to keep up with the public relations he does. And then there's me. I'm the viticulturalist, boots in the vineyard sort. Both of them are pressuring me. I'm having trouble sourcing enough grapes locally."

"It's interesting that you see the winery in terms of people," said Marty. "It's the way I see architecture. I've seen several firms fail and some succeed. But it all has to do with the people running them."

"Absolutely," said Doug. "It's all about people. I've been lucky. I hung in with the right sort. Winemaking in California was first treated seriously because of wines made in the Santa Cruz Mountains, by Paul Draper. His wines have held up over time against similar French vintages. I'm glad to be up in those mountains. The soils are spectacular, and the cool weather patterns good. We could do with some rain, though!" Doug buttered some bread as the words came tumbling out.

Doug did not need to tell Marty that years of drought had left all of California parched. "You irrigate, though, don't you?" she asked.

"Some," said Doug. "But dry-farmed grapes give better flavor, though we may have low yields some years. The roots go down deeper into those soils. But then we have the problem that not enough acreage is planted to vineyards around us. Housing gets preference. Vince is always on my tail. So that's why I'm out looking for grapes." Doug looked up at Marty. "Sorry," he said. "I'm talking a blue streak. But you seem interested."

"Oh yes," said Marty. "I hardly know anything about wine. I have some friends who get this amazing wine, from Bolinas I think. They talk about it and I hardly even understand. Orion, maybe? Taurus? It does taste wonderful with food."

"Sean Thackrey," said Doug. "I know him. Great maverick winemaker." He laughed. "Jeremy's jealous of him. Everyone wants Thackrey's wine, but he does exactly as he pleases. Doesn't answer to anyone."

"More people!" said Marty. "Personalities."

"It's a story," said Doug. "Wine is a story of the characters involved. And the soils, and the grapes, and the vintage year. At least that's how I read it."

Doug ordered a plate of pasta, agreeing to give Marty a part of it. The portions would be huge, and she didn't want more. She was surprised at their harmony, at the ease of their sharing.

"So tell me about your husband," said Doug. "What did he do?"

"He was an architect," said Marty. "He was good at sketching, though he let other people give him design ideas. His other 'business' ran away with him." Marty's fingers put quote marks around the world 'business.' She was surprised to find herself saying exactly what she thought to Doug. "He dealt drugs in the Seventies, and he drank too much."

"Wow," said Doug. "Sounds difficult."

"I was a stupid little girl," said Marty. "Fresh off the boat, so to speak. From Minnesota. But I did get an education out of all of it."

"I'll bet," said Doug. "And you've traveled I think Heather said? I feel like I know your niece pretty well."

"I was in Hong Kong recently," said Marty. "And of course I've traveled in Europe, England and around the Mediterranean a bit."

"Yeah," said Doug. "I worked the vendange in France one year myself, bummed around, learned a lot."

"I'll bet that was fun."

"Hard work!" said Doug.

"Did you do drugs when you were young?" Marty asked. She wondered if she appeared sophisticated to Doug. He seemed full of experience himself. His voice and appreciation for things opened Marty.

"Oh no," laughed Doug. "I was a dreamer. I didn't want to get away from reality. I took the opposite commute. I was always trying to get straight!"

Marty laughed, "Line's glad to be back in Santa Cruz," said Marty.

"Yes," said Doug. "It's a pretty great place."

"What I needed from California was the diversity," said Marty. "Different cultures around me."

"Well, we've got that," said Doug. "Not so much stability, though." He looked a little rueful. "I could do with a little more tradition. My mother's good, though. She's a rock. When my Dad died, she got a job, picked us up and moved us to Santa Cruz."

"When was that?" asked Marty, trying to get a sense of his life.

"I was 16," said Doug. "My sister was 18." He smiled. "I've had every kind of job. Picking artichokes, pumpkins, strawberries, worked in a window glass factory. Almost had a huge pane of glass fall on me. I liked to write too. Did some stringing for the newspaper in high school. My mother insisted I go to college. And I knew what I wanted to do."

"Not journalism?" asked Marty.

"No," said Doug. "I couldn't stand to ask people how they felt after their car crash, or a death. Hated it. I like exposing frauds, politicos and such. Justice. But viticulture is where it's at for me. Wine is a real thing, health and pleasure and conviviality. And, as I've said, I fell in with the right guys."

"My favorite Chinese poets are always looking up at the moon and writing poems about it, wine cup in hand," Marty smiled to herself. She wanted to sink deeper and deeper into this interesting guy. But what was she doing? Making another friend who couldn't be hers? She mentally shook herself. "Tell me about your kids," she said.

"Well!" said Doug. "Zoe is three and a half now, kicking butt and taking names! Amazing." Again Doug looked rueful. "I just don't see enough of the kids," he said. "I really want to stay home all the time, but I can't." He continued, wrapping his pasta around his fork quickly: "And the twins, Nic and Natasha, are not quite two. Quite a handful."

"Yeah," said Marty. "I'll bet they are. Twins are an instant family!"

"Yep!" said Doug. "Want some coffee? I've got a ways to go. I'd like a cup." He signaled the waiter.

The talk went on and on. Marty was mesmerized. She didn't want to move, but it was getting late. The waiter brought the check and, though Marty whipped out her VISA card, Doug said, "Don't worry. I'll expense it." He laughed. "You're a customer, right?"

They walked back to Marty's apartment, only a block away. "Do you know Robert Fripp?" Doug asked.

"No," said Marty.

"He's a guitar player. He was in a British band called King Crimson, and he's done stuff with Brian Eno and Peter Gabriel. Shows you my taste in music," he smiled as he stood outside Marty's dark entryway. "The weird ones. Yep, I was just a California boy, listening to my tapes and letting them take me away."

"I've heard of Brian Eno," said Marty doubtfully. "But I think the music I like is from earlier."

"The Sixties," said Doug. "Yeah. Anyway, I was thinking about this great song Fripp wrote: 'I smile like Chicago, she laughs like the breeze.' That's you," Doug said. "I can't sing worth a damn, but 'I'm a clown on a spree ... isn't it sweet to remember the way it might be?'" He took Marty's hand. "I better go," he said softly. "Thanks for the evening."

"Oh, thank you!" said Marty. "It was wonderful!" She stood there, watching as Doug loped up the street in the dark like a wild horse set free in the city. Then she put her key in the door and went upstairs.

That week Marty was caught up as usual in the thousand and one details of working at a large, ambitious architectural firm. She owed this job to her friend Lauren, the marketing director she had worked with at Whittaker Perotta, who spoke up when the company needed an office manager. It was sort of a catch-all job, with Marty hiring administrative staff and organizing facilities. Human resources and accounting were handled by the head office in Washington, D.C. For them, Marty was simply a liaison.

Facilities for the office were a big deal. Project teams were always moving and re-forming, the company expanding. Project managers and secretaries all had Mac computers, due to a forward-thinking systems manager who networked everything together. But much of the design process was done with drawings and models. The main principal of the firm, whom Lauren called the 'rain-maker' because he brought in many big Silicon Valley projects, liked nothing better than to gather a team of architects around him after hours to work on a model, cutting pieces of foam core and moving them around to determine what worked best.

Marty was proud of her administrative team and tried to be as communicative as possible about what was going on. Nora, the receptionist, a big Midwestern woman who described herself as 'bomb-proof,' had been with the company for ten years already. Everyone relied on her and the principals trusted her, but she also knew exactly how to put pins in their egos in a comic, friendly way. Architecture required a big ego. Marty had heard one of the principals tell a prospective employee categorically, "We are the best design firm in the city."

The firm seemed to run on competition and chaos. Somehow it all worked. Perhaps because the principals were so distributed. They took turns running the office, and Marty's boss was currently a Chinese-American architect who had gone to school at Berkeley. He was strait-laced, Confucian, and he had his own projects, but he met with Marty once a week, and Marty had his ear for problems. She liked him and got along with him better than Lauren did, who felt he was stingy.

Just before lunch, Marty ran across the street to the 'Annex' to find out how things were going with that project team, and to prove to them that people from the big office knew they existed. The Annex was the upper level of a barely-reconstructed building under the exposed wooden beams of the roof. It looked like an attic. Marty liked Amy, the thin dark girl she had hired to handle communications and files for them.

"Greetings from the exiles," called out one of the architects, as Marty's head popped up over the stairs. She waved and went over to Amy's desk in the sun-lit dusty room.

"Is everything okay over here?" she asked.

"I'm doing okay," said Amy. "But we need more paper, and foam core. Can you send Tyler over with them this afternoon?" She looked around, "And Jack says his phone isn't working."

"Cream and sugar too!" piped up a voice from a nearby desk. "We're running out."

"Sure," said Marty. She always had a free-roving assistant. Tyler was loved and petted by all of the administrative staff, a young man just out of high school. Marty picked up the phone at Jack's desk, but heard nothing. She borrowed Amy's phone to test the jack. When it worked, she determined she must send over another phone set also. Marty made some notes and then rushed off to lunch.

Japanese lunch, Marty decided. There were many choices, but she must move quickly. She walked down the street in the warm summer sun, taking the moment to remind herself who she was and what she was doing.

And that Doug Henderson had taken her to dinner! Marty knew she could not ascribe much importance to it. But the meeting showed Marty that the kind of man whom it was fun to be with and talk to, while at the same time a responsible grownup, a real person, existed. He seemed to enjoy everything. A natural-born Taoist, Marty thought to herself.

Marty ordered an unagi and avocado roll, which, dipped in soy sauce and followed by ginger was currently the most earthy, astonishing taste she could think of. She mapped the palimpsest of the city in her head. She and Nathan had once met for lunch at this very Japanese restaurant; she had eaten with Shannon, Philip and Matthew at the Italian restaurant she and Doug went to only a few weeks before. Everywhere she turned in the city, places revived a memory in her, of kisses, of talk, of things she had done with Erik, with Line, or even Mother. A geography of the heart.

The unagi was battered, fried and crispy, contrasting well with the unctuous avocado. Marty dipped a piece in the salty soy sauce with her chopsticks and popped it in her mouth.

The city was small. Marty could walk across it on a good day. Like the Paris of the surrealists, the flâneurs who walked around thinking and observing, San Francisco was endlessly interesting. But what were memories? Fleshless visuals by now. Marty wanted sensual pleasure, eating, sunshine, hands on her body, every day. How do we have room in our heads for this constant stream of sensuality, she wondered, one thing supplanting the next?

Marty didn't have much use for dreams, as some did. She enjoyed them and they were sometimes vivid, but she didn't ascribe much meaning to them. A vivid picture came to her of once waking with Erik at a friend's house. Marty remembered watching from a pallet on the floor as a Southern guy, barefoot in dirty white jeans, opened the refrigerator. He moved slowly and quietly, his veins full of mescaline, acid and grass. He was thin because drugs were more important than food. So long ago, thought Marty.

That was all behind her. Marty had many men friends, Matthew, Nathan, Will and Mark, who loved to practice tai chi san shou with her. But they were not for her. She was still hoping someone would come along who would be.

On Saturday morning, Marty was up early and off to join the motley crew of scholar warriors who met to practice tai chi. She carried a weapons bag she had made from the leg of an old pair of bluejeans with a wooden knife and the steel sword Sachiko had given her in it. At 50 Oak, Marty changed into her cotton tai chi clothes and shoes.

"Did you know that koalas are always high?" asked Stan when Marty came out of the dressing room. "They always have fermented leaves in their stomachs, because eucalyptus takes so long to digest."

"Hey," said Mark. "Maybe that's my problem." He was an athletic younger man with a head of silver hair who had started tai chi after Marty, but was ahead of her due to his competitive practice. Master Liu squelched competition. He said the person who started practice earlier was always ahead of someone who started later.

"Not yours," laughed Stan, stretching out first one leg and then the other. "You're on a permanent caffeine high."

"Looks like Clinton's got the Democratic nomination," said Mark, his legs in a horse stance, his arms swinging about his waist.

"Yeah, thought so," said Stan. "We need some new blood in Washington."

When Marty put down her things, Mark drew her into a push hands practice in which each person used the other's energy to circle and sink. "Soft, soft," he said. It was recommended that men work with women to soften their upper bodies, but Marty still felt some tension in her own shoulders. Asian people felt Americans were top heavy. Asians valued having a solid base, legs firm on the earth. Marty was working on it.

"Listen, surrender, transform and push," said Mark softly, repeating the push hands sequence they had been taught as his body moved forward and back.

After slow set, the group worked on knife. Tim and his wife had beautiful new steel knives, with red and gold silk handkerchiefs tacked on the ends. Unlike the sword, the knife had only one sharp edge and one held it differently. Marty recognized some slow set moves in the form. At one point she "unsheathed" the knife from an imaginary case strapped to her arm.

During a break, Anton borrowed Tim's new knife to try it, leaping through the air. The knife sliced the air dramatically, the red and yellow scarves flying. Most of the students rested in heaps about the room and on the minimal stage on one side. Marty and Ricka walked out through the marble foyer to feel the heat of the sunny front steps of the building.

"It's criminal for us to be inside on a day like this," said Ricka.

"Yeah," said Marty softly. "But tai chi is worth it." It was so often foggy now, that the sun felt wonderful on Marty's skin.

Sachiko and Diane followed them out to the front. "Could we do a bodywork session tomorrow?" asked Diane of Ricka, rubbing the back of her neck and her shoulders. "My job is killing me, I think."

After the break, Sachiko, Anton's Japanese wife, thin with a black bubble of well-cut hair around her face, took Marty aside to work on san shou. San shou meant 'dividing hands,' and was a choreographed set of moves. Sachiko felt just as she should to Marty, very heavy and based in her lower body. Sachiko showed Marty how to just sit back when pushed, straight back, not twisting and getting lopsided. Sachiko noticed the tiniest things Marty could improve. "Keep it simple," she said.

Marty was very slow. She did everything wrong several times before she did it right. She didn't have a strong connection to her body, she thought. The san shou rhythms, and the way you triggered the other person to move were hard to learn.

In partner work, the aggressor moved toward the other person, and they responded. Knowing the mirror moves didn't help Marty at all. She was hopeless, could not imagine them. She would just have to keep practicing. Once she got something, however, she did get it. In a way, her untrained body had no other ideas. Marty had been a lump, reading all the time, never studying a sport. Her body was empty, and accepted tai chi. It seemed that Sachiko and Anton found it worthwhile to work with her.

Marty loved how Sachiko and Anton were together. During breaks they sometimes pushed each other playfully, endlessly each other's best friend. They wore each other's clothes. Sachiko told Marty that Anton started tai chi first, and he was always more into it. But at some point she got hooked too.

People stood in the entrance to the big, wooden-floored ballroom, looking in, watching them. What did they see? Two long lines of men and women in loose clothing, making ritual contact with each other. San shou was highly choreographed. Marty loved the moves when she got them right.

Partner work worked out the middle of Marty's body, showed her where her waist was.

After class, Marty was exhausted. Her legs ached. Her hips joints were loosening, she thought, finally. But she felt weak in her middle and her legs tingled. Walking home up the hill from the bus, Marty's legs almost refused to budge.

Marty made herself a goat cheese and sage omelet for lunch, and then went down the hill to lie in the grass below the reservoir, looking out at the sunny Bay full of sailboats. It was all she could do. She looked longingly at Angel Island, a hump of green in the Bay below where the woods were wild and thick. Maybe tomorrow, she thought to herself.

Tai chi people said that once you started tai chi, you never got any older. Marty had been doing tai chi for more than two years. She had been 43 when she started. She was proud of her slow gains, the sets she had learned. Her body felt leaner, partly because she had been experimenting with fasting and limiting certain foods as well.

There was some chance that Marty was gaining a sound mind in a sound body. 'Mens sana in corpore sano,' as they used to say at Luther College. The long three-hour workouts, with breaks, every Saturday and one or two tai chi classes during the week was stretching and changing Marty. Perhaps she could, as she hoped, become impeccable, the whole person she was meant to be. Marty lay down on her rug, the sun and seawater glimpsed from under her hat shining below.

7

It was January and very dark in the morning before school. Rain poured down on the wooden decks outdoors. Line and Ivy stood near the big windows in the living room lit only by light from the kitchen. "Just for today," said Line quietly, her palms flat against each other in front of her heart, "I will let go of anger, I will let go of worry."

Ivy stood beside her, a little taller, blonde hair drawn back, her hands too in the Reiki self-healing posture Line was learning. "Today I will count my many blessings. I will do my work honestly. I will be kind to every living creature."

"Eyes," said Line, lifting her hands so her palms rested gently over her eyes. Ivy did the same. Line waited a minute, the sounds of the rain splatting heavy around them. "Temples," she said, moving her hands to warm the sides of her head. It felt wonderful.

"Back of the head," said Line, after a minute. Slowly their hands moved to the back of their heads, to the throat and then down, to heart, solar plexus, abdomen and groin. Ivy copied Line's moves, standing quietly beside her. "Kidneys," said Line and moved her hands to her back.

At the end, Line placed her palms together in front again. "Say it with me, Ivy. I seal this process with divine love and wisdom." Line repeated the phrase.

"Yes," said Ivy, as they finished. "It feels so nice." In the kitchen they could hear Stephen putting toast in the toaster. "I'm ready," Ivy said, putting her hands down, a note of determination in her voice.

Line planted a kiss on her daughter's forehead. "You'll be fine," she said. She could hear the noisy diesel engine of the school bus outdoors in the rain. "I'll be at the roller rink at 10:30 tonight, okay?"

Ivy put on her rain jacket, lifting its hood over her hair. "Yes, thank you Mom. I'll look for you at 10:30." She grabbed her backpack, which stood by the door. "Bye, Dad," she said as she rushed out the door.

"Have a good day, sunshine!" said Stephen from the kitchen.

Line joined Stephen where he sat reading the newspaper. "She and Emily are presenting their art ecology project today," Line said. For weeks, Ivy and Emily had been making tote bags, some from old clothing they bought at the Goodwill. They enhanced the bags with pockets, patches, ink stamps and experimented with different kinds of straps. The totes were meant to remind people they could shop without using paper or plastic bags. Line liked the ones they had sewn from oilcloth the best. They were sturdy and resisted damp. Ivy had given Line several for Christmas and even made a knapsack for Stephen.

"Always surprising, these kids!" said Line, pouring herself another cup of coffee. "Somehow I didn't think Ivy would become a sewer!"

"Artistic she is," said Stephen. He packed an apple and a sandwich into the little knapsack. Ivy had stamped the plain white oilcloth with hundreds of little books in black ink. It looked like a girl had made it, but Stephen carried it with pride. "I think that comes from your side of the family."

Line waggled her head. "Perhaps," she said. "It's nice to see her happy!" It was too wet for Stephen to ride his bike. Line needed the car to visit her hospice patients in their homes. She had two of them at the moment, one across town from the other. "I'll take you to school," she said.

"Thank you, my dear," said Stephen. "I'm ready when you are." He too pulled on rainwear and they went out to the driveway.

The sky was dark, but beautiful as Line and Stephen drove through the redwoods to campus. No one could complain about the rain. When the Cohens arrived home from Scotland six months ago, the state was still in a severe six-year drought. Even in November, clouds had hung ominous, but dry. In December the skies let loose. It had been raining ever since. There was snow in the mountains and rain all over the state. It began to look as though the drought could be broken.

After dropping Stephen at the library, Line turned back. The town of Santa Cruz had risen from the rubble of the 1989 earthquake. Pacific Avenue was pretty much rebuilt. The planning commission had straightened it out and it was no longer the forest it had once been. But there were sidewalk cafes, plenty of seating on the street, and new trees had been planted.

People Line knew were thriving too. Raven Lang was studying Traditional Chinese Medicine, applying it to her continuing work with mothers and babies. Paul Lee was chair of the citizens committee on the homeless, finding shelters and gardening projects for them. He also worked with the long-running Penny University and his many philanthropy and writing projects. He was full of ideas for the ecological use of the city's resources, currently bent on making a trail highlighting the town's natural beauty.

Santa Cruz was home to Line. She identified with the scrawny little fuyu persimmon tree she had planted before they left. It was alive only because it was down the hill from the plants on the decks, which Poppa had watered while they were gone. It was a tough little tree, living on the trickles of water flowing from above. And getting its fill of water now during the rains. Maybe next year there would be persimmons.

At home, Line got ready for her day. Poppa was up and hanging out in the kitchen. "Beautiful day," he sang out, as Line passed through. "There's flooding everywhere."

"Oh?" asked Line. "We didn't have any problem."

"Good," said Poppa. He wore a fluffy terrycloth bathrobe over his pajamas as he paged through the paper. "Looks like the weather might be nice for Clinton's inauguration next week. They're really making a big thing of it. Three days worth of concerts and events!"

"Do you wish you were there?" asked Line.

"Nope," said Poppa. "Let the youngsters have their fun. I've had mine."

Line packed up her nurse's bag and the lab coat she wore over her other clothes when she visited patients. She planned to stop by the hospice office and then make her patient visits for the day.

The community hospital where Line used to work had been sold to Dominican Hospital, and was now a rehabilitation facility. But Line found work with a hospice, which cared for terminally ill patients during their last days. The idea of hospice was that when someone was close to death they should be in their familiar home environment, protected from pain, leaving their minds free to make whatever journey they needed. Line was in the process of upgrading her nursing certification in order to dispense heavy drugs when needed as a palliative.

Line used an umbrella to slog from the car into the building in her rubber gardening shoes. The rain made her euphoric. She was looking forward to the green hills and the flowers the rain would bring. More storms were coming. She waited a moment for her supervisor, looking out the window at the sloshing water. From inside it was wonderful to watch people with umbrellas, cement flower planters soggy with water, the brave trees which spent their lives waiting for this moment.

And when the clouds retreated, the sun would be heading toward them. They had passed the year's solstice, which Line felt in her body. Even in California, which had more sun than Scotland, she felt the tilt of the earth as it swung around the sun strongly. My forty-ninth year, Line thought. Every seventh year was significant. Her return to Santa Cruz and beginning to work with the hospice had made it memorable.

When the supplies were ready, Line left, deciding to take the most difficult house call first. "Just for today," she said to herself as she drove. "I will do my work honestly. I will be kind to every living creature." She headed into the country a bit, toward a house which had once been a farmhouse before development began all around it.

It wasn't that old Mrs. Joris was a difficult patient; it was that her daughters were fighting over her. Line stood out of the rain on the front porch, with her bag, looking a bit damp, but as professional as possible in her white lab coat. It had a pin to identify her and big roomy pockets.

The atmosphere in the Joris house was not too bad. Only the older daughter, Nancy, was there. Mrs. Joris lay in state in a rented hospital bed in the middle of the living room. Line took her patient's hand, asking how she was, but Mrs. Joris, thin and wan under the bedclothes, only shook her head sadly, her big eyes looking fearful as they followed Line's movements. Her breathing was shallow and raspy. Line put her hands lightly on Mrs. Joris' forehead, her heart, her tummy.

"Did she have a good night?" asked Line of Nancy. Mrs. Joris looked like a flower that was drying up. She did not have any particular illness, beyond cardio-pulmonary disease. Line thought she might slip away at any moment, but bodies were strong. Often they did not want to give up.

"I don't know," said Nancy. "She doesn't say much."

Line filled the IV which gave Mrs. Joris some liquid, some nourishment and a morphine drip. She knew it prolonged life, which might not be the best thing under the circumstances, but it was hard to know. "She seems comfortable," said Line. "I'll just clean her up a little and change the sheets." She took blood pressure and other readings, entering them on a chart.

Nancy stood on the other side of the bed, helping Line, but when she started complaining about her sister, Line held her hand to her lips. "She hears everything," said Line. "Even if she can't talk." Family conflicts were not good for someone who was dying, even if they could not be avoided.

When she was finished, Line asked Nancy if she could have a cup of tea, to give Nancy a chance to talk. The problem in the Joris family went back to money, as always. Nancy had lived with her mother, now 98, for years, making little money but taking care of all of her needs. The other daughter, Diane, worked for the county and made money, including a pension she would soon get. She had a husband and children. Both sisters were at odds about what would happen after their mother died. The house must be sold and split between the two daughters. But Nancy felt she would have nothing to show for all her work. She would be homeless and bereft. In Diane's eyes, Nancy had taken advantage of her mother, spending time traveling and studying East Asian dances while living at home.

"I don't want her to go," said Nancy. "I just can't bear it." Tears slipped down her face as she sat at the kitchen table.

"She's had a good, long life," said Line. "You must let her make this journey." She sipped her tea. "Here," she stood up. "Let me put my hands on you for a moment." She stood up behind Nancy and put her hands over Nancy's eyes. "Just relax," she said. "Breathe." She moved her hands over to rest at the temples. "Take your time," she said. "It's all going to be fine."

Predictably the front door opened at that moment and Diane came in. She went over to her mother, and kissed her. Then bustled into the kitchen with her wet umbrella and bags. "How's it all going?" she asked. Diane's energy was high powered and controlling. Line was glad she had had time to speak to Nancy before Diane arrived.

"It's going well," said Line. "Your mother seems to be resting peacefully."

"How long do you think she'll last like this?" asked Diane.

But Line shook her head. Again she spoke very quietly. "She can hear everything," she said to Diane, indicating the bed in the nearby room. "Days, weeks. I'm not sure. Do you want the doctor to visit?"

"I'm wondering what to tell Pastor Ellis," said Diane. "He said he'd come when we needed him."

Nancy stood up, huffing over to the stove. Neither of the sisters were young any longer. Line wondered what Pastor Ellis meant to them both. She began to pack up her bag. "I'll be here again tomorrow morning," she said to the sisters. "Probably still be raining!" she smiled to break the tension. Before she left, she went in to Mrs. Joris and put her hands on her forehead for a few moments, blessing her as best she could.

Line tried to recoup her energy as she drove toward the neatly painted Victorian-style home of her second patient, Donnie. She was cautious in the rain, careful to give other drivers plenty of space. "Just for today," Line thought. "I will let go of anger; I will let go of worry." She parked. The front door was opened by Jeff, Donnie's partner.

"How are you doing?" asked Line.

Jeff looked long-faced, haggard, shaking his head. But the atmosphere in this home was tranquil. Zen sayings and paintings hung on the walls. "It's bad," said Jeff. "He's in a lot of pain. I just wish I could do more for him."

Line hugged the big, blonde man gently. "You're being with him," she said. "You're lending him your wonderful energy." She moved past him, becoming professional, taking her stethoscope out of her pocket.

Donnie was skin and bones, the shadow of a person. He was suffering from AIDS, the end stages of the human immunodeficiency virus. He could not stand needles or to have an IV and was subsisting on spoons of soup or gruel that Jeff, or their friend Marcia succeeded in getting into him. They ground up the heaviest painkillers they could get and put them in Donnie's broth.

68

For Donnie, Line could not do much either. He did not really want to be touched. Everything was painful. Line tried to swab his body lightly with a sponge, turning him in the sheets with Jeff's help as he moaned. But human dignity required cleanliness. Line did not think Donnie's suffering would last much longer. She smoothed down the clean sheets, cooing to him quietly. "Now it will be better," she said. "You'll be able to sleep."

Line placed her hands over Donnie's eyes lightly, moving them slowly down to rest very lightly on his heart, his tummy. "You can do this too," she told Jeff. "If he wants it. It's a Reiki process I'm learning. But it isn't different than any other energy or massage therapy. It's just addressing the whole person, sharing your body's healthy chi with his."

Line took Jeff's meaty hands and showed him how to lift them up to the universe, offering gratitude for life's healing energy. Then she placed them on Donnie's thin face. "Lightly," she said. "Lightly." She showed Jeff how to move them down.

When Donnie seemed to be resting, Jeff and Line went down the stairs and Jeff made another pot of coffee. Jeff worked over the hill for one of the big Silicon Valley data companies. He had been working at home as much as he could since it became clear that Donnie was dying. Jeff was also HIV positive, but he was taking AZT and in drug trials for a protease inhibitor called Saquinavir. "Why the hell not?" he had told Line. "What choice do I have?" The drugs were meant to block the virus from infecting cells and copying itself inside the body. There were high hopes that it would help reduce the progression of HIV, reducing the body's viral load, if not curing the disease.

"Do you want some of this in your coffee?" Jeff held up a bottle of Kahlua.

Line smiled. "Sure, why not." But she hoped Jeff wasn't using alcohol to cope. "Does it help with your drugs?"

"Maybe," said Jeff. "Things are so topsy turvy, I don't know any more. Nothing tastes right; my body's getting puffy; lots of things make me nauseous. Can't sleep."

"But they're keeping records of everything, right?" asked Line.

"Oh, I'm apparently doing pretty well. T-cells not dying off, and all that. I'm alive, a human specimen," said Jeff sardonically.

"So Marcia is spelling you?" asked Line. The Kahlua in her coffee made it go sweetly down her throat.

"Yeah," said Jeff. "She's been a big help." He stood at the butcher block in the middle of the beautiful kitchen. "And also some other members of our Zen sitting group. But Marcia has the most time."

"And Donnie's folks?" asked Line.

"His mother was divorced. He's not close to his father and his mother can't deal with it. I don't know if we'll see her or not. But Donnie doesn't care. He's beyond caring."

The AIDS epidemic had chastened and grown many people in the gay community. Most did not expect much for themselves or their partners. They had been blasted into the present, irredeemable reality, in which death was close and life was precious. Line felt grateful to be part of these stories, to be close to these brave and gallant people.

Line had always been the one to get a patient's story. When she worked at the hospital, the nurses would say, "That one seems interesting. She must have quite a past. Let's send Line down there. I'm sure she can get it out of them." Line saw the whole person. Mind as well as matter.

"I want to show you something," Line said. She pulled out her worn copy of Hands of Light, by Barbara Brennan, in which there were diagrams of energetic healing sessions. Line paged through the book. "I don't like to use the word 'healing' any more," she said. "Too many people mistake it for some magical moment of being healed, of being healthy again. That's not going to happen in a case like Donnie's. But we can share our energy field, our chi, with him. Our bodies are energy flows. Donnie's is drying up."

Jeff's eyes seemed to soften as he looked through the book.

"I don't have much use for the 'levels' of practice, and the hierarchies I see developing around Reiki," said Line. "But I do feel that humans touching each other is a sharing of solace and peace. And I do think we can get in touch with the universal life force for good."

"I agree," said Jeff. He slumped over his coffee. "The waiting is so hard though," he said. "I'm exhausted."

"It's a journey," said Line. "For all of us."

"Yes," said Jeff. "God help us."

Line stood up and hugged Jeff. She began to put her things away and pull on her outer clothes.

At home that afternoon, Line found a letter from Fern. Fern was good about writing, but it made Line suspicious. She felt Fern was keeping them at bay, not telling them everything that was going on. Phone calls betrayed one's voice, and they did talk to her occasionally. Line would have liked to talk to her more often. In letters, Fern tended to make nice, play up her accomplishments. And she asked for more money.

Line had expected that. You could not get a truly great education without spending money on it. Fern had found that the international archeological dig which had been going on for two years at the site once known as Troy, in Turkey, would take her on, if she could pay her own way. They needed students during the summers, but Fern would be on her own. She had several well-off friends who would also go. Even Line, with no historical background, could see that it was a powerful opportunity.

"That's our girl," said Stephen, when Line showed him the letter. He positively glowed with pride. "I'm sure we can come up with the money."

After dinner, which was a quick one because Poppa wanted to go to a movie, Stephen did the dishes, telling Line, "I'll wake you if you want to go lie down."

"Oh yes," said Line. "I think that would be a good idea. You won't forget? 10 o'clock?" Stephen did often get absorbed in his work. Line went off to their darkened bedroom and lay down, putting an afghan over her tired body. Her mind strayed over images of Fern in a sun-lit, rocky landscape, brushing dirt aside from the layer she was assigned to, looking for artifacts.

Stephen didn't forget. At 10 p.m. he came in and waked the sleeping Line. She got up in the dark and washed her face, smiling at Stephen in the mirror as he came up behind her and hugged her. "Jack Spratt and his wife," she said, laughing. It wasn't that she was overly heavy, but pounds did seem to stick to her pear-shaped body, and Stephen was as thin as a stick no matter what he ate.

Stephen smoothed his hands down Line's waist and hips. "I like it like that," he said.

Once again, Line dressed for going out in the thick, rainy weather. She drove over to the roller rink where Ivy was attending a skating party. She parked the car and went inside, braving the hordes of noisy teenagers who milled around outside and in. The building didn't close until 11, but Line wanted to be early. The building smelled of tomato pizza and the sickly smell of sweaty shoes and socks.

Ivy waved to Line from across the room, where she and her friends were taking off their rented laced-up roller skates. How many of them would she have to drop off, Line wondered. She baulked when two of the kids carried open soda cans out. "Not in my car, please," she said. She refrained from railing against the sodas, as she did in her own home. Sodas rotted people's bones.

It turned out to be four kids. Ivy in the front seat, and Emily, Randy and Melissa in the back. The arty kids, thought Line. "Seatbelts?" she questioned. She would get a ticket if everyone wasn't belted into their seats. It took a moment for the kids to find the middle seatbelt in back. "Ok, where am I going?" she asked. She knew Santa Cruz like the back of her hand by this time. She let Ivy direct, not really listening as the kids talked. She did prick up her ears, however, when she heard the name Mackenzie.

"Mackenzie?" Line asked Ivy. "Was she there?"

"Yeah," said Ivy quietly. "Not only that, she's preggers." In the back seat the kids were discussing how everyone they knew looked at the party.

"Pregnant?!" asked Line.

"Yeah," said Ivy. "She was with some swishy guys, surfers, I think."

Line looked toward the wet highway, the rain drizzling down her windshield. She knew much more about Mackenzie Henderson than she wanted to. Heather used to babysit for the Henderson kids and now Ivy sometimes did when Mackenzie brought them to Santa Cruz. Mackenzie was young, still in her 20's, Line was sure, but she did not act like a woman with three kids. She acted like a kid.

Even worse, Line thought, was the friendship she had seen growing between her sister Marty and Mackenzie's husband Doug. She had seen them talking, and Marty told her that Doug sometimes called her when he was in San Francisco and they went out for dinner. What did another pregnancy mean for Mackenzie and Doug, Line wondered.

It turned out that Randy lived near Emily, so that wasn't so bad. Melissa lived out on Pasatiempo, which took longer. The headlights shone on the water-slick roads and rain was batted off the windshield by the wipers. Line listened while Ivy and Melissa talked. She was happy that Ivy had lots of friends. It seemed that Ivy's circles had widened since returning from Scotland.

"Did you have a good day?" asked Line as she pulled away from Melissa's front door.

"Oh yes!" said Ivy. "I can't skate worth beans, but I think it got a little better after we went around a few times. It's fun!"

"I like your friends," said Line. "Emily is especially collected." Line winced at the thought that these kids only had a year left in high school after this one. Next year they would all be planning for college. But it was wonderful to see these young lives blooming as a contrast to the ones she saw in her hospice work.

"She knows exactly what she wants to do," said Ivy ruefully. "Not me."

"How did the bag project go over?" asked Line.

"Everyone liked it! But I think it was mostly Emily," said Ivy. "She knows what to say. I think she's going to be good at marketing or something."

"You had a lot of the ideas, though," reminded Line.

"Maybe," said Ivy. "You know Mom, I thought of one thing I've learned since we got back," she said.

Line looked at her expectantly. She turned onto their street and drove up the hill.

"I look at people's insides more now than I used to," said Ivy. "Like in Edinburgh, all those kids who dressed in leather and metal. Some of them were sweet underneath. And now, the kids that look really successful, with their perfect hair and perfect skin, don't always have much inside."

Line looked at her, nodding her head approvingly. "My wise girl," she said. She pulled up in the welcoming, lighted driveway and pushed the button that opened the garage door. "We got a letter from Fern today," she said. Ivy clapped her hands.

8

On an early June Saturday, Marty flopped down on her bed. At this time of year, a lozenge-shaped piece of sunshine came in through the window and lay flat on the puffy white comforter. Doug would arrive in half an hour and Marty was too excited to do anything but wait for him. She also wanted to close her eyes and relax them.

It had been almost four months since Doug had kissed Marty goodnight after one of their occasional dinners. They had not been able to let go of each other that night. Their long rambling conversations had fueled a bodily hunger which felt both wrong and terribly right to Marty. She felt helpless before it, and so, apparently, did Doug.

Marty felt that Doug was her match, as wild in his body and his thoughts as she was. That first night she woke up once to feel that he was absolutely familiar in her bed and again later to feel that he was absolutely unknown, magic, a prince. She had longed for love and was now overcome. It shook her to her foundations. Doug said she was only seeing the tip of the iceberg.

It began because Doug was angry at his wife. The baby Mackenzie was carrying had been conceived during crush the previous September, a time when Doug was never at home. In the intervening months, Mackenzie had confessed that she didn't exactly know who the father was either. She had been at a rock concert; things had happened afterwards; she did not know exactly what. Pregnancy was easy for Mackenzie and she was haphazard about it as she was about most things. The baby was expected in a couple of weeks.

"I can't talk to her," Doug told Marty. With Marty it was the opposite. He could say anything and he made her talk too. They were hard on each other. The first night, they shredded Marty's pantyhose, ripped her bra and Doug bit the pearls from her ears. They used the doorways, the walls, the bed, over and over. Marty's body shook as she remembered. But also, Doug said, "the mood I see us in is of these two people having tea and talking quietly."

"You are liberating me," Marty said. "I trust you enough to talk. And you're interested!" Marty felt he loved her naturally, simply. He was quite a bit younger than Marty, but the harmonic between them did not seem to quit. Marty was overwhelmed. She had never before had such access to her emotional life. She was trying to re-balance, find a place in her life for this extraordinary man. The process went on at a deep level, not conscious. It felt like structures shifting, like blockages vibrating free and blowing away. Each time they left each other it was more difficult.

"I'm not going anywhere," said Doug. "We've got time."

But did they?

When Doug arrived, he looked fresh and dapper, with a haircut, a white shirt open at the neck beneath a blazer. He wore jeans, of course, and lace-up boots. He sat down on one of Marty's wooden dining chairs, saying in his is rough Oakie voice, "Come here."

Marty came. He put his face into her bosom as she stood in front of him and reached his hands under her clothes, around her waist and down to her tummy. Marty felt his hands burning on her skin, the liquids sloshing around in her bottom. Marty kissed his ears, his neck, his mouth.

Despite the terrible sweetness Marty felt, they couldn't stay that way, holding each other. They must get up, as Doug said, eat solid food, go out into the world. They were going to the wine-tasting of the Family Winemakers organization at the Palace Hotel. Doug wanted to show Marty some of his world. "You look great!" he said, standing up.

Marty smiled at him. Doug always told her she looked beautiful, but she found it hard to believe. Beauty was mostly found in magazine photos. Marty did realize that her tai chi practice pushed the blood throughout her body, energizing her skin and thinning her waist. But it was one of the amazing things about Doug, that he appreciated life as he found it, as it really was in all of its three-dimensionality.

"We'll take a cab," said Doug. "Now that I have a parking place, I have to emigrate!" Finding a parking place on the top of Russian Hill where Marty lived was difficult and parking downtown would be expensive.

Marty called a cab and they went down into the street to wait for it. Marty took Doug's arm. She felt small beside him, wearing a short black linen coat dress, with white buttons down its front. Under it she wore white stockings and flat black shoes. Perhaps they did fit the profile of the well-heeled Russian Hill couple, for only a moment. It felt surreal to Marty. Nothing was ever as it seemed.

"The Palace Hotel," said Doug grandly to the cab driver.

Marty laughed. She knew that Doug had been poor, had eaten cheese from the welfare department when his mother didn't have much money. But here they were, sailing over Nob Hill on the leather seats of a taxicab. Doug held Marty close. A spatula could not have been inserted between them. "That you exist is a miracle," said Marty softly. But she felt that a sword hung over them.

"Yes," said Doug. His big hand sought the skin under Marty's clothes. "I will always say yes to you."

The summer streets were hushed, the traffic flowing down to the center of town, in the city that Marty loved.

At the hotel, they separated, walking self-consciously down the carpeted aisles of the corridor past the dark bar with its long painting of the Pied Piper toward the light at the other end. A ballroom had been laid out with long tables on either side. Each winery placed the wines it was pouring in rows behind phalanxes of glass stemware. Vases of flowers graced the tables and platters of bread and cheese helped people clear their palates between tastings.

Marty and Doug walked through the center of the room. A few people hailed Doug, but he quickly spotted his partner Jeremy behind a table, pouring wine for a small coterie of guests who were listening to his patter as he poured from a green bottle, one hand behind his back. He looked like a banker with his fine features, in a tightly-fitted blue blazer.

"This is Jeremy," said Doug, interrupting him. "My friend Marty."

Marty had heard a lot about Jeremy from Doug. He was the chief winemaker, educated in America and Europe, gifted in his tastebuds and able to blend great wines. He was meticulous in his work and did not mince words, but he was also knowledgeable enough to craft excellence from the grapes he was given. Doug admired him, had been working with him for almost ten years. Jeremy was the winemaking face of the company and got the accolades.

"A glass of our 1991 Pinot Noir?" asked Jeremy, holding out a gleaming green bottle to Marty. "Grown on the west side of the Santa Cruz mountains. Pretty good year: long growing season; a fragrant, complex wine." The people Jeremy had been talking to stood to one side, swirling the wine in their glasses, smelling it and then drinking.

"Thank you," said Marty. Jeremy could probably spot her relative innocence in this group. She was primed to listen and learn, keeping her eyes and ears open and her mouth shut. She took a glass from the array at the front of the table.

"You can just wander around," said Doug to Marty. "Pick up intel for us. Think of yourself as undercover," he said, conscripting Marty into the fold. He slipped behind the table, taking his place beside Jeremy and leaving Marty on the customer side.

Marty lifted her glass to the two of them. Her lover, Doug, and his partner Jeremy, who was smaller, more finely built.

Jeremy turned to Doug. "Where's that Vince? Have you seen him yet?"

"Oh, don't worry about him," said Doug airily, his smiling eyes on Marty as she sniffed the glass of Pinot Noir. "He's probably wandering around, buttonholing some investment banker or venture capitalist." To Marty he said, "Come back around five. We'll be packing up and then I'll take you somewhere for dinner."

Marty backed away. She was not a customer. She must give place to people who would buy. The atmosphere was festive, light gleaming on the glassware, people clustered around the tables, the beautiful bottles arrayed before them.

Though Marty too had grown up relatively poor and isolated, she felt that her education allowed her to go anywhere, do anything she wanted. She always felt comfortable slipping into posh hotels and restaurants, doing as she pleased. Now she looked around her, quite at home among the well-dressed people who would buy expensive bottles, perhaps place orders for cases of wine to put in their cellars. These were the connoisseurs, the collectors, the wine journalists and taste makers.

Marty swirled the wine in her glass, aerating it and looking at its color, the "legs" it left on the sides of the glass. Doug had taught Marty to taste wines in a simple, unpretentious way. The Pinot Noir smelled clean and fresh with mineral and herbal odors which came from the soil. Marty had no language for them, but she did enjoy the taste which moved from the front to the back of her mouth. Its soft, delicate texture wasn't acidic. Marty took a piece of cut up bread to eat with it.

Marty wandered around, looking for friendly faces. At the Kendall-Jackson Vineyards table, one she knew, she asked for a glass of Chardonnay. It too was clear and fresh, from a different part of California than Doug's wines, from the Napa Valley. "Try our new cool-climate Chardonnay, from the Russian River," said the smiling woman behind the table. Part of her long blonde hair was swept up behind her head in a comb. Marty wished she had a map with her. The label on the bottle said La Crema. Marty let the woman pour her another taste from this bottle.

Marty backed away. She was a lightweight, her head already buzzing. She walked out of the room and into the corridor. The Palace Hotel was famed for its Garden Court, a beautiful room domed in glass where Marty had had tea with Lana more than once. Long ago, she had also had lunch there when Cardigan Shores sent one of its venerable employees to celebrate her retirement with the women from the typing pool. Marty sat in the corridor on a large upholstered chair, holding her wineglass. The last part of wine tasting was thinking about the wine. What was your experience?

Marty knew that Doug had big notebooks full of information about the wines he had tasted, the vineyards and wineries he visited. Information he collected went into databases he had set up on his computer. "I'm an early adapter," he told Marty. Marty had set up employee databases at Whittaker Perotta, but it wasn't so necessary at her new company. Other people took care of this information now.

What Marty did appreciate however, was the fact that Doug used CompuServe to send her messages. She looked for one every day. It was a system whereby you wrote your thoughts to someone, as if in a letter, posted it to a hard disk somewhere in Ohio and the person it was addressed to received it when they signed in through a modem on their own computer. It was instant communication, a miracle. Marty had actually seen very little of Doug. He had come to the city five or six times since they began to be physically involved. It was very hard for Marty to see him so little. All of her thoughts centered on him.

In the world's terms, their alignment was not right. Marty was pretty sure Doug didn't think of their coming together as anything more than an affair. He was married and deeply involved with his family. He was completely honest about the fact that he had no heart for the 'D' word. He was doing the best he could.

But in nature's terms, Marty felt that the affair had gotten away from them. She felt a growing sense of their partnership. Doug felt like her match, unlike the other men friends she had. He was open and talkative and saw only the best in Marty. The bodily awareness Marty had found through tai chi opened her. She had taken him to the center of her heart. But it could not be. The uncertainty, the evanescence of the relationship contributed to the depth to which Marty had let Doug sink into her. A sense of doom hung over them, adding poignancy to their feelings.

By now, Marty knew a great deal more about Mackenzie. She was a lovely young girl who had married Doug in a romantic, flower-bedecked garden five years ago. Doug said that Mackenzie was a child, that he had wanted to take care of her. Since then they had had three children together.

Doug had found that, beyond having the babies, Mackenzie did not know what to do with them. Often enough, she dropped them off at Doug's mother's house in Santa Cruz and took off on adventures. Given his own need to work in the fields and scout vineyards around the state, Doug felt the family was fractured, the kids' most stable home with their grandmother. "It's not what I wanted," Doug told Marty.

Mackenzie was not easy to talk to. She hedged, agreed, pretended and then slipped out of any discussion they had. Marty had seen photographs in which the family looked, for all the world like a real family, kids ranged around their parents. She had also seen the kids with Heather the summer before: Zoe, who was bossy and talkative at three, and the twins, Nic and Natasha, sweet two-year-olds.

Marty knew, however, that Doug and Mackenzie were not partners, that Mackenzie wanted to be one of the kids. She liked Doug's attention, and Marty now knew how well Doug was able to pay attention! Once he had shined his light on you, how could anyone get along without it, she wondered.

As Marty watched, people circled in and out of the room where the wine tasting was going on, laughing and talking. Marty stood up. She went back into the ballroom and stood at the back of a queue for a glass of deep, dark Cabernet Sauvignon. Some of the wines poured were very expensive. She might never get another chance to taste them.

Across the room she caught Doug's eye. He came over to her. "Have you had enough of all this?" he asked. "I think I've done my duty here. We could leave."

"I know so little," said Marty, smiling up at him apologetically. "I have to figure out what an appellation is, what the grape varieties are. I feel quite out of my element."

"Wine is big business in California," said Doug. "It's worth knowing about. But people do fetishize it. It represents the 'good life.'" He laughed a bit sardonically. "They know little of the hard work in the fields, which is mostly done by Hispanic people."

"Yes," said Marty.

"Well, come on," said Doug. "I'm ready for a little of that good life. I'm hungry!" Doug did not seem the worse for the tasting he may have done. Mostly he had probably been talking.

"Shall we go say goodbye to Jeremy?" asked Marty.

"Oh, no," said Doug. "He knows. I have to get back tonight. I'm going to have crews out tomorrow morning for leafing and tucking. They know what they're doing, but it helps if I'm there."

Marty's heart sank. Doug would not come home with her. He would drop her at her apartment and go home to run his vineyard crews, which surely began at the crack of dawn. "What's leafing and tucking?" she asked as they left the hotel.

"We go through the vines, pulling leaves that are getting too big, letting air and light in on the clusters. We tuck the vines up on the guide wires of the trellis, so that they are five or six feet off the ground. All part of canopy management. Makes them easier to pick too. Sometimes we thin out bunches and shoots, but only a few guys can do that! We have to manage the harvest exactly, for weight, taste and color. It's really labor-intensive. All of the grapes for the wines you tasted today are treated with the greatest care." On the street he put up his hand, and a taxi pulled up alongside them.

"Yes," said Marty. "I had no idea, really."

"Someday I'll take you out to the vineyard," said Doug. But he did not say anything about when.

It was almost midsummer, the air warm and the leaves on the ficus trees on Hyde Street were thick and lush. The light lasted long in the evening. Doug and Marty ate a potato and pesto pizza at a small neighborhood pizza place near Marty's house. She loved this odd combination, but Doug did not want to take much time. Marty could feel in him the pull of his home and vineyards.

Primed for his leaving, Marty did not make a fuss. She wanted to beg him to tell her when she would see him again. She felt so lonely when he left. But it would do no good. If you had the guts to love like this, you had to have the guts to separate. The sun had not yet set when Doug left Marty at her door.

Two weeks later, Doug called. "Jason, our son, was born last night," he said softly. "I'll come and show you photographs on Saturday, if you're free."

The words "our son" fell like lead weights on Marty. "Of course," she said. Doug had accepted his new son into his family. She had known it would happen. She did not know what it meant for her, but she could guess. And of course, he would be right.

On Saturday, Marty did a long tai chi practice as she usually did. Her legs ached as she walked up the Union Street hill to her apartment, carrying the weapons bag she had made from some old blue jeans. What her legs really wanted was to have Marty sit with a blanket over them, warming their tingling, pulsing selves. But Marty made herself an omelet and a toasted bagel before she sat down.

When Doug arrived in the afternoon, Marty served tea and a piece of tangy lemon cake, Doug's favorite, with some fruit. Once again he was wearing city clothes, a crisp white shirt. He was going on to dinner with the wine buyer from a small local grocery that night, with Vince and Jeremy.

As Marty had suspected, Doug told her he could not sleep with her any more. He must recommit himself to his family. "But we can be friends," he said. "I will call now and then when I'm in town." They were sitting in each other's arms on the green velveteen sofa.

"Does Mackenzie know about me?" Marty asked.

"Maybe," said Doug. "The sad fact is, she doesn't care. She has no idea who I am or what I'm like. All she thinks about is what she needs and wants. She hasn't much sense of the kids either. I have to be both mother and father to them."

"And to her," said Marty. She shuddered to think how the kids managed. They were still small and Marty knew a Hispanic couple lived on Doug's ranch. They must be helping with the kids as well.

Talking to Doug, being in his presence was almost enough for Marty, however. She did not know what the pain would be like when he left. "We let the lions out," she said softly.

"You bet we did!" said Doug, talking in her ear. "Sort of hard to shove them back in their cages."

"But you will," said Marty. Doug was an honorable guy. He did what he said he would.

"Yes," said Doug. "It's a right pickle. You and me and my wife. You and I love each other, but she's my wife."

"I've been trying to let go," said Marty. "But it's hard. I love being with you so much, but I don't want to be stupid."

"What would be stupid?" asked Doug.

"If you didn't love me," said Marty. "But you do." The sweetness hung between and around them, thick with potentiality.

"Exactly as you are," said Doug. "As you love me."

Who knew, thought Marty. Who knew that she would fall for a much younger viticulturalist who didn't read books, but was intellectual in other ways. A big, fatherly Oakie who wanted her to call him 'honey.' As long as he was with her, Marty was okay.

"But you're going to leave," said Marty.

"Yes," said Doug. "We're each in our own pickle. A meta-pickle, I would say." He stood up, pulling Marty up with him. "You could have anyone you wanted, you know."

"But there isn't anyone else I do want," said Marty plaintively. The atmosphere around them was so thick Marty felt she must take her tai chi sword and cut it.

But this time, Doug did the cutting. He pushed Marty gently against the wall near the door and kissed her hard on the mouth. "Goodbye, my love," he said. "I'll send you a message. Or call you."

Marty melted. It felt so good to talk. "Thank you for stopping by," she said. She wanted to berate him for leaving, but what good would it do. None whatsoever. She must make what Doug gave her into what she needed. She listened to his footsteps as they fell away on the creaky, carpeted stairway and the front door closed behind him.

Marty had no plans for the evening. "Let go and let God," she thought to herself, as Al-Anon taught. The nobility of women was that of letting go. It was all they really had. Especially as I grow older, thought Marty. She didn't need to learn it just for Doug. She needed to learn it period.

On Sunday, Marty walked down the hill to the wharf and took a ferry to Angel Island. She climbed to the top of the mountain on the east side of the island where the grove of pines which Marty had once named for Dad had grown tall. She lay in the dappled shade of a tree, in the long grass and met her lover the sun, who kissed her body where it fell. She ate sensuous food, avocados, chocolate, pistachios and wet green grapes, which seemed especially wet in the dry grass. The trees were dark green above her and the sky a watery blue. Below, the bay was full of sailboats, and she could see the Oakland bridges. A bell buoy rang constantly, one high tone, with an answering low tone from another place.

Marty did not notice that she had been sleeping until she woke up and felt how delicious the sweetness of the heat was. She raised her head and moved the sweaty hair out of her mouth. She felt somewhat numb, could not remember where she was, what she should be doing, what to look forward to.

Sensuality is a beast, thought Marty. A cage of lions. Few people call them out and even fewer did Marty trust to let them play. She loved Doug Henderson. He passed both tests. But she wouldn't die of love, she did not suppose.

Lying on her rug in the grass Marty remembered that once, after one of their early meetings, she had looked in her own long mirror and seen Doug. He wasn't going anywhere. He existed. He had his family, his big life. Marty had simplified hers down to her work, tai chi, her friends, the natural world.

Hearing voices on the path above her, Marty turned over, so that some mother would not be horrified if her young son saw Marty's naked breasts glistening in the light. If my skin is ever beautiful, Marty thought, it is now. Butterflies and black dragonflies with translucent wings flew over her.

The sun was hot, but a breeze blew up in the afternoon. The chirping of the cicadas, which was loud in the heat of the sun, softened. The pines had long growing tips, shining as they reached toward the sun. Shadows were lengthening. The grasses were tall and golden, especially the beautiful quaking grass, or rattlesnake grass with its empty seed pods. I'm a naked little Taoist, Marty thought, laughing sardonically in the woods. Just off the path, within earshot of the world. She put on her clothes and rolled up her rug.

As Marty walked back over the hill and rounded the bend, she could see the ferry for San Francisco coming. She scurried down the hill, scaring a turkey buzzard who sat on a fence post. Purple ceanothus bloomed on the path and the tall purple plumes of Pride of Madeira rose from shrubs along the dock. Marty's legs tingled as she waited to board the boat. She was still talking herself down from the intensity of Doug. It would take a while. Somehow they had convinced each other that they were free to love. But they were not. Doug was not.

Marty thought of the two Old Testament women who quarreled over a baby, bringing him to King Saul to make a decision. "Here," said Saul, raising his blade. "I'll cut the baby in two and you can each have half." "No!" shrieked the true mother. "Let her have him." She wanted the baby to live. Marty felt like that mother. She must give up Doug, so that he could live.

9

Paul consulted his map of Bemidji and drove his Toyota Previa into the driveway of an apartment building. It was snowing, but there was no wind and the temperature was rather mild. He grabbed the bag full of dinners he was delivering and rang the bell on apartment 16. He handed two full Thanksgiving dinners to an older woman, who stood in the doorway, her ancient father in a wheelchair behind her.

"I hope they are still hot!" said Paul.

"Thank you, thank you for coming out in this snow!" the woman beamed. "If not, I can heat them up. Happy thanksgiving to you!"

Two other apartments in the building also got meals. Paul had been conscripted by Grace and her mother-in-law Jane into delivering meals as part of the big community Thanksgiving dinner Bemidji put on. This year it was being served at St. Philips, their very own Catholic church, to almost 600 people. It wasn't just for people who needed hot food. It was also for people who didn't have anyone to eat with, a demonstration of the town's solidarity. Paul had been helping at the social hall at St. Philips all morning and now had a mini-van full of meals to deliver to people who couldn't get to the church.

When Paul got back to St. Philips, he greeted his son-in-law Gerald and Gerald's daughter Dory, now eight, who were parking Gerald's Jeep. "Did you find all the places?" asked Gerald. Dory's brown face shone, her eyes very large. She wore a red parka and a ski hat with ear flaps.

"Probably not as fast as you did," said Paul. "But I got them." He had lived in Bemidji briefly ten years ago when he and Marie first moved back to Minnesota. "I bet you brought some sunshine into dark places today," Paul said to Dory.

Dory nodded and scampered into the church's open door.

"We had a few out in the country," said Gerald. "That took longer." But Gerald knew the place like the back of his hand. It was his home. He looked up at the sky. "I don't think this snow is going to quit," he said. "Not enough visibility to make it worth going up tomorrow, I don't think," he said.

Paul was disappointed. Gerald had offered to take him up in a small plane that belonged to the airport where he worked. Paul had looked forward to flying over the lake country he knew so well from the ground. "Snow check, I guess," he said. "We'll do it some other time. All right?"

"Sure thing!" said Gerald. "We'll get you up there one of these days." Gerald was a handsome young man in his early thirties, proud that he had recently gotten enough flying hours for his pilot's license. "How's that Previa doing?"

"Pretty good," said Paul. It was new to him, but a couple of years old. It had been a rental car. "Certainly more fun than the old Rabbit!" he said. "All-wheel drive. And warmer! Makes Marie happy." The teal-colored mini-van was streamlined and could carry seven people. But Paul did get some flack for buying a car which had been made in Japan. He brushed this off. It had been the best, cheapest deal he could find at the time. He had slept in it a few times already.

It had not been an easy year for Paul. Because Mother didn't have much help at the lake in the summers, Paul gave up his job at the canoe outfitters. He took an available science teaching job at the high school in Ely. It began in September, and Paul had worked hard all summer at the outfitting company. Next summer he would spend at the lake with Mother, but he had not had much time off this year. He was banking money, however, which felt good.

Paul and Gerald followed Dory into the church, where Grace and Gerald's mother Jane were cleaning up after the hundreds of people who had come to share food together. Grace's pregnancy had begun to show, her fourth baby due in March. She was energetic, washing big pots in the church kitchen. Gerald began to bag up the trash and Father Chuck handed Paul one of the wide dust mops that worked so well on large linoleum floors.

Paul liked what he saw of Father Chuck. He was genial and laid back, a far cry from the autocratic Monsignor who ran the parish Grace grew up in. Father Chuck was accessible, happy to work with his parishioners.

Dory stood next to her mother, wiping a huge pot with a dish towel. Paul heard Father Anthony, the other priest who helped out in the parish and its large elementary school, ask Dory about her Wednesday night class. "Got a vacation this week, didn't you?" he questioned. Dory was going to classes to prepare for her first communion in the spring.

When the social hall was mostly back to normal, Grace, Gerald and Dory drove back to the Hickman's apartment, and Paul followed with Jane, Gerald's mother. She was an attractive woman, dark, a little plump. The intense black hair she had firmly tamed into a bun at the back of her head had a few streaks of grey in it, as Marie's did.

"Good turnout today?" Paul asked. But Jane only smiled and nodded.

It was Paul's own Mother who had teased out Jane's story when Jane and her sister Louise visited at the lake. Jane had been a bright, attractive girl from the Leech Lake band of Ojibwe. She went to high school in Bemidji and worked at Bridgeman's, the sleek aluminum-clad ice cream parlor which had been a favorite of Aunt Rose. Every summer when Paul was small, Aunt Rose insisted the Mikkelsons drive to Bemidji and have ice cream sundaes, as well as visit the huge statue of Paul Bunyan and Babe, his blue ox, beside the lake. It was probably long before Jane began working at the ice cream parlor.

Jane had met Gerald's dad when he stopped by for pie and coffee. He drove trucks between Canada and Mexico, making sure to stop in Bemidji once he met Jane. They were married and had a son, Gerald. Gerald was only two when Mr. Hickman swerved on the highway to avoid hitting someone turning in front of him. He hit a guard rail and his truck jackknifed over the edge of a bridge, killing him.

Jane Hickman had been devastated. She quit working at Bridgeman's, where she met so many people, and now worked at a nursing home. Her sister Louise had moved in with her. The two of them brought up Gerald, finding comfort at St. Philips and living quietly, while supporting Gerald's athletic prowess in basketball and his dreams of flying.

Mother had been interested in Jane's parents, wanted to know more, but Jane and her sister weren't very talkative. They seemed to have a wry humor between themselves and Paul had caught them mentioning Nanabush, the Trickster, when something odd happened, but mostly they kept to a round of church activities, rosaries and masses. They were nearly as devout as Grace.

At Gerald and Grace's apartment, Archie came to meet Paul, snuffling at his hands to see what Paul had been up to. "Good dog," said Paul. "Did you take care of everything? Watched over everyone?" Tiny Andre, just up on his little legs was right behind Archie. Archie took care not to bump into him and make him fall.

The big room was full of people. Paul found Marie in the kitchen stirring the turkey gravy for their own feast. He put his hands around Marie's small waist, whispering, "I'm very grateful for you, you know." He liked it when her hands were busy!

Marie smiled back at him, but she was working another pan of Brussels sprouts on the stove, and then put on big oven mitts to take things out of the oven. "Help me," she said to Paul. The pan with the turkey in it was very heavy, and hot!

Louise, Jane's sister, sat in the corner by the television. Her feet and ankles were thick with water retention, an aspect of the Type II Diabetes she suffered from. She couldn't get around much, but she held some sway over the children. Besides Dory, there were Little John and Andre who was one. Paul spooned stuffing out of the turkey and into a bowl. He noticed that Marie had laced it with the precious wild rice harvested from Minnesota lakes.

Twilight was coming on by the time everyone crowded around the table, the snow at the windows soft and thick. As Gerald intoned a prayer of Thanksgiving before they ate, Paul thought that every one of the people at this table were grateful for each other. Gerald had been happy to find his Grace, an earnest young woman, now the mother of his children. Jane and Louise were grateful for this son, whose family had now grown to encompass them. Marie and he were grateful for each other, for the long years they had shared. Grace had found an unexpected family for herself as well. The children didn't know it, but they were lucky to be in this loving household. They would find out.

Paul also thought of the rest of his family, Mother who was celebrating in St. Paul with Ellie's family, Kristen's family and perhaps Christy, Line's eldest son. Christy was trying to finish his degree at the University of Minnesota. All over the country, it was family day.

Gerald and Grace's table was utilitarian. There were plastic dishes and paper napkins on the table, and it was too crowded for a centerpiece. But on the wall Dory had hung a picture she made at school of Native Americans and Pilgrims celebrating. "Tell your grandmas what they told you at school about Thanksgiving," prompted Gerald.

Dory piped up, as if reciting, "My teacher said there wouldn't be any Thanksgiving if it weren't for the Native Americans. The Pilgrims were cold and very hungry. The Native Americans brought them food and skins to wear."

The grownups smiled at each other. Paul was glad that this story had become truth told. He was sure he had been told this growing up as well, but it never seemed to make much difference. Native Americans were still discriminated against.

After eating, Paul felt like just sitting. He had eaten more than he needed to. But he stepped outside with Archie to get a breath of fresh air. He gave Archie some meat, as a treat, being careful to separate out the bones. The snow came down steadily, visible against the streetlights and people's lighted windows.

Inside everyone took a break before the pies were brought out, sitting like beached whales, Paul thought, around the living room. Marie, however, was full of energy. She never ate very much. "I've brought a new CD," she said to Dory. "It'll make you want to dance!" Gerald had all the latest entertainment equipment. Marie put her new ABBA Gold CD in the player and turned it on.

Disco music lit up the room and Marie and Dory danced wildly in the middle to "Dancing Queen" while everyone watched. Little Joe joined in and even Andre jigged at the edge of the room, fat little legs sticking out of his diaper. Paul clapped at the end of the song. He thought it was funny. Marie had never paid attention to ABBA before. But now that the group was long gone and all that was left was a CD full of hits, they became her favorite!

Marie let song after song play. Then she stopped the CD. "I'm going to play you my favorite now," she said. She hit the buttons on the player until she got to the one she wanted. "This is the reason I brought this CD. Just listen," she told the kids, standing in the middle of the room. "I'm going to sing along with it."

"I'm nothing special," Marie sang with one of the two women in the band. "In fact I'm a bit of a bore. If I tell a joke, you've probably heard it before. But I have a talent, a wonderful thing, 'cause everyone listens when I start to sing. I'm so grateful and proud. All I want is to sing it out loud." Marie knelt down on the level of Dory, Little John and Andre, who looked at her, rapt. "So I say thank you for the music, the songs we're singing. Thanks for all the joy they're bringing. Who can live without it, I ask in all honesty. What would I be? Without a song to sing what are we? . . ."

The song went on. Marie knew all the words, singing her heart out. Paul wondered if the Swedish girl, who was reputed not to know English well, knew what she was singing.

When the song was over, Marie turned off the player. "Isn't it wonderful?" she asked.

Grace clapped her hands. "Oh, Maman," she said in her softly accented English. "It's a beautiful song!"

Marie came over to her and hugged her. "I'm so happy!" she said. "You are all so delightful!" Everyone beamed at Marie's infectious performance, her happiness.

Marie turned around. "Come on, kids. Come on Paul. It's a Thanksgiving song! Let's do it again, just one more time." She started the song again and the music boomed out into the crowded apartment, the kids dancing.

Paul stood up and sang with Marie. It was hard to keep silent! When they finished, Paul reminded Marie. "We should do the companion to it, Pete Seeger's song, 'How Can I Keep from Singing.'" In his own strong tenor he began without any tuning note. "Since love is lord of Heaven and earth, how can I keep from singing."

The audience was the most quiet Paul and Marie had ever sung for. But, Paul thought, the most glad. Their faces shone in the lamp light. "So nice," said Jane, quietly. "So nice to hear you."

"Tante Louise," said Grace, "You could do the 'Women's Song.'" She turned to the others. "It's Ojibwe. I've heard them sing it."

Jane poked Louise, but Louise shook her head and the two of them giggled.

"Couldn't you do it together?" asked Grace. "They sing it to Andre when they want him to sleep."

But no, the older women did not want to sing it. Jane stood up, laughing. "Time to eat pie," she said.

That evening, Paul and Marie rolled out sleeping bags on the living room floor. Jane and Louise had gone home, so no one got to hear them singing at bedtime either. It's coming, thought Paul. Gerald's children, who were one quarter Ojibwe, would get some idea of Ojibwe culture, as well as their French Canadian backgrounds. All of them understood some French, especially Dory, as Grace spoke to her babies in French.

When Gerald was growing up, he pretended to know nothing about being Native American. Assimilation had been the best practice, the best way of getting ahead. But now, only a few years later, people were beginning to be proud of this background.

Gerald and Grace had enrolled their children in the Leech Lake Band of Ojibwe and given them Ojibwe names as well as the Catholic names they already had. Much of the Leech Lake reservation was Chippewa National Forest and lake, but there were several small communities offering social services. The Leech Lake Band operated gaming emporiums and hotels and had just opened a Tribal College in Cass Lake.

Lake Michigami, on the southern side of which was the Mikkelson cabin, was also in the Chippewa National Forest. Paul had never known much about the reservation, but he was excited to learn as Gerald and Grace became more involved.

In the morning Andre stood over Paul and Marie. "I can smell your poopy diaper," said Marie. Archie lay on the floor near the door, guarding the house. "Can you bring me a clean diaper and some wipes?" Marie asked Dory. "I'll clean him up." Dory had let down the side of Andre's crib so he could get out. All three of them slept in one bedroom, while their parents slept in the other.

When Andre was clean, Paul sat him on his stomach. "Look how he sits," he said to Marie. Andre's strong body and spine seemed to be balanced far over his fat little haunches. A more firm seat, Paul could not imagine.

Warmth and food smells filled the house. Wiry Little John climbed up on a kitchen chair to fetch down his cereal. Dory found bowls and poured milk for them. It reminded Paul of his own early years when Mother had stayed up late and slept in, letting the Mikkelson kids get their own breakfasts before school.

Paul fed Archie and stepped outside with him. Soft snow came down in feathery piles. "We best be getting on the road," said Paul to Archie. No one had to work that day and the snow wouldn't stop, but Paul wanted to drive during the daylight.

After a sleepy breakfast, Paul, Marie and Archie left, saying goodbye to the Hickmans and heading back to their own home three hours away in Ely. Paul could feel the pull of the cabin on Lake Michigami, only thirty miles south, but there was no heat or water there and snow might be heavy on the road. He drove resolutely east.

"I wish there was a way Gerald and Grace could buy a house," said Marie, as they headed out onto the highway, which was wet with the slush and the heat of cars and trucks that had gone before. "They're going to be bursting at the seams after the new baby comes."

"Oh, don't worry," said Paul. "I think Gerald has ideas. He's a smart cookie." He turned up the heater as the engine revved up. "Maybe we could help them a little. We'll see."

"Yes," said Marie. "Let's try."

"I cannot believe how isolated we Mikkelsons were when we grew up," said Paul. "Scandinavian Lutherans were almost the only people we knew! And Mother and Dad really pushed us to go to Lutheran colleges. Catholics were odd to us and I never knew a Native American. And we were surrounded!"

"Me too," said Marie, a trifle bitterly. "Stuck in our little Quebecois parishes. Didn't know a thing about the world."

"And then there was this opening," said Paul. "And me and Line and Marty rushed into it!"

"Yes," said Marie. "Me and Hanna too, a little later."

"Line's had my kids," said Paul. "And I think Marty's too. Mother's had eight grandkids from six of her own. And, of course Grace, who she sees more than any of them. And now there are these little great-grand kids! What an amazing world."

"I hope Grace doesn't overdo it," Marie worried. "Kids can be too much of a good thing. She's only 28!"

"Yes," said Paul. "Once the world needed all the kids we could come up with. But that's no longer true." Paul took his eyes off the straight wet highway ahead for a moment to look at his lively wife. Marie's dark curls framed her face. "Are you happy, my love? Do you feel at home here?"

"Oh yes, Paul," said Marie. "I'm very content."

Archie bedded down on the carpeted floor of the van behind their seats and Marie hummed to herself.

When they got home to Ely mid-afternoon, it was still snowing lightly. Paul took Archie with him for a quick walk around the sterile Miner's Lake near the house. He enjoyed seeing people, but for pure joy, Paul most loved walking out among trees and weather with his dog.

Paul paused at the large white pine before he crossed the road toward the lake. The pine was majestic standing tall and lonely, long a friend to Paul. Nearby Archie investigated a pileated woodpecker with its stiff red crown, drumming rat-a-tat at the top of a half-dead scrub oak.

"How you doing, old timer?" Paul asked the pine. "Ready for snow?" Pines, like other trees, went dormant during the winter, slowing down their metabolism and conserving food as if they were hibernating animals. They didn't lose their needles, like trees that sloughed off leaves it took energy to maintain. But they did give up on growth. Sap flowed more slowly. Paul put his hands on the bark, listening, feeling.

The scrub oak had no leaves at all and was quite dead on one side. It provided food and shelter, however. The area was neglected. Paul hoped it would continue to be.

A path wound around the small lake, bare sticks dusted with snow poking out. The trees were mostly scrub and thin stands of birch and aspen that had grown up since the mine had closed down. The lake looked frozen, but Paul didn't trust it. He saw tracks on the flat sugary surface, perhaps fox tracks, but he didn't let Archie go out on the ice. It was too early in the year.

They passed the place where Paul had had an experience with a fisher that fall, the first he had ever seen. It had crossed the path in front of him, seeming to flow with a smooth, undulating gait, at dusk. The animal was in the weasel family, too large to be anything but a fisher. It was at least three feet long, thick and dark. A few days later, he had seen it again in almost the same place, moving sinuously across the path.

And then, strangely enough, he found the body of a fisher near the side of the path in the same area a few weeks later. He picked it up to examine it, took it home and showed the pelt to a friend who cured animal skins. The friend said the pelt wasn't usable. It had been lying out in the sun too long. Paul buried the fisher in his yard near the garden, but as it grew colder, he dug it up. He wanted to keep the skull and certain of its bones.

Paul did not drag Marie into this activity, keeping the bones in the basement where he stored odd things for his own research. He had had to prevent Archie from getting too involved, as well. Archie did like to bury the odd bone, but there were so many smells and things to notice above ground that he didn't seem to bother much.

Paul kept his eyes on the edges of the path, where the undergrowth began. Above them, the sky was heavy and grey, growing darker, reflecting very little light. Paul could see tracks winding in and out of the sumac bushes. It looked like ruffed grouse had been feeding on the clumps of reddish seeds. There were even wing marks where they had flown up into the birches. Suddenly Archie startled one and it bounced out of the snow and flew into a tree in indignation. Paul laughed, but the grouse chewed at the leaf ends of the birch unconcernedly. Two more rose up as Paul came toward them, but then settled behind them back into the snow, where they had warm roosts. Paul was glad there were some left after hunting season, although he had heard that hunting didn't affect them much, due to the grouse population's cycles.

As it grew dark, Paul and Archie rounded the lake and returned home. Paul loved the dim, grey twilight, hesitating to go inside. Lights in the distance showed where the town was, but as it wasn't deeply cold, why go indoors? He walked around to the back of the house, where a flock of evening grosbeaks was picking about at the bird feeder and under it where seed casings had fallen.

Paul thought how deeply adapted to Minnesota he was. He'd been born across the Red River in North Dakota, very close to Minnesota, and here he was, home. Days, weeks, seasons passed with great rapidity. Soon the deep cold would start. But shortly afterward the solstice would come and the northern hemisphere tilt more toward the sun. It must surely be part of God's creation process that people adapt to the inexorable circling of the planets and stars.

Even as he reflected on it, Paul knew that scientists were working out where humans had originated, mostly due to the work of the Leakeys in East Africa. Humans had begun in rainforests, like their closest relatives the chimpanzees. But the earth's crust in Africa changed, throwing up the East African highlands and creating the Rift Valley.

Paul was fascinated by the subject, learning that, perhaps because of this climate change, the apes that moved into hot, dry climates on the savannahs of East Africa lost their fur and gained sweat glands, beginning to walk on two feet. This may have been the beginning of communication, hunting, the growth of the human brain. As there grew to be more of them, they had pushed into other parts of the world. Skin color was only one adaptation to environment. Dark skin was correlated with high levels of ultraviolet radiation from the sun.

Paul was happy to call the circling of deep space and life's evolutionary journey, God. Man would never get to the root of reality. There was always more. Paul did not have much problem teaching evolution in the Minnesota schools either. He had actually been somewhat depressed to find that there were few scholars or scientists among his high school students. Most were occupied in the primitive sports of football, hunting, fishing and snowmobiling and did not care about the environment. Those who did were a tiny minority. The environmentalist kids' parents often worked in the tourist industries instead of the nearby mines.

We're herd animals, Paul reminded himself. He didn't mind being at the edge of the herd, probably because of Dad's courageous example, but animals at the edge were more vulnerable.

Choice of habitat and adaptation to it was surely an aspect of being human. And habitat worked on a person. Line and Marty seemed to love the coastal climates they had chosen. Ellie was certainly happier since she had settled back in Minnesota. Paul wondered about Hanna. How was the cheese-making operation going on the farm in upstate New York?

These are my subjects, thought Paul, the people I know. He laughed to himself, stamping his wet feet as he walked into the house. I should ask more questions, he thought. It always felt invasive to ask questions, but he did want to know things. He began rubbing down Archie's wet fur with an old towel.

10

Line sat between Stephen and Mother at the University of Minnesota commencement program in June, flipping through the program as they waited for the exercise to start. There it was in black and white: Christopher Cohen, B.A. in History and Rhetoric.

Line nudged Stephen. "And what's rhetoric again?" She did not think anyone had studied it when she was going to college.

"The art of persuasion," said Stephen quietly. "It's a classical discipline, but nowadays everyone from public relations people to attorneys and lobbyists study it."

Line nodded, turning to Mother to see whether she had found Christy's name in the program. Mother was getting a little shaky, tottering on her uncertain feet. But she seemed thrilled to be dressed up and out in the world, seeing her grandchildren making their way. On the other side of

Mother sat Paul and his wife Marie. One the other side of Stephen, sat Poppa, Stephen's father.

"You can look at Nelson Mandela's speech for a powerful use of rhetoric," said Stephen insistently. Mandela had been elected in the first democratic election in South Africa and then inaugurated in Pretoria. South Africa was being watched closely, but as yet there had been no outbreak of terrible violence and retribution by the black majority who had been suppressed for so long. "A rainbow nation, at peace with itself and the world," quoted Stephen. "A real leader knows how to inspire and direct, using rhetoric."

Line nodded. The whole world had been impressed with Mandela. Stephen had pointed out how often the word 'peace' appeared in Mandela's address, though it did not deny that injustice and indignities had been done.

Line had no doubt that Christy had also studied Mandela's speech and actions. She spotted him in the large body of students in their caps and gowns. She was impressed Christy was even willing to participate! He was four years older than most of the other students. Indeed he and Heather were graduating the same year, Heather from U.C. Davis in two weeks.

Stephen had insisted they go to both graduations. "If that little so and so thinks he can graduate without us coming to see him, he has another think coming," Stephen had said vehemently of Christy. Neither Stephen nor Line had much say in Christy's life since he left home at 18. Christy supported himself by working on and off for various political figures. His favorite, Paul Wellstone, was now in the Senate. Poppa provided the money for Christy's education, and he bounced around, living with friends or his Minnesota relatives. Christy did not write home or call very often. He was a grownup.

Line did not expect much of the ceremony. The speaker was listed as Marvalene Hughes, V.P. for Student Affairs. When she stood up to speak, however, Line took notice. It wasn't what she said, Line thought, rhetoric aside. It was her presence. She was a small African American woman in a dark suit and pearls saying the usual things about leadership and how each student mattered as they went out into the world. But something about how she said them conveyed authority, commitment, certainty.

And then it was fun to watch the students parade across the podium and pick up their diplomas. Line wondered whether Christy's would go in a pile of forgotten things as soon as he left! Some of the students conveyed their egotism with a flourish of some kind or a glance to the audience, but Christy was business-like, his posture conveying a feeling of, ok, let's get it over with. Poppa stood up to take a photograph. Line was sure Christy was at least a little proud.

Afterward everyone stood out on the lawn in front of the auditorium talking while Poppa formed up groups to take more photos. The air felt moist and warm on Line's skin. She could smell the grass, which must have been cut recently.

"I was impressed with your speaker," Mother said to Christy.

"Yeah," said Christy. "She's a straight shooter. We all like her."

"She's on the list for the presidency of a Cal State college this year," said Stephen. "I hope she gets it!"

"And you're going to Peru in the fall with the Peace Corps?" asked Paul.

"Hope so," said Christy.

"Aren't things somewhat unstable there?" asked Mother. "Don't they have that Shining Path, or something, stirring up trouble?"

"All the more reason!" smiled Christy. "Actually, the leader of the Shining Path was captured and imprisoned by President Fujimori. It's quieter there now. But Peru has a lot of problems! We have quite a few Peace Corps volunteers there."

Line listened avidly to her son, wishing he would say more.

Beside her, Stephen stood with a knowing air. "Like everywhere, people in Peru are flocking to the cities where they think there will be work," he said. "But there's no housing and most of the economy is informal, outside the government's purview."

Line dug her elbow into Stephen's side, reminding him that it was Christy's moment. For once, he should let Christy know more than he did! But Christy didn't react.

"And why did you choose Peru?" asked Marie, who stood beside Paul in a pretty dress and little flat shoes, dark curls bobbing.

Christy dissembled, shifting his weight from one foot to the other. "Laziness," he said. "I'm not very good at languages, but I do have a little rudimentary Spanish, from growing up in California." He flashed a smile. "And they do need people."

Line smiled up at him. He looked so much like Stephen, though his hair was much thicker. Line knew he didn't particularly like to be the center of attention. "Proud of you, son," she said. "I am sure you will do well."

"We'd like to know what's going on there and how you're doing," said Paul. "Couldn't you send us round-robin emails or something?"

"Sure," said Christy nonchalantly. "I'll put you all on a list." He turned to Poppa. "Can I take off this monkey suit now?" he asked. "It's hot!"

"You bet," said Poppa. "I just had to get this one in the history books. I'm pleased as punch," he said. "Come on, let's all go and have drink on this kid." He went over and stood by Mother. "Hope I don't offend you," he said.

But Mother brushed it off, generously. "I'm pleased as punch too," she said. "And I would like to sit down!"

Line took Mother's arm and Paul took the other. Line was thinking how sad it was that she saw so little of Mother. I must come for a month sometime soon, Line thought. It was certainly possible, now that most of her chicks were out on their own. Only Ivy was at home, going to school and amusing herself with artwork in Santa Cruz. Fern was in Europe, where opportunities for archaeological digs kept presenting themselves.

But on that trip there was little time to talk to Mother or anyone else. The Cohens had little more than a long weekend. Stephen needed to wrap up the school year in Santa Cruz and two weeks later they would drive to Davis, where Heather would pick up a diploma in Viticulture and Enology.

At home, Line phoned Marty to see if she wanted to take the train to Davis and meet them for the ceremony.

"Well, actually," said Marty. "Doug said he would pick me up."

Line was not surprised. Her "Hmmmm" was eloquent. "I guess we'll see you there, then," she said. Doug had been something of a mentor to Heather, who often babysat for his children, and he had graduated from the very same viticulture program.

"I can't refuse to see him," said Marty. "Just being around him is worth it." Marty's voice sounded as if she were ashamed.

"Well," said Line. "Try to take care of yourself." She often listened to Marty's misery over her love for a married man who was committed to his family and much younger than Marty was. "Who else can I tell?" Marty had whimpered.

Line wondered if Doug would bring his kids. They loved Heather, but they might be a little young for a grownup ceremony. Zoe was only 5,

Line remembered and the twins were 4. The new baby must be a year old by now.

On Saturday, Davis was predictably gorgeous. Line loved the wide tree-lined streets of the flat valley town. The air was dry and aromatic. Bright poppies, roses or flowering sage bloomed in every yard. Poppa drove his red Acura, with Stephen beside him, and Ivy and Line in the back.

When they got to campus, Poppa stopped to ask directions, his preferred method of getting around. Reclusive Ivy cringed in the back and Line giggled.

"No wonder that girl got so good on a bike," Poppa said finally as they parked. Heather's only transportation in the spread-out town was by bicycle.

The campus did seem to be huge, and there were so many students that there were many graduation programs. Heather's was in the afternoon, for the College of Agricultural and Environmental Sciences.

Waiting outside by the front door to the hall stood Marty and Doug, for all the world like a couple. Doug was tall and forthright, his blondish hair burnished by the sun. Openness, honesty and not caring what other people thought kept his demeanor free and easy. Marty looked a little sheepish, thought Line, but pretty in a white linen jacket over a silky pink dress. Her hair was short and poufy. Line had put hers up on her head, as she usually did for work, and in hot weather. It was still long and red-gold. She liked it long, but she did find herself picking at the ends when she sat, brooding and thinking.

While they were greeting each other, along came Heather! "All of my favorite people!" she crowed, hugging everyone. In cap and gown, her budding beauty was hidden, except for her face, thought Line.

A professor who seemed to know Doug passed by, greeting him and asking "How's the war going?"

Doug's face darkened as he said, "Not good. We're looking to you guys for ideas!" The two of them stepped back into a conversation meant not to bother the cheery family group.

Heather interpreted: "They're talking about the sharpshooters, these little insects that carry a certain bacterium that attacks vines. They're especially bad up in the Santa Cruz Mountains right now."

"Why?" asked Stephen. "What happens?"

"First you notice leaf curl, the leaves drying up. Then the clusters dry up, becoming just like raisins. The bacteria affect the vine's vascular structure. Water can't get to the leaves and the fruit."

"That sounds terrible!" said Line. "Why is it happening up in the mountains?"

Doug had returned to the conversation by this time. "One idea is that our vineyards are surrounded by rough edges. They're small plots cut into mountainsides and right beside the forest. Not like the huge vineyards laid out in Napa and Sonoma, and the San Joaquin Valley. These native bluegreen sharpshooters may winter in the forest and then come down to the vineyard. Pierce's disease wiped out vineyards in Southern California in the last century, and we're having some disasters now. We have lost one vineyard already. And we can't afford it!"

"There's some cyclical pattern to it that no one understands," said Heather. "Might have to do with how cold the winter is, how heavy the rains."

"Does it spoil the wine?" asked Poppa.

"Actually, no," said Doug. "We don't harvest the affected grapes."

"UC Davis is all over it," said Heather. "But no one has figured it out. It's the reason there are quarantines on vines and stuff."

"We can't spray," said Doug, "because we mostly use predatory pests and parasites to keep disease in check. But some of us are trying things. Like ripping the soil around the vines, and pruning severely."

"One of my colleagues lost a small mountain vineyard a couple of years ago," said Stephen. "Even I heard about it, deep in the history department."

"Well, we'll figure it out," said Doug. "We're innovators. Never say die, and all that." He looked defiant, but he shook his head. "Tired of the subject," he said. "Let's go watch this girl graduate. Go New World wines!"

The group looked a little wilted by this discussion, but Heather joined her friends and the rest of them settled into seats. The speaker was an engaging member of the administration, but Line found her mind wandering. She had never heard of sharpshooters and did not really wish to know. As if Doug needed any other problems! Line did not think that he and Marty acted inappropriately. They kept their hands to themselves, could probably pass for friends.

In the middle of the ceremony, Line became worried that they did not have enough room in the car to transport back all of Heather's things.

The trunk of the car was roomy, but she had forgotten about Heather's bike! She did wake up and pay attention when the students filed across the stage and picked up their diplomas, but mostly her mind was roving.

Heather would also be going down to South America for an internship. She had wanted to go to France, but some French winemakers, friends of Jeremy at Boulder Creek Vineyards, had left France to try their hands at winemaking in Chile. They offered Heather a place. She would learn French techniques, applied to New World wines, would be gone at least a year.

"Except for the inverted seasons, it feels a lot like California there," Jeremy told Heather. He had been down to visit the operation. "West coast, beautiful cities. And the vineyards are backed up against the Andes." Chile, like Peru, had only recently voted a repressive dictator out of office, but Jeremy swore it was a stable country. Line sighed. Like Marty and herself, her children seemed bound and determined to go as far away from home as possible. Line looked over at Ivy, her youngest, so pretty in a sleeveless cotton dress, her light-colored long hair hanging down. So far Ivy seemed to prefer home, thriving best where she was appreciated.

After the ceremony, Poppa again popped out his 35mm Pentax and lined everyone up in the shade of a large oak tree for some photographs.

"Hey, if I'm not mistaken, this is a cork oak!" said Doug. "They were planted for shade in the 1920's, I think. It takes 50 years to grow cork!"

Poppa laughed. "It's all about wine for you, isn't it," he said.

"One way or another," said Doug. "Sorry!"

Later when Poppa had shepherded them into a small tavern, they ordered drinks and snacks and brought them to tables outdoors on the sidewalk, again in the shade of heavily-leafed trees. So pleasant, thought Line. But she asked Heather, "Are you all packed? I've been worrying whether we have enough space for your things on the way home."

"We came in style in Poppa's Acura Legend," said Stephen, smirking.

"The worst is probably my bicycle," said Heather. She looked around hesitantly. "Maybe I could take the train with it? Or something?" She sometimes took the train to San Jose and Line drove over the mountain to pick her up. It was much quicker than driving to Davis!

Again, Doug Henderson stepped in. "I brought my van," he said. "Plenty of room for whatever you've got."

Heather looked at him with relief. "That's great! I can't wait to get home," she said. "I can't believe I'm finally done with school!"

Doug looked quizzically at Marty. "Want to go to Santa Cruz?" he asked. "Stay with your sister for the night? I could get you back to the city in the morning."

Marty gave him a wide smile and Poppa said, "Okay! Now that that's settled. Anyone want another?"

But everyone knew they had a long way to go that evening. Who knew what traffic might be like. "We better get on the road," said Line. "And we still have to pick up Heather's stuff."

The drive was long, with Stephen scribbling notes in the front passenger seat, Ivy drawing and Line looking out of the window at the varied landscapes. The California hills were drying into the golden fur they sported in summers. Poppa twinkled along, sending out a thought to Stephen now and then. Heather had gone home in the van with Doug and Marty.

Line could not remember going to any other family graduations. They must have happened, she thought. Except for her own. She had gotten through three years of college, but had not gone for her final year. She slightly remembered her capping ceremony as a nurse in Chicago. But that had been obscured by finding she was pregnant with Christy while still unmarried. Line shook her head. Time was getting away from her.

The longest days of the year were upon them, but it was twilight when the little convoy arrived in Santa Cruz. It was cooler on the coast, of course. But Line could tell, as she opened the car door, that it had been a hot day. Doug helped unload Heather's things from the van into the driveway, but then rushed off to his own family and responsibilities, leaving a slight hole in the social fabric.

The Cohens' house was cool, having been shut up during the heat of the day. Line slipped out of the leather shoes she was wearing and into her ever-present flip-flops. She went about opening doors and windows to the evening breezes. The house was spacious and beautiful, swallowing up its occupants. Line preferred breezes, even if they were hot, to airlessness. "Come on, Marty," she said. "Let's go down and see how the garden is faring."

Marty was barefoot. "Everything is easy in the summer," she said. "Don't have to worry about shoes or sweaters or keeping the doors closed. I love California!"

Line looked over the planters on the shady side of the deck, pulling off dry leaves and deadheading roses with a small secateur. "I watered yesterday," she said. "I can't do it every day. But it is hard not to on these hot days." She looked at Marty's feet as she went down the wooden steps to the garden level below. "Do you need anything on your feet?" she asked.

"It's okay," said Marty, sitting on the last wooden step. "I'll just watch you from here."

The evening heat felt voluptuous. The sky in the west was blue and violet. The fog would roll in soon, Line thought. She looked over at Marty sitting in the shadows.

"It is really painful every time Doug leaves," said Marty. "But I can't refuse to be with him. I'm just so open to it. He's just a match for me, somehow."

"The Germans say there's a cover for every pot," said Line.

"But why does he have to be married and have kids?" cried Marty. "Doug always tells me I must find someone else. That we can only be friends. And of course he's right. But there's no one like him."

"Well, what is he like exactly?" Line asked. She could tell Marty wanted to talk about it, pick the open sore. The agapanthus would start soon, she noticed. The cistus was long gone, but there were poppies. The zucchini and squash flowers glowed in the growing darkness. Line's hands moved through them, picking a few zucchini with their flowers intact. So delicious at this time of year.

"It's something about order and pattern," said Marty. "He's got binders full of notes he takes on every vineyard he visits, every wine he tastes. I'm all about pattern too," Marty's face looked up at Line earnestly. "We're both hedonists, and we just trust each other emotionally. I got so open when we were together, like I've never been before! I guess that's why it's so painful. I didn't know a heart could hurt like this!"

"I'm sorry," said Line. She slowed down, turned toward Marty. A thin sickle moon was going down in the west, the evening star hanging beside it. "I was surprised by how my heart felt when I was away in Scotland for two years. It never felt at home, never felt really comfortable."

"This is where you're happiest," said Marty. "Isn't it?"

"Yes, definitely," said Line. "Hands in the dirt! Though it is always nicer when my kids are around. I mean, I want them to have lives of their own, too, of course."

"Yeah," said Marty softly. "It isn't that I expect anything. I've gotten kind of stoic. I try not to have any intentions toward Doug." Marty was very still in the twilight. "I've been surprised to find how much tai chi helps me. I can be miserable, but then I go off to class and by the end of it, the pall has lifted. It's taught me other things as well."

"Like what?" asked Line. She sat down on the wooden edge of one of the raised beds, her skirts full of zucchini. If I can't talk to Mother, she was thinking, I guess I should take time to talk to Marty.

"You know that I'm a two, on the Enneagram, for instance," said Marty. "Twos try to avoid their own feelings by becoming involved in other people's. But I've been noticing that when we all stand in a grid in tai chi, we strengthen each other's practice. And it seems that I have to occupy my own space, be my own person, instead of trying to take on someone else's emotions."

"That's interesting to learn," said Line. "The kind of thing it takes a long time to see in yourself!"

"Twos learn from being alone," said Marty. "But they hate it."

"I think I'm the four," said Line, "the 'tragic romantic.' Or, so I've been told. Do you know what sort of problems they have?"

"The enneagram describes our defenses," said Marty. "Ways we learn to protect our poor little personalities as they grow. And it was pretty overwhelming, that litter of kids growing up in North Dakota." She stood up. "I think the fours have trouble living in the present. I learned this from Nathan. He was so full of anticipation when I was planning a visit. But then when I got there, he seemed to want me to go away! It was easier to be in a relationship with him when I was far away!"

"That can't be true of me," said Line. "I'm surrounded! But I do have a habit of thinking that things are going to be great in the future. When I lose some weight. When I get home. When the kids are out of school. And then when they're in school! I can see that I have trouble staying with what is going on."

"It all gets away from us," said Marty. "Can't be helped." She raised her hands above her head, stretching.

Line stood up too, lifting her skirt so the zucchini wouldn't fall. "I learn from Reiki. The power of hands. Hands do so much."

"In tai chi they say that energy comes up from the earth," said Marty. "Gets directed by the waist and expressed in the hands." She sank a little on her legs, turning her waist with her hands following in a circle, the palms facing each other.

"Yes!" said Line. "All that we are is expressed in our hands."

"And voices," said Marty, quietly.

Line knew what she was thinking. She was thinking of Doug's rich, charismatic voice full of things he wanted to tell people. Line was thinking of Mother's hands, quick and intelligent, moving through yarn or cloth as she sewed. And Mother's voice. How it expressed her dignity, her strength. Line wondered about her own voice, which she never thought about. What had it become, since she no longer used it to shout at children? Perhaps it was time to pay attention to the self she was becoming. But then again, Line wasn't worried. It is what it is, she thought to herself.

11

When Paul heard the floorboards creak in the old farmhouse in the Mohawk Valley where he, Marie and Mother were staying, he slipped out of bed and joined Gary, Faith's father, for early morning chores. The sun had not come up, but the sky was pink and orange in the east. Heavy dew gave the lawn in front of the house a fresh look. Paul wanted to take off his shoes and walk in it.

But Paul also wanted to help Gary and Faith. The black and white cows were all crowded near the barn, knowing what time it was. Paul could hear them mooing and chewing when he got close. Gary waved when he saw Paul. Around the corner, from the separate studio where she slept with Hanna, came Faith. Gary would manage the cows, but Paul had learned he could be of some help to Faith.

"Morning," he said.

Faith smiled at him. "Here to help?" she asked. The long-haired East Friesian sheep were out cropping in the pasture. Paul and Faith rounded them up and directed them into the shed where they would be milked. Now that it was August, lambing was long past and milking was done only once a day. "The pastures have changed too," Faith told Paul. "There are not so many interesting wildflowers and herbs, which make the spring cheese taste almost floral. This time of year the cheese is going to taste grassy."

Faith made and sold three kinds of sheep cheese: a semi-hard cheese, aged about three months; a spreadable cheese made from pasteurized sheep milk and sometimes flavored with herbs or onions and garlic; and a feta, crumbled and aged.

In the shed, Faith lined up the sheep and Paul wiped down their udders, which were a bit greasy, before Faith hooked each one up to a milking machine. There were 20 ewes, their tails docked for cleanliness. The farm had a few Nubian goats too, but they were an experiment. "A giggle," as Faith called them. "Goats are silly!" They did look silly with their long floppy ears. Faith milked them by hand. The farm might get into goat cheese production, but the sheep operation, which was in its second year, was doing so well they weren't sure any more about the goats.

The milk was stored in a refrigerator in the gleaming stainless steel dairy. "On Friday," said Faith, "we'll make a vat of sheep cheese from what we got this week. We're getting to the end of the cycle."

They headed to the house, where Mother sat on the porch in a rocking chair. "So beautiful," she said. "The morning of the world." A plump grey cat with white feet and tail tip walked past her, its brushy tail in the air.

"Yes," said Faith. "And this is every morning!"

An August morning, though, Paul thought, was surely among the great experiences in life. The sun past its zenith, the waning moon high in the sky, the blue of the sky grew more intense, darker, at this time of year.

"I heard the apples plopping on the ground when I lay in bed," said Mother. She was sleeping on a daybed in the front room of Faith and Hanna's studio, as she did not think she could manage the steep stairs in the farmhouse. The studio was shaded by a large, old Baldwin apple tree.

"Oh yes," said Faith. "I must get out and prop up some skirts under that tree for them to fall into. Or we will lose them."

In the kitchen, Hanna and Marie were making pancakes. "An egg with yours?" Marie asked Paul.

"Sure," he said. The farm was a miracle of order and purpose. It had been in Gary's family for generations and was well-established. Seven plates were arranged around the wooden table in the big airy kitchen, for Gary and Martha, Hanna and Faith, Paul and Marie and Mother. The coffee tasted wonderful to Paul, as if he had earned it! He was hoping Archie was doing well this morning. He had left his dog at the lake with a neighbor as he did not know what he would be getting into on this trip.

Breakfast was a time for organizing the many operations which were all going on at once on the farm. Martha, Faith's mother, and Hanna took responsibility for sales and accounts. Hanna loaded available cheeses into a van twice weekly and delivered some to local stores, and sold some at a farmers' market. "I'm good at it!" she told Mother. The milk processing business was long established, but running the herds was plenty of work for Gary and Faith. And Faith made the cheese to precise microbiological and chemical specifications.

The big project that year was the cheese aging cave. Faith and Hanna had been in Europe the previous winter, visiting farms where cheeses were made and learning the many things Europeans had known forever.

"We have to keep it simple," said Faith. "We're not going to produce a thousand kinds of cheese, but what we do produce, we want to be great!" The cave was being dug into a low rise on the farm. It would be made of concrete with wooden shelves. But Faith had specified that it must have a rounded ceiling, like a real cave. "It promotes air circulation," she said. "Air trapped in corners gets stale and stagnant."

Added to all of this was the usual harvesting and preserving. Hanna also worked at a summer theater camp for all ages in Saratoga Springs. It was a lot of work, but she loved it. On the coming weekend, they would produce The Importance of Being Earnest. Mother didn't want to miss it.

"If you make the crust," Mother said to Marie, "I could peel the apples for a pie tonight." Mother couldn't help much as she couldn't stand for very long, but she loved all the activity.

Marie looked around for confirmation. "Sure," she said. "Sounds great!"

"This must be local maple syrup," said Mother as she poured some from a pitcher onto a pancake.

"We traded some cheese for it," smiled Faith. "With our neighbors. So much fun figuring out how to do this. They're both high value items nowadays."

"Cheese is going to keep this farm going," said Gary. "It retains its value with aging. Not like my volatile milk production. We're so glad Faith was willing to come back and work on it. And Hanna, too."

"Lots of outlay, though," said Faith ruefully.

"Not a problem," said Gary. He owned the farm, which had belonged to his uncle. A few loans on it wouldn't hurt, he had told Paul. "So," he turned to Mother, "Mrs. Mikkelson, Lois," he said bashfully. "We've been wondering whether you were going to write a memoir of your years as a pastor's wife. And raising six kids! Now that you have time." He cut his last pancake, expertly mopping up the rest of the egg and maple syrup.

"Oh no," said Mother, shaking her head, laughing. "I've really nothing to say."

Paul's ears pricked up. He had been wondering about this himself. Mother was a very good writer. It seemed to run in the Bakken family. Mother's father had been a gifted preacher and her brother wrote poetry and devotional books published by the Lutheran church.

"Quite the contrary," said Martha. "You always say such interesting things! I'd like to know more! Those far northern towns you lived in. Your Alaskan connections. Hanna told us you worked in an orphanage, and you took in an Estonian refugee after the war." Martha and Gary, Faith's parents, had been born in 1930, ten years after Mother.

"My sister Mabel wrote about her life as a missionary in Alaska," said Mother. "A much more interesting life than mine!"

So that was how Mother felt, Paul thought. She was self-effacing. But also she just seemed to have a different way of looking at herself than his own generation did. He sometimes thought about writing himself. And it all went back to Mother! It was she who had started him reading the literary naturalists as a young man, including Loren Eiseley, whose last collection he had with him.

"Quite an ornithologist, too, we've heard," said Gary.

Mother laughed again. "My youngest daughter has exaggerated my talents," she said. "Hanna is a dramatist. You mustn't listen to her!"

"And where did I get it, do you suppose, dear Mother," said Hanna.

"Oh, from your father, indeed!" said Mother.

"That's probably right," chimed in Paul, laughing. Dad was a warm and vibrant speaker himself and good at telling stories. A pang went through Paul. Could he remember them all? Dad's warm smile, his voice, stayed with him. But where were the many stories? "But you provided the intellectual spark, the drive to know, the curiosity," he said. "I remember the little tiny, spiral-bound notebooks you gave each of us to begin recording our Life List of birds." He turned to Hanna. "That was before even you came along, I think! I couldn't have been more than 10."

"Probably about what we could afford!" said Mother ruefully. "Have you still got it?" she asked.

"Oh," said Paul. "I probably do, if I hunt through every last box at the cabin!"

At this mention of the cabin, there seemed to be a collective sigh from the three Mikkelsons, Mother, Paul and Hanna. But Paul turned to their hosts. "I think we're getting too bogged down in family depths here!" he said. "I'll bet you all have things to do!"

"I love family depths!" said Faith. "Our family is small, but we have ours as well. You are right, though, breakfast might not be the place to bring them up!"

"Yup!" said Gary standing up. "I need to go have a look at that underground beehive they're building out there!"

"I'll come with you," said Faith. All of a sudden the table was all business.

"Paul and I will do the dishes," said Marie. "Breakfast was delicious!"

That suited Paul perfectly. He wanted to talk to Marie about their plans. Now that Mother was happily ensconced with Hanna, they planned to take a couple of side trips of their own. Marie wanted to go up to Drummondville in Canada, to see Gilberte, her sister. And Paul had been waffling about going to see Walden Pond. It wasn't that far away, could be done in a day trip. "If you can't decide about something," Marie told him, you should always lean more toward 'yes' than 'no'."

Paul was inclined to agree with her. They might not be this close to Concord again for a long while. It was really the only thing in New England that drew Paul. He knew Walden was just a small lake, and probably less interesting and beautiful than Lake Michigami. The significance of a place depended on the time you had spent there. But, lakes were "earth's eye, by looking into which the viewer measures the depth of his own nature," said Thoreau.

So they would go to Walden Pond. And to Drummondville. And to Saratoga Springs, to see Hanna's play. It had been quite a summer. Paul and Marie had managed to rent out their house in Ely to a wealthy Minneapolis man who was using it as a fishing camp, because of its access to the Boundary Waters Canoe Area. Paul and Marie had spent most of the summer at Lake Michigami with Mother.

The lake was lovely, as always, but the cabin was also fraught with looming problems. It had been good to get away! Mostly, it was clear to Paul that many of the things they had brought to the lake before Dad died, all the books and magazines, were rotting and molding in the damp. No one lived there for nine months of the year and it wasn't heated in the damp springs. After 35 snowy winters, the roof was not in great shape either. Even worse, Paul had found a small crack in the cement block foundation in the basement.

No one had money to maintain and preserve this legacy of their parents, except perhaps Ellie. But she and Bruce had taken to exploring the world on cruise ships. They thought the cabin uncomfortable and spent very little time there. Nevertheless, Ellie had mentioned making the cabin into a living trust for Mother. Paul planned to research this further with Ellie in the fall. Perhaps there would be a way of financing repairs. The cabin property was valuable to all of them. Lakefront property in Minnesota was no longer very easy to find.

As they washed and rinsed the dishes, Paul and Marie planned their days. On Friday, Faith donned her white lab coat, a hairnet, and made a batch of semi-hard cheese in the spotless dairy. She gave coats and hairnets to Paul and Marie also. "There'll be mold and microorganisms," she laughed. "But hopefully not from us."

The process was surprisingly simple. The sheep's milk was poured into a vat, along with whey from a previous batch as a starter. The mixture was gently heated. Faith used a thermometer to check the temperature and other lab instruments to determine its composition. As curds started to form, separating from the whey, Faith let out the liquid into a stainless steel can and collected the curds in colanders. The curds would continue to express the whey and dry.

The curds sat on a drain board for a little while, but then Faith showed Paul and Marie how to line a mold with cheesecloth and begin using gentle pressure to expel any further whey. They turned the cheeses several times in the molds, applying pressure until the cheeses took shape. "We'll clean them up in the end," said Faith. "But for now, all they have to do is sit there. It's called the affinage, or aging. Actually, they don't just sit there. I turn them every day, move them about. They're my babies!"

Faith let Paul and Marie help her carry the finished cheese to the farmhouse cellar, but she was finicky about the room where the cheeses were being aged. She didn't feel she had the control over the cellar that she hoped to have once the cheese cave was built. She was using an old refrigerator to store some of her cheese, but it wasn't big enough to hold all the cheese she made, so some was on wooden shelves.

The cellar had a musty smell, cobwebs in the corners. It must have been 150 years old, Paul thought. Lots of nice molds down there. He would have loved to stay and check out the insect life! Probably no mice, he thought. The two farmhouse cats saw to that.

That weekend, everyone went to see Hanna's production at a small theater associated with the Saratoga Performing Arts Center. The New York actors who ran the summer programs put on the play as a demonstration for their students.

"Most of us could probably not count on our fingers and toes the number of times we have played these characters," Hanna told them. "It's a master class in timing and elocution. Every word is important." She prepared to leave, taking Marie and Paul with her so there would be enough cars. "And each of us takes it very seriously!" she said mischievously.

Paul and Marie walked through the town which seemed to be drunk on summer. People wandered in the streets as if they had nothing to do. "As if they were on vacation," giggled Marie. They tasted the public springs which were strung along a fault line through the city and looked for Caffé Lena, which Marie had heard about back when she was 20 and singing in Montreal. It was still there, a small room at the top of a stairway which the legendary founder Lena Spencer had recently fallen down, dying shortly after.

The coffeehouse was open. The upstairs room had a small wooden stage at one end and room for less than a hundred on bentwood chairs around small tables. Large windows with open shutters looked out on the street. Posters showed that the McGarrigle sisters had recently played there and Nanci Griffith would play that night. "We won't be here," said Marie sadly.

Instead they joined the audience for Hanna's play. Paul, who did not pay much attention to theater, had never seen The Importance of Being Earnest. Mother said that if she had seen it, she had forgotten. They sat next to each other, rapt as the curtain went up. Hanna did not appear until the second act, as Cecily, a young heiress destined to be married off, though, like young Gwendolyn, she insisted that her husband be named Earnest!

Hanna's blonde hair was swept into a Victorian hairdo and she carried herself regally in a long pink dress with leg-of-mutton sleeves. When one of the young men pointed out her profile, she raised her nose in the air. The actors did not aim for British accents, but they did make sure that every word carried out into the small theater. Filled with students, everyone listened hard to make sure they didn't miss the word play.

"Wasn't that delicious?" said Marie, as they stood clapping at the end. "It went too quickly!"

"There isn't a shred of reality to it," Mother said as the players took their bows. "What makes it so much fun?!"

"The fact that the actors take it so seriously makes it funny. Every one of them is deadpan," said Paul.

"The wit turns on the idea of seriousness," said Marie. "Seriousness and earnestness are delightfully mocked! It's so frothy it makes me feel lighter!" She looked at Paul meaningfully. Was she thinking of writing a song, he wondered.

Hanna pounced on them when she came out to where they stood on the sidewalk in the warm summer night air. She wore heavy makeup, blue jeans with a hooded sweatshirt and carried a bouquet of roses wrapped in cellophane. Picking up Faith, who was tinier than she was, and swinging her around, she said, "that was really, really fun." No one doubted her! Hanna's family's smiles were as wide as their faces. "Did you like it, Mother?" she asked.

"Oh yes," said Mother. "You were just a dear!"

Hanna looked at Faith wildly and handed Mother her bouquet. "We're here," they chanted together. "We're deer." They knocked their wrists together like deer hooves. "Get used to it!"

Paul laughed. They looked so funny!

Paul and Marie left for Drummondville a few days later. Gilberte and her husband lived in the same house and were very relaxed. Pierre had the summer off from teaching and their two kids were now on their own. They gave Marie news from the farm (in English so Paul could understand) which was run by her two brothers since the death of her parents. Their quarrelsome sister Geraldine, who had never returned to the city, also lived on the farm, bitter and proud. "I don't think we'll go visit," Marie told Pierre and Bertie. "They don't really care about me."

"They do," said Pierre. "They will be happy to hear about you. Perhaps you could come to mass in the morning?"

Marie didn't believe her older siblings did care. "Is Monsignor Olivier still there?" she asked.

"He's very old now," said Bertie. "I think you would like young Father Jean."

Grace regularly wrote in French to Gilberte, and had sent photos of her latest baby, Jeanne. "She's making a dynasty of little Hickmans!" said Gilberte, wistfully. So far the Hickmans had not managed to visit Drummondville.

Paul and Marie did go to mass and met Marie's family, but they did not go out to the farm for Sunday dinner, pleading the long drive back to New York. Marie was pensive on the drive back, telling Paul, "They don't seem very powerful any more. Even Geraldine," she said. "Or maybe it is just that you and your family, and Grace, have filled my life to the brim."

"Good," said Paul. He knew that personal demons never went completely away, but seeing them in your rearview mirror might be a good thing. They drove back to the farm in the Mohawk Valley, where they found Mother and Hanna cutting heavy paper to make cheese wraps. "Never a dull moment," laughed Hanna. A cunning label designed for Shepherd Girl Cheeses held the wraps together. It was she who had thought up the name for Faith's cheese.

But then it was time to set the date for going to Walden. They would soon have to return to Minnesota. "Don't let's agonize over it," said Marie. "Let's just go."

"Okay," said Paul. He did not want anyone to think he was a celebrity seeker.

"I would like to go," said Mother. "But I'm probably better off here."

"You're going to drive through a lot of woods and mountains," said Gary, when they showed him their route on the map. "New England's going back to woods! It just isn't very easy to farm there. A lot of the land that was once stony fields is reverting."

Paul and Marie left before the day's milking got started, driving south. "I think we grew up in the age of photography," said Paul. "I'm not sure a writer like Thoreau would be read any longer."

"You told me he wasn't read much during his lifetime," said Marie.

"Nope," said Paul. "And it's taken a long time for people to realize the use of his science. Until the 1970's, really, when people started looking at the ecology of place. That's a hundred years after he died." The highway unrolled before them, surrounded by wooded hills. "But I was thinking, I've been reading the National Geographic since I was a kid. There were always color photographs! And I look for them in magazines. A picture often tells so much. Thoreau just had words!"

"Movies too," said Marie. "I've never seen any nature movie as good as that one Mother showed us this summer, Never Cry Wolf." Mother often taped movies off the television and took them with her to watch at the lake in the summer. There was no television reception there. Paul and Marie didn't take much time to watch television, except perhaps in the dead of winter when Paul was tired and Marie was knitting.

"Yes," said Paul. "Me either. That was an amazing movie." Never Cry Wolf told the story of a researcher who was let off in the wilds of Canada to investigate whether wolves were reducing the caribou herds. The researcher was overwhelmed by the amount of space around him, but in the end he proved that the predators of caribou were mostly on two legs. "It came from a book," said Paul. "Farley Mowat wrote the story."

As Paul drove, the visuals of the main character hiking with the Inuit man who helped him survive scrolled in front of his face. He could hear the narrator saying, "I decided to stay here until I get my bearings and have sorted out what constitutes reality." Paul's own experience resonated with this!

"It's the personal that gets you," said Paul. "This man, living alone in the wilderness and telling you how he feels." That's what Thoreau did, thought Paul. And Loren Eiseley. And Darwin. Observers, and writers, each of them. By this time the poignancy of their writing was partly due to how much was known about them, how their work was wrung from their souls. In a wonderful essay on Thoreau, Eiseley quoted him as saying, "There has been nothing but the sun and the eye since the beginning." Men were observers, thought Paul, and some became writers.

Not Mother, and not the Inuit, who, as Paul had learned in Alaska, did not particularly trust language. Indeed, language opened you to discredit. The world was ever-changing. Who could put it down in words? But Thoreau, in some 20 volumes of journals had tried to record what he saw. And people were still mining those volumes for what he had been able to see with his eyes and record with his hand.

"I don't think I'm like Mother," said Paul. "At least about writing. I want to put down what I think. It may be provisional. It may be partial. But it helps me think."

Marie smiled up at him. "I can never decide whether rhyming, in songs, helps or hinders you," she said. "Does it add to your ideas to have to think of a rhyme? Or does it squelch them?"

Paul smiled back at her. "I love us talking about this stuff," he said.

When they got to Walden, it was indeed a small, wooded lake. Paul was surprised to find a beach at one end, where people were swimming! The pond was a kettle hole, formed by retreating glaciers, a bit worn down by the season. It was too bad, thought Paul, that because they had come for the day they could only see it during the heat of the high sun. Surely, for Thoreau, its spiritual aspects were more evident in morning and evening light. Or in the winter.

"I'll sit here," said Marie, establishing herself at a picnic table near the beach, "while you walk around the lake." Paul realized she was giving him time to think. He gratefully took it.

The paths were dusty from traffic, the trees drying. At the north edge of the pond were granite posts showing where Thoreau had built his cabin, with three chairs in it: one for solitude, two for friendship and three for society. Paul thought of Archie, who had been his friend in the woods for a long time, though no speech passed between them. Thoreau had not had animals, as far as Paul knew.

I am an observer, though, Paul thought. I like my own thoughts, even if they aren't very interesting. It was really the three-dimensionality of experience that he enjoyed. It sometimes happened he could see himself walking through the woods from the outside, see the branches go by above him as he moved through them. It never lasted long. Paul recalled it most from the unforgettable nights of skiing through the ice fog near Fairbanks, using senses he barely knew he had. He had felt like a character in a game. Would he get home safely? One never knew. Until finally he quit, too frightened to go on pressing his luck.

I want to be the world, thought Paul. He wanted to dissolve in the world. Thoreau surely had. It was the kind of thing you could maybe hear or read about. But only if you were out in the world, walking a path around a famous lake, or an unknown one, could you do it.

12

Marty stopped at the Real Food Company on her way home from work. Her neighborhood grocery, with its forest green awning, stocked artisan breads, organic fruits and vegetables, grains and pastas, meat, fish, wine. All the things Marty loved to eat. It was harvest time and baskets of fresh apples, squash, and melons were ranged outside the door on the sidewalk, as well as buckets of zinnias and sunflowers.

As Marty hiked up the hill to her apartment, she realized she had grown up with what she now thought of as 'survival food.' Meat and potatoes, mostly unadorned, frozen vegetables during the winter. In the summer there were strawberries, fresh corn and lots of vegetables. Mother and Dad did like good food. But they did not eat the way Marty now did, small tasty bites of things, like the fig, walnut and gorgonzola appetizer she planned to serve her guests.

Opening the door to her apartment, Marty found Sabrina and Juliet, two French tai chi students, perched on her couch. She had left a key at the corner store for them, and there they were!

The French women rose and kissed Marty on both cheeks. Sabrina was a teacher, very close to Master Liu. Dark, perfect in body, Sabrina had grown up in Algeria and was a dancer. The year before, she had also stayed with Marty. Juliet, a sweet middle-aged woman, was her student.

"You must be exhausted from your trip," said Marty. Students were coming in from all over the United States and Europe to study with Master Liu. He had built up a large number of students in his Yang-style school. The annual tai chi gathering would be held at a rustic camp in La Honda, south of the city.

"Oh no," said Sabrina, stoically. "We're fine."

Marty remembered that jet lag wasn't as bad coming west with the sun. "I just came from the grocery store," she said. "Would you like some wine and snacks?"

"Thank you," said Sabrina. "We would appreciate it." Her English was very good, though she preferred to speak French.

Sabrina presented Marty with a lovely silk scarf wrapped in tissue paper, and Juliet handed Marty a box which held an antique pin. After admiring the presents, Marty turned on her oven. She cut the figs in half, drizzled them with salt and balsamic vinegar and topped each half with gorgonzola and a walnut piece, putting them in the oven.

Marty set out plates, a crusty sourdough baguette, wine glasses, green grapes. The Europeans taught us to eat, she thought. The Magnussons, with whom Marty had lived in England when she was just 20, had learned their habits from living in Germany. In California, people ate more like Italians. Once you had enough money and time to get past a 'survival culture,' you could begin to live.

"No wine for me," said Sabrina. "Too drying!"

Marty had thought of that. "Perrier?" she asked.

"Oh yes," said Sabrina.

They would meet Master Liu and other students for a Chinese meal in North Beach a little later. "We can walk down the hill to Yuet Lee," Marty told Sabrina and Juliet.

All three women were apprehensive about the week to come. Sabrina had brought Juliet with her because she wanted to speak French, but also, thought Marty, for protection! Camp was very intense. Not just the practice, which could be grueling, but also living together at close quarters in a primitive setting. There was also, as Marty had experienced, and pretty much managed to avoid, lots of competition, especially among the men.

Sabrina tried to explain it to Juliet. "They are all trying to find our who will become Master Liu's successor. Everyone wants to be close to him."

"I think of it as tai chi mania," said Marty. She had been at camp before. Just that week, Mark, while they playfully pushed hands, told her, "You're going to kick Valerie's ass this year!" Valerie was also French and started tai chi practice about the same time as Marty. Marty did not want to kick anyone's ass. Least of all Valerie's. Valerie was much younger, and beautiful, Marty thought. But Mark was one of the most competitive men Marty knew. It was the way he thought.

The dinner that night at the noisy Yuet Lee, known for its fish and shellfish, was a joyous occasion. Many of the students had not seen each other for a year. Others went to all the tai chi camps they could afford. The students, now teachers as well, who had been with Master Liu the longest sat nearest to him. Sabrina claimed a seat near him, introducing Juliet.

Though leavened with women students, perhaps a third, the atmosphere was macho and boisterous. At the big round tables, it was hard to talk across the platters of oysters, the fish, the chicken, duck and pork dishes. Two of the men brought out bottles of Remy Martin, which, with many toasts, were soon used up! Arthur, small, assertively Jewish and authoritative, went out for more.

Marty sat at the outermost edges, talking to the people on either side of her. "When he was growing up in Hong Kong with his grandfather," Malcolm, a teacher from Maine, told them, "Master Liu was treated like a rock star, or the dalai lama. He expects this."

Marty tasted things, not eating much. She loved the steamed dumplings especially, tasty bits of ground meat and herbs pinched into dough and sauced with ginger, vinegar and soy. She drank brandy too, but not too much. Arthur hung around Marty, trying to get her to talk. She was obviously single. What was the deal? Did she not want to be in the in-crowd where he was? Arthur had been to every La Honda camp since it began ten years before.

Sachiko, Marty's favorite teacher in San Francisco, picked up Sabrina, Juliet and Marty the next day and drove them down to La Honda camp. Hot sunshine in the middle of the day brought out the smells of the grasses and the tall redwoods. Sachiko helped check people in. She had a room in the lodge with her husband Anton, who would come later.

The other women found places to sleep in the dormitories set into the woods. Marty was surprised at how much some of them brought with them to comfort themselves, pillows, blankets, snacks and many bottles of cosmetics. Marty had her sleeping bag, her weapons and a few clothes. That was about it.

Arthur was mad at Marty because she wouldn't save a counselor's room for him, though she got there early. He had been drinking, called Marty 'stupid.' Marty was angry. She realized her passivity and acceptance had once again gotten her the attention of a most insistent person. She must set some boundaries, she thought. The tai chi group was a bunch of quarrelsome brothers and sisters. But it was also possible to just practice, to not get too involved with anyone.

Evening practice was in the crowded wooden dining hall, tables and benches pushed back. Ernesto told Marty that the camp deep in the redwoods had once been a logging camp, that the dining hall was built in the 1920's.

Master Liu, short with black hair and dressed in tailored Chinese clothes, helped them line up, drawing Marty toward the front, as she too was short. Sixty people did slow set together, the rhythm set by Master Liu on the corner. Marty became a beginner again, watching the senior students, imitating them as best she could, sinking, opening her hips and knees.

They did many fast sets too, one after another. Master Liu barked out the count with a deep voice. People's faces were lit from within, full of energy. "Camp begins!" said the person next to Marty, as Master Liu repeated, "One more time!" and they swung into position. They had already done five fast sets, feet pounding the floor at the jumps, everyone moving in unison.

Blood pulsed through Marty as she walked back to the dormitory cabins. The moon was almost full, shining through the trees. Abe, an attractive older guy who taught the Colorado class, sang out as they walked, "You're nobody if you don't make the 7 a.m. slow set!" Marty stood out in the moonlight for a moment, listening to the crickets and then went in to bed in her upper bunk.

Marty couldn't sleep though. All night she replayed her anger at Arthur, unable to calm herself. Early in the morning, she got up and went out to the stage built in the woods for slow set. A deer with very large ears stood and looked at her. Fog crept through the redwoods and hung around them, damp and cool. Slow set was lovely, people sleepy and tousled. Marty watched Abe, who wore a homemade cotton tai chi shirt and looked like one of the founding fathers with his rugged features and longish hair. Slowly Marty's tension released.

When she saw Arthur at breakfast, Marty asked him for an apology.

"I didn't call you anything," he said. "I don't remember that."

"Steve was with you," said Marty. "He heard you. It hurt me." Steve had acted apologetic all evening.

"Well, I didn't mean to hurt you," said Arthur. And that was that. Marty was free.

The main class of the day was at 10 a.m. on the stage in the woods. It was covered, so the hot sun didn't fall on the students, but the air was warm. The students just barely fit in the space. "You can accommodate the form to an environment," Master Liu told them, "but never try to adapt the form to your body."

After slow set there were many demonstrations. "All those over six feet," said Master Liu. And out into the middle came almost 20 guys! They did a family set together while everyone stood in a circle around them and watched. Marty watched Ted, a lanky golden boy from Colorado. His movements were simple, classical. Marty knew he liked her. They had talked last year.

Master Liu then asked three people to demonstrate the first section of slow set: First Mark, Marty's push hands partner, who loved to have an audience, though he began tai chi even more recently than Marty. Then Fred, who had been studying nine years. And finally Jim Bennett, from Phoenix, who had been studying for fifteen. Marty saw what Master Liu wanted them to. Mark was very good, but a little stiff and without a personal style. With Jim, Marty could see every vertebrae in his back articulating, soft and supple. He moved like a Russian bear. Tai chi clothes showed nothing and everything at the same time, if you knew how to look.

At lunch, Marty sat at a table near Fred, also from Colorado, eating salad. Abe had studied one year longer. "I'll never catch up to him," Fred said. Master Liu had told them that the person who has practiced tai chi for a shorter time would never catch up to the person who began practicing before him. It took the competition out of it. Master Tung considered tai chi to be a practice of the mind and spirit, as well as the body. He had told a group who wanted to do competitive push hands to go study elsewhere.

Marty took a nap after lunch, falling heavily asleep for a couple of hours. It felt wonderful. Sticky and sleepy in the heat, she took time for delicious thoughts of Doug. How he would love it here, she thought. The macho atmosphere. She imagined him listening to the guys talking about her. Only he knew what Marty was like beneath her glasses, that she could give as well as get, that she pushed people into doorways and demanded kisses.

But Doug was with his family and overwhelmed by crush which was intense at this time of year. When he came to the city, he stopped to see Marty. But they had agreed they couldn't sleep together again. That if they started once more, they would not be able to stop. Their love and friendship was strong, but it left Marty without a partner, in what she thought of as her prime.

When Marty waked up enough, she went over to the outdoor stage, where people were practicing on their own or in small groups. It wasn't a formal class, so Marty didn't wear her loose Chinese clothes. Just a long-sleeved t-shirt. Long sleeves were a courtesy to the other person so they didn't have to deal with each other's sweat. Marty's legs felt better than they had that morning.

Sabrina drew Marty into push hands practice, showing her how to keep the rounded space as she moved, the difference between the chest being open and being closed. She suggested Marty must turn out her ankles more, strengthening them. Sabrina gave Marty vivid esoteric images of the body as a skin bag full of fire, pushing out in all directions. "In order to go up, you sink down; in order to move forward, you sink back," she said.

Marty did her favorite two-person san shou with a guy named Greg. First one person was the aggressor in the choreographed application, then the other. Each move was initiated by the other person, but everyone was different. Different sizes, slightly different expectations of how the moves worked. They did it several times, trying to synch up. Marty's body knew the set better than her mind.

Later Valerie and Marty practiced partner knife. It was a beautiful set, the partners facing each other part of the time, passing each other, knives swishing through the air. People stopped to watch them. Valerie was slight, a little taller with beautiful cheekbones. Marty felt powerful, though, extending her arms to their maximum, turning on her heel to stretch out her knife. No 'tofu tai chi' here!

That evening at dinner they had moon cakes, heavy Chinese pastries filled with sweetened red bean paste. It wasn't quite time for the mid-autumn festival which moon cakes celebrated, but someone had found them for the group. Marty didn't like them. She tried to get away with one bite. After class, she noted that the moon was utterly full, a perfect round disk with the crispest edge she had ever seen. She sat watching it from under a tree, looking across the meadow full of tents. Many people stayed out all night, pushing hands and drinking. Marty went to bed, where she slept as sound as a rock.

The week went quickly with four practice times a day. Marty's legs got stronger. Having staved off the heavy artillery, Marty also felt she was getting some of the more subtle sexual attention. She told Abe that when she did cloud hands, she just kept going, her body growing lighter. "I'll get a rope and tie it around your middle," he said. "To keep you from flying away!"

"It's getting to the point at camp where everything is funny," said Ernesto. And indeed no one could stop laughing. Marty felt very emotional, open to everyone. Standing in their grid while they practiced together, Marty felt that each of them was mirroring the other. A forest of mirrors, she said to herself, each of us naked and vulnerable. Marty tried to look at herself as another person would. What did they see? A youngish woman with a pleasant face, grounded, simple, clear. Marty remembered the time she had looked into a mirror at home, and seen Doug! Her matchless twin. It had happened when she was first getting to know him.

After lunch Marty sat on a log in the woods, watching people walk by, writing in a spiral bound notebook. The breeze rustled in the trees, Canadian thistles blew past. It was very quiet. When big Daniel, an African-American acupuncturist, walked by, Marty stood up and he hugged her, commenting on what a beautiful afternoon it was. Everything felt sacred.

On the last morning, the class did 15 fast sets and then several family sets on the stage in the woods. Marty thought it was a record, but she managed each of them. Her endurance was good. Her legs pulsed and ached when they were still, but not in class. Many of the students planned to come to class in San Francisco after camp was over. "Now that we have our legs back," Ted told Marty, "we can't stop!" Valerie too told Marty, "We can't say goodbye!" Marty indeed knew how that felt. How she had had to cut the thick field between Doug and herself with an imaginary sword.

Marty had no strong attachments to anyone in this group. She was fascinated by how some of the teachers felt about their students. When Marty described how vulnerable she felt, Malcolm from Maine said, "Your teacher should hand carry you through it." He took notes when Master Liu taught, to bring them back to his students. Tai chi was an oral tradition, its transmission a sacred trust. Probably a stronger connection than sex! Malcolm wondered if, when Master Liu opened up his heart and invited you in, you could avoid it.

But there was also pain. One woman always seemed to be sad. She would have no life apart from Master Liu, Sabrina said. Sabrina told Marty her French students were in disarray. Two of her students wanted to move to Los Angeles, to study only with Master Liu. This saddened Sabrina, though she had many strong students.

Marty could see that some people made a guru of Master Liu, laying themselves at his feet. She was more interested in the relationship the Asian students had to him. They showed a reverence for their teacher, but were more circumspect. When they taught, they expected the same from their students. The tai chi group was very complex, however. Friendships, rivalries and just plain knowing too much about each other after all the years thickened the stew. Marty was sensitive to all of it. She felt she was on the edge of the group, independent but a member.

When they got back to San Francisco, Marty again felt there were tai chi people tucked into corners all over the city. Sabrina and Juliet remained at Marty's house. That evening there was another big banquet at a Chinese restaurant, Hakka, on Broadway, with big platters of fish and meat gracing the round tables. Remy Martin flowed, toasting Master Liu, the successful camp, teachers, even the fish and the pig on the table!

Ted and Arthur sat beside Marty, enumerating the five Chinese arts: martial, music, poetry, painting and medicine. In fact, Marty was surprised to find several guys circling, trying to sit beside her. Greg and Arthur watched as Ted kissed Marty's ear. Marty let him. They had noticed each other long ago. When the group paid up the bill with a heap of dollars and walked out into the streets in a gaggle, following Master Liu, Ted took Marty's hand and they ducked into the dark, off on a side street by themselves.

Ted hailed a long white limousine and asked the driver to take them to a nice bar. The driver didn't quite get Ted's request, and took them to a BART station on the train line! Next to it was the Hyatt Regency, however. That was good enough for Ted. They went in and had margaritas in the light of the plaza lounge, whispering to each other and listening to jazzy piano music. "Somehow I knew we would get together tonight," Ted told Marty. He put a sun-warmed arm around her. "Who taught you to kiss like that," he asked. "I hope it was someone you loved."

Ted wasn't fooled about how old Marty was. "You've done really well for 48," he said. He was in his early 40's, had just signed his divorce papers. "My wife wasn't happy," he said, "but I always am." He was a painting contractor in Colorado, had two sons and ten employees. He had grown up in Newport Beach, surfing and living on the beach as far down as Mexico. He knew Spanish, his mother had taught him calligraphy and he had done various martial arts for 20 years. "One of my watercolors won a prize recently," he said, explaining how he was working on the arts of the Chinese gentlemen.

Marty felt the sweet harmonic between Ted and herself. He was sensitive and good to her. Everything he did seemed right. "You might be pretty hard to resist," she told him.

"Don't resist me," Ted said. But he also seemed paranoid, worried that Marty might 'dump' him. When he left her for a few moments he told her, "Don't leave or I'll kill you." It was a contrast to the easy confidence in everything he did.

"I got us a room," Ted told Marty when he got back. "I deserve it, after sleeping on the dirt in a tent all week."

Marty did not resist. The bed was firm and lovely, and so was Ted. "You're enjoying this as much as I am, aren't you," he said. They were high up, looking out over the city. Marty didn't sleep much, but enjoyed waking up to Ted's sunny, heavy body. Morning sunlight stole in the from the side windows. "How well we fit together," Ted said.

But then Marty got up to go. She was worried about her guests. The last class of the week would be that morning.

Once more, tai chi students gathered at the big ballroom at 50 Oak Street. Ted did not come. Arthur asked Marty where he was, but Marty didn't know. She pushed hands with a guy who had broken his arm. It looked better than it had at the beginning of the week, but she knew he wanted her to be soft with him. Marty was short, and he was over six feet tall. He just had to sink down lower.

Marty's legs felt strange, disconnected. From the hip down they just throbbed. They looked fine from the outside, but when she stretched, the muscles hurt. Class was long, four hours of slow set, applications, family and fast sets. But then groups began to break up. The forest of mirrors was over. It was finally time to say goodbye.

At Marty's apartment, Sabrina packed. "I'm doing push hands with my luggage," she said. Indeed, one could find the tai chi in anything!

"I don't know how I'm going to learn to turn out my ankles," said Marty, referring to Sabrina's suggestion.

"You are strong," said Sabrina. "You'll figure it out. Do you know what the angel said to the human?" she asked. "The angel said, 'You are lucky you have form, shape, weight. Only with these can you evolve. Only with them can you refine your body.'"

Survival mode, thought Marty, did not only involve food. People who did not take time for the arts, for learning about their physical selves were in survival mode. Marty was glad she had a job which paid for some leisure, which allowed her to learn to live, to study the arts, to get beyond just existing.

When the French women were packed, the three of them waited, talking. Marty wasn't good at small talk, but she had learned from the French that you could talk about anything, any detail. She and Sabrina traded notes about the other teachers. Before long a big blue SuperShuttle van arrived outdoors to take them to the airport.

That afternoon Marty took to bed. Her legs felt wonderful under the warm feather coverlet. Her body was beaten and broken, but pleased with itself. She replayed the week, the practices, the banquets, the evenings. The evening with Ted was so quick, and what happened? He had acted homesick for salt water and beaches, after living landlocked in Colorado. He was a thousand miles away by now. Perhaps he would come back. Marty was surprised at having been chosen so publicly by one of the most attractive people at camp. But she also knew that tai chi had helped her to refine her body, that it was thinner, as attractive as it had ever been, despite her glasses. She would always have to wear them.

Marty felt spaced out after the week in camp, mentally loosened. When she went back to the office on Monday, however, reality hit pretty quickly! The office was expanding from the two floors it currently occupied into the whole building. The first floor was a construction site. The sandblasting the workers were doing rattled everyone. It wouldn't be long, though. The new floor would be beautiful with a long marble slab for the reception desk, dark colors, a conference room up front, and the partners' offices ranged along the interior corridor.

Marty listened to people's problems. If they were small, she tried to fix them immediately. She had recently taken to answering her phone, so as not to have to listen to the voice mails people left. Bigger problems did not always go away.

One of Marty's good friends had quit. She wanted to work from home, to contract rather than come in every day. Marty's boss Joe, the partner who ran office operations, felt she was deserting him. Diane was half Japanese, had an excellent design sense and had helped Joe prepare the interior design for the Shanghai opera house. Joe was tight about money, a patriarchal Confucian, though he was American-born Chinese. He did not want to pay the consulting fee Diane was asking.

Marty could not do much about this. As she had in the shifting tai chi group, Marty felt she was at the edge of the office. She actually thought her lack of deep involvement was a positive factor in her job. She loved the office, but mostly she didn't work overtime. Perhaps she was finally learning 'choiceless awareness,' Marty thought. To take what came and to leave the rest.

That night Marty left a message for Doug, telling him, "I had a wild and wonderful time at camp. It was like a film shoot, 60 people moving from place to place in the city and the country. Can't wait to tell you about it!" It was almost his birthday. Marty hoped he would let her celebrate with him.

Late that night he called, his voice tired but rich, telling Marty he missed her. "We lost a truck full of Sauvignon Blanc today, coming down from Healdsburg. What a mess!"

"It tipped over?" asked Marty.

"Overloaded," said Doug. "Grapes are slippery! But that's crush for you." He sounded exhilarated, loved hearing about Marty's camp exploits, about the forest of mirrors, how she felt about the teachers, how her legs felt.

"Do we get to celebrate your birthday?" asked Marty. "I'd love to take you to a restaurant where my friend is the sous chef. Le Trou."

"Le Trou?" asked Doug. "What does that mean?"

"Literally, a hole," said Marty. "Like a little hole in the wall, an unpretentious restaurant."

"Well my birthday season lasts a while," said Doug. "Somehow we'll find time to celebrate it. Can't say when just now."

Marty wished she could be as careless about Doug as she was about her place at work or in the tai chi group. But she had to be satisfied. That was just how it was.

13

Sometimes, what starts out as an ordinary party turns into something deeper. Which is what happened on Line's birthday in May. It was just Poppa, Stephen, Line and Ivy having a piece of cake after dinner. It wasn't even a 'big' birthday.

"I'm going to be so happy to be out of school!" said Ivy. She had been taking classes at the university that year, not a full load, but enough. Academics were not her strength and Line and Stephen hoped she would ease through school slowly, taking plenty of art classes, which made her happy. She picked at the cream cheese frosting on the chocolate cake she had made for her mother.

"I'll miss the school season," said Poppa. "My film series closes down so people can go on vacation. But," he said, pausing for effect, "I think I've got Phil Kaufman coming down to speak to us in a couple of weeks! Did I tell you? We're showing The Right Stuff and he'll be there to talk about it!" Poppa had curated a retrospective of Kaufman's films. He loved them. And it didn't hurt that Kaufman was Jewish.

"Good for you!" said Line. She tried to go to Poppa's films when she could. "This cake is so good, Ivy! Thank you!" She cleaned her plate carefully and licked her fork.

"That's quite a coup!" said Stephen. "I'm not surprised, though. You usually get what you want!" he laughed. Poppa had a persuasive approach, and he didn't quit either. If he wanted something, he went for it.

"Damn right," said Poppa. "Why not?" At 75, Poppa was as debonair and chipper as he had ever been. Each day he went out looking for adventure.

"If I survive the end of the school year," sighed Stephen, "it's going to be a summer of hard work. I've got to finish that book I researched in Edinburgh. And I've got an idea for another one too!"

"Oh?" asked Line. "Tell us about it."

"Well, you remember how hard everyone took it when the Labour leader John Smith died last year? And Tony Blair roared into #10 Downing Street? I've been thinking about how much I love contemporary history. And no one here understands the Brits really. I want to write a biography of John Smith and what a loss that was. It's a little bit about us too. Politics is changing as the Internet opens up. I've got the background and the distance to tell the story. It would be fun!"

Line bristled. "Does that mean going back to Scotland?" she asked.

"Probably," said Stephen mildly. "But not right away. I've got plenty to do here." He turned to Line. "I've been wondering, though, my dear, if I work all summer, what would you most like to do?"

Line had to think about it. It was not something she usually considered. Ordinarily, family plans were based around the kids, or Stephen's work. Almost anything except what Line might 'want.' "I really have no idea!" she said.

Poppa chimed in. "This time it's about you, Line," he said, smiling. "Today's your day. This time, you have to tell us what you want."

"Yes, Mum," said Ivy. "I would love to know!"

Line's face colored as her brain flew over her kids: Christy was in the peace corps in Peru, Heather was in Chile, but would be back in July, and Fern was back and forth between Edinburgh and Spain. But then there was Mother. Line had been thinking a lot about Mother. "I think," she said finally, "that I'd like to spend some time with my mother."

"Ahhh!" said Stephen. "Of course! What a good idea!"

"In Minnesota?" asked Poppa.

"Yes," said Line. She turned to Ivy. "Would you like to come with me? We could just go for a couple of weeks before Heather gets home."

"Mosquitoes!" said Ivy. "They're the worst in June. And it's too cold to swim!"

"Yes," said Line. "That's all true. But would you like to come anyway? We could see what Mother has on her loom."

"Of course," said Ivy. "Of course I'd like to come."

"I'll rub you down with eucalyptus essential oil," said Line. "Those Minnesota mosquitoes won't know what hit them!"

Two weeks later, Line rented a car at the Minneapolis airport and drove to Lake Michigami with Ivy. They got out of the car just as it was growing dark and smelled the deep spring forest around them, the fecund growth after the snow, mushrooms and lichens and soils buried in old leaves and pine duff. The sap flowing into new leaves on the poplars and birches contributed. It was intoxicating. Line lamented that once you were there, it became normal to your nose and you could not smell it as strongly again.

The porch lights were on and Archie, Paul's black and tan dog, bounded out to the car. Paul and Marie were right behind him to help with luggage. Inside, Mother sat in the big rocker by the window, a cup of tea at her elbow. She stood up with some difficulty, looking at Line with tears in her eyes. It made Line cry too. "It is so good to see you," said Mother, as she hugged Line's body to hers. "And my goodness, look at this girl!" she greeted Ivy.

Ivy stood there, shy in the lamplight. "It is good to see you, Grandma Mikkelson," said Ivy. "In your natural habitat too!" Line and Ivy had last seen Mother at Christy's graduation, but that was a quick trip and they had not left the Twin Cities.

"Would you guys like some tea?" asked Paul. Soon they were all seated in a group around Mother, on the shabby chairs and the jutting stone hearth of the Ben Franklin. Archie lay at their feet on the big rag rug which softened the cheap flooring.

"Can you tell if it is a mosquitoey year?" asked Line. Insects and moths flitted around the outdoor lights they could see through the window.

"Pretty normal winter," said Paul. "Ice-out was about six weeks ago, and we haven't had a lot of rain, so we should actually have a good year in terms of mosquitoes. This is peak season, though, as I'm sure you know."

"Yeah," said Ivy. "No picking blueberries! They grow right in the bogs with the mosquitoes, Mum said."

Marie laughed at them. "We know one little highland where there are blueberries. And it's dry there, under some pines. We could try there," she encouraged. "But it's really early for blueberries."

"Oh?" said Line. "I thought we used to look for them in June in the bogs, that bears come out of hibernation looking for them."

"Not quite," said Paul.

"We've had so many birds," said Mother, her face gentle in the light. "It's hard to do anything but sit here and peer through the binoculars, although the trees are getting pretty leafed out by now. Paul saw some wood ducks nesting in one of the Norway pines!"

Line was sure Mother did not do much except sit in that very chair and look through her binoculars. She was a sitting duck and Line would get to talk to her.

"It's new moon tonight," said Paul. "Would any of you like to come down and look at the stars with me? They're so bright here!"

"Me! me!" said Ivy, standing up. "I want to see the lake!"

"I'll watch you from here," said Mother, as Line and Marie made ready to go. They put on sweaters against the chilly air.

The four of them walked down the zig zag path to the lake Dad had made so many years ago, Archie following. The leaves of the trees whispered above them. Paul had a flashlight which helped to light the way. Line picked her way, looking at her feet, but Ivy sprang ahead like a young goat.

"Did you put out the dock yourself?" asked Line. She remembered how tough that had been when they helped Dad do it as kids. All the sections of the dock were out, letting them walk out onto the water. She looked up into the sky with its very bright stars. The Big Dipper shone, and the Milky Way was incredibly thick with stars. "So beautiful!"

"Well, I got Alf to help me," said Paul. "The lake isn't much fun until the dock is out." He stood behind Line at the end of the dock. "Starlight is really intense when nothing competes with it," he said.

"I can see Casseopia," said Line. "That 'W' over there, but that's about all I remember. See Ivy?" she asked.

Paul pointed out the summer triangle which could be seen at that time of year, Altair, Deneb and Vega, and how two stars in the Big Dipper pointed to the Pole star in the Little Dipper.

"I know it isn't," said Ivy, "But it reminds me of a bowl, turned upside down." She knelt down and put her hand in the water. "Pretty cold," she said. "I told Mum that. But who would I swim with anyway?"

"My grandkids will come one day," said Marie. "Grace's kids. There are five of them now, and they love the water!"

"Oh! Good!" said Ivy. "I can't wait to see them."

"There's a new baby, now," said Marie softly. "Mother and I can't get enough of holding the baby. Benjamin, he's called. Born in April."

Line could hear the love in her voice. "How wonderful," she said.

Time was different at the lake, thought Line, when she woke in the morning. Light streamed into the 'new room' from the east where she slept on a day bed. It was early but Line could not resist going down to the lake to watch the shining path the sun made directly to where she sat down in its warmth on the wooden dock. The water was green and glassy smooth. Line had no schedule to think about and no one to pack off to work or school.

She sat there, drifting. Don't think about what it is like in California, she told herself. Just be here.

Loons were laughing far across the lake, talking to each other. An ancient sound to Line. She wondered when she ever got to see that much sky. Ocean beach in Santa Cruz, of course, but Line had to admit she did not get there often.

Before long Archie and Paul arrived. "Canoe ride?" asked Paul. "It's so nice before the wind comes up."

"Oh yes," said Line. "I'd love that."

Paul righted the canoe and slipped it down the old rubber tires which served as a boat ramp into the water. Archie came out on the dock and snapped at a cloud of gnats. Paul held the canoe at the side of the dock and Line stepped in. "We'll just be along the shore," said Paul. "You don't need a paddle." They didn't take life jackets. They were grownups now, Line thought to herself, and could do things simply. They didn't even need to be an example to any kids this morning! They slipped quietly away, leaving Archie on the dock.

Line sat in front like an Indian princess, with Paul paddling east behind her, feathering his stroke at the end in order to steer. If he stayed close enough to shore, the sun was behind the pines. "You remind me of Dad," said Line. "I remember him teaching us to paddle."

"Yeah," said Paul. "I think of him all the time up here, how much he planned for this place. And how little I'm able to do anything about it. I guess he would have been about 76 now."

"No one knows how things are going to go," said Line. She felt far away from that situation. She would never be close enough to be able to help with the cabin. "How's Mother doing?" she asked.

"Well I can't get her in the canoe, no-how," said Paul. "Even getting her down to the dock isn't easy. She's arthritic, afraid of falling. Her knee hurts and she can't raise one of her arms. But her spirits put the rest of us to shame! She's as full of projects and ideas as ever!"

"I'm so glad to be able to spend some time with her," said Line. "And with you all. I'm excited to meet Grace and her family." Line trailed her hand in the water. She felt like a child. She could not remember when she had been as free of responsibility, her own children able to take care of themselves. But it wouldn't last. She must enjoy it. "Do you feel like Grace is your family?" she asked.

"I feel like sort of an uncle to Grace," said Paul. "She didn't grow up with us, so there's a lot I've missed. She's not like my own kid. But yes, she does feel like family. We're glad she settled in Minnesota. And those little kids are really fun!"

"I know Mother loves them. But isn't it interesting what happens, and how we are all getting so spread out? I'm worried about my own kids. Fern has spent so much time in Europe now, and Heather is bringing a guy with her from Chile. And Christy! Do you know any more about Christy than I do?" Line wondered.

"No," said Paul. "Don't think so. I think he likes being under the radar, keeping people guessing. And who knows what communications are like out of Peru. But you know Line, I've been thinking families are like Mandelbrot sets, intricate and ever-expanding."

"A Mandelbrot set?" Line asked, turning around to look at Paul. She had never heard of such a thing.

"I've been looking at all these beautifully colored graphic representations of sets of numbers. The simple equation for them was found by a man named Mandelbrot. When they're plotted by a computer they have this fine-grained detail showing the repeating fractal geometry along their boundaries. They remind me of the elements in families that repeat, more intricate as you go in and look deeper," said Paul. He had stopped paddling, letting the canoe be swept along toward the shore near a clear little creek which emptied into the lake.

Line was impressed with Paul's thoughts. She looked up at a weathered old building on the hillside. The Mikkelsons had stayed there when their cousins were building their own cabin, and once when Line was very small. She remembered that Mother put their milk and butter in the cold, rushing creek because there was no refrigerator.

"I always thought I was going to camp over here by this creek one night," said Paul. "I wanted to see what animals came down at night."

"And did you?" asked Line. She looked down into the mucky yellow-green water to see a leech, its black spots undulating up and down as it swam. But where were the schools of shiny little silver minnows she remembered?

"No," said Paul. "Not yet. Shows you I'm kind of lazy." He smiled.

"Paul," Line said, "you're a philosopher! And where do you get all this stuff? About these sets, and stuff?"

"I teach science!" said Paul. "I have to keep up! And lots of people are reading a book on chaos theory right now, including me. James Gleick. He clarifies a new way of looking at things that may have some impact. Always interesting."

The sun poured down on Line's back as Paul turned the canoe around with his paddle and headed back toward their own dock. A mother duck with small ducklings behind her swam close to the shore. The wind was coming up a little, pushing the canoe toward shore, so Paul had to steer, but also stay out of the troughs of the small current. The faithful Archie sat waiting on the dock.

"Chaos theory has some impact on weather forecasting," Paul went on as he stopped by the dock and let Line off.

Line crouched low in the canoe and transferred her weight to the dock. "Good dog," she said to Archie, patting him. "You are a good and loyal dog."

But Paul was on a roll. Line crossed her legs and sat down on the dock to listen.

"It proves that we can't know enough to predict weather long-range. We don't know enough about the oceans, which control the atmosphere, and we would have to have very precise understanding of the atmosphere to get it right. But we are getting better at prediction within a couple of weeks. Which has a big impact on economics! Surprised me to hear this," said Paul. He pulled up the canoe into the 'v' made by the rubber tires and snugged the canoe rope around a poplar.

"Mikkelsons don't care about economics," said Line. "That's obvious!"

"The fact that it is part of the whole, though. That's what's interesting. I never thought about the fact that knowing the weather helps companies make decisions and prevent losses."

Line rocked back on her heels. "I'm getting hungry," she said. "I'd like some of that homemade bread Marie makes. And some coffee!"

"Yeah," said Paul. "Sounds good." Archie followed behind him, wagging his tail.

Line walked along the path, listening to the water lapping on the stones and the breeze in the trees. "You guys are staying down at the beach house?" she asked. Paul must hear the water all night.

"Yep," said Paul. "Just about like a tent! It's cold this time of year, but we like it. We just have a ton of blankets on top of us."

Line waved to Mother who was sitting in the window, looking down on them coming up from the lake. In the cabin, everyone was up, having coffee and toast. "Did you sleep well?" Mother asked Line.

"Oh yes," said Line.

"Marie and I want to try out this little tea shop we saw in Walker the other day," said Mother. "It looked like a little cottage, flowers blooming around it. We thought you'd like it. And next door is a shop that sells quilting materials. Walker's trying to cater to tourists!"

"And residents," said Marie. "More people are living up here all year round now."

"It sounds fun," said Ivy. She was still wearing flannel pajama bottoms with a pink long-sleeved t-shirt on top.

After lunch the women got into Mother's big Plymouth, leaving Paul and Archie to man the fort. Mother let Marie drive. "I'm not quite as safe as I used to be," she said.

Line envied Mother's dependence on Marie, as if she were her own daughter. Marie had spent much more time recently with Mother than Line had. But it couldn't be helped. That was how life was.

Minnesota had wide, well-kept highways. Walker was small, but there, tucked into the woods behind the grocery store, was a little white frame house with lace curtains in the windows and a sign out front which said "Enchanted Tea Cottage"! Inside it was impossibly frou-frou, with flowered tablecloths on the few tables, a cupboard full of old china, beribboned garlands and pictures along the walls. A delicious smell of fresh bread hung about the room.

"Someone's idea of heaven, surely," said Mother.

"In Walker, Minnesota!" said Marie. "Who would have thought?"

Ivy tried on a flowered bonnet, in which she looked winsome and lovely. "I wish I had a camera," said Line. But she never thought about taking photographs. That was Marty's job.

A young girl wearing a flowered dress who seemed to be high school age came out to serve them. She looked to be part Native American, dark skinned, with thick long dark hair. She seated them, took their orders for cinnamon rolls, which turned out to be the specialty, and brought out a large yellow-gold ceramic pot of freshly made tea.

"I wish my hair was as thick as hers," said Ivy in a low voice when she had gone into the back.

Line poured tea into Mother, Marie and Ivy's china cups. They were mismatched but the effect was frothy and delightful. "So, Mother," asked Line. "Are you doing any weaving right now? Paul said you were full of projects."

Mother smiled. "No weaving projects right now," she said. "My current project involves videotape! I've taken all of the old Super-8 movies Aunt Mabel and later Dad made and converted them to tape. I'm going to copy them for each of you."

"Wow," said Line. "That does sound like a project!" Ever since they had gotten together to give her a VHS player/recorder, Mother had been taping movies off the television. It was often her Christmas present to each of them, a particular movie she thought they would like.

"Yes," said Mother. "Family history. There's footage of many of you on the first day of school each year. Remember Dad used to like to take those? I'm planning to make a voice tape to go with it, since some of the people you wouldn't even know. There are movies of Carl and I from before we got married and some very dark ones of our wedding. And then from our first trips up to the Rainy River Bible Camp when Ellie was 8 and you were 4. Paul was the baby. He got covered with mosquito bites!"

Line could almost see in her mind's eye a picture of a baby Paul covered with pink spots of calamine lotion, which is what they used to try to stop the itching. "I remember the smell of moldy mattresses on the bunk beds," said Line. "Jumping on them with cousins."

"You had a little red wool coat with white piping on it," said Mother. "Sailor style. And you can see that little red coat being passed down to the other kids! Marty and then later it appears on Kristen!"

"I can't wait to see it!" said Line.

The cinnamon rolls came on a plate for each, with plenty of butter. "This is my idea of heaven," said Ivy. "A whole cinnamon roll of my own!"

"It's not exactly health food," said Marie. "But it probably won't kill us." Line could tell that Marie was looking around with an appraising eye. Marie had a small delicatessen in Ely. Her staff were running it in the summer, but Marie sometimes took a weekend and went back to see how it was going.

"We don't usually eat this kind of thing, either," said Line. "But it is delicious." Line enjoyed the taste of the very white bread and the frosting on top. "We used to get sliced wheat bread, but all of a sudden now, we're getting these wonderful crusty loaves of focaccia and sourdoughs and wheat breads."

"Peasant breads," said Marie.

"Yes," said Line. "I don't even bake bread any more. The ones we can buy are so good." Line smiled at Marie who was dawdling over her roll. She had hardly eaten any of it, while the Mikkelsons had consumed theirs! "How does it feel to be a grandmother?" Line asked. "I've got four kids and any of them could be having kids, but no. Not a one!"

"It's amazing," said Marie. "I felt so cut off from my own family. But I get to watch these little kids. And be part of their lives." She shook her head as if in wonder. "A blessing I didn't expect."

"She's a very good grandmother," said Mother. "You should hear Marie sing to them!"

"I have heard Marie sing," said Line. "But I'd like to hear more!"

"We'll have time," said Marie. Her dark eyes were soft. "The tiniest one is Benjy. Big black button eyes! And long eyelashes." She broke off. "But every one of them is a darling. Dory has gotten them all into line. She's a little mama bear! Now I see what big families can be like for the kids. Like a litter of puppies when they all come so close." A shadow passed over her face. "But I am hoping Grace doesn't get worn out."

"You do get worn out," said Mother. "I can attest to that. But I wouldn't change a thing about our family. And look at all of you now!"

Line tried to see it from Mother's point of view. She and her siblings were each interesting and successful in their ways. But most of them had not done what was expected of them. There were eight grandchildren. A Mandelbrot set, as Paul described, repeating on itself. "More tea?" she asked, standing up to pour from the heavy teapot. Three generations at this table, she thought.

"We have one more baby project this year," said Mother conspiratorially. "Rhonda. You remember Ellie's daughter? And her husband Ethan? They live in Minneapolis, so it feels close," said Mother. "I'll get to see something of this baby."

Line only remembered Rhonda as a child, a little older than her own kids. "A great grandchild!" said Line. But she wondered if she had said something hurtful. All of Grace's children were, in a manner of speaking, Mother's great grandchildren. But it would take some explaining to say how! No one seemed worried about what Line had said, though.

There was only one other table of tea customers, but the waitresses bustled back and forth. Besides the dark-skinned waitress, there was a very blonde Scandinavian girl who looked like Ivy. Together they were as cute as bugs' ears. Line remembered that she had never known a black kid when she was growing up in the Midwest, or a Native American. Their waitress set out a fresh pot of tea, and took the yellow ceramic one away.

"This is so pleasant," said Mother, looking around with her intelligent eyes. "I don't even want to move!"

"We could just move down a place," said Ivy. "Like in the Mad Hatter's tea party. Maybe they would bring us another bit of food!"

Everyone laughed. Line was proud of her lively daughter, comporting herself like a grownup. She put a hand on Ivy's arm. "I don't doubt that they will do whatever you want," she said. She whispered in a lower voice, "As long as you don't come to expect it!"

14

It was after dinner, very late, but no one wanted to go home. Marty and her friends were drinking Sean Thackery's Pleiades wine, eating the dark chocolate Phil had brought, and talking about Flaubert. Marty figured she would never get to sleep anyway. Why not talk the night away?

"The hero of The Sentimental Education is despicable," said Matthew. "Does nothing, ignores the world. While Emma Bovary seizes life." Matthew was a year older than Marty, with long graying curls but no beard. His small North Beach apartment, where the four of them had just shared an excellent dinner, was stuffed with expensive photography books.

"I think quite the opposite," said Marty. "Emma Bovary destroyed her marriage and her husband, while the hero of The Sentimental Education saw and appreciated everything around him, to the point where he almost creates the atmospheres of the women he spends time with."

"It's really the number of layers and dimensions in a book that make it great," said Phil, Shannon's husband. The two of them lived only a few blocks away in a rent-controlled apartment on Nob Hill. Phil was handsome, lean and Mediterranean-looking. His mother, from Lebanon, had married a Norwegian. Marty had met both Phil's parents at their wedding, a simple, beautiful affair at the Swedenborgian church decorated with pine boughs and flowers.

Shannon had been the librarian at Whittaker Perotta when Marty was there. She too was thin, with finely-defined features, dark hair and a smile which occasionally flashed out of her careful, mindful demeanor. Marty had been impressed that, as a bride, Shannon wore a plain white dress without a shred of lace on it. She too had read Flaubert's novels. "Yes," she said. "Each of us takes something different from his books."

"I loved Salammbo," said Phil. "Such lush language! The complete opposite of Madame Bovary!"

Marty had not read Salammbo. She preferred Flaubert's realistic style. But it was the first time since being in California that she had been in a room with people who had read more than one of Flaubert's books and could discuss them!

"Cigarette?" asked Matthew of Phil, and the two of them went out to sit on the painted wooden landing at the back of Matthew's apartment. Smoke and the cold January air wafted in through the door. Phil was a cook and Marty was surprised that he was willing to corrupt his palate by smoking. Once at a party at Phil and Shannon's, Marty noticed that all of their friends, cooks, musicians, artists, and designers, smoked!

Most of these friends were younger than Marty, almost a different generation. But many of Marty's friends were now younger than she was. Will, whom she had gone out with; Lauren, who had recommended her for the job at Designers International; Shannon and Phil; and of course Doug. Marty ascribed the smoking to a kind of anger. "What if it does cause cancer. It's cool, it gives me something to do and I like it!" There was some grass at the party, but not as much as at parties Marty remembered from the years with Erik.

In fact, being hip had passed to this generation. It no longer belonged to Marty's. At Shannon and Phil's, a video of the party scene in Breakfast at Tiffany's, speeded or slowed in parts, played silently on a television screen, while great space music boomed out of large speakers hidden in the closet. For a coffee table, Shannon and Phil used a broken marble slab with a washing bucket for a stand. Their apartment felt Parisian, with large windows looking out on the city, cream-colored walls and old white linens in the bathroom. Reality for them was not enough. They were playing with it.

Shannon now worked at a gallery. The owner sold beautifully fashioned glass art objects in a trendy part of the city. The owner valued Shannon's meticulous skills, but she was also going to school to get a teaching credential. Everything she did was conscious, careful, focused. To Marty, who had pledged herself to become impeccable, her best self, Shannon was well on her way.

In fact, in one of the oddest circumstances Marty could remember, her friend Meredith from New York while visiting San Francisco had walked around looking at things she might use in her architectural practice.

In the evening Meredith told Marty about only one person who interested her. That person was Shannon, whom she had met in the glass gallery! Marty was sure it must be some level of intensity that she shared with both Meredith and Shannon, which had enabled them to find each other in the vast cornucopia of possibilities the city offered.

"To me," said Marty to Shannon as they sat, helpless at Matthew's kitchen table, "The Sentimental Education just feels more real than Madame Bovary. In Madame Bovary everything is mocked, including innocence and wonder. Country people, the salt of the earth, are mocked. Even Flaubert could not get into a book all that you can find in the country. I like Hardy much better for that."

"Oh?" asked Shannon. "I do like the detail in Madame Bovary, but it is very sad. The whole thing. Which doesn't seem very real in the end. Everything can't be sad!"

"Exactly," said Marty. "Nothing works for Frederic in The Sentimental Education, but you feel he understands a lot. That the world is worth contemplating. That's I think what I liked."

"I haven't read it yet," said Shannon.

Marty felt she had solved it, what she wanted to say. When Matthew and Phil returned, she tried to explain it, but got somewhat bogged down under Matthew's critical attack.

"Where's the moral fiber in Frederic?" asked Matthew.

"I don't think it is really about morality," said Marty. "Flaubert is trying to describe life precisely. It's more about reality, I think. And he finds beauty in it."

"But it is so disillusioning!"

"Yes," said Marty. "That's the point." But she gave up, turning to Shannon and Phil.

"I have to get up in the morning," said Phil. He stood up and he and Shannon began to collect their things. "Nice brisk walk in the night air will be good for us," he said. "Put us to sleep after all this exhilarating talk!"

"Take Pacific Street," said Matthew. "It's the easiest way to get over the hills."

Marty left with Phil and Shannon.

"Matthew's just a little too much sometimes," said Phil, by way of sympathy as they walked up the street.

"Amazing to be able to talk, though," said Marty. "He's really good at discourse. I'm not. I can't find the words quick enough."

"Me too," said Phil. "It is worth it, sometimes, to find words for feelings. But so is sleep!"

Their footsteps echoed on the cold concrete and the air had a bite to it. No one was on the streets this late, but cars did swish past on the damp roads. It was lovely to be out, wrapped in woolen coats and scarves. Marty kept her head down and kept going when the others veered off up Taylor Street toward their apartment. Energy pounded through her legs as she climbed Russian Hill. How amazing to have friends within walking distance, she thought. This is my city. I never want to live anywhere else.

The Museum of Modern Art opened its new building that month. Marty could not wait to see it. She asked Doug if they could visit it the next time he came and he sounded enthusiastic. Because she thought of him so often, time between Doug's visits was long for Marty. After each one she was relieved to find their passionate friendship intact, to learn that Doug still loved her. But after a few days of euphoria, Marty would have to again batten down her emotions and work with the pain of the inescapable fact that they were not together.

Late in January, Doug found a day to come to San Francisco. "We've decided not to prune until February," he told Marty on the phone. "It's the most important job of the year. Pruning sets the stage for the coming harvest. But it looks like I can take a day before it starts. And it's been raining."

When Doug arrived, he seemed tired, stressed out. He lay down on Marty's velveteen couch and took her in his arms. "Come here," he said, his voice thick. At their feet was the deep-colored Persian carpet which Marty had carried from place to place.

Marty's wild body was stilled lying next to Doug's. "We have a simple relation," he said. "But we have to honor each other's paths. We're not really so far apart about sex either. That part of my life is not so healthy. But it can't be helped."

"It's an aspect of my health and sanity," said Marty, low.

"Well, we get to talk to each other about anything, and everything," said Doug. "We're not having an affair if we don't lie about it. My wife and I are in counseling now, trying to be honest with other. It's not so hard for me. I'm willing to be open, trying to get to a place Mackenzie and I can talk to each other. But there's something blocking her and she won't say what it is. When we get to a difficult part, when we get through analyzing me, and the therapist turns to her, she gets up and walks out!"

Marty tried to imagine it. To her, the kids were what was important. She often thought about these kids she had only seen once or twice. Zoe would be six now, the twins five, while little Jason must be two. "How are your kids doing?"

Doug's face darkened and Marty could feel his body tighten. "It's hard to tell," he said. "Mackenzie ships them off to my mother often enough. We've got a good elementary school near us, but she doesn't seem very interested. Pays scattered attention. It's hard to know where her attention is! Doesn't tell me, that's for sure."

Hopefully the conventional home and school rituals were working for Doug and his kids. An older Hispanic woman whose husband managed Doug's ranch often cooked and cleaned, keeping an eye on the kids. Mackenzie had little to worry about. Marty could do nothing about Doug's home life. "I can accept the limits," she said. "I just don't like barriers." It felt very good to be talking, their bodies close.

"There's no barrier to me loving you," said Doug. "It's as natural as the sun rising in the morning. I think about you as I work. I imagine what you would do in a situation. But it's a fool's errand. You can't build your life around your love."

It was an odd thing to say. Marty felt she had. "I don't want to complicate your life," she said, "any more than I already have."

"Thank you," said Doug. "That's what I thought you would say."

That afternoon they went to the new museum, taking the cable car downtown. Marty wore black jeans and a cashmere sweater and carried an umbrella, as it was a grey, drizzling day. Cold air rushed at them as the cable car slid down the hill. "Good museum day," said Doug. He wore a black cotton shirt under his sports jacket, his city clothes. Marty loved how well they looked together in their minimalist colors.

The museum had a brick façade and a black and white stone array around a sliced-off central column. The foyer was open to the ceiling skylight, with stone flooring and wooden paneled walls. Doug let Marty lead him to the elevator. "We'll go straight to the top and walk down," said Marty. Architecture was her milieu.

In a gallery on the top floor they were accosted by a display of golden brown Kilpatrick's bread slices, toasted and arranged on shelves like books! Some toast slices were stacked around the room, carefully placed. In another room, a baby blanket was spread on the floor topped with two worn, stained stuffed animals.

They went out on a terrace which faced the street. Dual circular plexiglass enclosures invited reflection and distortion. It was called "The Kiss." Doug took advantage of it, holding Marty tight in his embrace. They barely looked at the paintings in the studios ranged around the central space. They went down a floor and sat on a bench made of two kinds of wood, looking through the frame made by a stairway at the people walking on the opposite side of the large atrium.

"It's like a playground," said Marty. "The whole place! I like the architecture more than what's in it!" One side of her body was snugged up against Doug's, tingling with juice.

"Yes," said Doug, carefully, looking at Marty.

Marty looked back at him. "I know what you're thinking," she said. "You're wondering whether I need this stuff. Whether I'm a culture vulture," she said.

"Yes," said Doug. "I do wonder that."

"Not really," said Marty. "I think of myself as an artist, not a connoisseur. I like primary experiences, don't have to see the world through someone else's eyes. It's what I like about us. We are simple, uncomplicated. And the world is a playground for us, all of it."

"I do like the city," said Doug, "as a contrast to how much time I spend outdoors. Jeremy pushes me to pay attention to art. Because of our clients. They're pretty sophisticated. But I wouldn't say that I am."

"Oh, you are," said Marty. "You learn from everyone and everything. I've never met anyone so open. You're a natural born Taoist!"

They sat for a moment, looking. "What I like," said Marty, "is seeing people framed in the walls of the stairwell. Framing directs a person's attention. That's all it is really about. Our eyes are cameras, but they can only take in so much. Art frames things, directs your thought. Most of the rest of it is hype."

"Yeah," said Doug. "According to Jeremy, wine is poetry. It enhances a meal, or an evening or a conversation. It must help to direct attention too, somehow." He laughed. "There's a lot of hype in there too, though, these days."

"I think Americans are missing taste," said Marty. "It's really important, something to teach our kids. How to distinguish what's good from the hype."

"Example," said Doug. "They learn that kind of thing from their folks. Or not."

"Exactly," said Marty. "They need so many different kinds of experiences." She did not tell Doug how much she would like to spend time with his kids. That would be complicating his life!

When Doug left that evening, after one of their intimate dinners set aglow by a glass of wine, he traced on his chest a little piece at the bottom of his heart with his finger. "This part is for you," he said. "It's okay for us to love each other."

"You have a big heart," said Marty hugging him. "I know you have room in it for me."

Doug didn't want to leave, but he did. Marty felt totally stoned. Her eyes were big and round and liquid and her legs throbbed with pleasure. Actually her whole body throbbed. Her life felt holy. She wanted to walk slowly, lie quietly. She felt that by this time she and Doug were complicit, could talk about anything. There had been a lot of pain, but both of them were equal to it.

Marty brushed and flossed her teeth, taking her time before getting into her big bed with its fluffy down comforter. The rain sounded loud on the concrete in the lightwell. There was a way in which Marty felt she was reintegrating, at a higher level of herself. It was partly because of tai chi, and partly because being with Doug had opened her emotionally, more than she had ever been in her life. Tai chi allowed her to keep to the standards she was setting for herself. It helped still her wild body and mind. And spending time with Doug helped her trust that he did love her, as he was able. She expected nothing of him physically any more, but she knew he needed their talk as much as she did.

It could not be said, however, that Marty wasn't busy. At work the pace was often heavy, but then slow, unpredictable. Sometimes there was nothing in front of her, but then she got a barrage of calls. While checking her message machine, she got more! She liked it that the people requesting her time were at least known to her. She was used to them.

Marty's boss Joe complained to her about the administrative staff. Designers International was a macho firm. The five partners resident in the office were all male, and so were many of the architects. It had begun as an interior design firm, but architectural design projects now eclipsed that part of the company.

"Your people don't realize that we are working all hours of the day and night to meet our deadlines!" Joe said. "They're loud and they act like their personal lives are more important than anything going on here. There's such a gap between them and us! They don't take things seriously. They need to remember they're here to help us!"

Marty agreed. "It could be we are losing perspective," she said. "I will speak to them." Many of her staff had lively personalities and could hold their own in the intellectual and artistic atmosphere of the best design firm in town. It was often a fun place to work. Never staid or rigid like financial companies.

When hiring, Marty looked for people who had wide-ranging skills. No one could predict what was needed on a day-to-day basis in architecture. But when they didn't have anything much to do, the staff visited with each other, laughing and yes, Marty often did hear women cackling loudly down the hall. They did get a little too loose sometimes. Marty would call a meeting, mention this conversation with her boss. But she didn't necessarily expect it to do much good.

Three times a week, Marty went to tai chi practice. On week nights, she did not bring her weapons, but only her tai chi clothes in a trusty black backpack. On Saturday, she carried the weapons bag she had made of old blue jeans, that once a grocery clerk had asked her to open, to prove to him that it wasn't a Smith and Wesson!

One weekend powerful tai chi students came up from Los Angeles for a workshop with Master Liu. When senior students were there, Marty could just watch and check herself against them. Tai chi practice was more concentrated when this happened, not so distracting as when new people kept turning up.

At the very last moment, Daniel came in and took the back right corner, the most Taoist position in the room. Master Liu asked Ernesto and Stan to do a partner knife demonstration. Ernesto's set was flawless, very beautiful.

They were studying several kinds of push hands, including what was called "three step" which morphed into "four corners." These were, of course, martial applications. With a good partner, Marty had no problem, but she found it hard to work with anyone who wasn't proficient. And there was always one side that was easier than the other. Luckily she got to work with Sachiko, who knew it perfectly, moving up and down the darkened ballroom floor.

The longer someone had studied, the simpler their tai chi was. Ricka told Marty that she was feeling more selfish. "I just want to practice, not teach." Sachiko said that she didn't think Master Liu had any secret to transmit to those who were waiting for it. "The secret is in the practice," she said. Marty was beginning to get used to feeling her legs, hips and bottom pulsing after class. It felt good. Mark told Marty her form looked strong.

At the evening Chinese banquet, Marty sat beside Daniel. He thought Deng Ming Dao's book The Wandering Taoist was a good introduction. "I knew I was Taoist very early," he said. He was studying acupuncture and practiced Traditional Chinese Medicine. "I really just want to spend more time with Master Liu. Have to be a world citizen to do that," he said.

"I don't want to be strung out with relationships on several continents," said Marty. She had seen this in several tai chi people, including Daniel. One of the Danish students spent half her life in Copenhagen, half in Buenos Aires. Marty did not tell anyone she had spent a night with Ted. They talked on the phone, but Ted had not been back to San Francisco.

After the banquet, everyone accepted that Marty went home on the bus, instead of walking out with them. Marty didn't say so out loud, but she had decided she would not go to camp any more. She would attend everything available in San Francisco to keep herself limber and light, but she did not have the time or the money to travel with the gypsy students. She no longer expected anyone from tai chi to be her partner. Nothing could rival the closeness she had with Doug.

Marty called Mother and was horrified to find that Mother was in a lot of pain. She had somehow damaged her sacroiliac. She was having trouble standing or lying down. She hardly slept. "I sit in the recliner and watch all those videos of you guys we've taken over the years," she said. "The older people I know all agree that it is our structure that gives out first. I do feel better when there are people around. Strange, isn't it?" She had gotten a wheelchair so that she could go shopping with Ellie. "I never used to be able to shop very long because of my legs," she said. "Now it's more fun. We can take our time."

Marty couldn't help it. She told Mother about Doug. She was ashamed that she was involved with someone who was married, but said she could not ignore how much fun it was to get together and talk. "It is nice to have someone who thinks the world of you," said Mother, "even if you can't be married."

Mother's encouragement allowed Marty to tell her about Doug's viticultural work, how he had mentored Heather and that he was an excellent father. "He must be quite a guy," said Mother. "There is certainly enough pain in the world, if you have opened your heart to love."

Marty made a fire in her fireplace that night and ate a plate of pasta with pesto. She wanted to say hard things to Doug, to tell him that if he really loved her, he would not abandon her to the world as he had. "You would care about me being with other guys." But of course he could not, in his position. He had told her he hoped that when she did find someone else that she would also keep a place in her heart for him.

But Marty could not split herself up. She had been making do with the unequal relationship. All Doug had done was love and want her. It had to be enough. She sobbed long and loudly, thanking her stars that she lived alone and did not disturb anyone with her floods of tears. She kept hearing Mother's gentle voice say, "If you have opened your heart to love." It was amazing that Mother didn't censure her or give advice. It could only mean that Mother, as Dad had before, trusted completely that God would one day right things. Marty hated knowing that Mother was in pain. She did not talk to Mother often enough. She resolved to call her every month on the 25th, her birth date.

Days without hearing from Doug were hard, though. Marty resolved not to call him, to let him experience her silence. In a way, silence refined their love. As the other half of Doug was his family, the other half of Marty was a wandering Taoist. I am not going to be with anyone else, she thought. My wholeness is with Doug. Silence allowed her to think of Doug in a healing way: What was it that she wanted from him that she didn't already have? What did she want from anyone?

It was another good reason to live alone. Marty could set the boundaries that freed her, partly based on what she felt was dignified, appropriate. She did not want to lose her human dignity in the battle with need and desire. Her strength, and Doug's too, was to be able to be open, hedonists, but then get up and leave each other, get up and go to work. This ability too, thought Marty, was a legacy from Mother, who remained for Marty a powerful example of dignity.

The weekend before Valentine's day, people rushed around with flowers, packages, wore red clothing. Marty went out to the pond at the back of the arboretum. She liked doing tai chi on the little bridge over it. The sun was about to set. The pond was still and sluggish, oily on top, a few willow catkins floating on the surface. The reeds were banks of standing sticks with tops bent in interesting patterns. A mallard and his spouse stood on the bank.

For the sake of her sad little heart, Marty tore the edges off of four leaves from the mulberry bush at the edge of the pond. She dropped them on the thick surface of the water, wondering why she still insisted on having four of them. One was for Nathan, ancient history; one for Matthew, who was too full a teacup for her to ever get close to him; one for Ted, who lived a thousand miles away. The last was for Doug, the only one it was easy to love. I have four of them to comfort myself for Doug's endless absence, she thought.

Marty could not send anyone a valentine. She watched as the four valentines slipped under the bridge on the pretense of a current. The sun sinking toward the horizon made the edges of the thick, furry catkins golden on the tree. She did not stay to watch the four leaves reappear on the other side. It would have taken hours.

15

Ellie found Mother slumped in her chair one day at the end of August. She called in an emergency, but when the EMTs arrived, they said Mother had been dead for several hours. Ellie called Paul. "I remember she complained of indigestion a couple of days ago," Ellie told him. "They think it was either a massive cardiac event or a blood clot somewhere in the brain."

Paul was shocked, but there was nothing to say. Mother had gone quickly and gracefully.

"Do you think we should do an autopsy?" asked Ellie.

"No," said Paul. "It wouldn't accomplish anything." He had just come home from school where he was cleaning up his science lab, preparing for the coming year.

"That's what I thought," said Ellie. Mikkelsons did not need to know everything.

Paul and Archie, his dog, left immediately, stopping at the co-op to tell Marie. He arrived in St. Paul in the middle of the night. He slept on the fold-out bed in Mother's apartment, as he had so often before. Archie sniffed around, looking for someone, but Mother wasn't there. Her body was at the funeral home. In a corner of the room stood her loom, warped for a colorful project. Her hymnbook lay open on the stand above the electronic keyboard.

Paul helped Ellie call all of their relatives in the morning, and make arrangements with Gloria Dei Lutheran Church, of which both Ellie and Mother were members, for the funeral. Marty and Hanna got flights that afternoon and Kristen, who was a busy nurse in the southwestern part of the state, would come with her family as soon as they could. No one could reach Line, who had, according to Marty, gone to Spain to visit her daughter Fern on an archeological dig.

That afternoon, Paul let Ellie man the phones, while he retreated to Mother's apartment, Archie at his feet. He dug through Mother's papers, finding the data he needed to write an obituary. She had been the wife of the pastor of small Lutheran churches in North Dakota, Minnesota, and Iowa for 37 years. Mother had also been a high school librarian and teacher for 20 years, her life touching thousands of others. She had six children, but there were few of her own generation left. Only her older sister Rose, who was in a nursing home and knew little of what was going on around her, one of Dad's sisters and the wives of Mother's brothers.

As for Mother's affairs, Paul and Ellie found them simple to wrap up. They had already put the Lake Michigami property into a living trust for Mother. Now it would be transferred to the family. Ellie had a power of attorney. Paul could not find a will or funeral instructions. Clearly, though living with chronic back pain, Mother had not expected to die suddenly. How simply and gracefully she left us, thought Paul again.

That night he went out to the airport and picked up Hanna, whose plane got in first. They were each dealing with the shock of Mother's death and there was little to say in the face of its mammoth impact upon them. Paul and Hanna stood outside of Marty's gate in the garish neon light, as rafts of people passed by in the corridors behind them. It was the end of summer and everyone was moving about.

Paul told Hanna as much as he knew about the circumstances. "Ellie thinks that either you or I should take her car," said Paul. Mother had a big old gas-guzzling Plymouth that she did not drive very much.

"Her car?" asked Hanna.

"Yeah," said Paul. "We're sure Marty doesn't want it, and no one else needs it."

"I don't think I want it either," said Hanna. "I use buses and trains to get around. And I drive our van to the markets to sell our cheeses."

"Think about it," said Paul. He and Marie were still using only one car and it did make things difficult. He would drive up to get Marie tomorrow. Perhaps it would be a good idea if they each had a car.

Marty got off the plane and fell into Paul and Hanna's arms. "I did finally get to talk to Line," she said. "I got a phone number from Poppa, Stephen's father. She won't make it back for the funeral, though."

"We didn't really expect her," said Paul. "But I'm glad she knows." It was too bad all the siblings would not be there, but it would have been horrible if Line had not known about Mother's death. Somehow she would participate, even while in Europe.

The funeral, at Gloria Dei church with its white painted columns and pews, magnificent altarpieces and large pipe organ, was attended by hundreds of people. Mother rested in an open coffin in the entry way, surrounded by baskets and mounds of autumn flowers. Paul and his brothers-in-law and Gerald would be pallbearers, as well as two of Paul's cousins. Kristen had provided a drawing of ducks migrating for the cover of the small printed funeral card. Inside was a poem by Mother's brother David.

Pastor Susan welcomed and greeted the family in her study before they were led in to the front pews. Paul noticed that his sisters could not help but sob when they were together, but he tried to stay aloof. He would speak for the family and needed all of his courage to address this large group.

Rhonda and her husband and baby sat beside Bruce and Ellie. Brenda too had come up from Dallas, where she had a job. Kristen's husband and teenage boys sat with her. Gerald and a tearful Grace sat on either end of a pew full of their five small children.

Hanna and Marie sang together, "Amazing Grace," and then Marie's extraordinary voice lifted up to the vaulted ceiling with the old Irish hymn "Be Thou My Vision." Mother hadn't chosen these songs, but Paul felt sure she would have liked them. A powerful folk rhythm pounded through the lyrics. "Be Thou my vision, oh Lord of my heart," Marie sang. "Naught be all else to me, save that Thou art. Thou my best thought, by day or by night; waking or sleeping, Thy presence my light."

Pastor Susan invited Paul to give the family eulogy. Paul and Marty had spent half the day before writing it. He began by explaining that Mother had recently asked him if he was happy. Later when Marie questioned her about why she had asked, Mother said. "What we want most for our children is their happiness, along with integrity and dignity." Paul continued: "In her own words she had characterized her life. These things, a capacity for happiness, joy, integrity and dignity, along with a deep faith, are the example she set us.

"We experienced her as a woman of wide and deep perspective, who followed us in our growing, reflecting and enhancing what she saw in each of us, giving us the freedom to follow different drummers and always welcoming us back. We learned from both her and our father the importance of loving relationships, the wealth that comes from family and community, the joys that can be found in music, literature and art, as well as a deep appreciation of the natural world. We saw in her quiet dignity, boundless curiosity about the world we all live in, and a mischievous wit.

"We go to her empty apartment. The loom is warped for the church paraments she was planning to weave. Two Bibles lie open, one next to her bed and one next to the recorder she used to make tapes for the blind. Her hymnal sits open on the piano. The refrigerator is full of milk. She wasn't expecting this to happen, and neither were we. Her first great-grandchild had recently been born. Mercifully she was taken quickly, though we all wished we could have said goodbye.

"We draw comfort and strength from the faith she bore witness to throughout her life. The faith which still proclaims that human brokenness was healed at a place called Golgotha and that the power of death was broken on Easter morning.

"We would like to express our gratitude for all she gave us, for being the central figure in our lives, both as a family and as individuals, for her sweetness of spirit."

Paul sat down, drained. Pastor Susan talked about how much she had enjoyed having Mother as a member of the church and appreciated her insights in Bible study. It was all a fitting tribute to an extraordinary woman, Paul thought.

After the service, the church ladies served coffee and cake for what became a family reunion. Paul had not seen some of his cousins for, as Dad used to say, "donkey's years." It always surprised Paul that the solemnity and grief which poured out at a funeral would be followed by what was really a party full of happy greetings and talk. Life was for the living, of course. And Mother would have wanted it that way.

Paul stood with Marie, who happily introduced her daughter and grandchildren to whoever stopped to talk. The kids were happy to eat cake and run around while Grace sat quietly breastfeeding Benjamin, the baby. Her face was red and puffy from crying. She had loved Mother, who had gently folded Grace and Gerald into the family. Paul and Gerald hung out protectively behind her, not saying much. Paul was deeply proud of this family, and he was also pleased that Gerald had told him privately, "There won't be any more kids. I had a vasectomy. I had to take the sin on myself. Couldn't ask Grace to do it."

But Paul, as the only son of Carl Mikkelson, got pulled into many conversations with Dad's side of the family, and a few former parishioners who had traveled to the funeral. He didn't look so much like Dad. Dad's hair was much darker, but Paul's blonde hair was getting a little grizzled by this time. It was more a manner. He was sure he walked like Dad, and talked like him. Dad's sister Hilda told Paul she was working on the Mikkelson family history, collecting documents and trying to communicate with the relatives who were spread out over the Dakotas, and in Norway.

That evening, Ellie asked all of the siblings to come to Mother's apartment below her house and take what they wanted of her things. "Her main legacy is the cabin," said Ellie. "And most of Mother and Dad's things are there where we can all use them. But some of her books and dishes should go to good homes," she said.

Paul waited, Archie at his feet, until others had had their chance. He did plan to take any field guides no one else wanted, and he thought Marie would like having the electronic keyboard. Marty took tablecloths and a few dishes she had given Mother when she returned from traveling. Kristen took any art books she could find. Mother had given each of them things she had woven. She had always been generous with her gifts to them, thinking of what each of them might especially like. They had plenty to remember her by.

Hanna found the large pictorial dog book they had all loved as children. Its pages were falling out. "Oh!" she cried, "Here's the teacup dog! Do you remember?" She pointed to the picture of a dog so small it could fit in a teacup.

Paul remembered many of the dogs. He had poured over them as a kid and traced them, making copies and coloring them. The images in the dog book had been burned into his brain at a young age. They reminded him too of his first dog, Foxy, who had been his best companion throughout school. He stroked Archie at his feet. "Do any of the dogs look like Archie?" he asked Hanna.

"Oh yes," said Hanna. "Here's Archie," pointing to a black and tan shepherd mix as she handed the book over Paul's shoulder.

"Remember how we used to put our finger on the globe and say that we were going to end up where it did when it stopped whirling?" asked Marty. "The house was full of National Geographics. I don't think Mother and Dad realized the wanderlust it might create in their kids!"

"Well I for one am glad to be home!" said Ellie. "I don't care if I ever leave Minnesota again." Paul had noticed that she was showing more interest in the cabin at Lake Michigami also. Perhaps due to the influence of grandchildren! The lake was a great place for kids.

The family began to disperse the next day. Mother would be cremated and interred beside Dad in a week at the country cemetery near Lake Michigami. Ellie would clear up what was left of Mother's belongings, giving away her clothes and paying her bills. They did not expect there would be much left of her bank account when she finished.

Paul and Marie took Hanna and Marty to the airport, stopping on the way for a farewell cup of coffee and a memorial piece of French silk pie at Baker's Square. Marie sniffed. She did not like any food that was made by a corporation.

"But it was Mother's favorite," said Hanna, sighing.

"The whipped cream is terrible," said Paul. "But I like the chocolate part." Big chocolate curls topped the pie.

"I must admit," said Marty, smiling mournfully, "it was fun to have 'church basement coffee' after the funeral. It's just the same as it always was! And it was great to see so many cousins."

"Yes," said Paul. "It's fun to see them in their grownup versions. But they're just the same as when we played anti-i-over Grandma Mikkelson's house years ago." All of Hilda's daughters had been there and so had the playful sons of Dad's other sister. Southern Minnesota was full of Mikkelson relatives. The Bakken cousins were more spread out across the country, but a few had come.

"Do you think Aunt Rose will be all right?" asked Marty. They had gone to visit her in the nursing home. She seemed to understand that Mother had died, that she was the last of her siblings. She was now 90.

"We'll take care of her," said Paul. "Ellie visits her quite often." He laced his coffee with milk, sipping it thoughtfully. He too tried to visit Aunt Rose when he could.

"I've been thinking about what makes the Mikkelson family culture," said Marty. "It's a meeting of two very particular people, Mother and Dad. And they were each powerful in their way."

"It's been great to live here in Minnesota," said Paul. "We're surrounded by their history. I take it in by osmosis. I've been realizing that, in addition to being the 'pastor's kids,' our family isolation has something to do with the intense pride Grandma Bakken carried on after the death of her husband. Her kids supported her and she didn't take anything from anyone. Mother was only 7, but Aunt Rose would have been 21 and she was probably teaching school already."

"Grandma Bakken was the aristocratic grandmother in my view," said Marty. "Certainly not because they were well-off, but it must have been because of her pride. It was the Depression. I'm sure they were poor, but I think you are right."

"She set high standards," said Paul. "Uncle David and Uncle Herb would have been in high school, but both of them managed to get a lot of schooling and became very successful. She also set a tight boundary around the family. They needed to work together. Like they worked together on the cabin." Uncle Herb had originally built the cabin and then sold it to Aunt Rose and Dad. Uncle David's log cabin was next door to theirs.

"Mother told me that, in Denmark, pastors were highly regarded as servants of the Crown," said Hanna. "Grandma Bakken must have wanted to keep that regard for her husband."

"I always felt Mother put a boundary around us," said Marty, taking a last forkful of pie. "She insisted we would become each other's best friends, especially when we were moving from place to place. It's hard to move in the Midwest. You're always the new people."

"The Mikkelson cousins seem pretty rooted," said Hanna.

"Yes," said Marty. "Dad's mother was more earthy. And I mean that in the most positive way. She was so physically capable. Her house was full of ancient walnut furniture, handmade rugs and embroidered linens with lace she had made. I think I get my physicality from Dad's side of the family, and my intellect from Mother. A rich heritage."

"I remember the garden full of strawberries," said Paul. "Luscious. She used to sell them for pin money, I think."

"I never saw that house!" wailed Hanna. "I never got any strawberries!" Grandma and Grandpa Mikkelson had sold their house and lived in a nursing home by the time Hanna was old enough to remember.

"It was interesting to me that your family didn't need an autopsy," said Marie. "And I know you have family secrets, but no one presses on them or worries about them." She was only picking at her pie.

"Forgiveness is more important," said Paul. "In this family."

"No one talks about things in my family either," said Marie. "But it just drags everything down. It gets very dour sometimes."

"We do talk about things," said Marty. "But it takes time, and understanding."

Hanna's eyes were wide as she listened. "I love hearing you guys talk. I feel like I missed out on so much of this!"

"Well," said Marty. "You got the whole megillah. You got Mother and Dad by themselves. All that weaving and spinning and craft work. And you got to laze around the cabin all summer with nothing to worry about!"

"Hah!" said Hanna. "'Twas a mixed blessing indeed! They were kind of exhausted by the time they got to me and Kristen!"

"All the same," said Marty. "We are all some version of Mikkelson. I took back my maiden name recently, because I like having that quality of ethnicity that it has. And then there's the alliteration that I like. Marty Mikkelson."

"I like being a Mikkelson myself!" said Marie, playfully. "And what do you want your name for, Marty Mikkelson?"

"God knows," said Marty. "I'm kind of a scholar warrior, as you know. Probably don't need my name for any particular reason. I just like it. I like calligraphing it."

"You're the youngest," said Paul to Hanna. "Does it feel tough to be an orphan? Mother and Dad were each relatively young when they died."

"I don't know how I feel yet." said Hanna. Her eyes were red, and she used a paper napkin to blow her nose. "I need some time to think about it. But all of us have to see Mother and Dad in each other from now on. That's the best we can do."

"Yes," said Marty, softly. "Us older kids preserve a sense of how Mother and Dad were when they were younger, and you saw them when they were older. We need each other."

"I am sure it was exhausting to have all those kids," said Paul. "Mother has only eight grandchildren of her own, from six kids!"

"You guys are acting pretty relaxed for people who have to get on airplanes," said Marie. "Shouldn't we be going?"

Marie was right. They all stood up and pulled themselves together. At the airport, it was hard to say goodbye. It had been a real Mikkelson gathering. Marie and Paul went back to Mother's old apartment to pack up and drive north. There was, as usual, a great deal to do.

Paul and Marie loaded the electronic keyboard, a few dishes and a box of books into the Previa, which Marie would drive north. "I'm feeling very tender toward you," Paul told Marie as he hugged her goodbye and bid her drive safely. "Thank you so much for being a daughter to Mother."

Marie was crying as she looked into his eyes. "It's because she was such a wonderful mother to me," she said. "She was a mentor for me. And I needed one."

"Yes," said Paul. "To all of us."

Marie ruffed up Archie's face, putting her hands around his muzzle. "Take care of my boy," she said to him. "I love him so much." She got in the mini-van and drove off.

"Okay, Archie," said Paul finally. "These are our new wheels!" He let Archie into the cushy back seat where he could lie down, and rolled down the window. "Enjoy the air!" Paul told him. Archie sniffed all over before he settled down. Paul wondered what he made of the smells.

Paul stepped on the gas. The air was warm and the sky very clear with the intense fall blueness beginning. A few puffy cumulus drifted along the horizon. Driving by himself gave Paul a chance to think about everything. It was like some bottom had dropped out. In many ways Mother had leaned on him and now that pleasant weight was gone.

When Ellie called, Paul had been working on his science lab. He had missed a couple of days of teachers' meetings, but he would be back for the beginning of school. The past three years of teaching had been easier in some ways than working for Canoe Country Outfitters, though he still had a hand in there too, helping them with their computers and databases on weekends. With teaching, there were lots of vacation days and open days. Paul often wondered how anyone ever learned anything at school.

Paul had begun teaching in order to spend summers with Mother at the lake. Would that change? He was still the chief maintenance and support person at the cabin, such as it was. There was never much money to do anything with anyway. He did think maybe they needed a new roof, though. Mold and water damage were seeping in. He resolved to talk to Ellie about it. Maybe the family trust could come up with the money. Maybe this weekend, when she and Bruce came up for the interment. They needed a stone to mark Mother and Dad's burial place. But there might be enough in Mother's account for that.

Paul drove steadily on, happier as he got further from the city. Cornfields were dry and golden and the soybean plants were beginning to yellow too. On Paul's other side was the pleasant weight of Marie. It wasn't very heavy, and she had been a wonderful partner. It was just that she wasn't as happy when she wasn't working or surrounded by people.

Marie had a darker side, sometimes simply took to bed and lay there. She did not seem to have the supports and interests which made her happy as she grew older. She did hang around a knitting shop in Ely, and was working on a quilt with the women there during the winter. She was quite unlike Paul, who could have holed up all winter with some binoculars, a pile of books and his skis, not seeing another person. It did worry him a little. He actually felt he was part of the problem for her. He tried to be amenable to her sociability, however. Though they weren't always regular at church, they did have a membership and enjoyed singing in the choir.

Paul sighed. He felt very lucky to have Marie, who cared for him as he did for her. She was always cooking wonderful food for them. When he came home and only wanted to put his aching legs up, she rubbed them for him and reminded him to stretch, though he didn't always do it. I also need to start an exercise program, thought Paul. He had heard of post-polio syndrome, which affected polio victims as they aged. Not going to be me, thought Paul to himself. He was going to fight it to the death.

The landscape changed as Paul drove north. The farms were scrubbier and hay sat in the fields in big rolls, not in bales. The deciduous trees that lined the roadways changed to pines and scrub. There were more lakes, dotted with ducks and herons. Paul looked back to see that Archie had his head out the window. "Smell that northern air, do you?" he said.

When he got to Ely, Marie had arrived before him. They unloaded and Marie made them a simple supper of pasta and tomato sauce with cooked corn on the cob. They sat outside on the back steps in the evening, Archie beside them. A thin sickle moon was visible as it crested the sky and a cricket was singing over near the dried-up garden. Since they had been gone during the summer, the garden wasn't up to much, but maybe that could be remedied now.

"You know that book of Thoreau's journals for 1851 that I've been reading?" Paul asked. "I was surprised to have him say that he thinks of those to whom he is truly related when falling asleep at night."

"That's lovely," said Marie. "And a little sad."

"He was a prickly guy," said Paul. "And I was impressed he said that. Mother is missing now, but I can think of her in peace and know that she is not in pain. That makes me happy."

"Yes," said Marie. "I hold her in my heart. A lovely thing to think of before going to sleep." She rested her head on Paul's shoulder. "I'm glad you are right here, though."

Line threw a hood over her head and dashed through the rain from her car into the Boulder Creek winery. "Heather," she called into the large seemingly empty room full of upright stainless steel tanks. "I'm here!"

Heather's head popped around a tank, her hair bound back in a tight bun. "Ok, Mom!" she called back. "We'll be out in a minute."

Line went back out to the car, which was actually a sizable mini-van, to wait. The rain washed down the windshield, pounding on the metal roof over Line's head. But she was always happy about rain. This year she felt it was helping dispel the heaviness of her sorrow about Mother's death.

When Mother died only months ago, Line had been staying in a small city on Menorca, one of the islands in the Mediterranean belonging to Spain, where she and Stephen had gone to see what Fern was doing. It was not an easy place to get to and Line had not been able to go to the funeral. Grieving alone had felt surreal, as Line was mentally in Minnesota as well as on Menorca, touring the extensive archaeological site of the Roman city of Sanisera. The site, spread out along the sea, had grown so large and needed so many workers that a school had been started to train archaeologists in field work. Fern had been there for several years, getting in on the beginning of the school.

Stephen told Line that this was what being a world citizen felt like. But Stephen was very grounded, his head settled clearly in the present, though he immersed himself in time past, seeing human movements and currents across both space and time. Line herself had more trouble staying in the present. She was always sending her mind out after her kids, or in this case, her siblings, imagining where they were and what they were doing based on what she knew of them. The rain helped Line because it meant so much to the gardens and trees of California. This year it cleansed her own sad thinking.

Line did not expect the surrealism of sending herself out in time and space to quit. It was only getting stronger as she could see that Heather would marry her boyfriend Pablo and move back to Chile where Pablo's family had vineyards. He had come to California to see how vineyards and wineries were managed, but he was living two lives as well. One in the southern hemisphere and one in front of him. He had a New World orientation, he told Line, but it was tempered by the reversed seasons. He was constantly worrying about what was happening in his vineyards during his absence.

Pablo and Heather were cellar rats at the winery that winter, racking and re-racking wines to get the sediment out and endlessly cleaning everything to keep the bad microflora from interfering with the good microflora which made the wine.

Heather had called Line that afternoon, a wet Saturday in January, asking whether someone could drive the winding 14 miles up the mountain to collect her and Pablo. The car they usually used was needed and they wanted to come home for a day off, Sunday. Their weekday accommodations, a kind of bunkhouse on the ranch used when there were big crews in to work on the grapes, was somewhat austere. Especially when you knew that your parents' comfortable and opulent house was close by!

No one expected Poppa to go. He was a fine driver, but his eyes were not very good in the dark, and the road to Boulder Creek during the winter storms was not easy. Stephen was at the university, as usual. He liked doing most of his work there, coming home to relax. Ivy was home, but she wasn't an experienced driver. Line, the adventurer, elected herself.

Heather and Pablo emerged from the lighted doorway, running through the rain. The three of them drove home slowly. "I don't care how long it takes," said Line. Indeed, the car's headlamps lit up a sapling lying in the road as they came down the mountain. "That wasn't there when I came up," said Line.

It wasn't very big. Heather and Pablo got out and pushed it to the side of the road. It was springy, Line could see from inside the car, her lights trained on the wet forest darkness beside the curving asphalt. Pablo tried to pin it behind another tree so it couldn't get away and surprise the next driver.

"I'm glad you saw that!" said Heather, climbing back into the car dripping with water.

"That wasn't so bad," said Pablo in his slightly accented English.

Line was thinking of the wind and water damage still remaining from the intense New Year's storm. "It is brave of people to live up in these mountains," she said. "Especially in the winter."

"Yeah," said Pablo. "We've had a few days lately where we lost power and had to turn on the generators. The road is good, though."

In town they usually didn't have trouble with electricity. Line was relieved to see all the lights on in their own house on its ridgetop when they drove up Beel Drive and into their garage.

Inside, Ivy was washing lettuce and laying it out on towels. She had made Basmati rice to go with the curry Line had put together that afternoon.

Poppa played bartender, mixing the pre-dinner drinks with great care as people turned up. Stephen had caught a ride home with a colleague. He wanted a simple drink, an old favorite, Scotch on the rocks with a little vermouth and a bit of Angostura bitters floated on top. Poppa made one for himself and one for Pablo. "Line? Heather?" he asked as Line, Pablo and Heather washed up and dried themselves off.

"I'll have one," said Heather. "It sounds like civilization!"

Line demurred. She would have a glass of wine with dinner. She did not enjoy the hard stuff much any more.

"Everything's ready," said Ivy from the kitchen. The table was laid with plates, wineglasses, napkins, silver in appropriate places.

Line looked around at her attractive family. Pablo was dark, long and thin, with curly hair, drops of water hanging in his small mustache and goatee. Beside the golden Heather, he looked like a young Castilian count. They stayed close to each other, brimming with some shared delight.

"Time is time," said Poppa, his bow tie bobbling below his Adam's apple. He called the shots about dinner when he was around. His neck was getting a little stringier as he got older, though he still seemed to be a young 76. Because he was dressed up, Line suspected he had a film night planned.

When everyone sat down, Poppa raised his glass, "L'Chaim," he said.

"L'Chaim," echoed back. Line took a sip of the Merlot they were drinking that night. "Bottled poetry," Jeremy, the winemaker up on the hill called it. He never tired of discussing how wine affected an evening, lending it warmth, light and spirit.

"Quite a dark night up on the mountain, right?" asked Poppa.

"Good for us," said Pablo. "Can't have too much rain." He looked at Heather conspiratorially. "You tell them," he said.

"No, you," said Heather, looking down at her plate. Bread and olives, appetizers sat in front of them.

"Okay," said Pablo. "Heather has agreed to marry me. We'd like to have the wedding quite soon, as my parents can come in February, before harvest gets started. February is like your September. They can take a week at the beginning of the month."

Line was not surprised, but it was sudden. "Oh Heather! That's so soon!" she said. "There's hardly time to plan!"

"You don't need to plan," said Heather. "We just want it to be small. Just our family and a few friends would be lovely. Can we do it here?"

"Congratulations! We would certainly like to meet your parents," said Stephen to Pablo, shaking his hand. "She's a treasure, I can assure you."

"I know," said Pablo. "How could I be so lucky?"

Stephen stood up and hugged Heather. "Of course you can do it here. My dearest girl."

Tears rose to Line's eyes as she watched, shaking her head. She too stood up and hugged her eldest daughter.

"It's just wonderful!" said Poppa. Line knew the gleam in his eye. Privately he had begun to wonder when Stephen and Line's kids would have kids. He wanted to see them!

"You could marry us," said Heather to Poppa. "Remember how you became a deputy for a day and married those friends of yours? Could you do that for us?"

"Certainly!" said Poppa. "I would be honored."

"Ivy can be bridesmaid," said Heather, "and maybe we'll get Doug to stand up beside Pablo. We just need to get married so that when we go back to Chile we aren't looked upon as fallen people." She smiled.

Line put her hand on her heart. It was all happening so fast. It would be done before she even thought about it!

Ivy was up and hugging Heather. "I can't wait! It'll be so much fun!" she said. She danced around the room, waving her hands. "Now that you've gotten everyone to their feet, come and have some curry," she begged them. "Mother made it this afternoon."

The family and its new-found member went into the kitchen and dipped into the curry and rice kettles. Rain pounded on the wooden decks outdoors and Line could hear the wind in the trees. Life, she thought. Rushing through us. When they sat down again, Heather went over a brief guest list. Ivy planned the flowers. Food would be easy, and Heather had heard of someone who could make a cake. Perhaps there wasn't much to worry about after all.

"Can I help you find a dress?" asked Ivy. "I would be so good at it!"

"I would love that," said Heather. "But nothing special. This will be just small. We'll have a Catholic ceremony when we get to Chile, after I've studied."

"After you've studied?!" said Stephen.

"With Father Raul Maria," said Heather innocently. "He's Pablo's parish priest."

Line and Stephen looked at each other. Heather a Catholic?! Now that was surprising! Line said nothing, absorbing the information.

Poppa, the world citizen, took up the challenge. In Poppa's eyes, anything and everything could be, and should be, discussed. "Are you sure you know what you're doing, Heather girl?" he asked. "Catholicism is serious!" He looked at Pablo. "No offense!" he smiled.

"I know," said Heather. "I went to church a lot in Chile. It helped me with my Spanish," she said. She and Pablo had met while working in the vineyards of some French friends of Jeremy who had established a winery in Chile. "The churches in Santiago are very old, and very beautiful."

"But don't you have to believe, confess certain things?" asked Stephen.

"It's complicated," said Pablo. "We do and we don't. The Catholic Church plays a different part in Chile than it does here, I think. Much more integral. You know I was born at the time Pinochet became president. Until he was ousted in 1990, the Catholic Church was our best defense against abduction and ill treatment by the government. My father worked for the Vicariate of Solidarity. We all revered Cardinal Raul Silva Enriquez, who asked the Pope to create it. My father worked as a lawyer with hundreds of people. The Vicariate was supported internationally, and it didn't disband until five years ago."

"I had no idea!" said Poppa, looking around at the family members at the table. "We know about Pinochet's repressions. But I didn't realize the role the Catholic Church was playing."

"We might still have Pinochet hanging over us if it weren't for Pope John Paul. When he visited in 1987, he pushed Pinochet to open to democracy. A referendum was scheduled on his presidency. That was what led to the amendment of the constitution. He is still commander of the army. But, you can see, the Catholic Church in Chile is our benefactor in many ways. I grew up in it."

"I have a feeling all of us are going to pay more attention to Chilean politics from now on!" said Stephen.

Line was impressed that Pablo had instinctively known how to sway this family. They had talked with him often, of course. His family was part of the European elite, his father of ancient Spanish ancestry and his mother Austrian. He was open and eager to learn about California, but his heart and his life were in Chile, near Santiago.

"My sister lived in Chile for a little while," said Line. "But I always felt she didn't know anything. She was in an American bubble, her husband working for an American corporation. They wanted the copper and magnesium for their magnetic tapes."

"Yes," said Pablo. "We've got the mines. But we've also got weather like California in the Valle Central. It's perfect. I wish you could see our vineyards!"

"They're in a flat valley, with the Andes rising up behind them," said Heather. "Spectacular!"

"You are talking us into it!" said Stephen. "Could happen."

Late that night, when Stephen was propped in bed with a news magazine, Line put on a nightdress, interrupting him. "I'm more surprised about Heather turning Catholic than about the marriage," she said.

"Sounds like a cultural thing," said Stephen.

"I'm not so sure," said Line. For her, religion had always been about belief. Only faith, taught Martin Luther, was needed to attain salvation. "She's young and we haven't insisted the kids believe in anything."

"Just your normal, humanist virtues," said Stephen. "Courtesy and high standards. You're quite high-minded yourself, my young wife."

Line smiled. "The kids are wonderful," she said. "I trust them and we've certainly opened them to what we could."

"There's no harm done," said Stephen. "Heather's going to have to deal with that culture one way or another."

"I suppose," said Line. She slipped into the warm bed beside Stephen.

The next few weeks were hectic. In the vineyards, pruning began and Heather was too busy to worry about anything. Line made phone calls, calling in her troops. Marty would do casual photographs. Pablo found recorded music, though Line hoped that Christy would be home to manage it during the actual wedding. It would have been nice to have Paul and Marie, or Hanna to sing, but Line didn't expect so much. She was most worried about hosting Pablo's parents, who she expected to be considerably more formal than the Cohen family.

Thoughts of Mother kept coming to Line as she planned the wedding. Mother had quickly adapted and put together Line's own wedding so many years ago. Mother had once told Line that when she was young and had so many children in quick succession, a doctor had prescribed Librium for her anxiety. They were the original Valiums, a bit more heavy duty, Line guessed. Mother had taken them for a little while, but then quit because she didn't like how they made her feel. The idea of Mother being anxious was foreign to Line in the first place. Mother had always seemed so powerful and collected.

Everyone, including Poppa, became involved in the wedding. Poppa thought there should be a professional photographer, though he promised Line that the person would be unobtrusive and not make the wedding into a show. "Just a few nice photos of our first wedding," he said. Line acquiesced. They were still hippies, she thought, interested in authenticity and simplicity. But they were not poor.

When Heather and Ivy couldn't find a simple white dress in all of Santa Cruz, they found a pattern Heather liked, and Ivy cut it out. "I want it to be about the flowers," said Heather. "Not the dress." The flowers would mostly be hothouse roses.

Ivy made a sleeveless sheath of heavy, textured white cotton, with a filmy organza stole to wear over it. "It's going to look so good with her skin," she told Line. Heather spent so much time outdoors her tan almost never faded.

Line did convince Christy to come and Poppa sent him money for a ticket. Christy had been back from his Peace Corps years in Peru only a few months. He was working for the Democratic Farmer Labor party in Minnesota. Paul Wellstone had asked Christy to come along on his cross-country speaking and listening tour during the coming summer, an exploration for his presidential aspirations. Wellstone planned to tour the places Bobby Kennedy had in 1966, talking especially to poor people. Christy was to take notes and do publicity.

The guest list for the wedding took on a life of its own. Friends Heather had met at the university, her old friend Allison from Santa Cruz, and others wanted to come. But when everyone gathered on a Saturday afternoon, it was still quite relaxed, just a big family party. The sun even deigned to come out, though the decks were damp and the trees glistened with moisture.

Line had left the decorations to Ivy, while she and Stephen devoted themselves to the Valenzuelas, who had come from Chile. Mr. Valenzuela spoke English better than his wife, though she was pretty and well-dressed. Line showed them around the house and garden, dragging Christy with her to translate.

Seeing it through foreign eyes, Line was proud of her household. The house, with its big windows open to the air and light, looked wonderful. Ivy and Poppa had spared no expense on the flowers, mostly red and white roses, with a striking white Phalaenopsis in bloom on a little table where Poppa had put his books near the fireplace.

Line rushed around, begging Christy, who stood by the stereo equipment, not to wait. She did not want the sun to go down until after the ceremony. It slipped away so fast during the winter. Marty, in a slim black dress, had been making the most of it, photographing everyone in the afternoon light.

But then, Christy set the needle of the phonograph on the wedding march. Heather emerged from down the hall into the spacious room where everyone sat on sofas and chairs waiting. She walked slowly to the pompous strains on the arm of her father.

Poppa, at the front of the room, stood waiting with his book, along with Ivy, in pink, on one side and Pablo and Doug on the other. Seven-year-old Zoe, Doug's oldest daughter in a white dress with a red sash, strewed rose petals from a flower basket on the carpet in front of Heather.

Poppa made the most of the civil ceremony. Doug passed the rings to Poppa, and Heather and Pablo spoke their vows to each other clearly, so everyone could hear them. Afterwards Poppa said a few words, bidding his granddaughter and her husband happiness. He had enlisted Stephen to make the traditional Jewish exclamation, "Mazel tov!"

Line was sure that the Valenzuelas would be scandalized by the brief formalities, but she herself felt that Heather and Pablo had been well and truly married. They allowed the photographer half an hour after the ceremony, but then he left, and everyone was free to eat and talk, drink and dance.

Line felt some relief. There was champagne and wedding cake, but everyone behaved themselves. Line wasn't sure Doug's wife Mackenzie had ever been in the same room with Marty, but Marty gave no sign that she was madly in love with Mackenzie's husband. Marty was still photographing, though the light was low and candles gleamed on the tables. Mackenzie's four children circled around Alice Henderson, Doug's mother, who was a stout, comfortable presence.

Mackenzie, in a filmy dress, her auburn hair long enough to be half way down her back, seemed young and a little disassociated. She paid no attention to her kids, but hung around Christy by the stereo. Perhaps because he was being the DJ. Christy kept the music coming, some of it soft rock, some more energetic. Line wondered what the Valenzuelas thought of The Gypsy Kings, whose powerful guitars sounded very authentic to Line.

The Valenzuelas stuck together, enjoying their handsome son. The little Henderson kids hung on Heather, whom they loved. "I want to take them outdoors," Heather told Line, "but it is getting dark and cold."

"We need you here," said Line. "Without you, there's no party!"

Poppa pressed Christy to play whatever dancing music he had. When the strains of "Sweet Caroline" came over the speakers, he pulled Pablo and Heather into the center of the hardwood floor for the first dance. So beautiful they were, Heather blonde and Pablo dark.

The next song was Frank Sinatra, with Poppa claiming the dance from Heather. "Look at this guy," said Line to Marty. "He's the same age as Mother was." Poppa was sweet, thin, dapper and dancing.

"Yeah," said Marty. "He certainly looks happy out there."

"Poppa has made his luck and his life," said Line. "I think it was that northern diet of Mother's. She never quit drinking milk!" Line herself had been deeply influenced by all the nutrition winds that blew through California. She often tried to diet, but felt best when she and her family stuck to a regimen which was somewhat Italian, with lots of fruits and vegetables.

"Her circulation did not look good the last time I saw her," said Marty. "I am glad she is no longer in pain, though. It was hard for me to know. She was someone who didn't deserve it."

"I know what you mean," said Line. Poppa and Heather were laughing as they danced. Beside them were the Valenzuelas in their elegant clothes, considerably younger than Poppa. Line looked around for Stephen. He was talking to Allison, who was a neighbor when they lived in their previous house.

There were more dancing songs, ABBA and Journey and others. Zoe, the oldest of the Henderson kids, danced in a circle with the twins, who must now be six. Chubby little Jason, four, sat in Alice Henderson, his grandmother's lap. Where was Ivy? Line wondered. She was in the lighted kitchen, talking to Heather's friends from Davis about the university in Santa Cruz, a champagne glass in her hand.

Pablo took a long-stemmed red rose in his teeth and tried to do a tango with Heather to the Gypsy Kings guitars, but Line could tell they did not really know what they were doing. They laughed and clowned. Heather let Pablo swing her around, turning swiftly and putting her leg up as he pulled her toward him.

When the unmistakable sounds of Eric Clapton's guitar wafted through the room, Line went to find Stephen, pulling him into the circle. They didn't dance much, but she loved Clapton.

"Oh my darling, you were wonderful tonight," sang Clapton. Line clung to her skinny husband who had pulled off his tie and opened his shirt. They moved slowly, Line's hand on his shoulder. Stephen sang along. Clapton took his good, sweet time, with guitar solos in between.

Line looked around. Mackenzie had pulled Christy onto the floor, and there indeed were Marty and Doug, standing in the dark of the hall, dancing. Oh dear, thought Line, it's really time for this to be over. When the song stopped, she began to gather dishes and glasses, napkins and plates off the tables. She turned on lights and asked Zoe and the twins to help her blow out candles. The mood was broken and people began to recover themselves, looking for their coats and possessions.

Heather and Pablo stood at the door. "I'm sure you'll be very happy," said Alice, bidding the young couple goodbye. When the group of Hendersons Doug gathered up left, the party seemed much smaller!

Line was sure Heather and Pablo would be happy too. They had managed to find each other across the miles. Line thought of Mother once more, who had always expected the best. It wasn't what you thought would happen, usually. It was often more and better than what you could imagine. Line had seen it herself, had tried to be open to this unfolding, unknown future. Seeing how Mother's story ended gave Line confidence. Mother was, hopefully, right.

17

At the arboretum in San Francisco, Marty showed her cousin Sarah, her partner Abbie, and their toddling daughter Gloria the "hippopotamus" rocks. They were a series of rounded off rocks poking up from the ground under a gorgeous California buckeye. Gloria climbed on one of them, riding it as if it were one of the big animals half submerged in a pool. She looked up at the three adults, a big smile on her round, pink face.

"It was Christy who used to love them," Marty said, remembering the days when she and Line had lived nearby with Christy, at about the same age as Gloria was now. Creamy fragrant buckeye blossoms, just finishing their summer bloom in June, littered the rocky ground just off the path. The day was chilly, the sun beginning to burn through the persistent morning fog.

"Come on Glory," said Abbie. "Let's go have something to drink." She collected the little girl in her arms and they all walked over to the circle of stones brought from a Spanish monastery which set off the California native plants section. The stones formed a low wall, perfect to sit on and just the right height for Gloria to waddle alongside, holding herself upright, her little diaper sagging.

Sarah opened a small backpack and took out crackers and juice for Gloria. Abbie and Marty brought out sandwiches and fruit, a picnic. "Everything tastes better outdoors," said Marty as she ate bread with cheese and avocado.

"Yes," said Sarah. All of them wore sweaters, casual clothes, sneakers, though Marty's feet were bare in her favorite teva sandals. "I'm glad the sun is coming out!"

Abbie and Sarah had conceived Gloria with the help of two gay male friends who also wanted a child. Gloria spent her weeks with Abbie and Sarah, her weekends with her fathers. Abbie was the pastor of St. Francis Lutheran Church in the Castro area of San Francisco while Sarah did stained glass work and stayed home with Gloria.

They had initially shared the pastor's job, their hands full at the height of the AIDS epidemic, providing counseling and community for gays who were dying. The church had been put on trial and expelled, as Abbie and Sarah would not agree to the Lutheran policy of celibacy for gay pastors, but it continued to exist independently. It was a place of sanctuary not only for those with AIDS and their partners, but for the whole community, including parents who came out from the Midwest to spend time and grieve with their sons.

Things were a little quieter by this time and Gloria was an answer to prayers. It was clear to Marty that Sarah and Abbie now had the problems all parents had. They lived in an apartment right behind the church, which Sarah had made into a home with artfully painted furniture, candles in the unused fireplace and lovely linens and china. But there was no attached yard or garden as there would have been had they lived in a suburb.

The arboretum was for Sarah and Abbie, as well as for Marty, a woodsy place to relax in the city. Marty resented the fact she had to take two buses to get to it, but that could not be helped. The city, in all its density, gave her so much. She supposed it wasn't reasonable to require a park with huge trees and luscious grass within walking distance of your house.

Marty told Sarah and Abbie about Heather's wedding that spring. "Ivy made Heather's dress, I believe," said Marty. "And did the flowers. Heather looked lovely with her handsome Chilean husband. I got to see Christy too. Line's kids are growing up!"

"I was just telling Sarah to look closely at our daughter," said Abbie. "They grow up so fast!"

"It seems incredible," said Marty. "I can see Christy so clearly playing on those rocks! And now he's just come back from Peru. He told me that he really appreciated government since coming back. About half of Peru is anarchic, he says, even the traffic! But they do seem to be getting to the bottom of their terrorist problems. He says he learned a great deal in those two years."

"What's he doing now?" asked Sarah.

"He's in Minnesota, working in politics I think," said Marty.

"We're thinking of moving back to Minnesota," said Sarah. "We just don't think we can afford to have Gloria grow up here. And we miss the lake," she said. Sarah's father, Marty's Uncle David, had built the beautiful log cabin next to the Mikkelson cabin on Lake Michigami. "Maybe we just miss Minnesota!"

"It's been a difficult time," said Abbie. She had long, thick curly hair which flowed freely around her pale face. "We have formed a wonderful community around us at the church. But we're starting to look ahead."

"It's kind of odd," said Sarah. "Everyone here is massed around one issue. We don't feel melded into a bigger picture the way we are in Minnesota. An extended family. Here, we've become 'professional lesbians'!" She laughed. "Not that it's a bad thing."

"I'll miss you if you move back," said Marty. Sarah and Abbie sometimes had her over for Christmas, a day when it was nice to be around

165

any family you might have. Sarah loved the holidays and made a lot out of decorating and having a big tree full of the ornaments she had collected over the years. Her manger scene had three wise women in it, instead of three wise men!

Sarah and Abbie let Marty talk about Doug, for which she felt grateful. Sarah explained how Abbie had confronted her about their growing love at a time when Sarah was about to make another commitment. "I am so glad she did!" Sarah had told Marty.

Abbie and Sarah were very close, both deeply into counseling and dealing with emotions. "Emotions aren't allowed in my family," Sarah said. "So everyone is full of opinions! And they need to be right! So they have trouble relating to each other." Marty's family saw Sarah's from a distance. She had no idea of their problems.

"Well we might not move for a couple of years," said Sarah, picking up little Gloria, who was sitting in the dirt, playing with gravel. "Everything takes a while. But, it's good to have plans." She put her nose in Gloria's soft neck. "You smell so nice, baby girl," she said. "Even when you're dirty!"

"Plans!" said Marty. She was a little shocked. Of course people needed to have plans, but at the moment she hadn't a one. "I have small plans," she said. "But no big ones."

Marty's plans involved staying where she was, working at Designers International, living in her spacious apartment on Russian Hill, practicing tai chi and being friends with Doug. It was all she could imagine at the moment. She had made more money than she needed that year and was wondering what to do with it. She knew one thing she did not want to do: she did not want to travel by herself any more. She had done enough of that.

After the picnic, the women wandered through the gardens and out toward a pond where ducks were being fed. Their feet clopped musically on a wooden bridge built across the pond. The sight of seagulls and ducks rising together and wheeling over them and then settling on the water was exhilarating, but Gloria was getting sleepy.

Abbie tucked Gloria into her stroller. Marty bid them goodbye. "I'm going to stay a little longer," she said, "walk through the Japanese tea garden before going home."

"Lovely to see you," said Sarah, hugging Marty. "We'll have you over soon!" They headed out into the tree-lined street toward their car.

The Japanese tea garden was a famous landmark, but when Marty had lived near it, she had come to love it intimately. She walked down all the well-known paths, noting that the iris was flowering at the edge of the stream. Huge, ugly orange carp floated in it. The garden had just had its centenary, had been made by the Hagiwara family. Though its tea house served thousands of people, the garden always looked wonderful, as it was meticulously manicured and tended.

Marty differentiated herself from Sarah as she walked. Sarah and Abbie were out in the world, confronting institutions, taking positions, working outwardly. They were of the world, held by the world's things, its realities, its Christmas ornaments, and the things they wanted for their daughter. Marty had the luxury of being a maverick, a Taoist and scholar warrior. Her feet were planted on the earth, rooted in a value system which involved life itself more than any resulting artifacts.

Marty sat down on a stool beside the long wooden counter under the light colored eaves of the tea house, looking out into the sun-filled air. A young girl in a blue kimono splashed with flowers came up to her and asked if she wanted tea and cookies.

The world did come to meet you when you were alone, Marty thought. A blackbird strutted along the counter that served as a table, a nearby guest batting at it. She tried to slow herself down, experience each sensation, smelling the hot jasmine tea as she poured it from its small ceramic pot, tasting the almond cookie, feeling the chill on her skin and looking out at the azalea, the people on the paths with bamboo railings, the high round moon bridge with children climbing on it. It all looked wonderful. It was reality, a kind of Zen reality as Marty had taught herself to see it. The thin skin of the world which perfectly expressed the depths beneath.

One of Marty's small plans was to take a calligraphy class. Diane, who was half-Japanese and had worked at Designers International, was entranced with the art of making letters with ink on white paper. In the East, as far back as Murasaki's Tale of Genji, the way someone wrote, the paper and the unique human handmade characters were as important as the idea in a poem. They were often messages between people. In the West, however, Diane said that people calligraphed texts that touched them, hardly ever their own thoughts. Marty liked the idea of writing her own poems. She had even heard a Korean use the term "writer" to mean calligrapher.

Diane took Marty to a meeting of the Friends of Calligraphy at which Brody Neuenschwander described his work on Peter Greenaway's movies. Marty had seen Prospero's Books, thought it highly stylized and un-involving. He was now working on another one based on The Pillow Book. In it, a book becomes a metaphor for a man. The body is a book. Is it created from the outside in or the inside out? How would a book speak? The images Neuenschwander projected were beautiful, as he talked of painting letters and words on skin, the sexual fetish of the woman character in the movie.

Calligraphy seemed to relate to tai chi for Marty. Choreographed tai chi movements cut out the space around them, perfectly, cleanly. Done well, they were always the same, simple, made with the whole body. Calligraphy too must be done from the dan-tien, the seat of one's power in the lower abdomen.

Marty drank her tea and chewed her almond cookies slowly. People streamed around her, changing seats, walking up the paths. It did not feel impersonal, however. It felt intimate to sit in the open air, looking out. Water trickled down over rocks in the garden in front, past a little carefully-clipped pine tree and a pink flowering azalea. Somehow, hordes of tourists could not overwhelm the lovely place.

Living on the Pacific Rim had begun to hit Marty very hard. Much of what she saw of the East made more sense than what she knew of the West. A friend of hers had become a student of the Urasenke Foundation, which sought to keep alive the tradition of Sen Rikyu, a famous 16th century tea master. She invited Marty to a tea ceremony. Everything about it was ritualized: the utensils, the artwork and flowers in the tea room reflecting the season, the movements of the participants, even the conversation, expertly led by the host. It was a supreme exercise in consciousness.

Marty had found the powdered green matcha tea delicious, but very intense. Recently after a ceremony she had felt her brains practically burning up! There was nothing she could do about it but wait until they settled down. Marty knew herself to be sensitive. Red wine and chocolate kept her from sleeping, and by this time she only allowed herself caffeine on rare occasions. She did not think she could become a tea student, though she loved the fact that all of life, the physical and the mindful, entered into a properly-done tea ceremony.

Leaning East was another way Marty was different from her cousin Sarah. Sarah still used the Christian language, adapting it to be more inclusive, praying to "Father/Mother God," for instance. Marty no longer thought in the Christian language. She had been pleased to find that John Blofeld, her favorite interpreter of Eastern thought, suggested that, for Taoists, "life itself, flowing in accordance with mysterious natural laws that operate in sweeping cycles of change, is charged with spiritual significance." Belief was hardly a necessity.

Tea drinking, in which one could come to taste "sunlight, wind and clouds," had long been a part of the Taoist Way, as pointed out by Blofeld. The Japanese had refined it into a ceremony. But in a humble way, as Marty sat surrounded by people she didn't know in a public garden in San Francisco, she could drink mindfully, consciously. At home too, she had ritualized her morning tea, green tea on weekdays, and the smoky black lapsang souchong on Sundays. It would have been nicer if Doug shared it, but that could not be helped.

In fact, Marty was becoming more relaxed about Doug. Partly because he did not seem to back off their relationship, though it complicated his life. He needed their talk as much as she did. She acted as if she was married, though she only got about 3.5% of his time, according to her calculations! If that was all she could have, she would make the most of it. She had finally realized, that, in the Sufi poet Rumi's words, "a man and a woman together always have a spiritual result." Marty did not want to sleep with anyone again until it was part of a whole, committed relationship.

Marty's generation had thought sex was simply a matter of health. Sex was a need. If one didn't have a regular sexual life, one was not living in one's body! By this time, even though she was older and felt her sexuality had been more awakened than ever during the brief time she spent with Doug, Marty felt sexuality was an expression, not a need. Realizing this was part of the difficult path she was walking. She had pledged herself that she would no longer casually sleep with anyone. She had taken the last blood test to make sure she was not HIV positive, she told herself.

Marty had been astounded to learn that Ted, with whom she had woken up at the Hyatt Regency one morning after a tai chi banquet, died of alcoholism in Colorado. He had gone very quickly, surprising his raft of friends. Half the town had apparently turned out for his funeral. Marty could not believe it. She had not known he was an alcoholic, had not seen the signs, though she ought to have with her experience. He was so attractive, charismatic, but also needy, she remembered.

Marty had not seen Ted after the night they spent together. They had talked on the phone, but Ted had not come back to the Bay Area for tai chi workshops. Abe said he had quit coming to tai chi when he could no longer hide the shakes. He died of a hemorrhage in his forties, having tried over and over to overcome his problem. It had sobered the whole tai chi community. Even Master Liu was a little less anxious to drink all night with his students, friends told Marty.

Marty finished her tea and left the tea garden, lost in thought, taking her two buses back home through the vibrant San Francisco streets.

On Monday she walked down the hill in the fog to work. That was reality too, the necessity of the ants who said as they passed each other, "bread and butter, bread and butter."

A big presentation was to happen at Designers International the following day for a prospective client. Richard, the youngest partner, was preparing for it. He had all of a sudden been inundated with projects. Any extra space in the office was given over to his work. The third floor had been trashed. Even the large conference room which was supposed to always be clean and available was covered with model bits and pieces of Styrofoam.

Richard was completing a master plan for the UCSF Life Sciences campus, which would take up a good part of the re-developed east side of the city. The plans and renderings were pinned on the wall. It was very exciting. Everyone loved working with Richard. But he was wrecked. When no one was available to go out and get him a sandwich, Marty did it herself. She handed him the sandwich; he took it, but he didn't even look up!

That day the architects all had deadlines, so Marty and Sebastian rushed around, moving models from one place to another, cleaning surfaces, throwing things out and stacking things so they looked neater. Sebastian was the office archivist, which wasn't very exciting. Red-haired and well-educated, he loved it when there was physical work to do.

The two of them went shopping for the dishes the office didn't have and, towards the end of the day Marty found herself, at Richard's urging, pulling the handicapped information signs off the building. They were much too big, he said. Richard, looking around at the newly clean office, said, "We should have done this long ago!" When Marty went home that evening, she could hardly walk up the hill!

The next day the prospective clients came for an hour in the morning, but then everything settled back into its usual chaos. Marty looked out of her office and saw Michelle's lovely white orchid glowing on her desk in the light. Michelle had been worrying how to care for it, as if it were a child or a pet. Sebastian, Michelle and Anna carried on loudly, teasing each other in the corridor. Michelle was always laughing.

Marty especially appreciated Anna, whom she had hired as a project secretary just out of college. Anna got excited about everything. Sometimes Marty had to talk her down. But she brought things out into the open, then dealt with them with total common sense. She had great rapport with the architects she worked with. She was just the kind of person Marty usually tried to hire.

Marty felt her staff was great at the moment, with the exception, of course, of Erica. Erica was older, worked for the two main principals. She was already there when Marty arrived. Marty tried to be friends with her, but Erica could be bitter, unhappy and often felt victimized. Marty remembered a week that Erica refused to speak to her, believing that Marty had done something to make the work environment toxic for her. Marty was surprised how painful it was. Erica told the younger staff that it was terrible to grow old, that she was miserable. She said, right out loud, "I hate this job, I hate my life, if I didn't believe in karma, I'd kill myself." It shocked Marty.

That morning Marty noticed that one of the photographs of projects in her office was missing. Richard must have hidden it when he took the prospective clients through, not wanting anyone to know Designers International did conservative law firms! In fact Designers International, according to Richard, didn't want to provide a product. The firm was particularly good at looking at the social aspects of their clients. They showed people how to get flexibility in an environment that wasn't static. In its campus work, the firm had gotten good at providing village environments. Many Silicon Valley companies lapped it right up.

Clients hired Designers International because they didn't want the same old thing. The word was out about the company. "Those guys are dangerous!" Marty found it exciting. She was also impressed to hear her boss Joe, uptight Confucian Chinese that he was, tell someone unequivocally, "We are the best design firm in the city!"

On Saturday that week, Marty did not want to get out of bed. But Ernesto had moved north and did not usually come down to teach tai chi any longer. Stan had taken over the class, but he was not able to be there. Marty had promised to go as senior student. She often found herself teaching new people lately, when the class was split so everyone could get the instruction they needed. Marty did not really like taking responsibility for the whole class. It scared her, though she did it when she had to. She took the bus, changed into her cotton tai chi clothes and flat velveteen Chinese shoes, and took the ancient elevator to the third floor of 50 Oak Street where class was now held in a room with big windows and a linoleum floor.

Marty had just clapped her hands for class to come to order, when who should appear but Anton and Sachiko! They traveled a lot, so didn't come often. Marty was thrilled. Anton and Sachiko took over, taking the corners of the grid of people in order to set the rhythm of slow set.

Marty was mesmerized by Anton's command of the group, by his lightness and the power of his energy. Many of the new people had never had him for a teacher. He emphasized different things than Stan did, always reminding students that each movement had a martial application. "Push from the back foot," he said. "Your opponent is in front of you. Don't turn too much. You must sit, or everything else will be wrong." Marty loved him as a teacher, though she did get much from Ernesto and Stan as well. She could see that Anton loved teaching too!

At lunch there were ten people around the table at Eliza's, the only place nearby Anton was willing to eat. He knew all the Chinese restaurants in the city and the status of their kitchens and chefs. Eliza's wasn't as authentic as some, but better than others. Marty was thrilled with the lotus root and pork soup. The lotus root tasted a little like a potato, though it was crisper.

Marty didn't talk much over lunch, mostly listening. Someone asked Cliff if he wanted to have children, but he said, "No, I want to keep doing tai chi." It was amazing. Even after studying for years, tai chi still had so much depth in it for so many of the students. Marty was impressed with the quality of all of these friendships, but also she was pleased that she had won the right to come and go, was not part of the integral tai chi group around Master Liu.

Marty loved Anton and Sachiko, who were inherently upper class, but had a great warmth to them nevertheless. These are the people, they seemed to say to themselves. Those who are willing to study tai chi. They had chosen to live in California, after all. Sachiko had come during high school, had lived with a Jewish family whom she was still close to. Marty thought she liked the freedom she had as a woman in the United States.

Evening calligraphy classes began in a room in the reclaimed Fort Mason on the shoreline below Russian Hill. Besides Marty, there were two other people she knew that Diane's enthusiasm had seduced into coming to the class. Marty brought a large tablet of thin art paper, black ink and a pen with a set of flat nibs. Kathy McNicholas, the teacher, asked what each of them was expecting from the class. She gave them sets of ruled guide lines to put beneath their paper for using with Italic letters and another for Roman capitals. She demonstrated how to make the fluid letters, dipping a pen into an ink bottle, and then set them to copying, practicing Roman capitals from a handout.

Marty could tell immediately that it would take years to make letters with any mastery. Endless repetition. Just as in tai chi. Every stroke reflected the hand that made it, its strength and its weakness. She did love the thickness of some strokes, the thinness of others. Strokes were made in an order Marty didn't anticipate. She practiced, remembering how she had sat in junior high school, writing her own name endlessly under the eyes of an English teacher.

After class, Marty was surprised to find herself climbing up the steep outdoor steps at Fort Mason almost as fast as Ken. At work the next day, Ken said, "I woke up tracing the letter strokes in my head!"

"Me too!" said Marty. "I see the letters with new eyes. You have to be so conscious! I can see the negative space as well as the positive."

"That's what art is about," said Ken. "Calligraphy feels like drawing, to me." He was an architect, but occupied himself with the office computers and networks.

As class progressed, Kathy showed them various handmade fonts. Marty loved uncial the best, a script of capital letters found in European manuscripts of the 4th to 8th centuries. Kathy got them to make little accordion books and also gave them a Shakespeare sonnet to prepare and calligraph onto a sheet of heavy paper. "If it turns out well you could frame it and hang it on your wall," she said.

Marty never had enough time to practice. She realized that she could not work full time, do tai chi so often, have a life and also do calligraphy. In tai chi people often said to each other that you could only do five things well in life. Marty enumerated her own five things: cooking, gardening, writing, tai chi and Doug. She had barely kept up with the calligraphy homework and she did not think she would take the next class.

But Marty did finish her sonnet. She loved the way it began. "So are you to my thoughts as food to life, or as sweet seasoned showers are to the ground" went the text. She took time with the letters, finding the rhythm. As in tai chi she took as much time as each movement needed. It's for Doug, she thought to herself. It was he who was the food of her thoughts.

18

Paul woke up in his sleeping bag in the back of the van on a cold September morning in the campground near the Minnesota Renaissance Festival. Marie was beside him, dark curling hair falling over her flushed, sleeping face, Archie at their feet. Around him, Paul could hear people moving about, talking, pans clanking as the artists and performers who transformed themselves into 16th century people during the day woke up in their campers and tents.

Paul was tired and the morning was crisp. He tucked his feather bag up around his neck and turned over on the comfy mat below him. He could smell the coffee someone was making nearby. A whiff of tobacco on the air also smelled good. They had driven down the night before after Paul's day of teaching. It was a little hard to do, but there were only a few more weeks of the fair. Marie had gotten them a gig singing and performing on one of the festival's many stages.

Paul felt Marie's arm slipping into his bag. Her kiss on the back of his neck gave him goosebumps. He turned to face her. "Did you sleep well, my love?" he asked. His own hair was a bit shaggier than usual, he thought, but he loved Marie's long dark hair.

Marie stretched. "Well enough," she said. She unzipped bag and went off to the restrooms, taking her soap and towels.

Paul had been worrying about her. Her energy was almost manic, so excited was she, and she seemed to have trouble resting. Paul also got out of his bag, putting on a sweatshirt and swinging his arms a bit to keep warm. He roughed up Archie, by way of good morning. The sun was just topping up over the trees to the east. Paul rustled up the granola and milk, and put out food and water for Archie. They would have coffee a little later at a makeshift vendor's booth in the campground. Archie would spend the day on a long leash in the shade of the car. It was humiliating, Paul knew, but he thought Archie would rather be with them, than left at home with a neighbor.

Marie dressed in a muslin peasant blouse, pulled tight at her waist by a black and lavender printed cotton bodice over a long muslin skirt. So pretty, thought Paul. He too wore a muslin peasant shirt with a jerkin over it, loose trousers and leather shoes. They didn't sing until the middle of the afternoon, so they used the mornings to practice and watch other artists.

The festival had been going on for a long time in the same place. It had many buildings and an entrance that looked like a castle. Once you were on the grounds, everyone strove to give paying visitors the feeling that they had stepped back into the time of Shakespeare, of Queen Elizabeth and her court. A few people dressed in rich velvets and doublets, accompanying the queen on her rounds. Trumpets signaled her approach. But most, like Paul and Marie, dressed as peasants and craftsmen, setting up booths and entertainments in the woods at the edges of the grounds.

Paul wasn't thrilled by the food, barbecued meats and sausages, big turkey drumsticks, corn on the cob, deep fried onions and shepherd's pie.

Plenty of ale and mead made with honey to drink. All manner of clothing, jewelry, ribbons, mirrors, pewter tankards, children's toys, lotions and potions, candles, soaps and leather ware were sold. In the afternoons there was jousting on a field with men on horseback dressed as knights, as well as dancing and juggling, music and theatre. A great deal of historical scholarship had gone into the alternative reality created for the fair. Many people made their living at this fair and traveled to others like it.

Paul was continually astonished at the depth of what people were doing. He loved the booth where paper was made from rags beaten to a pulp, treated with gelatin, pressed into flat paper on a big, flat press, and hung to dry. He also loved watching the falconers, a man and his wife dressed in leather jerkins, who had a Harris hawk, a falcon with its powerful beak and a great horned owl, its golden eyes pointed forward as its neck swiveled. The couple were very quiet and respectful of these great hunters, educating people as they explained what they were doing. They allowed Paul to look at the raptors up close, at the hoods and jesses attached to their legs.

Paul felt bad about the birds' captivity but he sensed complicity between the birds and their keepers. He hoped that they were allowed to hunt at times. The great tawny birds were beautiful. It took some courage, Paul thought, but also lots of patience. During their act, the couple flew the birds off leather gloves, long jesses trailing.

That morning Paul hung out with Rodney who made medieval instruments. Paul and Marie had researched and practiced their songs all summer, but Paul had an idea. He wanted to put a drum behind the slow ballad of "Lord Randall" which he and Marie sang as a duet. The song was a bit of a dirge, and Paul thought a drum would give it more rhythmic power. Rodney agreed to lend Paul one of the drums, which had a light, resonant sound.

Paul had never drummed before. He practiced, Rodney suggesting some licks. The drum had a light skin head stretched over wooden hoops that fitted together like embroidery hoops with a melodic sound that reverberated through its closed head. Rodney showed Paul the ancient method of playing a pipe with one hand, while the tabor, the drum, hung on one's shoulder and was hit with a stick in the other hand. Paul didn't want to try that, but he did want to get some varied drumbeats.

Medieval music all had strong rhythms, meant for dancing, Paul thought. Rodney had made many drums of different kinds. He told Paul about a wooden box with a sound hole which you sat on and drummed with your hands, a cajon. "It comes out of South America," Rodney said. "I can't bring them here, into the 16th century. But they're very simple. Anyone can drum."

Paul met Marie for a snack at lunchtime to get ready for their set. She came walking through the crowds with a little crown of pink roses and colored ribbons on her dark curls. Paul showed her the drum he had borrowed and explained what he planned. "Lord Randall" would be a capella, a duet between them, with the resonant drum behind it.

The paths thronged with people, the dust they raised visible on the sunny day. Sunlight played through the trees, as it must have in medieval times. They passed the group of male Morris dancers who were performing in a circle, bells on their legs. A tableau of peasants lounging around a table, tankards and mounds of food in front of them, depicted the seven deadly sins, one pointing dramatically at his codpiece. Lust, gluttony, greed, pride, sloth, wrath, envy. One man raised a tankard sleepily, shouting, "Huzzah!" and fell back on the table, as if asleep.

"My sin is probably envy," said Marie as they passed.

"I've been surprised at how Midwesterners become positively bawdy in this setting!" said Paul. Women allowed their breasts to pop boldly out of their bodices, men were suggestive and swore by "God's blood," "God's bodkins" and other parts of His anatomy.

"Yes," Marie smiled. "I think I can sing my song today." Marie had found one early song which shocked both her and Paul. Whether she sang it or not depended on how bold and mischievous she felt that day. They found their stage and stood in the space behind it, hidden by little wooden wings, preparing themselves and their instruments.

"You look beautiful," Paul told Marie. Light shown through the trees on her face.

They took the stage. A few people sat on benches below them, and others stood at the back, tentative, trying to decide whether they wanted to stay.

Without preamble, they sang "Fair Phyllis," an a capella duet with lots of calling back and forth. It actually had four voices, but they had adapted it. It was difficult to sing. It seemed Fair Phyllis, a shepherdess, had wandered off. Her lover went looking for her, up and down, up and down, and when he found her "they fell a-kissing." Marie was all joy. She effervesced and shimmered, Paul being the solid background.

Marie explained, "This is one of our happiest songs. A madrigal, or polyphonic motet from the 16th century. It's so short, I want to sing it again!" she said. Paul tried to throw his voice out into the audience as they

176

sang the difficult triple and double beats, "up and down, up and down," as the shepherdess' lover went looking for her.

The morbid "Lord Randall" in which a young man is poisoned by his lover did sound better propelled along by the drum. Paul was pleased, though they hadn't had much time to practice.

Paul sang "Wild Rover," an old Irish drinking song with a guitar accompaniment and Marie on a tambourine. They also had a version of "Scarborough Faire" and a Scottish song called "Wind and Rain," which was also not very cheerful. Most of the songs they had found were dour, Paul thought. They didn't have many songs, since they were trying to be authentic to the period.

Marie ended with the odd song she had found sung by a young maiden. "A sweet-scented courtier did give me a kiss, And promised me mountains if I would be his, But I'll not believe him, for it is too true, Courtiers promise much more than they do." The chorus followed. "My thing is my own," Marie sang, deadpan, "and I keep it so still. Other young lasses may do what they will." Paul stood beside her, innocently strumming his guitar as she continued to sing the other verses.

The faces below them laughed, appreciating the way the young girl spoke so openly of her sexuality.

They closed with the short powerful song someone had made of a fragmentary poem: "O Western wind when wilt thou blow, that the small rain down can rain. Christ, if my love were in my arms, and I in my bed again," singing it twice, once just Paul intoning the dark cadence, and then the two of them in harmony, Paul beating his drum softly.

Paul and Marie bowed in response to the applause, holding their hands and instruments up. They backed off stage, where Paul gave Marie a kiss. "Up and down, up and down," he sang to her.

Marie laughed. "Time for a little something?" she said.

"Yes," said Paul. "We need to wet our whistles! Meet you at the grass hummock, okay?" He stopped to drop off the drum he had borrowed with Rodney while Marie went to an alehouse to get them each a glass of mead.

The hummock of grass at the edge of the Faire where they often rested was set a little away off from the hubbub. Paul fell back on the grass, looking up at the blue sky. Singing was exhilarating, but then he was tired. They had nothing to worry about any more that day. Their next set would be tomorrow.

Marie put down the glass tankards of golden liquid on the grass and took her little crown of paper flowers and ribbons off. The mead was not sweet, but crisp, light and dry as a bone. Paul leaned on one arm, drinking. The sun was warm where it shone on them.

"Happy?" Paul asked, looking into Marie's rosy face.

"Oh, yes," said Marie. "I love the feeling. Giving people something."

"Yes," said Paul. In the distance they could hear trumpets, announcing the royal party walking through the shire.

"I can't help it. It makes me think of Diana," said Marie.

Only a couple of weeks ago, when Paul and Marie were settling back into their house in Ely for the winter, Marie had called Paul to tell him Princess Diana of England had been killed in a car crash. Paul had had no idea how much Marie felt for the princess. Marie watched hours of the television coverage.

Early in the morning, the first weekend of the fair, Marie had dragged Paul out to watch a tiny portable television one of the performers had put just outside his camper. People had gathered around it. On the tiny screen, replayed footage of Diana's long funeral cortege passed Buckingham Palace on its way to Westminster Abbey. Diana's sons and her ex-husband Charles walked behind her coffin, the Windsors all coming out to pay their respects.

"So young," said Paul. Diana was a year younger than Paul's sister Hanna.

"And Mother Teresa," said Marie. "The two of them seem linked in some way." Mother Teresa had died the day before Diana's funeral.

Paul lay back on the grass, Marie's head on his arm, dozing like a 16th century shepherd, and thinking about the summer. They had spent it at the lake, though Mother had been gone for a year. They had again rented out their Ely house to an outdoorsman who used it as a fishing camp, a jumping off place for the Boundary Waters. The rent paid their mortgage and even a little extra for themselves.

The summer had been damp and mosquitoy. Rain hung around late into the summer. But Hanna and her partner Faith had come for a vacation, and so had Marty and Kristen's family. Ellie and her daughters came occasionally on the weekend. Line had not come that summer, as she and Stephen were on their way to Edinburgh once more. Grace's kids, now ranging in age from 12 to two, had enjoyed the place the most.

One day Ellie passed three crisp $100 bills to each of the siblings, the last remnants of Mother's bank account. They laughed and explained what they would do with the cash which felt like a lot to each of them. Kristen and Mike wanted it for a satellite dish, Marty wanted a Scandinavian teak coffee table for her apartment, and Hanna said she would buy a beautiful, purebred dog. Paul planned to buy books with his money, and a little something for Marie. In fact he was watching her, to see what she liked from the crafts displayed at the Renaissance Faire.

Mother and Dad's real legacy was the cabin, and there was much talk about what was to become of it. It didn't seem that money was the biggest problem, in the end. Decision-making in a consortium was the sticking point. No one wanted to share decision-making with Mike, Kristen's husband. He had put the dock out one year with a broken piece on it, cobbling it together. Bruce, Ellie's husband, didn't like the discomfort and crowdedness of the lake cabin. Of the local families, it was really up to Paul.

Paul had found a crack in the cement foundation at the back of the cabin, where it was built into the ground. Weather and winters had built up the pressure behind the foundation, which had not been anticipated. Paul calculated that the cabin was almost 40 years old. He thought that, even if they did nothing, if they just let the cabin molder into the ground, it was still an amazing legacy and family investment. Lakeshore property was hardly even available in Minnesota any longer, and then it was expensive.

Uncle David's log cabin next to the Mikkelson cabin was still beautiful and sturdy. It had a clear purpose as a summer place. The Lande cabin down the lake by the creek, where the Mikkelsons had stayed in the early years, was probably 50 years old. Decrepit but standing, it might not have a foundation below ground. The Mikkelson cabin, as it stood, along with the unfinished craft barn and the simple beach house, had gone through many iterations of Dad's ideas. All of them were dependent upon his presence.

Paul thought that what was needed was some serious collective thinking about the cabin. He did not like the staircase which had been built between the basement and the upper floor. It was an afterthought and took up space with an ugly protective railing. The basement was hardly used any more, anyway. It was impossible to keep it dry enough. Paul and Ellie agreed that they did not want to put a new roof on the place as long as the foundation was buckling, but they had patched it.

New, winterized cabins had been built recently along the lake, and a few people were taking up permanent residence. Paul knew that would be a possibility for him, but there was no work for him nearby, and he was a long ways from retirement. He also didn't want to condemn Marie to a life in a makeshift house, far from people and community. He probably would have liked it himself.

Indeed, one of the highlights of the summer had been camping by himself for a few days deep in the woods, and then coming back during a terrific thunderstorm. He had gone swimming in the lake and felt the electricity crackling in the air and surging through his body, which was especially receptive after spending time alone. He had loved watching the storm roll across the lake at him, and the feeling of freedom that he didn't need to take shelter. He just let it roll over him. He capped it off by standing under the eve spout and letting the rainwater from the storm pour over his head in a delicious cold shower. He had gone inside, cooked up a package of mushrooms in butter and ate them with a glass of white wine.

Paul rolled over on the grass, looking at Marie. The cold was seeping up through the ground in the late afternoon and the shadows of the trees lengthened. "Come on," he said. "Let's go find some dinner." After their set on Sunday, they drove home to Ely.

Monday afternoon found Paul in the newly-designated high school computer lab, for which he and the other science and math teachers were now responsible. President Clinton had made over $2 billion in grants available through the Technology Literacy Challenge Fund and no self-respecting high school had missed out, Ely Memorial High School among them. The big push was to get students connected to the outside world, to the World Wide Web for purposes of research and learning.

It was early in the year and Paul was installing software and faster modems. The little Apple farm they had had thanks to Steve Jobs now felt quaint, the little box computers underpowered and connectable only to each other. What people wanted now was speed and disk space as bigger applications, with more features were developed every year.

Only one other student sat in the room. Most were either at football practice, or band practice, or had already gone home.

"What are you doing there, Steve?" Paul asked.

"Oh, I'm on a Star Wars forum," said Steve, a nerdy looking senior whom Paul suspected knew a lot about both hardware and software. "They're discussing whether George Lucas should have changed the original film for this year's re-release."

"Oh?" asked Paul.

"Mostly people don't like how it now looks as though Han Solo didn't shoot first against Greedo in the bar," said Steve.

Paul smiled. Steve acted as if Paul of course knew exactly what he was talking about! Paul did know, generally, who Han Solo was, having seen the blockbuster movie twenty years ago. But he knew nothing of the changes. "Why did Lucas change it?"

"He didn't want people to think Han Solo was a cold-blooded killer," said Steve patiently. "But other people say that then his becoming a hero later doesn't mean as much."

Paul scratched his head. "What do you think?" he asked.

"Oh," said Steve, "I don't care. I was just reading about it."

"Sounds more like a literature problem than a scientific one," Paul said, going back to his work. If this was what students were using the Web for, it did not seem to him that innovation and productivity were going to be served!

The new computer lab was in the Industrial Arts building of the high school complex, which had been erected, along with the school itself, in the 1920's as a memorial to Ely's World War I losses. The buildings were spacious and still serviceable for the almost 200 kids in grades 9 to 12, with big windows, wide marble staircases and high ceilings. Paul thought it was the perfect building for a high school.

It was the perfect size for a high school too. Paul loved the kids, several big families of whom passed through his classes. Each had distinct personalities, but also a familiar cast to them which harkened back to their brothers and sisters. They were the mining families who had been there forever. The political divide which separated these families from those they called the 'packsackers,' or environmentalists, was visible even in the high school, however. Paul, who was generally on the side of the wilderness protectors, tried to find the common ground between them, but it wasn't easy.

The relentless march of the school year bothered Paul, with each of the events marked off and celebrated exactly as they had been year after year. Football games, homecoming, classes, tests, semesters giving way to the Thanksgiving and Christmas holidays. Paul sometimes thought the year had been designed so no one had very long to think about it!

Homecoming was coming up, impossible for the teachers to avoid. The whole town took part. One of the teachers who was avid about football described it to Paul as an intellectual game. But only one person, the quarterback, got to play at this high level. Paul hated to see the kids crashing into each other and getting bunged up.

But they were out there at it this very afternoon, the Timberwolves drilling and throwing themselves at each other, practicing in the chilly evening air. Paul could hear the thwack of their pads and helmets as he walked past the football field home.

Archie was, as always, faithful and glad to see Paul. "Good dog," said Paul. "We'll w-a-l-k around the lake tonight, I promise," he told Archie, who knew the word 'walk.' Paul could not use it until he was ready to go.

Marie brought home meat loaf from her delicatessen, putting it into the oven to warm with some baked potatoes. She was working less and less, but liked organizing her young helpers. And she did feel she was offering a valuable service to the town, making delicious soups, breads and other things for people who didn't have time to cook.

After supper Paul and Archie walked out around what was now called the Trezona Trail around Miner's Lake. The air didn't seem quite as cold as it should have been on an October night, Paul thought. The sky was too overcast to see much, humidity hanging in the air. Archie nosed about in the bushes along the trail, scaring up a squirrel and chasing it. Archie had no chance against a squirrel. He just liked tracking it. Like Paul.

Paul had been hearing about the El Niño effect which had probably helped bring about the warm wet summer, and might lead to a mild winter. It was an actual warming of the Pacific Ocean, noticed by South American fisherman and named, because it happened around Christmas, for the Christ Child. Abnormally warm water in the Pacific changed the path of the jet stream, the atmospheric current high in the sky. A mild winter would be nice, Paul thought.

Paul was pleased with the place he had found for himself in the community. He liked being able to choose his persona, hide out and think. Being the pastor's kid in small towns had been tough. It still influenced Paul's demeanor all these years later. Since Mother's death, Paul found himself thinking about these things more and more.

Paul had been interested in Marty's description of what she called her tai chi practice. 'Practice' was a good description of how he felt about Christianity, these days. Choir and church attendance contributed to Paul's feeling that the school year galloped along, but he and Marie did not shirk. Singing was life and health.

Marty had explained that the Christian idea that God sent his only Son to become a human exemplar and save people through his death in only one location in the world was something she could not personally confess. Paul had heard it called 'the scandal of the particular.' Paul was happy to live with the question. The Gospel was beautiful because it extended this mystery, confounded normal human expectation. Turning human logic on its head, God had allowed himself to take on humanity's weakness.

But we really don't understand much at all, Paul thought. God acted in Jesus, the Christ Child, reaching out to us and showing us his love. The question was, how many other times had He done this throughout history. To me, Paul thought, He does it all the time. We can't figure these things out and we don't need to.

Paul remembered Line's problem with Mother telling her animals didn't have souls. That was a mystery too. Here he was, walking along with Archie, as much in tune with him as he was with any human. And evolutionary science was pretty certain by this time that some of the great apes were humans' nearest relatives. That growing a brain whose chief feature was the understanding and making of language hadn't happened over night, but was an exemplar of the mystery of becoming the human species.

Paul turned around, wondering how long it would take Archie to see that he had done so. He was the leader of the pack. It was Archie's duty to follow him. And sure enough, here came Archie tearing past him, nosing in the bushes.

Little pools of light penetrated the thick darkness. Lamps had been placed along the trail which were probably what had given it a name with a capital letter. Humans, Paul thought sardonically. Mapping and naming, pointing and de-mystifying. The Native Americans had certainly named things, though their knowledge was passed on verbally. They didn't mind mystery. And they didn't need to leave tracks and traces. Paul was conflicted. A science teacher, he was committed to truth. But he was also perfectly happy with the unknown.

At home, the porch light was on. A porch light, thought Paul, as he opened the door and let Archie in. 'All ye know of truth, and all ye need to know.' Who said that, Paul wondered. He had no idea.

19

Line reached for the tea canister on the shelf at Kerry's father's cottage at the edge of Edinburgh early on a dark morning in February. Gusts of wind blew the rain against the windows. A light outdoors shone on the rivulets as they ran down the glass. Stephen would come in a moment, and they would breakfast together before he left for the university.

I'm measuring my life in cups of tea, thought Line. Red rose tea. She put two teabags in the ceramic pot and poured in the hot water. Where was Kerry this morning, she wondered. Having tea somewhere in Bosnia at the field station where she was working with Doctors Without Borders? Line did not think she would be very comfortable.

When Stephen planned their second trip to Edinburgh, Line said she did not want to live in an apartment again. She wanted a bit of garden of her own to tend. She wrote to her friend Kerry and asked her to look around for a small rental house with a garden for the duration of Stephen's two-year lectureship.

Kerry responded immediately, asking Line and Stephen to live in her father's cottage, as he was in ill health. Line knew the place. Kerry herself lived in a small, separate addition and wanted the extra help. Line approved of the idea, but by the time she and Stephen arrived, Mr. McLachlan had died. Stephen and Line had the cottage to themselves, as well as his garden, which had been his pride. It was full of vegetables and wonderful flowers.

Line harvested what she could when she arrived, making beetroot and cucumber pickles, and sauerkraut for the winter with Kerry's help. She was now planning next summer's garden. Kerry herself, adventurous and feeling free since her father's death, had joined Doctors Without Borders and been sent to help in the endless conflicts in Bosnia and Serbia. Kerry was delighted that Stephen and Line could watch over her home.

It was an odd situation for Line. She sometimes thought of her own home as 'Poppa's,' but it wasn't really. It was equally hers and Stephen's, and she had set up the kitchen for her own convenience. This one was not. It was quaint, rustic and authentic. A few copper pans hung on the walls and dishes were exposed on an old wooden cupboard. Every time she wanted to use a dish, Line felt she should wash it first to get the dust off.

The stove was clean and serviceable, the sink had a cotton curtain hiding the trash bins below it. A white painted table was big enough for two to eat on, and flower patterned curtains hung at the windows. It looked to Line like a kitchen from 1950's America. She was happy to have a kitchen, and a garden, but it was odd to work in a place which did not belong to her, one she couldn't change.

Line put out the plates, waiting until Stephen came to dish the hot oatmeal and put in the toast. The fresh oranges she had cut into pieces looked very bright on the table under the electric light. At the windows, the sky was dark, the rain streaking down.

"Tea, my love?" asked Line when Stephen came into the room, wearing his coat and muffler against the chill. Line too wore a heavy sweater over her pajamas.

Stephen nodded. He looked pensive, as usual.

"It's really pouring out there," said Line. The telly had reported that the jet stream would bring rain for the next week. "How are your classes going?"

Stephen laughed. "All they want to talk about is Monica Lewinsky!" he said. "And if not her, they want to talk about whether Jefferson kept a slave as a concubine. My classes are not very sophisticated!" He was teaching American history, while doing his own research for a biography of John Smith, a Scottish MP who had just missed becoming Prime Minister of England when he died.

"But what is there to say about Monica Lewinsky?" asked Line. Monica's friend had tape recorded a discussion about her affair with President Clinton and turned it over to the investigator in an Arkansas land use case against the Clintons. The investigator promptly broadened the case to include misconduct and possible perjury by the President. When Line and Stephen had talked to Poppa and Ivy on the phone the previous weekend, Poppa said, "It's embarrassing to have a president with his pants down all the time!"

"Very little to say," said Stephen. "Unless you are in a roomful of sniggering young adults!" He spooned brown sugar and put milk on his oatmeal. "But I do think it's a sad thing to ruin what might have been a successful presidency with a sex scandal!"

"And what about Jefferson?" asked Line.

"You remember I told you about that black woman historian last year who reviewed the controversy over whether Jefferson lived with Sally Hemings. She did it like a lawyer reviewing evidence in a case, analyzing all the writings and notes and interviews she could find. The Jefferson family has always denied that Jefferson fathered Sally Hemings' children, but this book was so thorough it opened up the question again."

"And what do you think?" asked Line.

"I think Jefferson did," said Stephen. "He never said a thing about his involvement with Hemings, but he was a deeply interesting guy, full of conflicts and paradoxes. Probably too smart to talk about it. Gordon-Reed points out that historians ignored the black testimony, while, if you pay attention, it makes perfect sense."

"Hmmm," said Line. "I'd like to know more."

"Yeah," said Stephen. "You couldn't really expect Jefferson, a bachelor, to be alone all that time, I guess."

"People are only human," said Line. She buttered her toast, smiling. "I'm glad I just have my seed catalog order to worry about! But I do feel a little odd doing it without Kerry."

Stephen stood up. "My dearest," he said. "Maybe there will be a letter from her. I'd like to know how things are going with her too."

"Or any of the kids," said Line. She had to admit that she had gotten to the point of watching for the mailman. So many people she loved were far away and she felt a bit housebound during the dark, cold days. "I hope you don't mind if I turn up the heater," she said. "Though I do feel it's extravagant when I'm the only person here."

"Don't worry about it," said Stephen. "Just take care of yourself." He gave Line a peck on the cheek, put on his galoshes and headed out to drive Kerry's tiny car to the university. It was not a day for riding a bicycle in the wind and rain.

Line put her feet in their heavy woolen socks up on the chair Stephen had left and poured another cup of tea. It was kind of nice, having no one to worry about until she made dinner in the evening. She got out her pile of seed catalogs with the colorful photos of flowers and vegetables in them. She did feel she had gotten stuck in someone else's life.

Time was rather odd, on a dark, dank day too. In California time never felt empty. Line had stuffed it with relationships and responsibilities, large and small. In Edinburgh, Line had to make the most of all of them, even going to the grocery store. Oh well, she thought. She did have things to look forward to.

The Winter Olympics was on, for instance. Line loved watching the interviews with the young sports people competing in Japan, especially the rivalry between two young figure skaters, Michelle Kwan and Tara

Lipinsky. Both from the United States, Kwan had been a star for a while, but the 15-year-old Lipinsky was competing hard, with a smile that seemed to take up her whole face!

Then there was the mail, and the Daphne Du Maurier book she had found on Kerry's shelf about an adventurous woman who joins a group of French pirates. It wasn't hard to imagine Kerry loving that one! On the weekend Stephen and Line would go to Glasgow. Stephen wanted to see where John Smith grew up and went to school. The Glaswegians were supposed to be more Scottish than the cosmopolitan Edinburgh residents. In fact, it was said that it was hard to find a native on the streets of Edinburgh.

Stephen and Line had been to Glasgow in the fall, to a football match when Scotland qualified for the coming World Cup. Line could not now think of that city without remembering the afternoon in Celtic Park with 50,000 people singing "Walk on, walk on, with hope in your heart, and you'll never walk alone." Incredibly moving. Line remembered that she and Marty had sung it walking home from high school.

Kerry's father had been Glaswegian. He had lost an eye in World War II and came home to live quietly with his wife and work as an accountant. Line did not know much more about him, though she had looked through the photograph albums. Kerry was a post-war baby, the only daughter. She was as thin as a stick and, like Line, interested in alternative health care, studying acupuncture and massage. But she also loved traveling, using her parents' home as her base.

Line cleaned up the kitchen, put on a pair of Kerry's old Wellingtons and a macintosh and went out in the rain. The birds flitted around the feeders, even in the wet, which was now more like mist; not so heavy. She went up the walk to the little shed which was glassed-in on the south side to catch any winter sun. The seedlings she was putting out for the summer were arrayed in tiny pots and flats, which covered the surface under the paned windows. The little sprigs of leaves in the damp dirt looked brave and hopeful.

In Scotland, Line did not have to worry about drought! In California too, she knew that El Niño had brought many storms that winter, filling the reservoirs and saturating the dry earth. Ivy had complained about it on the phone: "My feet are always wet!" But that was because Californians didn't buy Wellingtons, didn't expect storms.

Hands in the dirt, separating plants that were too close and tamping the dirt around others, Line thought that people were really just like plants. Marty had told her that in tai chi they imagined energy bubbling up from the earth through the feet, and moving up into the body. Carolyn Myss, on tapes Line had been listening to, described energy coming in through the top of the head and dropping down to the various chakras in the body, many volts of electricity.

The two ways of visualizing energy showed Line that, like plants, people get their energy from earth and sky. People needed their roots to be deep in the earth, and to have the sun and rain pour down on them. It is incredible, she thought. Each person can be connected to the Source themselves, flowering and blooming where they were planted. People needed the thick fabric of community laid across the earth, family, friends and others. But each of us stands upright by ourselves, Line thought, like flowers or trees.

It was something Line needed to remember. For many, many years, she had based her actions on the needs of her children. Christy, who had bitten deep into Minnesota Democratic politics, was working with Paul Wellstone to get money for a presidential run. Heather was probably enjoying summer and harvest time in Chile at her new husband's winery. Fern had spent the Christmas holidays with them, though it was colder in Edinburgh than on Menorca, where she was working on an archeological dig and school. And Ivy was in school in Santa Cruz that spring, arriving soon for a vacation during the long days of the Scottish summer. Ivy was less certain than any of the others about what she wanted to do with an art degree. Line was glad this youngest daughter remained close.

Nevertheless, Line thought that she must find her own Source. She was happy, had been very lucky to have a husband who loved her and loved their far-flung kids. Was this the bloom that was expected of her, she wondered? Was she giving enough, doing enough good in the world? It was hard to know. And who could tell her? Perhaps she could only tell herself whether she was becoming the flower she expected to be. She had hardly ever spent much time alone. Now was the time, she thought.

Line also felt well-based in family. Mother and Dad's legacy was one of health and happiness, though they had both died younger than they should have. Paul and Ellie had sent Line a document for her to sign which established a Mikkelson Family Trust for the sake of the cabin. It could never be encumbered or sold, but would remain on the lake, to be used by whichever of the Mikkelson siblings and their children wanted. Maintenance fees would be shared. Line thought that it was possible Christy might want to spend more time there, if the others didn't. He might have children himself one day. Line thought it was a wonderful idea.

Mother and Dad now were visible only in Line's siblings. Paul was more and more like Dad, Line thought. Perhaps because she didn't get to see much of him. Ellie was more like Mother, though perhaps more well-off. Kristen also retained the Midwestern stamp, while Line herself, Marty and Hanna were far afield. Line was always inviting her siblings to come, either to Scotland or to California, but at this point, most seemed to be absorbed by their own lives.

And then there was Poppa, Poppa their benefactor, who grew older but was still healthy. He and his red Acura Legend were seen all over Santa Cruz. He had found a student couple to live with him and Ivy when Line and Stephen left, to help with cleaning and cooking for a reduced rent. The woman was pregnant and would have her baby in Line's house that summer.

The world just rolled right along, Line thought. You had to have your feet deep in the ground not to get uprooted or washed out. Mother and Dad had provided good soil for their kids, and Line felt that she and Stephen had done the same. Their kids were confident enough to follow their dreams, though Line was a bit rueful to see how far away their dreams carried them.

The mail, which fell through a slot in the front door, did bring letters. Line swept them up, flipping through them. There was one from Kerry and one from Fern! Line made herself a cup of tea and settled down with a shortbread and her letters. She opened the blue aerogram from her daughter carefully, slipping her finger under the seal. Fern's own hands had written these words with a pen. One of the words was obscured by a water mark. Perhaps Fern also had a cup of tea while she wrote?

"Sit yourself down, Mama and Papa," she wrote dramatically. "This is me, the real me on a wintry night, with nothing to do but write to you."

Fern had never said so, but Line inferred that she was involved with the Spanish archaeologist who ran the school. Line had met him and could see the attraction. Fern was among the first students he worked with on Menorca and she had now been involved in this complex dig for several years. Line felt sad about it. Fern deserved someone of her own. But Fern was also ferocious about her work.

Sanisera was the civilian community on the north side of Menora which grew up next to a Roman military camp at Sanitja, in a natural port. The Romans had colonized the island in the first century B.C., as it was becoming infested with pirates. When Rome fell, it continued to be used. Fern had chosen ceramics as her specialty, and archeologists were finding amphorae from many locations and times, as well as other lamps and ceramic figures. Many were found in the sea.

Like her father, Fern did not display a lot of emotion about people. She had stumbled into a place where there was a lot of work to be done, on a sunny island off Spain. Line hoped the best for Fern, that the education she was getting was worth it. Stephen was pleased that she was so committed. Her work would surely hold up well on a professional resume.

Fern wrote that the Tremontana, the north wind, had been strong in February and the island was especially quiet. The island is a biosphere reserve designated by UNESCO, she said, and people were quite ecologically aware. When a winter storm came through, the archaeologists retreated to their offices and spent time drawing, measuring, and cataloging their finds. "This place is so rich," Fern wrote. "Remains layered for 2000 years, and abandoned. We've found a basilica as well as a necropolis. You can imagine that the bone people are thrilled!"

Fern had loved being in Scotland at Christmas and couldn't wait for Ivy's arrival. "I hope she comes to see me," she said. "It is such a beautiful place! So many great people!" Line shook her head in fondness for her intense daughter, happy Fern had found a place and a work that meant so much to her.

Kerry's letter, written on a piece of plain white paper, was much less sanguine. She wrote that the Albanian rebels known as the Kosovo Liberation Army were fighting in the Drenica valley, and the Serbs had massacred a number of women and children in retaliation. This had been in the news, as Line well knew. The long-standing ethnic strife, mostly based along religious lines, had simply not abated with the recent Dayton accords which ended the Bosnian war.

Kerry was based in Bosnia, just over the border from Serbia, in Sarajevo where a family medical program trained doctors and nurses, and provided care to the gypsy population. They were hoping to turn the operation over to the local population soon. Kerry had not been there long, and was on the administrative side of things in the now quiet city. "I see lots of shell shock," she wrote. "And yesterday, this lovely family of Rom made me think of you. Stoic, silent kids. One of them, age 10, had lost his hand. The mother was pregnant."

Line put away the letters carefully. She stood up and there it was, a flash of heat washing through her body. She thought momentarily of the little tube of Progesterone she had to get her through menopause. But really, she decided, it was nothing. The heat dissipated slowly as she washed up. All the hype about menopause had frightened her, but in the end she hardly noticed it. She did not mind that her periods no longer came! It made things simpler.

On the weekend, Line and Stephen drove over to Glasgow. Stephen had been following John Smith when he and Line were first in Scotland, and had been saddened by his death from a heart attack. Smith's slow but steady reforms were welcome, though Tony Blair, the current prime minister for Labour had chafed under his leadership, thinking them too slow.

Stephen wanted to visit Glasgow University, which Smith had attended after a childhood in the Highlands. Stephen's forte was contemporary biography. He and his publisher also thought that a thorough biography of Smith would help Americans understand the British government and its rich heritage. Line was tagging along. She was always ready for new places and people.

But when Line saw the large collection of imposing Gothic stone buildings Stephen was proposing to visit, she balked. It was raining, or she would have just walked around. But who knew how long Stephen would be. "I saw a big glasshouse nearby, I think," she said. "Could you drop me off there?"

Line asked a passing stranger, who said, "The Botanical Garden is just over there, you can't miss it." The large white-painted glasshouse looked very inviting, and searching for an entrance, Line saw a tea room. "There," she said to Stephen. "Perfect. You can find me there. How long do you think you will need?"

They agreed to meet in a couple of hours at the tea room and Line hopped out of the car, free to wander under the Victorian painted gingerbread and glass. The air was warm and humid inside for the sake of the tropical and carnivorous plants, very pleasant. Inevitably, when she looked at the succulents, Line thought of California, of the large outdoor cactus garden in the arboretum in San Francisco.

At the tea room, Line ordered a cup of tea and a scone. It was rather empty, but an older woman, who heard Line's American accent, came over to sit down with her.

"Why have you come to our fair city on this rainy day?" the woman asked, arranging herself on a chair with difficulty and putting her two canes down beside her. She had a pink, wrinkled face, surrounded by white curls under an upturned green bowl-shaped hat.

Line smiled. Listening carefully, she understood the accent. "I'm from California," she said. "Sunny California! But my husband is lecturing in Edinburgh. We just came over for the day."

"Ah, California," said the lady, nodding. "I've never been. But I've been to Italy. They say it is similar, though without the history."

"Oh yes," said Line. "We love Italy. But you have lovely gardens here. And never a lack of water! California droughts can be awful." She was thinking about how many times in her life she had sat down by strangers, or they had come up to her. How interesting they were.

"I dare say," said the woman.

"My husband is writing about John Smith," Line said, expanding into her American act. "He was beloved here, wasn't he?"

"Seems like yesterday," said the older woman. "You never saw such a funeral. I went over to Edinburgh for it, Cluny Parish Church. He's buried on Iona with all the Scottish kings." She shook her head sadly. "Such a loss."

"Well now you have Tony Blair," said Line.

The old woman sniffed. "Could have been so much better. We trusted John."

"Did you know him?" asked Line. The lady must be in her 80's or 90's, she thought.

"I've seen him speak," she said. "And I taught his wife at Hutcheson Girls Grammar, just down the road. Elizabeth. Now there's a girl! They just made her a Baroness! Out of Gilmorehill, right here in Glasgow. She was the smartest of my girls. I've kept my eye on her."

"Does she live here now?" asked Line, a little awed at the woman's experience.

"Edinburgh," said the older woman. "Runs the Fringe Festival, I believe. She could speak like anyone. No fear. And her daughters! Three beautiful daughters."

"Ah yes," said Line. "It's sad they lost their dad. I have three wonderful daughters myself. And one son. They are all far away, though. Living their lives."

"California is a big place," said the woman. "I don't think I'll get there. My knees are gone." She indicated her knobby legs under a flowered skirt. "But I still need to get out of the house. I like meeting people."

"I'm so happy to talk to you!" said Line. "I'll tell my husband that you taught John Smith's wife as a child!"

"Just after the war," said the woman, shaking her head. "Ah, that was a difficult time. We were all a little hungry, with the rationing. But proud. Proud of standing up to the Germans. And it doesn't hurt to be hungry sometimes. I don't think anyone is hungry here any more."

"I hope not," said Line, though she knew more than she let on. Ivy's experience a few years ago with kids on welfare had taught her that the food people ate wasn't always the best. You could see it in their bodies, big and pasty, like the chips they lived on. "It's nice to meet a teacher," she said. "Education is so important."

The old lady stood up creakily and put out her hand. "Yes!" she said. "You young people must carry the torch! Keep it burning!" She looked around. "My son is going to pick me up. I think I better go out to the road. So nice to meet you!" She picked up her two canes and walked toward the door. Line could see her in the entry way, struggling to pull the hood of her macintosh up over her hat. Line wanted to go out and help her, but she knew better.

Stephen picked Line up a little later in Kerry's tiny car. When she told Stephen about meeting the lady, Stephen laughed. "Trust you, my wonderful wife, to run into live informants right on the street! I have to find everything in books!"

Line knew Stephen's style. He liked to be in the background. When they were together, it was always Line who smiled and acted approachable, while Stephen hung back. "You never know," she said.

"I've made overtures to Elizabeth Smith's office," said Stephen. "I'm hoping to interview her."

"I almost want to go along," said Line, "to meet this wonderful woman."

"It's probably a little premature," said Stephen, "my biography. Time always seems to settle things, and there hasn't been much time. But it is interesting how much people regret Smith's death."

"Yeah," said Line. "She didn't seem too happy about Blair."

"Well," said Stephen. "I'm for him. The time is right for decentralization, and he's doing it. I'm not sure about him personally, but Labour's doing the right thing."

"He did seem to bring the Queen around after Diana died," said Line. "She was having a hard time admitting how popular Diana was."

"It's a civilized country," said Stephen. "Post-imperialism. I can't wait until the United States gets there!"

193

Line smiled at him. Stephen knew that she couldn't wait to get back to the United States, their raw, adolescent, uncivilized country. But she wasn't going to say so again.

20

"I can do it! I can do it!" said sturdy three-year-old Benji, trying to wrest a peeled stick with a marshmallow on the end from his father, Gerald, as they stood by the fire at the edge of the cabin clearing on Lake Michigami.

"Yup," said his Dad, his arms encircling Benji's. "You can do it." But the stick smashed into the rocks around the edge of the fire ring and the marshmallow was covered with ash. Benji's small, dark face, framed in a mop of thick hair, looked stricken.

Paul watched and listened as he helped four-year-old Jeanne pull her half-burnt marshmallow from its stick and squeeze it between two graham crackers (one with a square of Hershey's chocolate on it). One thing that hadn't changed since he was a small boy himself in long-ago North Dakota, was S'mores. They were made of exactly the same things, and required exactly the same amount of care.

"Ooooh!" said Jeanne sadly as she took a bite, and hot marshmallow dripped down on her shirt. The light behind her glistened in the curly tendrils of her dark braids.

"Eat it quick," said Little Joe, her oldest brother, now ten. Marie noticed and came over to help the little girl, scrubbing at the spot with a damp napkin.

Little Joe expertly threaded another marshmallow on a stick and held it against the hot stones of the fire ring. "I like mine just perfect," he said to Paul. "Lightly browned. And then I toast the next layer lightly. I don't even care about the rest of it."

"That's one way to do it!" said Paul. He was trying to make sure that Andre, Grace's six-year-old middle kid, who was opening another package of graham crackers, didn't reduce them all to crumbs.

Marie took little Jeanne on her lap, where she and her daughter Grace sat in the lengthening shadows on lawn chairs near the table which held the food. Dory stood over them eating a S'more. Dory was now 13 and trying to distance herself from the younger kids, the Fearsome Foursome, as Paul thought of them. All of the kids had been at the cabin for the last four weeks, however, and Dory had done her share of watching over the younger ones.

Dory was a very pretty young girl, with long dark hair flowing down her back. Grace had matured into a soft, winsome mother, but she had never been the beauty her daughter was. Or her mother, Paul thought. Grace was simply more retiring, while Marie's flashing eyes and high coloring came out to meet you.

Archie, Paul's black and golden dog, lay on the lawn beside the women, his border collie ears flopped down around his face. Archie was definitely older now. He loved having a family to shepherd, but he was slower about it.

"Have you had enough?" Paul asked Marie. "Do you want another one?"

"No thanks," said Marie. "It's so much fun to watch these kids! I never got to do this as a kid!"

"Nor I," said Grace, quietly in her French accent. "It's very American, no?"

Gerald brought Benjy over to the table to help him make another S'more. "We did," said Gerald, a trifle grimly. "At Boy Scouts and CYO. Must be pretty American." He had grown up Catholic in Bemidji with his Ojibwe mother, his father having died when he was only three.

"Remember last year when it was so buggy we couldn't even eat out here?" asked Paul.

"Yes!" said Marie. "We roasted our hot dogs outside and then took them inside to eat them! Much better this year."

Every summer was different. It was what Paul loved, gauging each summer against previous ones. At this point in August the late summer sun was beginning to go down noticeably earlier. Paul looked toward the cabin, where a long ladder leaned against the wall. He was almost finished painting it; just the undersides of eaves and some trim left. A sort of muddy yellow-green, Paul had chosen the color so that the cabin would recede into the woods. It had been dark brown, but the old paint was peeling and cracking. Paul took on the job.

Marie stood up and began to put the food on a tray to take it into the cabin. Grace helped Benjy, whose tousled hair stood up. "You're so sticky!" she said. "Come with me. We'll wash some of that marshmallow off." The screen door slammed behind them. Archie looked back and forth between his people, and came to stand beside Paul.

"The sunset is so beautiful, Dad," said Dory. You have to see it!" Gerald had not been with the family most of the time. He had come to take Grace and the kids home to Bemidji. As Dory said, the sun quite predictably dropped into the western horizon on Lake Michigami, pink and gold clouds circling it. "The sun makes a shining path on the water straight to you," Dory insisted.

"Not tonight," said Gerald, decisively. "I have an early morning flight. We have to go home. You've had a great summer. Go help your mother pack up." Gerald worked at the Bemidji airport, doing maintenance and sometimes piloting small planes on short hops around the state.

That summer, Gerald had taken Paul with him when he took another passenger to Ely. They flew quite low and Paul had his face pressed to the window the whole time. He was fascinated by the color of the lakes, quite green the day they flew, and the thickly wooded areas between them.

Gerald flew south first so they could see the expanse of Leech Lake and Lake Michigami's distinctive outline. When they flew over the Mesabi range, near Hibbing and Virginia, Paul saw the huge swaths of land cleared by blasting and the garish tailings basin lakes created by taconite mining. He had visited a mine, and knew the taconite rock was blasted out of the ground and crushed. Iron concentrate was pulled out of the taconite through magnetism. Even from what was once considered waste rock, Minnesota still produced a significant portion of the country's iron ore.

This evening, Dory made a face and stood near Little John, who was tracing his burning stick through the air. It was too light to see an ember trail, however.

"Go! Both of you!" said Gerald quietly. "Get your stuff together." The kids ran off toward the cabin.

"They do seem anxious for school to start," said Paul. He would soon have to get back to Ely and ready his classroom for another year himself. He began folding up the card table and lawn chairs.

Gerald laughed, helping him. "I'll bet Grace is more ready than they are! But they are excited. The first thing they showed me when I got here was the school supplies they bought yesterday. Poor little Jeanne was admiring them. And Andre strutted around with his tablets and color crayons. He can't wait!"

"I was the fourth one," said Paul. "I remember watching the other kids leave every day, and sitting on the porch steps waiting for them to come back. Your kids are great. I'm so glad we get to have them here. Though Marie is getting pretty tired."

Gerald nodded modestly, as if he was doing the best he could. "They love coming here. There's not much to worry about in Bemidji, but it seems they are even more carefree here. And there's so much for them to do!"

The cabin and the half-built craft barn were stuffed full of the interesting collections the Mikkelsons had built up over the years, books, games, archery equipment, crafts, old magazines. All summer there had been small bathing suits on the line. The kids went in swimming twice a day, or played about in the inner-tubes and the canoe. Paul painted in the morning, and after lunch everyone napped, even the grownups! Dory, who had claimed the beach house, and Little John occupied themselves reading. In the late afternoon, everyone was usually down by the water.

"Andre's the one after my own heart," said Paul. "We've been going out in the woods, identifying bugs and wildflowers. He never tires of it." Poor Dory had gotten poison ivy on her bare ankles, and often sat around with her feet in a bath of Epsom salts.

"Glad to see it," said Gerald. "Andre gets lost in the shuffle sometimes, I think."

"Three adults to five kids," said Paul. "Plus Archie shadows Little John. And Dory sort of takes care of herself. It's been a good summer."

Paul made sure the fire was out. Then he and Gerald carried the lawn chairs up to the patio and put the table inside the lower level of the house. It was chock full of things, firewood, shelves full of books, old file cabinets, tools, fishing equipment. Paul sighed. It was a mess. But soon he would be home in Ely, where his things were more in order.

Paul and Archie followed Gerald up to the main part of the cabin where Grace was gathering up the kids. "Take some of the corn," said Marie. "I think we bought too much." Soon the bits and pieces of luggage were stowed and everyone stood out by the Jeep, hugging goodbye. Paul swung little Jeanne and Benjy up in his arms, holding them close and kissing their sweet faces.

"I guess we won't see you now until Thanksgiving, maybe?" said Gerald to Paul.

Paul shook his head noncommittally. "No idea," he said. "I leave all that to Marie." He and Gerald smiled at each other complicitly, guys, happy to cede the social field to their wives.

Paul helped the little kids buckle their seatbelts. There weren't enough, so Benjy sat in his mother's lap and Andre and Jeanne were buckled up in the middle of the back seat as if they were one person. Dory and Little John each claimed a window.

Looking back Gerald shook his head. "One of these days they're going to catch me," he said. "I really need a new car." The car doors shut.

Little Joe's hand fluttered out the window. "Catch you later, alligator!" he shouted. The Jeep turned on the gravel and headed down the two-rutted road, over the grass growing down the middle. Archie barked after them, his tail vigorously waving.

Paul and Marie, stood beside the white birches in front of the cabin, waving. When the car was gone, Paul looked toward the lake. "Evening swim," he said. "Want to come?" The water was the warmest in the evening and he was amazed how much he could see trolling about the shallows with a mask and snorkel.

"No, thanks," said Marie. "I'll come down to the dock, though. Not many more evenings like this." She leaned down and gave Archie's neck a roughing up. "Lots of kids, wasn't it," she said to him. "And now all you've got left is us."

A few moments later, Paul came down to the lake with his flippers, snorkel and mask. He jumped into the warm lake while Marie stood watching the sinking sun, Archie at her feet. Paul stayed near the shore, looking at the seaweed, rocks, the occasional clam, leech or crayfish, the ridges on the sandy bottom of the lake. Few actual fish came this close to the docks.

What Paul loved about snorkeling had again to do with three-dimensionsality. As he dove down and came up, he felt he was actually moving in more than two dimensions, as people did on land. He imagined himself a fish in its element. It was freeing not to have to stump about on his mismatched legs, and he hoped swimming strengthened them.

Paul surfaced, watching his love, her arms encircling her head. A loon called, far out from them. The air was moist and warm and the blaze of color in the west was mirrored in the opalescent-colored water. A light breeze rustled in the treetops, but the water was smooth, just undulating, the reflected colors pooling on the broken surfaces.

"You missed the heron," said Marie, pointing up. "Just flapped its way across the lake."

"Herons have habits," said Paul. "Just like we do." He climbed, dripping, onto the dock and rubbed himself down with a towel. He was remembering the Great Backyard Bird Count he and Marie had helped with in February. The idea was that for two weeks, you recorded every species you saw in your backyard and input them into a computer operated by Cornell University. The Audubon Society had helped publicize the event and many people had participated. Paul had tried to interest his biology classes. Citizen science, he had heard it called.

Twilight came on, bluer and then blacker, but it took a while for the stars to come out. Paul determined he would come back in a while and have a look. He hurried up to the cabin in his wet bathing suit. When he was warm and dry, he brought out the thick book he was reading to Marie in the evenings, Tolstoy's War and Peace. Often she fell asleep, but then he had the pleasure of telling her what she had missed.

Marie sat in her rocker under the lamp, knitting, Archie splayed out below on the rug. Paul pulled a chair over and began a chapter. When they had started it, Paul hadn't been very enthusiastic: a story about a lot of princes and princesses it seemed to be. But when Pierre began to bumble his way through the pages, making mistakes he was unable to do anything about, Paul got more interested.

That evening Paul read a chapter in which Nikolai, fresh from falling off his horse in a fight with the French, bursts in on his friends in the Guards in Austria. Nikolai, whom Paul knew to be the beloved eldest son of the Rostovs, tells them stories of his battle exploits. When Prince Andrei, something of a philosopher, comes in, Nikolai takes a dislike to him and nearly insults him. Prince Andrei demurs, telling the young hothead Nikolai that they are all about to take part in a much larger duel in a few days.

Paul looked up, but Marie was asleep in the rocker. He put the book away. It was astonishing how much Tolstoy was able to characterize each of these men, including both their actions and their inner thoughts! It was easy to picture the scene.

Telling Archie to stay and watch over Marie, Paul slipped out of the house and picked his way down the steep path to the lake in the dark. The Milky Way was thrown out across the sky like a handful of bright dust. Paul stood out at the end of the dock and looked up. As always, he oriented himself by the Little Dipper with its Pole star, and by the bright stars of the summer triangle, Altair, Vega and Deneb, now high overhead. The moon was not up yet. Wind and water undulated softly and Paul breathed the moist air, his life.

Walking back up the hill toward the cabin, Paul thought how much he loved the quiet of the great north, the feeling of being almost alone in the northern forests of birch, poplar and pine. The lights in the cabin above were pinpoints, the tiniest bit of civilization, just enough.

Paul moved quietly, gently waking Marie. She went off to lay down in what had always been Mother and Dad's room, the bed covered by a quilt made by Paul's grandmother. Paul was brushing his teeth when he heard car tires crunching on the gravel outdoors. Archie stood by the screen door, barking. Astonishing! The woods was as quiet as it ever was and Paul didn't expect anyone.

Paul turned on the porch light and opened the screen door. There, pulling a rucksack from the trunk of his car, stood Christopher Cohen! Beside him was a thin girl with long, kinky curls.

"Calm down, Archie," said Paul. The girl smiled widely as Paul came toward them. He put his arms around Christy's thin shoulders. "Howdy, partner," he said.

"I'm so glad you're still here!" said Christy, returning the hug. "I was a little afraid you'd already have gone back to Ely." He turned toward the girl. "This is Emily. We're doing some rallies in this part of the state, and of course I wanted to come."

"Yeah," said Paul. "So glad you did! We've got a couple of days left." He shook Emily's hand. "My wife's already in bed, but come in, come in!"

In the cabin, Marie was up, wrapped in a terrycloth robe, running water into a teakettle. She too hugged Christy and greeted Emily. "Tea?" she asked. "Cocoa?"

"We'd love some cocoa," said Christy, looking at Emily, who nodded.

Marie got out a saucepan, some milk and the cocoa tin, arranging mugs for each of them. The four of them sat around the old table. It was the middle of the night, but who cared? Paul thought of Tolstoy, like him offering civilization in the middle of a dark northern woods.

"Well, who is it this time?" asked Paul, wondering who the rally was for. There was a governor's race going on. Christy managed data and information for the Democratic Farm-Labor Party in the state.

"Skip Humphrey," said Christy, looking at Emily. "He's a good guy, but his rallies are not nearly as interesting as it was to travel around with Wellstone last summer."

"And what's Wellstone doing this summer?" asked Paul.

"Oh, he's still trying to figure out whether the country could handle a progressive president. He's traveling in his big green bus somewhere. Marcia, his daughter, is with him. But I have to do what the DFL tells me.

We're trying to get Humphrey into the governor's seat," said Christy. "Plus some representatives riding on his coattails."

"You know how Jesse Ventura goes around saying, 'don't vote for politics as usual'?" asked Emily. "Skip Humphrey is politics as usual!"

Everyone laughed. Humphrey was the son of Hubert Humphrey, who had been vice president under Lyndon Johnson.

"Nothing wrong with that," said Marie. She had waked up completely, Paul could see, her eyes sparkling. "Son of his father, and all." She stood up. "I can make more cocoa, if anyone wants it." But people shook their heads.

"Humphrey's a nice guy," said Christy. "And I admire how he has stood up to the tobacco companies, but you know he's kind of low-key. Polite, deferential. He just isn't interesting!" Christy, a younger version of his father in jeans and a t-shirt, looked energized. He probably never thought about how late the hour might be.

"Well, I guess after what you've said about Wellstone," said Paul, "he's a hard act to follow."

"For me, certainly," said Christy. "No one forgets Wellstone once you've been around him. He's got big ideas, not small ones. He's looking at the big picture."

"That is certainly a big question," said Paul. "Whether the US could handle a progressive president."

"So, I watched him," said Christy. "He'd take someone's hand, or put a hand on their shoulder, and then ask, 'Don't you think we should stop paying big subsidies to corporations and start protecting farmers who want to grow safe, healthy food?' And then he'd wait. He'd listen as if he really wanted an answer. He'd ask teachers 'How do we talk about education in a way that gets us beyond false choices?' or he'd ask a businessman, 'Don't you think people are more concerned about monopolies than most politicians imagine?' I was there," Christy continued. "Me and Marcia would both take down the answers and compare them later."

"I love Paul Wellstone," said Emily. "When he speaks, you hear optimism, you hear possibility. He never whines about his opponents. And in the Senate, he votes with his head!"

"Even Clinton," said Christy hotly. "He lets the conservatives set the agenda and tries to work around it. Wellstone wants to change the agenda! 'Course, Clinton's lucky he's still president." He looked around the table darkly.

Paul looked at Marie. "I've been fascinated by Minnesota politics since I moved back to the state," he said. "How much of it comes out of the Iron Range! When I was growing up, it was all about the farmers who lived all around us. But the farms were 160 acres! Now they're huge, and the number of farmers is dwindling. Also, I've realized how important the mining interests are up in our part of the state, the unions. Perpich came out of Hibbing. And he had really big ideas. International ideas."

Rudy Perpich had been a transformative force in Minnesota. His father was a miner from Croatia, but Perpich rose from a school board, to the Minnesota senate, and was governor for just over ten years. He had helped Paul Wellstone get started, before his recent death.

"That doesn't mean our Paul does anything about politics," smiled Marie. "We vote, of course, but we don't join anything."

"Except choir!" said Paul. "We do like choir!"

Christy laughed. "I know you pretty well, Uncle Paul," he said. "You're a progressive, if I ever met one!"

"It all goes back to this guy I knew in Alaska," Paul said. "Arvi Kukkonen. He was a Quaker, and involved in everything. He opened me up in a lot of ways."

"Yeah," said Christy. "You used to tell me about him." Paul and Christy had had many political discussions.

"Your Dad would be proud of you, Christy," said Paul. "You are doing great work."

Christy sunk into himself a little at the mention of his father. "Probably wonders when I'm going to settle down and make some money," he said with a trace of bitterness. Christy and his father still communicated mostly through other people, especially Line, his mother.

"Money's over-rated," said Paul. "Family is more important, and I'm sure your father thinks so too." Though none of them mentioned it, they all knew that Christy's grandfather had bankrolled Christy through college, and still did somewhat. But what else was Poppa supposed to do with his money?

Marie stood up. "I'm going to bed," she said. "You can sleep wherever you want, Christy. You know where the sheets and blankets are."

"The beach house?" Christy asked. He looked at Emily. "It's like sleeping in a treehouse," he told her.

"Sure," said Paul. "The kids have been down there, and we haven't had a chance to clean up. But you can go down and have a look." He stood up. "I'll find you a flashlight," he said, rummaging in the middle room where many things that had never gotten absorbed from Mother and Dad's house still crowded the shelves and cabinets. He wasn't going to ask whether Christy and Emily would be sleeping in the same bed. Christy was a grownup. "The lights down there should work," he said.

The moist night air felt great as Paul stood at the door, watching Christy and Emily go down the path. Moths crowded around the porch light, banging into it. He was thinking about how great conversation was when people hadn't seen each other for a while. Important things came right out.

In the morning, the sun was up before Paul. He lay in bed listening. Archie was up, padding around, and so was Christy, probably making coffee. Paul heard him talking on the phone. "I'll be right over," Christy said. The phone was the only communication device in the cabin. Christy must have arranged with someone to use their modem to allow his computer to connect with some network.

"Those kids can't live without the almighty internet," Paul teased, talking softly to Marie, who was stretching in bed beside him.

Marie smiled. "They're political!" she said. "I don't blame them." She got up and put on her robe. "It feels so weird without kids all over the place!" she said.

"I have to tell you, I'm glad," said Paul. "I love them, but I think they wear you out!" There were dark circles under Marie's eyes if you looked closely.

"Oh, I'll catch up," said Marie. "Don't worry. I wouldn't give up our summers with the kids for anything." Her eyes looked back, as if she were remembering. "Dory is so smart and lovely," she said. "I didn't know Grace had it in her!"

"Well Gerald is a fine father," said Paul. "Dotes on them all!"

"Yes," said Marie. "I guess we all have to get back to our lives." She had reached an agreement about her delicatessen business with the young people who were running it. Marie planned to keep working there, but they would be paying her from now on. It had never made much money anyhow.

They heard car tires crunching away in the sandy drive out front. When they went out to the kitchen, the cabin was empty, except for Archie, lying by the door.

That day Paul climbed ladders with his paint bucket, working on the undersides of the eaves. Painting was certainly not his favorite job, but he was the one available. He had been painting every morning for weeks. But it was almost done.

In the cabin, Marie was singing as she swept the sandy floors. "Black bird singing in the dead of night. Take these broken wings and learn to fly. All your life," she sang, "you were only waiting for this moment to arise." Whisk, whisk, the broom sounded in between notes. "Black bird fly, into the light of the dark black night."

Paul always thought of an actual blackbird, but Marie had explained it was about civil rights, that Paul McCartney had written it in Scotland in the late Sixties. It was the kind of thing Marie knew.

The sun hit Paul as he climbed down the ladder. He looked up at his paint job. It'll pass in the dark, he thought, as Mother used to say. It would serve to keep some of the weather out. He had sanded off the worst of the cracked and peeled older coat. If he had the gumption, he might put on another one next summer. He thought of Aunt Rose, who had moved into the cabin with her gaily-colored gold gingham curtains when she and the Mikkelsons had taken over from their brother. Aunt Rose had died that year, in April. Paul often found himself thinking of her generosity to his family.

Marie came out the door with the big rag rug. "Can I shake this here?" she asked. The rug looked way too big for her slight frame to carry.

Paul came up to grab it. "Let's take it over on the other side of the driveway," he said. "I'll help you."

Marie smiled as they shook the dust out into the light. "Into the light of the dark black night," she sang. The trees above them rustled. It was the end of summer, but the cabin wasn't going anywhere. They would all be back.

21

Marty got into the office car with Ken and two other Christmas party committee members and went to the LIMN gallery after work. An exhibit of photographs was opening that night, and, through friends, the committee had found they could rent the gallery for their office party. It was the end of November, the year turning toward the holidays.

The gallery was an old warehouse, converted into a white room with odd shapes and a few big paned windows. The large photographs were all black and white images of ballet dancers. The committee had come up with a spy theme for the party involving a Russian dancer and a current mystery. Carla, who was very pregnant and scheduled to have her baby the next day, had brought her husband Charles, a wild Irish Protestant. Ken's wife Stacy had also come, as well as members of the band they had hired and Lawrence, from Dance Through Time. Stuart was planning the lighting.

The group walked through the rooms, determining where things would happen in the elaborate skit they had planned. Charles gesticulated wildly. "The checkpoints should be here!" he noted. "The dancers should harass people here, but not here," he pointed. Carla decided where to put the bar and the food. There would be a mock assassination. Of whom? Werner of course! The partner who currently controlled Designers International, who was getting most of the jobs. Lauren called him "the rainmaker."

As a Christmas present that year the partners wanted to purchase Palm Pilots for each employee. These were handheld computers on which a client list could be uploaded. It had a stylus for making notes and learned to read your handwriting as it got to know you. Ken and Joe were terribly excited about them. Marty was skeptical. She knew people would complain that they would rather have had a bonus. She could just hear Nora's acid comments. But when she asked whether any women were interested in these devices, her boss Joe said that in the Washington office women told Mitch the idea made them want to kiss him!

Part of the conspiracy theme, the Palm Pilots would be handed out with a "dossier" as an invitation to the party. Marty had written the "mission" for it, a two page memo from the CIA describing what was required "should you choose to accept it." It noted the unexplained death of a Russian dancer, the description of the double-agent Lawrence, and his intentions toward a well-known architect, as well as the clues hidden in the photographs.

Everyone had had ideas: secret agents in mirror shades running around, dancers in costume to check each person in, an old black and white film projected on white walls, lots of deep red roses to give a dark, glamorous feel to the rooms. The partners were always willing to spend money on having a fabulous Christmas party. Marty had helped put on many of these parties over the years. She loved the committee meetings, finding she had much to contribute, collaboration at its best. Designers International thrived on chaos. Out of it came hot projects!

Ken and Marty stood in a room where stylized text was embossed into prints. Since they had taken a calligraphy class together, Ken was all about typefaces and their meaning. So was Stacy, who was studying graphic design. Though Marty's "mission statement" had been written on a computer, Ken explained: "I'm going to doctor it so it looks as if it were typed on an ancient CIA typewriter." He was also making a Russian passport in Photoshop, which got one in to the party.

Because of the gallery opening, hors d'oeuvres were being served, and Marty had a glass of wine. "I doubt that the party will be as much fun as planning it," Marty told Carla.

Carla looked like a melon, ready to split, but she was game, walking around. "Maybe we could get some briefcases and have the waiters serve dessert out of them," she said.

Marty took the cable car home. It was full of college sorority girls, holiday makers teaching each other a drinking song. They looked so fresh, as if they had come from a magazine shoot, each perfectly made up, cuddling up to each other and taking photographs. The night time air was crisp and dry.

"Suck it up girls," teased the grip man. "Help us get over the hill!" He wore suspenders to hold up his large pants, and leather gloves. As the cable car climbed the hill, he engaged the car with the cable beneath the street. When they came down a hill, he braked. The car was going down to Fisherman's Wharf, but it dropped Marty at her corner, a local with a key to an apartment on Russian Hill.

On the top landing, Marty noticed that mail was piling up outside Dorysse's door. Each floor of the building held two apartments, one facing east and one west. Dorysse, who was probably in her 80's, had been a well-off woman. When Marty first lived in the apartment, she would see Dorysse downstairs, sitting for a while before she climbed the four flights of stairs after a walk around the neighborhood. Dorysse liked talking to Marty. She complained that her family was restricting her allowance. She had lived in the apartment for goodness knows how many years.

Recently, Marty hadn't seen her downstairs. She heard Dorysse sending out for food, and paying for it when it arrived. She seemed to live on hamburgers and Orange Crush! When Marty asked her to tea, because how hard could it be to step across the hall to Marty's apartment, Dorysse slipped a note under her door, thanking her, but saying she was ill and couldn't come.

Marty was a little worried about her. It seemed pretty quiet over there. Marty worried whether she was paying her bills, whether she had electricity or even her phone. When she asked John, who lived below her, what to do, John shook his head. He had lived in the building almost as long as Dorysse, but "All we do is yell at each other," he said.

In her own apartment, Marty turned on the heater, trying to warm the place up. She folded a blanket around herself and sat on the hardwood floor, checking her phone messages. She had not seen much of Doug lately, but they frequently talked on the phone. And he would come during one of the four days Marty had off for their own private Thanksgiving. "I need to see you," Doug's message said. "When I don't get to see you, I want to. And when I do see you, I want to see more of you." I guess I'm safe then, Marty thought to herself, wrapping his thick, warm voice around her. It was lovely to go to bed with Doug's voice in her ear.

Despite the fun of planning the Christmas party, Designers International had not been a good place for Marty that fall. Joe, her boss, had given her a critical review, saying she was "reactive," that her "leadership was not apparent." He wanted her to be more of a strategic planner. He did not want to see her at the front desk, filling in for Nora the receptionist! He wanted to see Marty take her staff beyond the status quo.

It was upsetting to have Joe confirm what Marty knew to be true. She knew she was reactive. She had always felt that the high-powered architects at Designers International needed people to absorb their intensity. Marty was an implementer. She had solved some of their problems: stabilized the administrative staff, bought a fire safe for slides, gotten them through many moves and changes, and worked well with the Washington office. She had realized right away that she did not want to deal with the massive conflicts between offices and partners which seemed to fuel the place.

Now, however, Joe had voiced their expectations. Marty felt miserable at work. She did not like being unappreciated. She had thought about countering Joe's statements, but then decided against it. Her time at Designers International was probably over. She would never be able to please Werner, and Joe wasn't much of an advocate under the best of circumstances. Joe had always seemed to like her, but Marty could hear Werner's voice in this review.

Marty also felt feisty and angry. She would stick it out, learn from it. She would leave on her own timetable, perhaps next spring. She was terribly busy at the moment, doing billing, budgets, interviewing people, since Erica had finally left. People were charretting up on her floor, working day and night. Marty wasn't sure what was driving it.

In interviews for an executive assistant for the senior partners, Joe rejected the younger ones and looked for experience. They were all anxious to find someone. Marty was struggling to keep up with their needs. The closer she got to Werner, however, the more she liked him. He was a decent guy, though driven and difficult, desperate to keep in touch with his clients. She watched helplessly while he mashed his Wizard to a pulp, trying to put new batteries into it. He was endearing and dependent. He and Erica had trusted each other, each weirdly paranoid.

Nora, the rock solid receptionist whom Marty relied on, was worried Marty would lose her sense of humor while she ran around, trying to take care of everyone's needs. "Don't worry about them so much," she told Marty.

"I understand why you've been able to stay here so long," Marty told her.

"Tough love, baby," said Nora. "Tough love." She was good at handling the partners, with humor as well as kindness. Like Marty, she had grown up in Iowa.

Marty laughed at her.

Difficult as the work was, it showed Marty something about herself. The firm rubbed off on her, and she pushed through to her own excellence, stopped indulging herself in food, hardly having any sweets. She got to the office at 8 a.m. and worked all day without much break, cutting through all kinds of problems. Things would slow down in December.

On Saturday, Marty went to tai chi practice as usual. Class began with the Tiger Mountain Qigong Master Liu had made up, a series of movements done while standing in the horse stance. In the middle of a grid of people, Marty moved with them, raising her arms in the postures. Usually they did no more than four repeats of each movement. That day they did eight. By the time they got to the slow set, energy pulsed all around Marty. Her body felt thick with it. It was almost too much to handle.

When they finished and stood around talking, Marty found others had also felt the powerful energy. Vanessa had thought to herself, I can't finish this. The energy felt wonderful, thick and juicy. But it was unfamiliar, hard to get used to.

After slow set, the group did five fast sets, repeating all the movements in the slow set very rapidly to disperse the energy. The sets became easier with each one, but it was a workout!

No one stuck around for lunch that day. As she did most Saturdays, Marty took the bus, then walked up the Union Street hill to Hyde

Street, carrying her weapons in the long bag she had made of an old pair of blue jeans. It was a damp day, and clouds hung low in the sky. The sidewalks were full of puddles. By the time she got to her apartment and climbed four flights of stairs, Marty was starving and her legs were exhausted! She made herself a quick omelet with sage and goat cheese. Then, covering her throbbing legs with a quilt, she sat on the sofa, sticking them straight out to rest them.

At Thanksgiving Marty and Doug celebrated on the Saturday after the holiday. Doug opened the door to Marty's apartment, bringing in the fresh smell of the cold outdoors. Marty's body thrilled to his physical warmth as he wrapped his big arms around her. "It's my favorite holiday," he said. "Thanksgiving. But I'm not sure I know anyone who is as thankful as you." He handed her a couple of bottles of Beaujolais Nouveau, the first pressing of the year's vintage in France. "Put them in the fridge," he said. "Jeremy gave them to me."

They went down the hill to Real Foods and stood reverently amid the bountiful shelves of vegetables. Marty loved watching Doug in a store like this, wondering what he would choose. But he wanted to eat simply after the big Thanksgiving events. He picked out a butternut squash, a yam, an onion and a loaf of their current favorite Pugilese bread. At home Marty had already collected a rich salad of figs, gorgonzola and walnuts, and prepared everything she needed for a French apple tart. She had only to assemble and bake it.

Marty made a fire and they lay on the couch in front of it, drinking a glass of the Harvey's Bristol Cream Marty had bought for her throat. She was wearing the black jeans architects favored, and a creamy grey cashmere sweater. Marty took the elastic out of Doug's ponytail, letting his long brown curly hair settle around his shoulders.

"I'll tell first," Marty said. She explained how she had rented a car and driven down to Santa Cruz on Thanksgiving Day, where Poppa and Ivy were celebrating. "It was an odd little gathering, with an older friend of Poppa's and two students Ivy had collected, far from their home in China.

"Ivy set bouquets of fall greens and nandina with its red berries around the house. I love Line's house," said Marty, seeing it in her mind's eye. "The Chinese kids called nandina 'heavenly bamboo.' They said in China they all think it protects the house. We roasted the turkey, and served it with cranberries, stuffing, gravy, greens and mashed potatoes. Poppa made drinks, and he and Arthur reminisced about Brooklyn and told all the funny stories they could think of. It was a blast!"

"I love hearing about Poppa," said Doug. He had met him at Heather's wedding. "And all of your family."

"I brought a pumpkin pie," Marty said. "My one requirement for Thanksgiving. It all got eaten." She stood up and put on another log from the bundle she had bought at the corner store. "Your turn," she said, sitting back down. "Tell me about the kids," she begged. "About everyone."

Doug had been in Santa Cruz also, at his mother's house. She baked the traditional turkey for his family. His sister Eva, an anesthesiologist who lived near Sacramento, had come with her husband and kids.

"My mother's fine," he said. "She just pretends everything's fine. And so it usually is! On the surface. Mackenzie was there, but kind of checked out. I have no idea what she thinks any more. Mother did all the cooking, except Eva brought a ham, and two pies. And Mother got Zoe to help her, which was great."

"She must be about nine?" asked Marty.

"Yes," said Doug. "Exactly. And the twins are eight. It was a nice day, so the kids were out on their bicycles. Jason can ride too, now. I got him a little one, because he can't stand being left behind."

"We were so close to each other!" said Marty. "I wish I could have visited."

"Best not," said Doug. "My marriage is hanging by a thread. The 'D' word is in the air, but I can't bear to think of the kids without me around. I don't think Mackenzie cares about them. She really just wants money. But it is possible she would use them to get it."

"She's like your fifth kid," said Marty.

"Yes," said Doug. "When she's taking care of them, it's every man for himself. She does like to dress them up. Like dolls. And put them on stools for her tea party. Poor little Jason eats it up. But the older kids are more savvy. They resist."

Finally, Doug picked Marty up and carried her into the kitchen! Marty squealed. But Doug said, "You're my baby."

"Yes," said Marty, softly. "I am." She loved the fact that she had found the last patriarch for a lover. And he was much younger than she was!

Marty took the large All-Clad frying pan she had given Doug to use at her house down from the refrigerator. "For you," she said. The pan was a miracle of thick laminated metals, which heated evenly and was easy to clean.

Doug was riffing in a voice Marty hadn't heard before. "I loves my baby," he said. "We go out. We go dancing. I say, 'Bandleader, this my baby.' Bandleader say, 'Crazy.' 'Waiter, could you bring me a glass of milk!' It's word jazz," Doug confided. "Ken Nordine. A national treasure."

Marty was mystified. Doug was full of references to movies and music she had never heard. Perhaps also because he had come of age in a slightly different time.

Doug peeled and grated the yam and the squash, sautéing them with onion and garlic and marjoram. Marty peeled the last two apples and sliced them thinly, fanning the slices out across the top of the tart. She spread melted butter and sugar over them and put the whole thing in the oven. Somehow, they did not get in each other's way in the small kitchen. Bumping into each other was a pleasure in any case.

Light for the table was three votive candles. The simple food was lovely with the light, fresh tasting Beaujolais. They ate the rich gorgonzola and walnut salad with thick slices of bread dipped in olive oil. "With utmost thanks," said Doug, raising his glass of wine. "Especially for you." He swirled the slightly chilled wine. "It's a little thin," he said. "But I like it."

Doug had brought a videotape his kids liked, Totorro, an animated Japanese movie. "We've watched it many times," he said. Curled up on the couch together, Marty felt that lying in Doug's arms was as fine as any more intimate adventure. It was like being cooked over a low burner, slowly. Marty became a thick, stewy mess. She remembered the hot fire of Erik, but liked this better. No one had loved Marty quite the way Doug did, knowing exactly who she was.

The kids in the movie were loud and silly, the houses set in the Japanese countryside. But there were quiet times also. The graphics were beautiful, entirely original. But all too soon, even before it was finished, Doug decided he must leave.

They stood in the hall outside Marty's apartment, saying goodbye. Doug turned to look up at Marty when he was halfway down the stairs. They had both remembered his hair at the same time. "Oh!" Marty said, handing him the black elastic which she was wearing around her wrist.

"One of these days we'll forget," said Doug. He tied up his hair as he usually did and went down the stairs.

Marty went to bed. She had opened to him, as always. Like a flower. It was painful to be left alone. But it made another visit possible. She was stoic, accepting. There was nothing else to do.

On Sunday night, Marty went in to the Designers International office. With her fellow committee members (except for Carla, who was recovering from having her baby), she wrapped Palm Pilots in brown paper and tied them with string. In her best calligraphy, she wrote the "agents'" names on them in black marker. Slightly over one hundred packages. Thrilling to the secrecy and anticipation, Marty and Ken put copies of the "dossier" they had put together, the invitation, along with a Palm Pilot on each person's desk. No one seemed to suspect what they had been whispering about for weeks.

Christmas had begun. The office was full of gifts, chocolate, food, wine. It became harder to concentrate, and there was also less need to. Work slowed down. Marty brought in the packages she wanted to send to her family and put them in FedEx boxes, stacking them neatly on the front desk for pickup. It was an extravagance to send them that way, but she felt it was worth it.

When Marty arrived at the LIMN gallery for the party, she found that the caterer had not arrived to set up. She held Carla's baby, the little Charlotte, who was by now pink and white and beautiful in her blanket, and worried. George, the caterer, was the partner of an architect at the company. He had often catered their events.

The band was playing, the sounds reverberating off the concrete walls, and people were arriving. But George and his helpers did arrive, quickly setting up. Carla ran around, checking the big vases of long-stemmed red roses, their color intense in the monochromatic rooms. They had had to lop off some expenses, but not the roses. The dancers they had hired wore tights, tutus and ballet shoes. They were stationed at the entrances to check and frisk the "agents" as they arrived.

Winston, the oldest partner, looked fabulous with a small phalanx of medals on his chest and a commissar's hat. He and his wife had been to Russia, and she also looked lovely in a wooly coat. Others wore fedoras, shades and Kevin wore his "godfather's suit." Anna had a wonderful low-cut red dress trimmed with white rabbit's fur. Stacy, Ken's wife, had spent the day in a beauty parlor, having her hair put up. She wore a leopardskin coat and white go-go boots.

The bar and the food people were all professionals, Marty was happy to note. But the food was a little chi-chi, and probably not enough. Marty would hear Nora grousing, about it on Monday. She had two martinis with olives. The band played, and a few people danced. Stuart had brought red gels for the lights, and used strobes for some songs. Marty loved watching people dance in the light.

Marty held Charlotte while Carla and Ken orchestrated the assassination of Werner with a rubber gun. The band had stopped and a shot rang out. Everyone screamed and dispersed. The harsh overhead lights came on. Everyone knew Werner was the target, but there he was, walking away. He would come back as Santa Claus at the end of the party. If there was anyone left, Marty thought.

The band began to play again, and the lights went down. The music pounded on the concrete walls and the low ceiling. Most people weren't dancing. They stood outdoors in the chill and talked. Marty noticed that Joe, her boss, came without his wife. "She had her office party this evening also," he said. "Did you try your Palm Pilot?" he asked. "I think they are great."

Marty wasn't very interested in inputting all of her addresses and phone numbers to the little electronic device. She was perfectly happy with her address book, full of lines drawn through the ones where people had moved and their phone numbers had changed. She tried to seem enthusiastic.

Ken and Stacy were dancing, having a wonderful time. "It's just like I hoped," he told Marty, when they stopped to take a break. "It'll go down as one of the great Designers International parties." Marty agreed. She wished Doug had been there. We would have danced, she thought to herself. She might even have bought a dress and high heels. Without an escort she felt odd. She didn't like having people wonder whether she was all right. She was all right, especially when she could leave. As soon as she felt she could, she slipped out into the cool evening and took a bus home.

That night Marty was woken at 2 a.m. by Kristie, one of her downstairs neighbors pounding on Dorysse's door, telling her she was getting help. Kristie had heard Dorysse's voice yelling over the lightwell. Dorysse said she had fallen and couldn't get up, that she had been there for three days.

The police came first, a young man and two women, but they had no authorization to break down the door. No one could get into the back door either. Eventually the fire department came with the paramedics. They broke the frosted glass in a panel of the door and opened it. Marty, and everyone in her house who had gathered in the hall, was startled to see Dorysse sitting in a heap in the tiny space that was left in front of her door.

The entire rest of the apartment was piled with bags of garbage. There was literally nowhere in the house you could walk.

The paramedics put Dorysse in a little seat and carried her downstairs. "Don't take me to the hospital," she said. "It gets me all out of kilter."

"You're out of kilter already," said the young, blonde paramedic.

The paramedics had Dorysse out by 2:30 a.m. Marty and her neighbors, stood around for a few minutes, horrified by the state of the apartment. "Mrs. Chin, the landlord, keeps asking what she can do," said John. "It's been a fire trap for ages." The neighbors went back to bed, but Marty couldn't sleep for a long while.

In the morning, Marty took a good look at Dorysse's place. It was an odd mixture of gentility and trash. At the back of the apartment you could see a china cabinet in the kitchen, dishes behind its glass doors, teacups hanging in a row on little hooks. But the kitchen, the hallway, every room was stacked with trash. You could not even walk in.

In the living room Marty could see china lamps, leatherbound books on the mantelpiece. In the bedroom a wonderful painting, reminiscent of Georgia O'Keefe, hung over a carved bedroom set. The bathtub was stuffed with dirty diapers. Indeed the whole bathroom was.

Late that afternoon, Mrs. Chin came and talked to Marty and John. He explained how badly Dorysse treated anyone who tried to help her. "The trash pattern has been going on for a long time," said Mrs. Chin. "I've cleaned it out twice." They all agreed that Dorysse should go to a nursing home, but what would that take? "I will try to speak to her family," said Mrs. Chin.

"Life in the city," said John, when Mrs. Chin had gone. "You never know." He was a historian, his own apartment below dark and filled with books.

Marty shook her head. It was hard for her to get her head around. "What combination of personal characteristics could get you to this point?" she wondered.

"Arrogance," said John. "Being spoiled and idle and never having to take care of yourself."

Marty could not imagine it. She went back to her own apartment. It was almost Christmas. She resolved to bring home some lovely flowers, perhaps some roses, to clear her head and heart of this sad incident.

22

In the spring, Line felt lifted and light. The April sun came up just when Line and Stephen were getting up, and stuck around until after 8 p.m. Line was planting. In the middle of the day, the sun felt like a hot human hand on her back, like an embrace. The sun's heat brought out the smell of the dark, loamy soil which Line had prepared for the seedlings she had reared in the nursery shed.

For once, however, Line would not be there to see her harvest, since she and Stephen would leave Kerry's house in Edinburgh in a month or so. But Line didn't care. The vegetables she had set over the winter needed planting. Someone, probably Kerry, would be there to eat them in the fall.

Birds fluttered and twittered around the garden, a noisy little kaffeklatch. Line kept the feeders full, so the brilliant goldfinches and chaffinches came, as well as sparrows, of course. She loved the blue tits with their little crowns of color. At least one pair nested among the blossoms of the apple tree. She even loved the blackbirds for their full-throated, varying songs, though they weren't as welcome at the feeders. Line was afraid they kept the small songbirds away with their great black shadows.

Kerry's father had been especially interested in his collection of hellebores, which bloomed even in the winter, waxy blossoms in all colors, from creamy to pale pinks and purples, to a few dark magenta ones. But there were also crocuses and daffodils. April was such a feast of blossoms, one almost took them for granted. A brilliant yellow forsythia bush lightened Line's walks to the market. And one day she had gone to the Meadows near the university, where ancient cherry trees blazed out over the walks, meeting in arcs over your head in profusion, an extravagance of delicate pink color.

Line's secret favorite was a magnolia with creamy white blooms, growing in a nearby sheltered garden. It reminded her of California. She had first seen it when the blooms were like candle flames, standing alone on their branches, ready to open. So beautiful. They held the secret which made Line happiest. In a few weeks, she would be back in Santa Cruz. Stephen had begun to worry a little about Poppa, who was growing older, 79 now. He had promised they would not leave again soon. "I can't keep doing this to Poppa," he said.

Stephen was ready to go home too. He had the material he needed for his book on John Smith, which filled in much that Americans didn't know about contemporary British politics. Smith had risen in the Labour Party, up through the shadow cabinet while the Conservatives were in power. He had been just ready to move into 10 Downing Street, the first Scottish prime minister of the United Kingdom since Ramsey Macdonald in 1935, when he was felled by heart attack. Tony Blair, the current prime minister, had actually been born in Edinburgh, but his parents moved the family to Durham when he was five. No one really thought of him as Scottish.

Line got up off her knees. Yes, there were the blue tits circling and chattering. On her way back to the house, she passed the small shed-like cottage where Kerry lived. Kerry had returned from Sarajevo and was now working with the Scottish Refugee Council to help the thousands of refugees who were pouring out of Kosovo. She was at work at the moment, but she would have dinner with Line and Stephen that night, as she often did.

Line packed herself a sandwich and walked over to the brook Kerry had shown her where she could gather watercress. Some days were windy and wet, but that left skies full of color and change. Line was out in all weathers, but today was a blessing, dry and warm. She loved the paths through the woods, which followed the little beck, thickly overgrown.

Keeping her eyes open for blossoms, Line scattered seed from a can of wildflower seed she had brought. Wildflower blooms helped the bees. It wasn't quite time for the hawthorns, but pink sloe blossoms hung from bare branches of a blackthorn. She loved the fact that walks and byways were available to people everywhere in Scotland. It was called "freedom to roam" and allowed people access for walking, cycling, horse-riding and primitive camping almost anywhere in the country. In the United States, everything was owned. It was only in national and state parks that you could really roam.

Line went down to the clear running stream and gathered a few clumps of the tangy green watercress. She was putting it into everything, sandwiches, salads and on top of the meat. Stephen loved it. He was sure the cresses were full of minerals their bodies needed after the dark winter. The Scots got their Vitamin D from fish in the winter, but also from eggs and mushrooms.

Line put the cresses into her collecting bag. She sat for a moment on the rock wall at the back of a garden arranging herself and her bags. She got up quickly when she saw tiny blue marsh violets growing in the stone. Was she sitting on some of them? No, they mostly grew on the sunny side of the wall. "And who appreciates you?" she asked the small, delicate flowers. She was sure someone knew they were there. Scottish people were extremely sensitive to their surroundings. "I do," she said.

On her way home, Line stopped at the home of her nearby neighbor, a 96-year-old woman who lived with her daughter. She went up the little walk to the back door, which was on the latch. The daughter was working and appreciated it when Line stopped by during the day to see if her mother needed anything.

Line bustled into the living room noisily, where Mrs. Daiches sat in a chintz-covered chair, looking out the window at the street. "And how are you today, Mrs. Daiches?" she asked.

"Middling," said Mrs. Daiches, a tiny woman with white hair which waved around her pale face. "Not bad." She did not get out of her chair, and Line leaned down to take her hand.

"It's a beautiful day!" said Line. "I brought you some watercress. Can I make you a sandwich?"

Mrs. Daiches brightened. "Oh yes, my dear. Bread and butter and cress. That sounds nice." She stood up and went into the kitchen with hesitant steps, her back bent.

"Do you want your shawl?" Line asked, following behind her.

Mrs. Daiches sat at the little table and ate the sandwich Line made. Line lived quite far to the east of the city. Rather than take up the volunteer work she had done for the NHS the last time she was in Scotland, she had found volunteer opportunities right in her neighborhood. Line sat with Mrs. Daiches, sharing a slice of white bread with butter and the peppery-tasting cress.

"The sloe tree is in blossom," said Line. "I remember you told me you used to make sloe wine. Or maybe Clarissa told me."

"Oh yes," said Mrs. Daiches. "That was hard. Those trees have thorns! And then you have to wait. The wine takes at least a year to age. But we liked it. Especially with pheasant, when my husband brought one home. Or a rabbit."

"I love elderberry cordial," said Line. "I buy the concentrate at the store. So cool and lovely on a hot day." A picture of Ivy drinking it with her last summer rose in her mind, a lazy afternoon when they had sat in Kerry's garden, glasses of the silvery liquid in hand. Wouldn't she soon be drinking something with Ivy on their spacious deck in Santa Cruz? Was it the space that bothered Line in Scotland? Everything seemed tiny, the rooms cluttered with furniture.

Line stood up. "Is there anything else I can get you before I go?" she asked. Mrs. Daiches needed little.

"Oh no," said Mrs. Daiches. "I want my nap! That's all." She stood up and shuffled back into the living room. "Thank you, my dear. That was delicious." She lay down on the stiff couch and Line wrapped a blanket around her and left by the back door.

Scottish people certainly knew their wild herbs and made the most of the lush woodlands, thought Line as she walked up the lane toward home. She was not sure the young people were getting that kind of learning. It was one thing Line would miss: the delicate, ancient relationship to the world around them the Scots had. But home to Line was California, the no-holds-barred, full catastrophe living in that last frontier state.

The other person Line didn't so much help, as simply check in on, was Rosemary, a woman she had met tooling around the streets in her motorized wheelchair. Rosemary was probably about the same age as Line, but she had been diagnosed with progressive MS a few years ago. She had the use of most of her upper body, but not her legs.

Rosemary lived alone, and had been assessed a careworker for a few hours in the morning by the NHS, but Line liked to stop by in the late afternoon, to see whether she could help Rosemary with her tea. Rosemary didn't eat much, but Line liked to lift the heavy kettle full of water onto the flame, get the milk from the refrigerator. Rosemary could do it all herself, and insisted that she wanted to be self-sufficient. But she was often weary from exertion and Line liked to spoil her a little. Sometimes, on long, dark rainy days, they shared a bar of chocolate!

It did seem to Line unfair that so many good people had such a hard time, while often the worst people had it easy. The villains in Line's life were people like Nixon, who had prevented peace in Vietnam, then continued to bomb it unmercifully. Or Ronald Reagan, who had ceased to house and care for the mentally and physically ill, unloosing a plague of homelessness everywhere in the U.S. during his presidency. He gave everyone his big California smile, but underhandedly prevented democracy in Nicaragua. Like Margaret Thatcher's in England, Reagan's conservative policies robbed the poor, while helping the rich.

Now, of course, those in power were centrist, but a little more turned toward human rights. Line was on the side of human rights for all people. From Kerry, she had learned that the Serbian president, Milosevic, was the bad guy in the current war. He had signed the Dayton Accords to stop the war in Bosnia, but continued to consolidate his power, condoning atrocities and genocide against the ethnic Albanians in Kosovo.

That night, when Kerry walked over from her little cottage, both Line and Stephen could see how tightly wound she was, the lines on her forehead deep and the movements of her thin body brittle.

"I think you need a drink," said Stephen. "Scotch? Or a gin and tonic?" he asked, rising to greet her. He and Line had the television on, watching the BBC nightly news.

"They bombed a refugee convoy!" said Kerry. "Are they admitting it?" she asked, sitting abruptly on a hassock in the tiny living room.

"Yes," said Stephen quietly. "American reporters went in there and interviewed people, so no one could pretend otherwise. NATO is expressing regret. They mistook it for a Yugoslavian military convoy." NATO was using F-16s in aerial strikes aimed at the bridges, public buildings, barracks and military installations of the Serbs who were persecuting the Albanians in Kosovo, trying to get them stop.

Kerry shook her head. "When will it end?!" she asked. She took the small glass of Scotch Stephen offered her and drank it in one quick tip of her head. Then held it out for more. "I'm feeling so helpless!"

It was true. Here they were, sitting on a large, peaceful island high above Europe, in relative safety. But television cameras and interviewers brought the faces, the struggling lines of Albanians trying to leave their country right into the room. Line knew that it wouldn't stop soon. Education, she thought, was the answer. But Kerry did not want to hear the long view right now, Line was sure.

"You are doing what you can," said Line. She stood up and turned off the television, looking at Stephen and Kerry questioningly. But yes, they had all had enough of a dose for the day. "Tell us about it," she said, as they adjourned to the little dining room where Line had laid out the plates. The sun slanted in, giving the glassed-in cupboard, with its collection of unused china, the lamps, the fruit on the table a warm glow.

"It's kind of chaos over at the shelter," said Kerry. "There aren't enough interpreters. We're trying to make lists of people's names, helping them find each other. But then, we need places for them. And money. They're glad they are in a place of safety, but they are bewildered!"

The three of them tucked in to the baked fish and jacket potatoes Line had made, plus a salad, laced with the fresh, bitter watercress. "I would be," said Line. She could easily imagine arriving in a cold northern country, shut out from the places that you knew, with nothing of your own. "Disoriented," she said.

"Yes," said Kerry. "I like that feeling. It's why I travel. To shake myself up. But I have a home. It's always been my refuge. These people were in camps where they were mistreated. Hungry. Cold. Trust is going to be hard for the kids I'm seeing."

"That part is hard for me to imagine," said Line. "Neighbors against each other. They've lived together, but all of a sudden they hate each other?"

"I don't get it either," said Kerry. "So, why is this happening, Mr. Historian?"

Stephen sat back. "Well, the quick answer is that communism held down all these ethnic hatreds with its ideological control, its secret police and top-down organization. But now that the people in Eastern Europe can vote, they're splitting into their ethnic groups and nations, mostly along religious lines. The Kosovars are mostly Muslim, I think, right? It's going to take a while for this all to settle. And, you are right, Milosevic isn't helping one bit," he said, referring to earlier conversations.

"He's unprincipled, people say," said Kerry. "Just wants the power. The more the better."

"I don't know about the air strikes," said Stephen, "whether they will accomplish what they set out to do."

"I'm thinking that when you leave, I'll take in some refugee family," said Kerry.

"Good idea," said Line. "It might be temporary. I am sure most of them want to go home, once they can." She spooned out more of the salad onto her plate. "They can help eat up all the vegetables I've been planting!"

"A few stay," said Kerry. "If they want education for their kids, or something."

"This cress is so delicious," said Stephen. "We don't usually get it in California."

"I saw the marsh violet, Kerry," Line said. "The one you showed me. So tiny!"

"Good!" said Kerry. "April in England. It's usually a good time."

Later that evening, as Line made the rounds of the house in her pajamas, making sure lights were off and doors were locked, the telephone rang. Line picked it up.

"Oh hello, Line," said her brother Paul's diffident voice.

"Paul!" said Line. "It's so good to hear from you!" She wondered why he was calling. It must be important, as Paul would never normally spend money on a trans-Atlantic phone call.

"What time is it there?" Paul asked. "Did I wake you up or anything?"

"10:30 at night," said Line. "Is everything okay there? Where are you?"

"I'm in St. Paul," said Paul. "At Ellie's house. Marie's in the hospital. She's been diagnosed with breast cancer and will have a double mastectomy in the morning. I just wanted to ask you about it Line."

"Oh Paul!" said Line. "I'm sorry! Double? Is there cancer in both her breasts?"

"Yeah," said Paul. "Lumps. According to the CAT scan. She's at the university hospital. Couldn't be in a better place. But it's thrown us both for a loop."

"Is it in the lymph?" asked Line. Breast cancer could be contained, but if it began to metastasize, it would be deadly.

"Don't think so," said Paul. "They're talking treatment plans. But Marie's got her own ideas. That's why I'm calling you. I wanted to know what you think."

"I bet they want to do chemotherapy, and radiation," said Line.

"Probably," said Paul. "Marie wants to refuse. She thinks a good healthy dose of sunshine and an antioxidant diet would be better than trying to deal with all that poison in her body."

Line sighed. "Oh Paul. I see what a problem you have. But there aren't any easy answers. And I bet the doctors don't know exactly what they're dealing with yet."

"Right," said Paul. "I just thought I'd ask what you think. You know, you had those healing methods, like Reiki. And other alternatives." His voice sounded tired, but not hysterical.

"When did all this happen?" asked Line.

"This week," said Paul. "Marie found the lumps and we scheduled the appointment. I'm just trying to figure out what I think."

Line had been on both sides of this situation. "The doctors will tell you that outcomes will be better and life might be prolonged by a full treatment plan," she said. "On the other hand, they are experimenting. No one knows enough about cancer. I have to say," said Line carefully, "I take very seriously what the patient wants. There's more to it than just the treatment. There's also whether you want to fall into their hands, live the life being in and out of hospital." Line sank down on the couch, wrapping an afghan around herself in the chilly air. "Could you call me again when they've done the surgery and another CAT scan?" she begged. "I don't think we know enough just now."

"You're right," said Paul, sighing audibly. "It's kind of early to tell. But I thought it would be good to talk to you." Line could hear the anguish in his voice.

"Oh yes!" said Line. "I wish I could be more help. But it's a journey. I'll try to make it with you. Did you anticipate any of this? Like over the winter?"

Paul seemed uncertain. "Over the years," he said, "it has seemed to me that she's been less animated, maybe. And in the winter, we're all a little sluggish. But Marie's got that energy. She can turn it on and it shines! Maybe there's been a little less of that. Or maybe a little more! Maybe she's been spending it. Seems so bright sometimes, dark others."

"Well, don't despair," said Line. "We'll get through it. I'll be coming home soon. Maybe I can come out to see you all."

"Yeah," said Paul. "One way or another. I guess we'll be at the lake this summer as usual. I'm glad it's almost the end of the school year. Things are starting to be a blur." He seemed to shift his thoughts. "I better go," he said. "This is probably getting expensive. But it is good to talk to you, Line. Thanks for your support."

Line wished Paul a good night, and said she would be thinking of them both during Marie's surgery. They both hung up. Line could hear the utter quiet of the house around her. What a blow to her darling brother and his wife. Cancer sounded like a death knell to most people, though doctors were getting better at dealing with it. It wasn't something you could cure, but only manage.

When Line went into the bedroom, Stephen was awake, reading in bed. He looked up expectantly. Line sat on the bed, explaining everything to him, the anguish creeping into her own voice and face.

"Line," said Stephen reasonably. "It's the middle of April. We have only a few weeks left here. You have been so helpful to me, making us a home away from home. Why don't you go to Minnesota now, and we'll meet in California as soon as I get there?"

Tears dripped down Line's cheeks and she brushed them away with her hand. "I never would have thought of it," she said. "But I would really like to go. It's such a wild card, cancer," she said. "So hard to deal with. Thank you, Stephen." She was thinking back to the deaths of her parents, how profound they had been. She had missed Mother's. But so had everyone; it had been so sudden.

Line went over to her side of the bed and lay down.

"Ready?" asked Stephen, his hand on the light switch.

"Remember when you came to Alaska?" asked Line curling up towards him. "Paul took me in when Marty had all those druggies at her place, and I still wasn't sure about you?" She and Stephen had gone over it many times. It had been like a completely new love affair when they got back together, both of them more grownup. Christy had resisted Stephen's intrusion into his intimate life with Line, but eventually, with more kids coming along, he had had to grow up too.

"I remember," said Stephen. "It would be great if you could help Paul. And when we meet in Santa Cruz, everything will be new again for us too."

Line drifted off. Life was amazing. How it twisted, and no one could follow it.

It took a couple of weeks to get reservations and plane tickets. Line was surprised at how many friendships she had to gently close. Milkmen, shopkeepers, neighbors with dogs. She said goodbye to trees and gardens she had loved. Birds. It was unlikely she would ever see Mrs. Daiches again. Rosemary, possibly. Kerry, certainly. Kerry was a traveler. Line also bid a fond farewell to Kerry's little house and garden.

By May, Line was in Minnesota. Paul picked her up at the airport and took her to Ellie's house in St. Paul where Marie was lying out on the newly green lawn on a chaise lounge soaking up the afternoon sun. Her eyes looked listless, her face pale, but she smiled at Line and the sun glinted in her dark curls.

Line bent down and kissed Marie's cheek, careful not to touch her anywhere else. "My poor darling," she said. "You've had a rough time."

Marie looked down at her flat chest. She had always been small. "As you see," she said, ruefully. She was wearing a loose, button-down shirt. "The teacup is cracked and broken."

"Let me know how I can help," said Line. Unfair, unfair, she was thinking. Here was another lovely person, leveled by the rough injustice of the world.

"I'd love it if you could help me wash my hair," Marie said. "I can't take a shower until the stitches come out. They kept me in the hospital while things were draining. What is that stuff anyhow?"

"It's excess blood and lymphatic fluid," said Line. "Most surgeries have some drainage."

"Ugh," said Marie. "I don't have so much pain. It's more just tight and uncomfortable."

"Exercise?" asked Line.

"Marty sent us this videotape of some Qigong exercises her teacher made," said Paul. "They're good for stretching. We do them in the morning. And some walking."

"Exercise is good," said Line. "Whatever you can stand."

"I'm just glad to be home," said Marie. "Well, not exactly home. But almost. Ellie has been great." Ellie had no need to rent out Mother's downstairs apartment. Most of the time it sat empty, unless her daughter who lived in Texas came up, or other Mikkelsons came through. Ellie was teaching in a high school, bustling, confident and happy.

Line slept that night on the pull-out couch in the living room. She was glad to be almost home too. In the U.S., surrounded by family. She and Paul made a merry breakfast in the morning for the three of them.

"It's like we revert to being a bunch of kids!" said Line.

"Please!" said Marie. "It hurts to laugh!"

"I don't think we would act like this if our kids or grandkids were around," Paul said. "Interesting!"

Line made herself a cup of coffee. So good! After breakfast they sent Paul to the store and Line found a chair so Marie could hang her head over the wash basin while Line soaped and rinsed her hair.

Marie sat on the bed, breathing deeply, psyching herself up for the effort. Line saw a copy of The Imitation of Christ on the bedside table. "Grace sent that," said Marie.

"Have you seen her?" asked Line. "Since the surgery, I mean?"

"Oh, yes," said Marie. "All the kids came." She moved into the bathroom. "Maybe if I sit this way," she said. "Like in a hairdressing place."

"Good," said Line. "Shall I get a pillow to make you higher?"

But it worked. She poured warm water from a pitcher over Marie's head and began to work the shampoo in.

"So Paul tells me you don't want chemo or radiation," Line began.

"I'm really not too optimistic," confided Marie. "They took out some lymph nodes too. Did you know I lost my uterus 25 years ago? I really gave myself up then. I was so sick. The last twenty years with Paul have been just grace. And of course, watching my daughter have all these kids. I'll fight this, but in my own way."

"I guess they'll do another CAT scan," said Line. "To find out how it's going?"

"Yes," said Marie. "But I'm not good at hospitals. Sunshine, family, good food. I'll be fine."

"You're a brave lassie," said Line. She poured rinse water through Marie's thick, dark hair. "There," she said. "I think that's got it. Easy does it." She helped Marie to sit up and toweled off her damp head. "Comb?"

"Let me do it," said Marie. She grimaced as she tried to stretch her arms up to run the comb through her hair. "Oh, Line," she said. "Why don't you do it."

Line silently combed the tangles out of Marie's hair. Unfair, she thought. Unfair.

23

Marty looked out over the parking lot below her as she ran down the steps to Fort Mason on a brilliant sunny day. Doug was leaning on his white minivan, talking on his mobile phone, waving at her. The Bay was green beyond the piers and the wind coursed gently over the hills. Above, gulls wheeled and shrieked, dropping down to scrabble for food.

Doug had asked Marty to meet him "if at all possible," at Greens, a vegetarian restaurant opened by the Zen Center in the decommissioned fort at the end of one of the piers. Marty, who already had one foot out the door at Designers International, told her office she had a doctor's appointment and left at lunch time. And there he was! The doctor, looking tan and vital. He hung up his phone as Marty approached and gathered her into his arms. "How's my girl?" he asked. "You look like a total fox. I love watching you come toward me."

"Wonderful," said Marty, made shy by his compliments. "So happy to see you!"

"Well," said Doug. "I have a beat-up car and I'm broke, but you still love me," he said. He used to begin with "I'm married," but he didn't today.

"Yes," said Marty, looking up into his smiling face. "I do."

They walked into the wooden doors of the spacious restaurant where a spectacular bouquet of shrubs and long-stemmed desert flowers greeted them. The hostess seemed to Marty to have a secret smile on her face as she led them triumphantly to a table by the window. Doug must have charmed her, in his way. She pulled the shade against the intense afternoon sun. In the little harbor beyond the window, Marty pointed out a sailboat with a wooden mast and blue canvas sail covers belonging to a friend of hers.

Seated across from each other, Doug took both Marty's hands in his across the table. "I have something to ask you," he said. "Mackenzie is going to leave. She wants a divorce. It'll take time, but do you want to come and live with me?" he asked. "With us, me and my kids?"

Marty breathed heavily. In her wilder dreams, this was what she hoped for. "Yes," she said. "That is exactly what I want." What Marty wanted most in life was to be what she thought of as a 'real woman.' She hadn't felt she was in her first marriage. She had had to be more like a grownup with a child. Partnership had eluded her.

"It won't be easy," cautioned Doug. "My finances are a terrible mess. And I'd be taking you away from the city. And we haven't told the kids anything yet. But Mackenzie wants out. She's met some musician. Wants to go live with him in LA. It leaves us free, my dearest."

"I don't care about the city," said Marty. "If I ever get out of Designers International, I can come!" She had told them she was leaving, hoping to take the summer off and think about her life, but Designers International was baulking. They were interviewing for her position, but it was going slowly.

"A partner," said Doug. "You've felt like a partner to me, and that is what I want." He looked down. "I'm sorry I can't be more romantic about it."

Marty laughed and shook her head. "Neither of us is a romantic. I'll leave that to Mackenzie! But we have a harmonic between us that won't quit. In spite of our age difference and everything else. You know how much I have so wanted to pursue it!"

"Dear God," said Doug, taking his hands away and heaving a sigh. "What a relief." He must have known what Marty would say, but when it actually came down to it, when the words were actually spoken, it wasn't the same as what one imagined.

The waiter came over and they ordered a plate of Mediterranean tastes, roasted eggplant, filo pastries, pickled beets, delicately flavored lentil salad, and a green salad with papaya and mango. Every taste was heightened by Doug's news, by the clarity of the air, by the golden afternoon.

Doug became more relaxed. "We're past the point of talking," he said about himself and his wife. "Our actions speak louder than words. She's a dramatic girl and she wants to play out the story her way. But in the end, I think you and I will be together."

"She doesn't want to share custody of the kids?" asked Marty. To her the kids were the most worrisome thing about living with Doug. The four of them ranged in age from ten to six, and had had a checkered childhood. Doug's work kept him away from home a lot. The kids felt that Alice Henderson, Doug's mother, was their own. Marty had seen little of the kids, and she liked Alice, but it was complicated. Would the kids come to like her?

"Mackenzie wants to be free," said Doug. He shook his head. "Not my idea of freedom," he said. "It will work out. I can imagine you and I making a real family together."

"But your Mother?" asked Marty. "Isn't she their real mother?"

"Mom's getting tired," said Doug. "She's 69. I know she'd like some help."

Marty too began to relax. Everything was opening. There were possibly bad times ahead, but nothing could stop their relationship now. How long it had been. Marty had fallen in love with Doug years ago. Perhaps finally they would be able to grow together.

When Marty stood up, she bent to kiss Doug. He put his head between her breasts as naturally as if they were at home. It seemed to her that everyone in the restaurant noticed this simple gesture, that everyone looked up as they processed toward the door.

They went home and lay on Marty's long, velveteen-covered couch, Doug with his computer and a book on stock trading at one end, and Marty with her book at the other. Their tevas were on the carpet below, their bare feet touching. Something about synchronicity, Marty thought. Things just worked between them. She felt peaceful, her usual restlessness tamed. At

4:00 o'clock Doug left. One day at a time, thought Marty. Neither of them knew how it would all happen.

At work, two of Marty's administrative staff gave notice. It felt to her as if everything was in shambles. She worked harder than ever, afraid she couldn't leave. But she was also less intent on setting precedents and standards, felt she could be a little bit looser. Someone else would be in her office soon.

Marty's boss told Nora how sorry he was Marty was leaving. Ken told Marty he couldn't imagine the office without her. Everyone talked about what sort of person should replace her. Robin, in Washington, wanted someone to "whip the guys into shape." She wants a Confucian, thought Marty. That was not her.

Marty was a Taoist. She felt she hadn't done much. She had just been there a long time and the odd patterns of Designers International were laid down in her soul. She knew everyone, plus their preoccupations. When she walked into the office in the mornings, she whisked through the place, setting it to rights. It would take someone else a while to be able to do this, but Marty felt that change was good.

Werner's new administrative assistant Tania came and cried in Marty's office. "My stomach hurts when I come to work," she said. Marty wondered why she stayed, but the place was compelling. "It's character-building," said Tania. Marty prepped for a big office move, in which new project teams would coalesce around each other. She gave her thoughts completely to the housekeeping of Designers International while the architects kept crashing ahead on their projects. Marty was exhausted, her head like a cabbage.

But the weeks went on. Marty hired two new project assistants and began training them. They were full of energy, reminding Marty of when she first arrived at the company, how she had bounced around the place. One was a squat little dyke with bleached, cropped hair. Big, stiff-toed Doc Martin shoes, laced up in front looked kind of normal on her. The other was small, thin, and feminine with long dark hair. She too wore Doc Martins, but they made her look like a cartoon character. She was coming down from the mountains, where she had spent the winter. Marty watched them, took pleasure in them, though she was feeling quite disinterested.

At last a woman named Carol was hired to replace Marty and she was able to set the date of her last day. Marty tried to leave as clear a trail as she could, all the public information available to Carol. The administrative staff was still not in good shape, but it could not be helped. At least there wasn't as much bickering and whining as there had been when Erica was there. In two short weeks Marty would be free to think her own thoughts.

Marty talked to Doug almost every night. She couldn't wait to tell him things. He and Mackenzie were in mediation. Mackenzie kept waffling, perhaps worrying that her new friend would not take care of her. In fact, at first the mediation lawyers told them they were too confused. But gradually Mackenzie admitted the marriage was over. Doug wanted to do right by her. He was taking it slow. "I'm feeling free," he told Marty. "Free of obligation and guilt, but not of responsibility." He said responsibility was what you took on yourself, while obligation and guilt were what other people tried to give you.

Marty's last day at Designers International finally came. Three big banks of flowers for her stood on the reception desk, one from the Washington office, one from her own office and one from Tania, a fall of irises, daisies and small sunflowers. Someone gave her chocolates. Marty's boss, Joe, took her to lunch where they had the predictable talk. It was the day of the monthly staff meeting, when everyone came down and shared food and information. There was champagne to celebrate the selection of new associates. Marty's contribution to the firm was recognized. Marty felt good, that she had finished her course, that she had done what she set out to do.

And then Marty was free, at last. She began to feel what she thought of as 'normal.' There had been so much stress and drama that she had come to expect it! 'Normal' had to do with her body feeling simple and healthy.

Tai chi class was held in the gym in the old 50 Oak Street building which seemed to be crumbling. Sun shone in on the class, dressed mostly in dark cotton clothes. There was lots of space and good energy. Stan convinced Anton to begin teaching them 'hard set,' also called 'open-close.' Anton explained the essentials, opening and closing the body, and keeping the "tiger-mouse" point on the hand open, the fingers spread. Marty felt it all the way up to her spine. "The hands are small," said Anton. The 'hard set' was the last of the many sets Master Liu's students learned, the most esoteric, full of deep body knowledge.

Leo wanted Marty to work on sword with him, but sword was a fog. Marty had not done it for some time, could not put the moves together. She realized again that her body sometimes learned things that her mind didn't. Once she had done sword with others a few times, she would get it back. I must rely less on class, thought Marty. Now she had the time. If she moved away from the city, she must cultivate her own relationship to tai chi.

Doug did not want Marty to let go of tai chi, though there were no classes near Boulder Creek. He promised that if she would set up her own daily practice, he would join in. Marty had been religious about class for years, using it to help with her need for people, for family. Many times she had gone to class desperately unhappy or full of longing. She had left rejuvenated, the soggy feelings turning around and lightening. Tai chi energized the whole person, the emotions and intellect, as well as the body.

But everything was changing. Doug suggested Marty go to camp once a year to connect with the group and brush up on the sets. Marty also worried about what she would do for money, but Doug told her he needed her. "I just want you to be there for me," he said. "And I want to take care of you." Marty knew he needed her help with the kids, and in the tasting room. They would share the household money. "I'm afraid you'll be as busy as I am," he said. "It's just not like an office. It doesn't go like clockwork."

Marty laughed. "Nothing goes like clockwork," she said.

Since quitting work, Marty found it wonderful to think her own thoughts. She felt more responsive to things, since she wasn't as stressed. People greeted her as she walked around the city, noticing. One night she walked by a restaurant up the street where people danced to salsa music around a table laid out on the sidewalk. They wore lampshades on their heads! My neighborhood has more spirit than I thought, Marty said to herself. My city. At least for the moment.

Marty went to the farmers' market and spent time with her friends. Shannon was pregnant and she and Phil had gotten an allotment in the community garden just above Fort Mason. Marty met them at the garden for a picnic on one of the long June evenings. Shannon wore brown coveralls over her slightly bulging tummy.

The rhododendrons and callas were blooming wildly, the convection wind loud in the Monterey cypress as the fog rolled in. The grass was lush, but beginning to dry. The smells of the weeds and grasses made Marty feel a part of everything, more than just human. The wind blew the graceful, aromatic eucalyptus branches above them as they sat on a blanket.

Phil was slightly deferential to Shannon. "We have many more girls' names in mind than boys'," he confided to Marty. He spread out the food they had brought.

"Look," said Marty. "We've got bitter, the arugula; salty, French ham; sweet Pugilese bread; and pungent radishes! We're only missing the sour, of the five Chinese tastes."

"Pickles," said Shannon. But no one had brought any. "I'm finicky about eating," she said. "Sometimes I want one thing, then another. I have strong reactions to smells." The smell of rosemary made her nauseous. Below spread the lovely panorama of the Bay, with Angel Island a massive green hump, hardly distinguishable from the land to the north. A big container boat came in under the Golden Gate Bridge and smaller boats too were beginning to be swallowed up by the fog.

One day Marty took the ferry to Sausalito. Sachiko picked her up in a new Mercedes 4x4 van and took her to the house on a hill where she and Anton lived. She wanted Marty to look in on the house now and then, feed the coy and water the plants while she and Anton were in Europe. She had just come from Florence and Venice, but would go back, as Anton's work for an international duty-free consortium took them everywhere.

Marty shared the Joseph Schmidt chocolates she had been given, and Sachiko brought out some she had bought in Paris from Pierre Hermé. She made a lovely herbal tea called Melissa, serving it in some of the unique, delicate cups and saucers she collected on her travels. It was minty and made Marty yawn.

Sachiko's house was in a bit of disarray, as it was meant only for her and Anton, but it totally reflected them. A large part of the living room was empty, but a delightful troop of tiny animals marched across the beautiful wooden sideboard. The book nook in front of the fireplace seemed to be the most used place, books spilling off the shelves and ottomans. Big windows looked out on a deck, with vegetation cascading down the incline below it and the horizon a long stretch of hills.

Sachiko talked to her plants, to the vegetables, to inanimate objects as if they were people, calling them pet names and cajoling them. "Don't do that to me, darling," she said. Everything responded to her playfulness. It made for a human atmosphere! Plants were everywhere, violets in the kitchen window. She took Marty out to the deck to see the David Austin roses. She explained exactly how much food to give the coy, which swam, small and golden, in a deep ceramic pool. Sachiko's whimsy combined with her artfulness was so attractive. She dedicated herself to her husband. But also to tai chi, which she took very seriously.

Doug came to the city on a Friday night. He did not let go of Marty for a minute. "I'm getting impatient!" he told Marty, holding her in greeting. "I'm past thinking about the divorce," he said. "But of course, I have to pay attention."

Paradoxically, Marty had become more patient! "I have all my life to love you," she told Doug.

They talked and talked. It was so much fun to make plans! They could hardly leave the house. On the staircase, Marty waylaid Doug. She tried to tell him about what she considered her liabilities. "I want us to be real, and in order to do that, I need you to know you can leave me at any time." She did not want to tell him this, but she was worried their interests and abilities might change as they grew older, hers much quicker than his.

"We've been having this passionate time," said Doug. "But I want it to be real, too. I want to settle down and have a boring life with you."

Marty laughed. "I'm not the least bit worried about aging," she said. "But you mustn't feel guilty if you feel you need to leave. The only way I will feel comfortable living, working, fighting together is if I know you have chosen it." The future was vastly unpredictable. Marty felt that if she had Doug for a little while, she would have him for always.

They walked down the hill to the Tango Grill on Columbus Street. They sat in the window and were served by a thin Argentinian waiter with a heavy silver cross hanging around his neck. His voice was low and thick and Marty had to listen closely to understand him. They had clams in broth, dipping their bread into a piquant parsley, garlic, olive oil. Drinking only a half glass of Chilean chardonnay each, they became quite drunk, on each other.

"I think you can call me your boyfriend now," Doug said. "I want to take us somewhere, to get away from everything for a weekend before we settle in and become real and boring. I have an idea about it too." He would not tell Marty more.

"I am worried about how to introduce you to the kids, though," he said. "I think they should come to San Francisco. We could all go to a museum, or to the aquarium or something. Maybe a couple of times before you move in to our house."

"Yes," said Marty.

"It isn't as though I have to ask their permission to bring home a stepmother," he said. "But I want to be courteous, to them and to you. Even for me," he continued, "if I spend time with them, they authorize me. But if I'm not around much, they turn their backs! Jason acts out and Zoe gets bitter."

"Exactly," said Marty, thoughtfully. "I think it will go slowly," she said. "It's usually that way with me."

"I'm just glad to feel so certain about this," said Doug. "It's very different from how we were before."

Marty hardly noticed walking back up the hill. They stood leaning on Doug's car, a man, a woman and a car. All it took for a story, Doug said. Marty felt dazed. She was totally in love. This was her life. She had wanted it, but it was beginning to fall heavily upon her. She would be a real woman after all. She did not know how she had found Doug but she knew that their conversation could go on forever.

When Doug left, Marty felt terribly open, the sap rising all over her body. Her bottom and legs were warm and tingling, her eyes soft, starry. She and Doug would come together, soon. Marty went to bed, the delicious feeling of Doug's hands, Doug's body imprinted on her. She enjoyed the feeling, fell asleep. At midnight she woke to a pain in her buttocks, the hormones draining away. But she slept again, all night, and in the morning felt rested.

Doug told Marty he felt she was always waiting for him. "It's because you have a complex life, and I have a simple one," said Marty. She was sleeping a lot and enjoying it. She did tai chi by herself every morning on a playground under a spill of bougainvillea. Around Doug, she sometimes felt overwhelmed, they were so sensitive to each other. They allowed, respected and cherished each other. They talked endlessly, Doug referring to music, Marty to movies and books.

Standing waiting for the bus one day Marty could not believe her life. A wild, sexy, rock star sort of guy was now her boyfriend openly. She stood very tall, enjoying the secret feeling that she was special, whether anyone knew it or not. She felt very sexual in a mundane world, with a double-edged power which she now knew how to use for good. She had felt sexy when she was younger, but now, she thought, when she finally felt safe and her emotions were open, sexuality was more intense. A whole person at last.

Marty even realized that she was less concerned that these feelings were hers. She felt diffuse, a part of everything, without a need to be a fixed, definite self. She could lend her secret feeling of power to the old Chinese women who were going out to shop, to the tourists with their maps who were not sure where they were going, to the people on her street with briefcases.

The surprise Doug had for Marty involved a bed and breakfast in the little town of Freestone, north of the city. Their room was in a Victorian house, painted in delightful colors. "This isn't the real thing," Doug told her, "but it will do for a start. I want to pamper you." They drove down the road and had a small relaxed supper before going to bed, where they were finally, after all the years, able to enjoy each other fully.

After a relaxed breakfast, they drove to a day spa called Osmosis. The atmosphere was very quiet. They were served green tea in beautiful ceramics in a room whose moon-shaped window opened on a deck and a lovely garden full of herbs and flowers. Marty felt a bit bewildered. Bees buzzed in the flowers and there was the sound of water pouring from a fountain. A small bronze Buddha was seated in a niche on one side of the room. In the distance they heard subdued voices. They were very far from normal life, from traffic noises, the clatter and clash of people and dishes. It was hard for Marty to quiet down enough to enjoy it!

They changed into the thick cotton robes they were given and were led out into an open wooden shed, where they were asked to disrobe and climb into a bin full of cedar dust and shavings. They wrapped their hair in towels and lay down. An attendant heaped cedar shavings over them so only their heads stuck out. The attendant left and Marty and Doug lay there, the skin of their bodies absorbing the enzymes and sap from the trees.

"I read about this," said Doug softly, "and I really wanted to try it! The Japanese have adopted these baths all over the country. They offer them to recovering athletes and to people with all kinds of stress. The owner of Osmosis experienced them when he was studying gardening and Zen in Japan."

"It's quite amazing," said Marty. She was struggling to take it all in. The landscape in front of her was of a beautiful garden with a creek trickling through it. She listened to the water, trying to inquire of each of her senses what she felt. The smell of the cedar was like incense.

After an hour, Doug and Marty were directed to an outdoor shower, where they washed the cedar dust off each other, taking their time. Doug was playful in the sun, Marty shy. They put on their robes and two attendants intercepted them. A tall, blonde man who said his name was Kurt took Marty into one room, and a short dark lady took Doug into another.

Marty lay face down on the massage table, trying to give herself up to the quiet insistence of hands. She remembered the first time she had visited the tai chi class, thinking to herself that she would never be able to get used to touching people she didn't know. She had quite gotten past that one! She pushed hands with everyone now, even a guy who had visible Karposi's lesions on his arms.

I have taken Tara's vow, thought Marty. She had read it in Gary Snyder's book, a poem which had been written over a period of forty years, Mountains and Rivers Without End. She had tried to memorize it, and now knew it well enough to repeat it to herself: "Those who wish to attain

234

supreme enlightenment in a man's body are many … therefore may I, until this world is emptied out, serve the needs of beings with my body of a woman."

Kurt's hands moved over Marty's body. He didn't talk much, but asked a few questions. Marty told him a little of her story, that she had recently quit a stressful job, that she had studied tai chi for ten years.

"I'm not finding much tension to worry about," said Kurt. "Maybe a little in your neck. Must be the tai chi," he said.

Marty agreed. She felt that tai chi had helped her in every way, her posture, her circulation and her openness to the world. She remembered the ingrown, shy creature she had once been. She was still shy in response to Doug's compliments. And she still wore glasses, but up close she didn't need them! And she was very close to Doug.

Kurt's hands were respectful, as quiet as he was. He took a very long time, giving Marty a full rub-down. When she finally emerged in her robe, there was Doug. They met in the dressing room where they changed into their ordinary clothes. Neither of them had much to say. It was so outside normal experience. They were let out into the sunshine, out of the amazing atmosphere and back into their car.

"Thank you, Doug," breathed Marty. "I really don't know how to thank you."

"All your life to love me," said Doug. "That's what you said. I'm going to hold you to it." He gave her a mischievous smile.

"We shall be one person," said Marty. It was amazing how fast they were melding together.

24

The fact that, already in October, Marie didn't want to go out to choir practice, struck a chill in Paul's heart. "Too cold," she said. "Too dark."

Not go to choir practice? Unheard of! But Paul had been hatching a plan. He was not without ideas. He began to put them in place. He talked the outfitting company he had worked for into taking over the mortgage on the house for the time being. The company could possibly rent it out to ice fishermen or skiers over the winter. He took an indeterminate leave of absence from teaching and fitted out the Previa for a long drive south, down into Mexico, to Oaxaca.

Marie looked at him wistfully, hopeful, but not quite certain they could pull it off. "All I really want is heat and sunshine," she said one night after dinner. She was too tired to do much more than mope around the house most of the time. Sometimes even too tired to cook.

Paul, as ever, was optimistic. "We'll be snowbirds," he said. He had first read about Oaxaca in the Audubon magazine. It seemed to be well set up for people who wanted to avoid the cold of winter. "We can study Spanish in some of those language schools they have down there, and look for birds we've never seen."

From research he had concluded that rents in Oaxaca were very low. It might chew through his savings, but it would probably be worth it. Paul felt he had entered into a desperate pact with Marie to give her whatever felt good to her.

"Migrating birds," said Marie. "That's us." She lay on the couch in the late evening, wrapped in a wool blanket though the heater was on.

Being migratory was the last thing Paul had expected in his life, but he would make the best of it. "I don't think we can take you, Archie," he said, laying a hand on Archie at his feet. Archie was too old for adventure and who knew what they would run in to. "Do you think Grace and Gerald and the kids could take him?"

"I do," said Marie. Gerald and Grace now lived in a suburban house with a yard. Their kids, except for Benjamin, the littlest, were in school. "Plenty of room for Archie now in Bemidji. And the kids love him." The kids knew Archie well from playing with him at the lake during the summers.

Ellie felt Marie should stay and take the cancer treatments the doctors recommended, but when Paul said they were going, Ellie offered financial help. "Not now," said Paul. "We can make it through the winter. Maybe later." He looked doubtful. Who knew what later meant. He also had a plan to see if he could send out articles to magazines, make a few dollars that way. He had long ago learned to make a dollar go a long way. Surely it would in Mexico.

By Halloween, Paul and Marie were on the road. "It's a long, long way," he cautioned Marie. He was remembering the bus trip down to Texas his college choir had taken. Once they got past Texas, Oaxaca was another thousand miles into Mexico.

But Marie said she would have nothing to do but rest and look out the window when she felt like it. "I'll be fine," she told Paul.

When they stopped in Bemidji to say goodbye, the grandkids dressed up in their costumes so Marie could see them. Paul took a photo of Dory, in a little white nurse costume; Joe and Andre, who wore slick little Batman and Robin costumes; Jeanne, who was a princess; and Benjamin, who was dressed in a tiger costume. They were terribly proud. "We got lots of candy," confided Jeanne. "But we can't have it. Only on Saturday," she said dolefully.

Grace was tearful when they left. The grownups knew that Marie's health was critical. There was even a question about whether they would see each other again. Marie too was sorrowful, but she put on a brave face. "See you in the spring!" she said lightly. "We'll send you something from Mexico at Christmas."

"Take good care of Archie," said Paul. "Or get him to take care of you!" He did not like leaving his long-time companion.

They drove down through Kansas, Oklahoma and into Texas. In Austin, the temperature was 70 degrees Fahrenheit. As long as they were in the U.S., Paul thought it safe to sleep in the car. He drove steadily, taking only three days to get to Laredo.

Triple A had advised Paul to stick with the toll roads once he was in Mexico. They were expensive, but he would arrive in Oaxaca more quickly, and then could settle. They did not need passports, but Paul had to have all his vehicle paperwork in order, and extra insurance. Unlike his well-traveled sisters, Paul had never had a passport.

Paul pushed hard the first day in Mexico, driving ten hours to Santiago de Querétaro, where they found a hotel. They were just north of Mexico City, where the difficult driving would begin, but past the northern part of the country, where drugs were being grown and sold.

Marie thrilled to the Spanish names and cathedrals when they got off the highway. Santiago de Querétaro had a long pink stone aqueduct from colonial times strung through it, its lovely arches lit up at night. Marie wanted to go into one of the many churches they passed. She had begun to look for angels, paintings and sculptures of angels everywhere.

"We can't really take time tonight," Paul told her. He was disconcerted by this longing for angels. "I promise you all the angels you could want, as soon as we get to Oaxaca tomorrow." His legs and buttocks ached from the tension of driving and pressing his foot on the accelerator. Luckily, his right leg was the stronger one.

In the morning, Paul felt rested. They took showers and had breakfast, arming themselves for the road. Everything felt different. Paul found that he could buy quite a bit with the pesos he had exchanged for dollars. He had also been told that they shouldn't drink the water. Paul was being extra careful. Marie was not well. Bottled water was part of the deal.

"Let's try the Mexican chocolate," said Marie. "I've heard about it." Flavored with cinnamon, sugar and almonds, the chocolate came in a pottery bowl and was delicious.

"What is it that makes the atmosphere of another country so different?" Paul wondered.

"Here especially," said Marie. "It's like we are all humans. We need the same things, food and water. But there are so many ways to do it!"

"I wish my Spanish was better," said Paul. He had taken it in college, but never used it.

"My French helps a little," said Marie. "But not much."

They switched from the 57 toll road to the 40 to Puebla, driving through the afternoon. Relieved to be so close, Paul slowed down and began to enjoy the dry mountainous terrain of the Sierra Madre. By evening they dipped down into the high valley of Oaxaca. Paul was elated. The car had made it. They had made it. They found a small hotel which seemed inexpensive. The temperature in the evening was almost 75 degrees!

In the morning, they went to mass at the nearby Templo y Convento de San Augustin. Its façade was covered with carved figures. Inside the high white-painted arched ceiling led the eye to a magnificent altarpiece. The ecclesiastical language of the Spanish mass was easy to understand, the sonorous chanting peaceful. Marie lit a candle in a crypt in front of a statue of the Virgin Mary.

Leaving Marie to rest at the hotel, Paul walked through the narrow streets to the Oaxaca Lending Library. Church bells rang out, dogs skittered in the road and traffic cops blew their whistles. The few cars were tiny. Gas and water vendors hawked their wares. The low buildings were painted in bright colors, their walls coming right down to the sidewalk. It was just past the Días de Muertos and evidence of paper skeletons could still be seen, as well as the white frosted 'bread for the dead' and wreaths of drying marigolds.

The venerable Lending Library helped expatriates and snowbirds to acclimate themselves to the city. It had a bulletin board where rentals were advertised, computers where you could connect to the World Wide Web, and English books. Quite a few of them.

Paul copied addresses and phone numbers into his notebook. A vivacious lady noticed him and started a conversation. Paul quickly explained he was looking for a small rental for himself and his wife.

"Oh!" said the lady, who said her name was Janice. "Maybe I can help. There's a rental available in my building. Small kitchenette. Bedroom and living room."

"Does it have access to a garden or some sunshine?" asked Paul.

"Oh yes," said the lady. "It opens out onto a little cactus garden and patio. And then there's the azotea, the roof where you could sun yourself."

"Wow," said Paul. "It sounds like it's old. Adobe?"

Janice laughed. "I doubt it," she said. She was dressed in bright colors, her white hair cut so it framed her face. "But stucco, you know. Painted bright colors. Lovely tiles in the garden."

"Sounds like heaven," said Paul. "Is it far?" He was wary. Could it really be so easy to find a place to live?

Turned out it was. They were early, for snowbirds. Most didn't come until after Thanksgiving, Janice told him. The building was northeast of town, in the Barrio de Jalatlaco, near a lovely old church on a cobblestone street, Hidalgo Street.

Marie loved the place. The wooden entry doors were painted blue, the walls yellow and salmon. Their apartment opened onto a large courtyard with a garden where Marie could rest in the sun. Bird of paradise plants bloomed in the courtyard, flamboyant green beaks opening with orange petals and a slim blue crest. "Looks exactly like a bird," said Paul.

"We'll have to be careful," said Marie. "At least you will. My skin turns brown quickly. But you, Mr. Norwegian, will fry like a pancake!"

Paul laughed at her. "Don't worry," he said. "It will be quite a novelty to sit in the shade in a t-shirt in November."

Paul went down the street looking for food. He could see trees a few blocks away, and realized that behind the colorful walls were surprising courtyards. He found a corner grocery and bought a rotisseried chicken, with spicy sauces, rice, beans and tortillas. The little apartment, though sparsely furnished, was equipped with a few painted pottery dishes. There were even cotton napkins!

"I feel quite at home!" Paul said as they sat down to eat.

"Tastes much fresher than the food at Zona Rosa's!" said Marie, naming the Mexican restaurant near Lake Michigami where they sometimes went in the summer. "I'm sure Zona Rosa's uses canned beans." She picked at her food. Afterwards she went into the bedroom and lay down for a nap.

Paul tucked a woven cotton blanket around Marie's thin body, noticing her collarbones standing out under her thin shirt. He felt the greatest tenderness toward her. "Sleep well, my love," he said. "I'm going to look around some more."

By himself, Paul walked over to the small park. He sat in the shade of one of the trees with its sparse leaves. Sunshine and shadow washed over him and he heard birdsong. There was little grass, only concrete around a central statue, with the few trees on the perimeter standing in the dusty dirt. From what Paul understood, the wet season in Oaxaca was in the summer. By the fall, there was little rain. They were also so close to the equator that there was only about an hour of variation in sunrise and sunset times over the year.

A bird with a cinnamon-colored back and belly and a strong orange beak picked at a branch. It looked much like the American robin, except for the coloring on its back. Paul leafed through the Oaxaca guidebook he had brought, but it didn't identify birds.

The statue in the middle of the park was of Benito Juarez, a president and reformer of Mexico. He had been born of Zapotec parents, but was educated by the priests in Oaxaca. So much to learn, thought Paul. He sat, letting himself relax for a moment. It was all so strange, the color, the warmth. Nearby a dark young man was playing a guitar, singing softly in Spanish. Perhaps practicing. He didn't seem to be soliciting money.

Whenever he was alone, the stark reality of what he and Marie were doing struck Paul. When Dad was dying, Paul remembered, no one was allowed to say so. Even a week before his death, Dad was insisting he was going to beat his liver cancer. Paul remembered that Kristen had made an ink drawing of Dad, emaciated, with a dark little beanie covering his bald head. In the picture you could see that he was going, but no one was allowed to say so. Saying so might cause it to happen.

In Marie's case, it was a matter of surrender. Line had told Paul that breast cancer, if it metastasized, could spread to the liver, lungs, bones, lymph or kidneys. Even the brain. There were nodules in Marie's armpits. There was not much question but that it was spreading. Paul was worried Marie would be in pain, but at least so far she assured him she was fine. Her color was pretty good, Paul thought, but she was so thin. As if her spirit was eating her body.

Toward the end of the week, while Marie rested in the afternoon, Paul wrote to Line and Marty, who were now living in the same town. "I've taken over our lives," he wrote. "Marie is happy just to be here. And our days are filled with color, warmth, light, music. I'm very glad we came.

"In the mornings we go to mass at this old church near us, San Matias Jalatlaco. It is very peaceful and quiet and it soothes Marie. Even in Spanish. Maybe more because it is in Spanish! Then we lie in the sun for a while, though Marie likes the heat more than I do. I've been reading to her, but I'm not always sure she's awake.

"Then I go out and find us some food, which is pretty easy. After lunch, she rests, while I go to the library to read the newspapers and try my hand at Spanish conversation. In the evenings, we come out to the park and listen to the mariachi bands going up and down the streets, serenading people in restaurants. The temperature is very mild in the evenings, and the air is dry and pleasant here. We're in a valley in the Sierra Madre, kind of high up at 5,000 ft.

"The musicians are dressed in embroidered suits with short jackets, white shirts and lavish ties. They play either strings or horns, which makes a very distinctive sound, and they all sing. Great harmonies. I'm sure you've heard the kind of music I'm talking about.

"Marie seems fine, not getting any worse, or any better. She doesn't eat much and rests all the time, but she says she isn't in pain. I understand now why she didn't want to live that life, in and out of hospitals, clinics, doctors' offices. It's a kind of waiting for life. A hope and a promise she didn't trust. Here we feel we are living. Remember how Mother used to say, 'This isn't living, this is just existing,' when she was unhappy? I think she may have been quoting her own mother. In Oaxaca, we feel very alive.

"Please write. Everything feels strange here and it helps to think of you," Paul wrote.

Days began to take on sameness, a simplicity. Paul kept notebooks, but he did not have the energy to write anything formal. He did manage to write a short article on how it felt to be a snowbird for The Ely Echo. Paul had not thought they would stay in Mexico long enough to subscribe to things, but the editor sent him a copy of the newspaper with his article in it.

The bird turned out to be a rufous-backed warbler, a relative of the American robin and quite common. There were crows and sparrows aplenty in town. It would have been fun to get out of town, visit the Zapotec ruins and the desert and forest habitats nearby, but Paul did not want to leave Marie. He also did not have a lot of money for such things. The town was big enough and strange enough for the time being, he felt.

Grace wrote letters frequently, telling Paul and Marie how the children were doing and how Archie was. Line didn't write. Paul hardly expected her to, but they did get a letter Marty had dashed off.

"I'm writing you from the tasting room," said Marty's letter. "I have this letter tucked under the bar and when there aren't any clients, I pull it up and write!

"I've been terribly busy since moving to Boulder Creek, but I love hearing your news and I'm glad you are both together and enjoying a quiet time. The kids are in school during the day, so I spend the mornings in the tasting room and then walk home, so I can be there when they get home from school. The Boulder Creek elementary school is pretty good. We are way up a mountain road from Santa Cruz, though. Doug is worried that when the kids go to high school, it will be too far away. But that is a few years off. Zoe, the oldest, is ten this year.

"I'm in the PTA! We've just had a cake auction to raise money. You wouldn't believe some of the silly cakes people made. Jason raised his hand at the wrong time, and we ended up with a bunny cake covered with coconut! But Doug doesn't care. He is so happy we are doing things as a family, that nothing fazes him.

"It has been quite a shock to me to be surrounded by people, and I haven't quite found my bearings. But I'm very happy. The kids are a challenge, especially Zoe, who had begun to assume she ruled the roost. Not that I actively dissuade her from thinking this. I am trying to work with her, find ways to help her. And what Doug says rules. Doug is gone a lot, but when he is here, there is nothing more delightful than sitting at one end of the dinner table with him at the other, the kids ranged in between. They adore him and he is a wonderful father. I try to work with the patterns he has set up which the kids expect."

There were three little stars and then the letter continued:

"Well, I just spent some time talking with a young man about our Pinot Noir. He's catering a wedding. I hope he buys a lot! The harvest this year is tough. Cool weather and even now the grapes are not all in. We are toughing out a long hang time to see what will ripen. Doug is a nervous wreck. But the winemaker, Jeremy Barnes, tells him that the wines from this year are going to have a lot of staying power.

"Take good care of yourselves, Paul and Marie," Marty signed off. "Loved your letter. We are thinking of you every day."

Even in Mexico, Paul found, people were worried about 1999 turning over to 2000. Computers were not as ubiquitous as they were in the

United States. But the government, the airlines, any international businesses had to pay attention to the fact that computer files could not get by with treating a year as two digits. Paul was amused to find that his expat neighbors talked more about the end of the Mayan calendar in 2012. They were not exactly in Mayan territory, but it was very close. In Oaxaca, the Olmec and Zapotec cultures dominated.

Janice proved to be a good friend and interpreter of local customs. She had worked in California, but made her home in Oaxaca for the five years since she retired. She brought tea into the garden to share with Marie, and sometimes Paul, in the late afternoons. "I feel more alive here than anywhere," she told them.

It was Janice who explained that the days of the dead, which seemed to be a bit macabre to Paul's northern sensibility, were really a happy time. "People believe the dead have permission to visit their friends and relations once a year," she explained.

"On November 1, the children who have passed away visit in the evening, and then adults come on November 2. People visit the cemeteries, and welcome their relatives' souls with flowers, food, candles and incense. It is a time of peace and happiness." Janice picked up her teacup, her silver bracelets jingling. "Even I," she said, "agnostic that I am, have come to enjoy this idea that there is a crack in the worlds once a year. That there are other worlds than this one. Mexicans are far more familiar with death than we are. I think it's healthy."

Janice also introduced Paul and Marie to the famous Oaxacan mole sauces. Every restaurant had different recipes. Old family recipes from aunts, grandfathers, and grandmothers. The sauces had dark tastes of chiles, nuts and spices. They were served with pork or chicken and rice. Some of them were laced with chocolate.

For Paul and Marie, life went on rather simply against the colorful, noisy backdrop of the town. In late November Marie told Paul, "Janice says there is going to be a calenda, a parade tomorrow. It's for my favorite saint, St. Cecilia's day! The patron saint of musicians. I used to pray to her as a little girl. There'll be floats and children marching. I can't wait to see it!"

Paul asked questions and plotted the best place from which to watch the calenda. They set off early, as Marie thought she could walk if they took it slowly and rested on the way. Marie looked like a Mexican waif with her dark curls. She was dressed in a white cotton embroidered blouse Janice, who seemed to have lots of resources, had given her. She wore it with jeans and wrapped a shawl around her. From a tulipan tree on the patio, Marie tucked a large red-orange flower behind her ear against her dark hair.

Mass was held at the church of San Felipe Neri, filled with color and music. Mariachi bands played. Afterwards the shrine of the saint wended its way down the steps, out through the iron gates and into the street. Paul found a place for them to watch the procession and laid a little rug down at the edge of the sidewalk so Marie could sit down.

A statue of St. Cecilia, in a white dress with a gold halo around her head, led the procession ensconced on a float decorated with lilies and palm leaves. "She's so beautiful!" said Marie. "Look at that sweet lovely face." Priests and altar boys followed.

Musicians played as they walked behind St. Cecilia. A group of little girls dressed in embroidered blouses and red woolen skirts stood patiently waiting to be told where to go. Behind them were boys in serapes carrying crosses on poles. Huge papier-mache masked figures were manned by people underneath their voluminous robes. As the procession got going, everyone in town followed it. Rockets and firecrackers boomed around them and church bells pealed.

"St. Cecilia was singing when they beheaded her," Marie leaned over to tell Paul amidst the cacophony. "One of the early Christian martyrs."

"This isn't just about a Catholic saint, though," said Paul. Clearly the excuse for a parade came up often in Oaxaca and was taken up by everyone, indigenous, Spanish, and expatriate people alike! When did the kids go to school, Paul wondered. The evidence of the Días de Muertos had just barely subsided.

Paul tried to ask a young woman in broken Spanish what she hoped for from the saint. "My father is a músico," she said. "St. Cecilia will find him work. She takes care of us all year."

As the procession moved away, Marie stood up. "Come on!" she said, wrapping her shawl around her scrawny body. "We have to follow them! Come on my gringo husband!"

Paul didn't like it. The crowd was moving in the opposite direction of their apartment. How would he get Marie home? But Marie's eyes snapped with fun. Paul stepped up beside her and they moved out into the procession walking down the street as the sun sank behind the mountains.

25

Clearing up Christmas took a good day at Line's house in Santa Cruz. It was Poppa who loved having a Christmas tree with all the trimmings, presents, cards, candles and carols. And this year, all of Line's daughters were home!

Line and Heather boxed up decorations and sorted cards. A wood fire burned in the fireplace. It was a cold, clear day with people coming and going, all the doors open. If you were active, you stayed warm, but Line wore two sweaters. Outdoors, Poppa chopped up the drying noble fir into pieces which could be used in the fireplace. Good kindling and starter fuel, though you had to be careful.

"I'll keep all the photographs," said Line, sorting them from the piles of cards. "I love having them to remind me of all of you." Her little desk in an alcove off the kitchen was festooned with photographs both new and old; even a few of the bright faces of the kids' ancient grade school pictures.

"I do that too," said Heather. "My desk is a shrine to all I left behind in California." She smiled at her mother. She and her husband were visiting from Chile, where Pablo's family had vineyards and a winemaking operation. Heather too wore sweaters, her long golden hair falling over her shoulders. She kept reminding them that it was full summer in Chile, that she had given up its warmth and light to come and see her family.

From the kitchen, where Fern was organizing pans to make brownies and Ivy was making chili, Fern called, "Shall I make a double recipe?" It was New Year's Eve and Marty's birthday. Line planned to serve the brownies with ice cream and a fudge sauce that night when the Hendersons came for dinner. Line's brownies came from The Joy of Cooking.

"Oh, why not," said Line. "There'll be 14 of us tonight. We'll probably need it." The brownies were very rich, but it was the last gasp of the holidays and Line was willing to pull out all the stops. It was the night people had been fearing. Y2K it was called. Would the computer systems everyone increasingly relied on cause any trouble? When computers began, apparently no one thought very far ahead! But here they were, with the date rolling over from 1999 to 2000. Programmers had been working for months to remedy the situation.

"That is a hell of a lot of eggs and sugar!" said Fern. She judged everything by the situation she had been living in on Menorca, where there were apparently not many sweets. Not much birth control either. Oddly,

Fern was five months pregnant, whereas Heather, who was married (and Catholic!), was not. Line and Stephen's first grandchild would be born out of wedlock.

It was a long story. At the archaeological dig on Menorca where Fern worked, she had fallen in love with the Italian director. They had been more or less together for years. But the dig was partially funded by the director's wife's foundation and when Fern's pregnancy began to show, she and the director had parted. Even in Europe, apparently, it wouldn't do for children of the director, but not his wife, to be running around. Fern had come home to have her baby and figure out what to do next.

Line didn't mind. She had been waiting for grandchildren. And Poppa was ecstatic. He was always putting in his two cents: "Where are the progeny?" he lamented. He had four grandchildren, any one of whom could have had children. But Heather was the only one who was married and she and Pablo seemed to be taking their time.

"These brownies are kind of a meringue," said Line going into the kitchen. "The sugar provides the structure, makes them stand up. And they are Marty's favorite."

"No problem," said Fern. "I'll do exactly as Mrs. Rombauer says." Fern's brown hair was tied carelessly in back with an elastic, her thin face a little sallow. She was completely unrepentant, though grateful her family had taken her in. Line saw her own young and arrogant self in Fern.

Ivy giggled. She too was thrilled that Fern would be around for a while. Of all of the kids, Ivy seemed the least likely to leave home. She had strung out her degree, and would probably graduate. But her interests in textiles and weaving did not translate into obvious kinds of work. Stephen was worried about her, but Line wasn't. Ivy could take as long as she wanted, as far as Line was concerned.

Poppa came in and laid a few of the fir branches on the fire. They were still fresh and damp, but they quickly dried and popped like firecrackers in the fire. "Snap, crackle, pop!" he said. "Like rice krispies!" Poppa was 79, but no one noticed. He still looked jaunty and did exactly as he pleased, driving his red Acura around town. He had lady friends, but no intention of compromising his comfortable family situation with new attachments.

Line noticed the beautiful old menorah, crafted to look like the tree of life, on the mantel. Hanukkah was long over. It had been early this year. I must put that away, she thought. They did not display lights outside, as many people did. Christmas trees, candles and wreaths were quite enough, in Line's mind.

A car could be heard in the driveway and Stephen and Pablo appeared. Stephen had taken his son-in-law over to show him the university. Pablo, affable and dark, bearded, his hair a bit shaggy, was a contrast to Heather, whose blonde hair and tawny skin clearly came from northern Europe.

"Let the party begin!" said Poppa excitedly, going over to the bar to prepare drinks.

Line beamed at her family. It had been a long time since so many of them had assembled. Only Christy was missing. He was in Minnesota, hopefully with friends or with Mikkelsons. Sadly, Paul and Marie had gone down to Mexico that winter, but there were still other Mikkelsons to make Christy welcome.

Pablo came over to Heather and hugged her. Heather looked up at him and spoke to the group. "We want to go to the vigil for peace tonight at 8 o'clock at Holy Cross," she told them. The two of them had discovered the beleaguered church built on the site of the first Misson Santa Cruz, for which the town was named. Services had been moved to the parish hall from the church, deemed unsafe after the earthquake ten years ago. And then the parish hall burned down! Services had been in a tent pavilion for several years. Now, however, the church was repaired and retrofitted.

"I guess we could have a drink now and not spoil our meditation," said Pablo.

"We might need to eat a little early," said Heather. "What time are the Hendersons coming?"

"Around five," said Line. "Don't worry. It will all work out. But you know how anxious to see you those kids are," she reminded Heather. Heather had babysat for the little Hendersons quite a bit when they were being shunted between their home in Boulder Creek and their grandmother's house in Santa Cruz. Zoe especially loved Heather.

"Zoe can come with me," said Heather. "She's not too little."

"We'll see what Doug thinks," said Line.

"I'd like to go," said Ivy. "I don't think I've ever been in that church. I've heard it has beautiful stained glass windows." The Catholic complex on the site of the ancient mission had schools, gardens and a replica mission and museum.

"I'll come with you guys," said Fern.

Line walked out onto the deck. It was a beautiful day, but they were beginning to need rain again. Leaves, brown and curling, skittered across the deck in the light breeze. Pine needles too lay in piles. Line could never sweep the decks enough. She went down the steps to have a look at what was left of the garden. The herbs did well all winter, and she had a few winter greens too. She watered a bit and then looked further down to where the persimmon stood, bare except for a few orange globes. Line had taken some and left the rest for the birds. They were the non-astringent Fuyu variety. Delicious in salads, or eaten like a fruit.

How did her kids get so religious, Line wondered. And Catholic at that! She and Stephen had never said much about religion, one way or another. Perhaps that left them free to be interested. The year had turned for Line at the time of the solstice, beginning a new round of the earth's journey round the sun. Christmas was like a freight train, pounding into your life. It was impossible to avoid, to try to remember what you were working on! But it was wonderful to have so many family members gathering and to hear from friends far and near.

What was I doing, anyway, wondered Line. Since returning from Scotland, she had slowly been getting back to hospice work. As always during the winter, she had a few serious cases. Winter had a way of taking people with it, dry leaves whisked away by the wind. But today Line didn't need to think of them. She had taken herself off the on-call list. Having family around was compelling.

By the time the Hendersons arrived, twilight had come, blue mists settling in the woods around the house. The sky was thick with atmosphere, the moon waning. It would not be up for hours.

"Come in! Come in," said Line. "Happy new year!" she hugged Marty, "Happy birthday," she whispered. "I didn't forget."

"And to you," said Marty, hugging her. "It's been a wonderful birthday."

Doug ushered in his mother, Alice, a thin older woman who Line knew to be a hard worker. Her hair was permed and she wore a bit of makeup, lipstick and color on her cheeks, though she wore pants and a sweater like the rest of them. She pressed a large bag of lemons on Line. "From my tree," she said. "It's overflowing!"

"Thank you," said Line. Behind Alice were the little Hendersons; Zoe in a black velvet top and taffeta skirt, a ribbon in her hair; Nic and

Natasha, both dressed in jeans with colorful long-sleeved cotton t-shirts; and Jason, his skin and mop-top hair darker than the rest, dressed in jeans and a little hooded shirt.

Heather scooped up Zoe. "I guess you knew we might take you to church!" she said.

"These are my Christmas clothes," said Zoe importantly. "I hardly ever get to wear them."

"You look terrific," said Poppa, hugging her. He leaned down to shake Jason's hand. "Happy new year," he said. "Are you going to beat me at mancala?"

Jason nodded gravely. He didn't say anything, but Nic faced Poppa. "I'll beat you for sure!" The twins were nine.

"Me too!" said Natasha staunchly. "I'll beat you."

"One at a time," said Poppa. "One at a time. Everyone plays the winner." Mancala was a two-person game.

"Come in by the fire!" said Line. "I guess kids don't get cold." She was surprised none of them wore coats.

"Where's your Christmas tree?" asked Zoe, standing in the middle of the room.

"We took it down today," said Line. "Time for a new year." She looked at Doug and Marty, who stood off to the side, smiling. Doug looked dapper in a sportcoat and Marty, the new step-mother, was small and pretty, her pink cheeks glowing. "Drinks?" Line asked. "We have everything: sparkling water, apple cider, wine, and, of course, gin!"

People ranged themselves around the big room. Poppa put the wooden mancala board out on a table and showed the twins how many stones to put in each pocket. Small, Jason watched raptly. It was a new thing. Poppa had gotten the set for Ivy for Christmas, and loved to play. "Not quite like African kids playing with pebbles in the dirt," he said to Alice, who was watching. "But close."

Alice looked indulgent. She had seen a lot of life in her 69 years as well.

"The colors don't matter," Poppa told Natasha, who fondled a blue stone.

Marty and Line watched from the kitchen counter where Line was lining up glasses. "Natasha always wants her hair short," said Marty. "'As short as a boy's,' she says." It wasn't quite that short, but much shorter than Zoe's long wafts of curl. "Doug calls them 'Zoe and her three little brothers,'" laughed Marty. Little Jason stuck close to the twins.

"How's it going?" asked Line quietly, hoping the sisters could talk privately in the family cacophony.

"I'm very happy," said Marty. "I feel like a real woman, with all those problems. Drawn between yourself, your husband, your kids. They don't feel quite like my kids, of course. I feel more like an aunt. But it has been quite a year!"

"For all of us," said Line. "I'm so glad to be home. And hopefully we won't be traveling so much in the future. It's such a wrench! Traveling is like a dream. Home is where things feel real."

"Big changes in life make you think, though," said Marty. "I think I had this idea that Doug and I would continue that idyllic sweetness between us, that when we got together it would be just the two of us. That idea was crazy! But we are partners, strong in all the chaos."

"The kids are okay?" asked Line. She knew Marty worried that she wouldn't be able to manage them.

"Remember The Little Prince?" said Marty. "He said it was the time that he spent with his rose that mattered. The kids are accepting me, but it will be a while before we all meld together." Marty turned back to the living room where everyone was talking, playing, putting on music. "I've had this one idea, though, that's been helping me. I think that the world you create around you is your self, not the limited little interior body we all think of as our precious selves." She looked at Line quizzically. "You've known that for a long time, haven't you?"

Line hugged her beloved younger sister. "I never think about it," she said. "The world runs away with me and I just try to do the most good I can!"

Marty shook her head. "And I went looking for my self in all the wrong places!"

"You're on the right track now," said Line. "Things are going to be fine. I think you came into Doug's family just in time, before the kids become teenagers."

"They are each their own person already," said Marty.

"Gin and tonic?" asked Stephen, coming over to the two sisters.

Line considered. She didn't drink much hard stuff lately, but tonight was special. "Sure," she said. "Sounds good."

The evening rolled on. After their dinner of chili with rice, a big salad, and Marty's brownie dessert, Heather and Pablo left for church, taking Fern, Ivy and Zoe with them. The little kids fell asleep on various sofas and in various laps, little Jason in Alice's.

"Do you remember when Dad took us over to the church in Bryson at midnight and rang the bell?" Marty asked Line as the six remaining grownups sat around talking. She turned toward the others. "It was snowing in this little tiny town in North Dakota. We climbed up into the wooden steeple, and a thick rope hung down from the bell. As thick as my leg!"

"Kind of," said Line. "We would have been about ten or so?"

"I remember it just like yesterday," said Marty. "He looked at his watch and when it was midnight, he rang the bell. And then he jumped on the big knotted rope and swung up high into the belfry! He wouldn't let us get too close."

"Yeah," said Line. "I do remember."

"Mid-Fifties?" asked Poppa. "I remember that time perfectly too. I was working like a dog. We were trying to get rid of Joe McCarthy. He self-destructed pretty fast, but his red-scare tactics lasted a long time." He turned to Alice. "What were you doing in the mid-Fifties?" he asked.

Alice smiled. "I was thinking about getting married," she said. "Had my girl Eva in 1957. And then Doug," she said looking at him. "No end of trouble," she kidded. Alice's husband had died when her kids were young. Alice had moved to Santa Cruz and gotten a job in the high school lunchroom. She and her kids had taken care of each other ever since.

"And how about this year?" asked Marty. "What's the best movie you saw this year, Poppa?" she asked.

Poppa looked thoughtful. "Hmmm," he said. "That's a hard one. Modern or older?" he asked. Poppa was now an authority, as he was still running his film club at a local theater.

"From this year," said Marty, decisively.

"There were a few good ones," said Poppa. "But the one that had the most effect might be The Matrix, I have to say. What do you think?"

"Wow," said Doug. "I haven't had a chance to see it, but that's quite a statement! I do hear people talking about taking the red pill. What's the red pill?"

Line had seen The Matrix with Ivy and Stephen. She was pleased she knew.

"It's what you take when you want to see behind the rosy curtains of pseudo-reality," Stephen said. "The blue pill keeps you silent, working for institutions, but sated and happy. You think," said Stephen. "The red pill wakes you up to what's really going on! And it isn't pretty," he finished.

"I may be Jewish," said Poppa, "but I don't put much stock in the idea of a 'chosen one.' Neo, in the movie, is revealed as chosen. I didn't like that part. But the idea of waking up is perennially important."

"What's the year been like for you, Doug?" asked Stephen.

Doug shook his head expressively. "Banner year," he said. He and Marty sat beside each other, his arm around her, their sides melded together. "Really tough harvest. Cold and we just weren't sure anything would get ripe. But then there is Marty!" he smiled at her. "Hardly believed she'd come." He leaned down and kissed Marty on the cheek.

"There's no place I'd rather be," said Marty, her face shining.

"So the vintage is going to be a good one?" asked Poppa. Wineries were big business for California and Poppa was full of respect for Doug.

"Not as good as 1997," said Doug. "That was a year to treasure. But this vintage will be good."

"I'm glad we're back in Santa Cruz," said Line. "I loved Scotland. It's something of a big garden. But, home feels so wonderful. You never see it as sharply as you do when you've been away for a while."

"Yes!" said Poppa. "I'm glad you're home too!" He had had students living in the big house while Line and Stephen were gone. They were interesting, he told Line, but not family.

"So you finished the Scottish project? What are you working on again Stephen?" asked Doug.

"I'm finishing up a book on a guy named John Smith," said Stephen. "He was born in Scotland, and he almost became prime minister of the United Kingdom. But he had a heart attack. It's a biography. A really interesting family. And also illuminates the British government."

"How was this year for you, Alice?" asked Line, trying to be a hostess.

"It's been great," replied Alice. "I don't mind saying that I hope I've seen the last of that Mackenzie! Quite a piece of work, she was."

Line was surprised. She had not expected Alice to be so outspoken. But it was true. Everyone was glad Mackenzie was no longer a factor in Doug's complicated life. The divorce would go on forever, since his finances could hardly be sorted out. He owned the ranch with two partners, and he lived there. But it was very hard to know what community property he and Mackenzie had shared, if any. They had been married ten years, though. And Doug had been her sole support.

Doug looked haggard when the subject was raised. Line called him over to help stir up the fire. "It's lovely to have you here tonight," she said. "Your kids seem to be thriving." Marty was always telling Line about them, about how Doug managed, what a good father he was.

"They're confused still," said Doug looking at Line squarely. "But I think we're stabilizing. Christmas was a good test. Marty made frosted gingerbread men with the kids and we trimmed the tree with them, and cranberry and popcorn strings. And there were less presents. Less Santa! Marty read the Christmas story to show the kids what it was all about originally. It felt more real to me. And less tense!"

"Mikkelsons have pretty strong Christmas traditions!" said Line. "If she starts making lefse you'll know you're in trouble!" She was thinking about how she had melded the Mikkelson traditions in with Poppa and Stephen's lightly Jewish ones. But her own kids had not had to deal with an erratic mother.

Heather and Pablo, Fern, Ivy and Zoe arrived rather late. Doug went over to them. "Are you falling asleep?" he asked Zoe. "See, the others are all asleep." He indicated the forms of Zoe's 'little brothers' asleep under blankets on the sofa. "We better get you all home to Grandma's."

Zoe clung to Heather, acting as if she didn't want to leave. "I want to see the new year," she said.

But Doug was insistent. "Come on, Marty, we should get these kids to bed."

"How was the service?" Line asked.

"Very fine," said Heather. "I like this church." Pablo, by her side, nodded.

"There were all denominations," said Fern. "Jewish, Hindu, Christian, Buddhist. People prayed in all kinds of languages. And the music too."

"Oh," said Line. "Sounds nice."

Marty and Alice stood up and began rousing the little kids. They were going to Alice's house, not too far away. With choruses of 'happy new year' and 'happy birthday,' the grownups and kids were accompanied out to the car.

"See you in the new year!" said Doug. "Thanks for all the fish!"

Everyone laughed. Line was pleased she knew what he was talking about, how the dolphins had left earth in The Hitchhiker's Guide to the Galaxy. Not that she had read the book.

When the Hendersons were gone, Poppa said, "Well, I think we may as well turn on the television. See what's going on the in the world."

"Yes," said Fern. "I want to know whether it is going to fall apart at the seams."

"Nightcap, anyone?" asked Stephen. Several people wanted one.

The family went down to Poppa's den, where a television with a quite large screen graced one side of the room. Poppa turned it on. Stephen, Ivy and Fern lounged on the sofa and Heather and Pablo shared one large chair.

Television news readers acted excited as coverage of cities across the globe was displayed. But none of them had anything substantive to say. It was just a moment, anticipated for its mark on people, a way to take a snapshot at a particular time in the world.

Not much happened. Firecrackers and fireworks were the main celebratory spectacular, most memorably from the Eiffel Tower in Paris. New York had an amazingly quiet, benign celebration. London tried to light up the Thames, though it wasn't very successful. Cecil Williams had put together a unity celebration in Union Square in San Francisco.

"People really like getting together," said Line, as they watched the traditional lighted ball drop in Times Square, New York, and everyone counted down the last few seconds of the millennium. The news readers said over a million people were crowded into the square and the surrounding streets.

"My goodness," said Poppa. "Such a to-do!"

Fern stood up and stretched. "Life doesn't feel any different in 2000," she said a little sourly.

"Oh," said Ivy, popping up to hug her. "It will. Especially for you."

"Yes," said Fern, turning to embrace her sister. "I am sure it will."

"So, could we go to bed?" Heather asked plaintively. She and Pablo were sleeping on the hide-a-bed in the den.

Line looked at them all fondly. Marty was right. Nothing made you feel more like a real person than having your family safe and happy and gathered around.

ACKNOWLEDGEMENTS

The author would like to thank her siblings, cousins and friends who have shared in the experiences of which this is a fictionalized account. She would especially like to thank the teachers and classmates with whom she has practiced tai chi for more than 25 years. She would also like to thank Don Starnes for his cover design, and for his support throughout the project.

Connie Kronlokken

ABOUT THE AUTHOR

Connie Kronlokken grew up in a large Norwegian/Danish Lutheran family. She spent her childhood in small towns across Minnesota, North Dakota and Iowa. In 1969 she moved to the San Francisco Bay Area and now lives in San Rafael with her husband Don Starnes. Connie studied filmmaking in Denmark and has been a student of yang style tai chi for more than 25 years. She loves being with her family, the march of the seasons, cooking and gardening. She has been parsing romance from reality for most of her life.

www.ingramcontent.com/pod-product-compliance
Lightning Source LLC
Chambersburg PA
CBHW02074525O626
47155CB00003B/920